BILLIONAIRE'S CONTRACT ENGAGEMENT

BY
MAYA BANKS

AND

MONEY MAN'S FIANCÉE NEGOTIATION

BY
MICHELLE CELMER

BILLIONAIRE'S CONTRACT ENGAGEMENT

BY
MAYA BANKS

Published in Great Britain 2011
Harlequin Mills & Boon Limited,
Eton House, 18-24 Paradise Road, Richmond, Surrey TW9 1SR

BILLIONAIRE'S CONTRACT ENGAGEMENT © Harlequin Books S.A. 2010

Special thanks and acknowledgment to Maya Banks for her contribution to the KINGS OF THE BOARDROOM series.

ISBN: 978 0 263 88092 2

51-0211

Harlequin Mills & Boon policy is to use papers that are natural, renewable and recyclable products and made from wood grown in sustainable forests. The logging and manufacturing processes conform to the legal environmental regulations of the country of origin.

Printed and bound in Spain
by Litografia Rosés S.A., Barcelona

To Elizabeth Edwards —
Thank you so much for allowing me to pick your brain.
The information was invaluable and helped me to
really wrap my mind around these characters.

And for Diana —
you'll be missed!

Maya Banks has loved romance novels from a very
(very) early age, and almost from the start, she dreamed
of writing them, as well. In her teens she filled countless
notebooks with overdramatic stories of love and passion.
Today her stories are only slightly less dramatic, but no
less romantic.

She lives in Texas with her husband and three children
and wouldn't contemplate living anywhere other than the
South. When she's not writing, she's usually hunting, fish-
ing or playing poker. She loves to hear from readers, and
she can be found online at either www.mayabanks.com
or www.writemindedblog.com, or you can e-mail her at
maya@mayabanks.com.

Dear Reader,

Temptation is hard to overcome, as Celia Taylor is about to find out. Even the best of intentions can't hold up against the persuasive powers of tall, wealthy, gorgeous Evan Reese. But really, what's a girl to do when it's clear the man is very hungry and she's on the menu?

Celia has some very important lessons to learn — about just who's important in the scheme of things and what she isn't willing to give up ... for anyone. Evan? He knows what he wants. He just has to persuade a certain someone of that.

Evan and Celia have a fun but very passionate flirtation. They dance around each other — not so delicately — but that's what made this book so fun to write. It is my hope that they charm you as much as they did me and that you enjoy their journey to happily ever after.

Enjoy Evan and Celia's story!

Until next time,

Maya Banks

One

The vultures were circling.

Celia Taylor stood back, wineglass in hand, and surveyed the crowded ballroom. The fund-raiser was supposed to be more pleasure than business, but business was uppermost on the minds of her competition.

Across the room, Evan Reese stood in a large group of people. He looked relaxed, seemingly in his element, an easy smile making his extraordinarily handsome face even more gorgeous.

It should be a crime for a man to be that good-looking. Tall, rugged, he looked every inch the kind of man who'd be at home in the athletic wear his company designed and sold. There was an aura of confidence and power around him, and above all, Celia loved a man who was sure of himself.

Given the long, searching glances they'd exchanged over the last few weeks, she'd be a fool not to entertain the idea of seeing where things could lead.

If he wasn't a prospective client.

A client she wanted to land very much.

She wanted the account—her boss and the agency was counting on her—but she drew the line at sleeping with a man to get what she wanted.

Celia turned away from the sight of Evan Reese before she became too enthralled in just watching him. They'd performed a delicate dance around each other ever since he'd fired his last advertising agency. He knew she wanted him—in the professional sense of course. Hell, he probably knew she wanted him naked and in bed too, but she wasn't going to dwell on that. Maybe later tonight when she could afford to indulge in a little fantasy.

The problem was, anytime a big company like Reese Enterprises fired an agency, it became open season. The other agencies circled like sharks. It was a dog-eat-dog world, and in reality, she should be over there, shoving herself down his throat like the rest of her competition, but she couldn't help but believe Evan Reese was secretly amused by the attention. He took a different hand. She was sure of it.

"Celia, glad you made it. Have you spoken to Reese yet?"

Celia turned to see her boss, Brock Maddox, standing a foot away. He wasn't drinking. He didn't even look particularly thrilled to be here.

Her eyebrow rose. "A tux. Why, Brock, you look positively decadent. However are you keeping the ladies at bay?"

He grunted in response, his lips curling in distaste. "Cut it out, Celia. I brought Elle along."

Celia looked beyond his shoulder to see his pretty assistant standing a few feet away. When Elle looked her way, Celia smiled and waved.

"You look beautiful," Celia mouthed.

Elle smiled and ducked her head self-consciously but not before Celia saw the faint blush that colored her cheeks.

Brock gestured impatiently toward Evan. "Why are you standing over here while Evan Reese is over there?" Brock scanned the room and his expression hardened. "I should have known the old bastard would be here."

Celia followed his gaze to see Athos Koteas holding court within hearing distance of Evan. Though she wouldn't admit it to Brock, it made her extremely nervous to see their business rival hammering so relentlessly on Evan Reese. Koteas owned Golden Gate Promotions, and not only had Koteas lured away a few of Maddox's top clients in recent months, he'd also launched a PR campaign against Maddox. It was dirty pool, but it in no way surprised Celia. Koteas was ruthless, and he'd do anything to win.

"Well, yes," Celia murmured. "His ad execs are busy working Evan over."

"Any reason you aren't?"

She laid her hand on his forearm. She knew how important this account was to Brock—to everyone at Maddox Communications. "I need you to trust me, Brock. I've studied Evan Reese extensively. He knows I'm interested. He'll come to me eventually. I'm sure of it."

"Are you fifty million dollars sure, Celia? Maddox is small, and this kind of deal means our employees keep their jobs whereas if we continue to lose clients and accounts, I can't make any guarantees."

"I know I'm asking a lot," she said in a low voice. "But I can't walk over there and pull out the seductive wiles." She gestured toward the women standing around Evan. They weren't making any bones as to how far they'd go to sign him. "It's what he expects, and you of all people know I can't do it. I can land this account on the *ideas,* Brock. I've spent every waking minute putting this pitch together. There's no way he won't go for it."

Brock studied her for a long moment, his eyes gleaming with what looked like respect. She loved working for him. He was hard. He was demanding. And he was the only person she'd presented her side of what had happened in New York in her last advertising job.

"I never expected you to land the account on anything less than your brilliance, Celia," Brock said softly. "I hope I never gave you any other impression."

"I know. I appreciate your confidence more than you know. I won't let you down. I won't let Maddox Communications down."

Brock ran a hand through his hair and glanced once more across the room. He looked tired. It was true he worked hard. The agency was everything to him. But in the last few months new lines had appeared around his eyes. More than anything Celia wanted to be able to hand this account to him. He had believed in her when everyone else was willing to think the worst.

She glanced up to see Evan threading his way through the throng of people. "Don't look now, but he's headed our way. Maybe you should take Elle and go dance or something."

As quickly as he'd approached, Brock turned and melted back into the crowd.

Celia sipped at her wine and practiced nonchalance as she literally felt Evan close in. It was impossible to miss him. Her body always seemed to heat up about five degrees whenever he was anywhere near.

And his smell. Even amid the hustle and bustle of the crowded room, the mix of so many feminine perfumes, she could pick out his unique scent. Rough. Masculine and mouthwateringly sexy. It made no sense to her, but she was attuned to his every nuance, and that had nothing to do with all the studying up she'd done on him and his company.

"Celia," he murmured.

She turned with a welcoming smile. "Hello, Evan. Enjoying the evening?"

"I think you know I'm not."

She raised one eyebrow and stared at him over the rim of her glass. "Do I?"

Evan snagged a flute from a passing waiter and turned his attention fully on her. It was all she could do not to gasp under his heated scrutiny. It was as if he undressed her right then and there in front of a roomful of people. Her blood simmered and pooled low in her belly. He had beautiful eyes, and they were currently devouring her, delving beneath the modest evening gown she'd chosen. He made it seem like she wore the most scanty, revealing dress imaginable. She felt nude and vulnerable under his searing gaze.

"Tell me something, Celia. Why aren't you over with the rest of the piranhas convincing me that your ad agency will take Reese Enterprises straight to the top?"

Her lips curved upward into a smile. "Because you already are at the top?"

"You're such a tease."

At that her smile faded. He was right. She was flirting, and it was the last thing she wanted to do.

She glanced across the room to where the other ad execs stood staring holes through her and Evan.

"I'm not desperate, Evan. I know I'm good. I know my ideas for your ad campaign are spectacular. Does that make me arrogant? Maybe. But I don't need to sell you on a load of malarkey. All I need is the time to show you what Maddox Communications can do for you."

"What *you* can do for me, Celia."

Her eyes widened in surprise at the blatant innuendo. And then he went on to correct the errant assumption she'd just made.

"If the ideas are yours and are as brilliant as you say, I'd hardly be taking on Maddox and what the agency could do for me. I'd be hiring you."

She frowned and hated that she suddenly felt at a disadvantage. Her fingers curled a little tighter around the glass, and she prayed they wouldn't shake and betray her unease.

He studied her curiously, having obviously picked up on her discomfort.

"It wasn't a proposition, Celia. Believe me, you'd know the difference."

In a daring move, he reached a finger out and traced a line down the bare skin of her arm. She was unable to call back the shiver, or the sprinkling of chill bumps that danced over her flesh.

"I only meant that if you wow me with a pitch and I sign on with Maddox, you won't pawn me off to some junior executive. I'd expect you to oversee the campaign at every level."

"And do you anticipate signing with Maddox Communications?" she asked huskily.

There was a gleam of amusement in his green eyes. He took a measured sip of his wine and then regarded her lazily. "If your pitch is good enough. Golden Gate has some good ideas. I'm considering them."

Her lips tightened. "Only because you haven't seen mine yet."

He smiled again. "I like confidence. I don't like false modesty. I look forward to seeing what you have in mind, Celia Taylor. I have a feeling you put every bit of that passion I see burning in your eyes into your work. Brock Maddox is a lucky man to have such a fierce employee. I wonder if he knows it."

"Are we moving into the appointment phase?" she asked lightly. "I have to admit, I've enjoyed watching you surrounded by the piranhas as you call them."

He put his glass down on a nearby table. "Dance with me and we'll discuss appointment times."

Her eyes narrowed.

He lifted one finely constructed eyebrow into what looked like a challenge.

"I've also danced with female ad executives from Golden Gate, Primrose, San Fran Media—"

She held up her hand. "Okay, okay, I get it. You're making your selection on who's the best dance partner."

He threw back his head and laughed. Several people around them turned to stare, and she had to resist the strong urge to flee the room. She hated the attention that Evan seemed to have no issue with whatsoever. How nice it must be not to have to worry what people thought about you. To have your reputation intact and not have suffered the stupidity and vindictiveness of others. But then men rarely suffered in cases like hers. It was always the woman. The vilified other woman.

Knowing no graceful way to bow out of the dance, she set down her own glass and allowed Evan to lead her onto the ballroom floor.

To her relief, he held her loosely. To anyone looking on, they could find no fault or impropriety. She and Evan didn't look like lovers, but she knew the thought was present in both their minds. She could see the desire in his eyes and knew he could probably see it in hers.

She wasn't practiced at hiding her emotions. Maybe being the only girl in an all-male household growing up was the reason. Her family was a loud, demonstrative lot, and she'd always been regarded as the precious daughter and sister.

It would make her life easier to be able to hide her thoughts from this man. Then she wouldn't concern herself over whether he was giving her a shot because he thought she deserved it or whether he was thinking only of the powerful sexual pull between them and how best to capitalize on it.

Wow, Celia. Lump him in with all the other jerks you've known, why don't you? Nothing like being tried and convicted based on your gender.

"Relax. You're thinking way too much," Evan murmured close to her ear.

She forced herself to do as he'd instructed and gave herself over to the beautiful music and the sheer enjoyment of dancing with a man who took her breath away.

"So how is next week? I have Friday free."

She jerked back to reality, and for a moment couldn't for the life of her figure out what he was talking about. Some professional she was.

"I was thinking we could meet informally and you could

go over what you have in mind. If I'm interested we could do the whole shebang at your agency. Maybe that'll save us both a lot of time and hassle if I'm not loving your ideas."

"Sure. I can do Friday. Friday is good."

The music ended, and he held her just a bit longer than necessary, but she was so affected by the intensity of his gaze that she couldn't formulate a single objection.

"I'll have my assistant call you with the time and location then."

He picked up her hand and brought it to his lips. The warm brush of his mouth over the back of her hand sent a bolt of pleasure straight down her spine.

"Until Friday."

She watched wordlessly as he strolled away. He was immediately swallowed up by a crowd of people again, but he turned and found her gaze. For a moment they simply stared at one another and then the corners of his mouth lifted into a half smile.

Oh, yes, he knew. He knew exactly what her reaction to him was. He'd have to be a complete moron not to. And he was anything but. The man was smart. He was driven. And he had a reputation for being ruthless. He was the perfect client.

She turned to walk toward the exit. She'd done what she'd come for. There was no reason to stick around and be social. If there was any gossip over her dance with Evan, she certainly didn't want to hear it.

On the way, she passed Brock and Elle, who were standing somewhat awkwardly to the side. Brock didn't say anything. He just lifted an inquiring brow. Of course he would have seen her dancing with Evan. Brock probably hadn't looked at anyone but Evan all night. A shame, really, since Elle looked fabulous in her black sheath.

"Friday," she said in a low voice. "I meet with him Friday. No formal pitch. He wants to hear my ideas first. If he likes them, he'll arrange a time for us to hit him with both barrels."

Brock nodded, and she saw the gleam of satisfaction light his eyes.

"Good work, Celia."

Celia smiled and resumed her path to the door. She had a lot to do before next Friday.

Evan Reese loosened his tie as soon as he walked into his hotel suite. He left a trail of clothing from the door, where he threw his jacket over one of the chairs, to the bedroom where he peeled off his socks and left them on the floor.

The desk with his laptop and briefcase beckoned, but for once, the idea of work didn't appeal to him. He was too preoccupied with thoughts of Celia Taylor.

Beautiful, seductive, impossibly aloof Celia Taylor.

His body had been on heightened sense of alert ever since she walked into the ballroom, and though he'd known the moment she left, he was still tense and painfully aware of her scent, how she felt in his arms, how her skin felt under his fingers the one time he'd been bold enough to touch her.

He wanted to do a hell of a lot more than just touch. He wanted to taste her. He wanted her underneath him, making all those feminine, breathy sounds of a woman being pleasured.

He wanted to slide his hand between those gorgeous legs and spread her thighs. He would spend all night making love to her. A woman such as Celia wasn't to be rushed. No, he'd get to know every inch of her body. Find out where she liked to be touched and kissed.

His fixation with her couldn't be readily explained. It wasn't as though he lived as a monk. He had sex. He never lacked for partners. Sex was good. But he knew that sex with Celia would never be just good. It would be lush and delicious. The kind of experience a man would sell his soul for.

She was indeed a beautiful woman. Tall, but not too tall.

She would fit perfectly against him, her head tucked just underneath his chin. She often wore her long red hair up in a loose style that told him she didn't pay a lot of attention to whether every strand was in place.

He wanted to take that damn clip out, toss it in the garbage and watch as her silken mass spilled down her back. Or better yet, let it spill over him while they made love.

He cursed under his breath when his body reacted to that image. Cold showers didn't do a thing for his hunger. He ought to know. He'd taken enough of them over the last few weeks.

Perhaps her most mesmerizing feature was her eyes. An unusual shade of green. At times they looked more blue but in certain lighting they were vivid green.

The more cynical side of him wondered why a woman that beautiful hadn't tried to seduce him into hiring her agency. It wasn't like it hadn't been attempted before. In fact, he'd received two such propositions tonight at the fund-raiser.

He wasn't saying he'd mind. Right now he'd use just about any reason to get into Celia Taylor's bed. But there was a reserve about her that intrigued him. She was a cool customer, and he admired that. She wanted the account. She'd made no bones about that. But she hadn't actively pursued him.

No, she'd waited for him to come to her, and maybe that made her damn smart since he'd done just that.

The ring of his BlackBerry disturbed his fantasy and brought him sharply back to the present. He looked down in disgust at the unmistakable ridge in his trousers then reached into his pocket for his phone.

His mother. He frowned. He wasn't really in the mood for anything to do with his family, but he loved his mother dearly, and he couldn't very well ignore her.

With a resigned sigh, he punched the answer button and put the phone to his ear.

"Hello, Mom."

"Evan! I'm so glad I caught you. You're so busy these days."

He could hear the disapproval and worry in her voice.

"The business doesn't run itself," he reminded her.

She made a low sound of exasperation. "You sound so much like your father."

He winced. That wasn't exactly at the top of the list of things he wanted to hear.

"I wanted to call to make sure you hadn't forgotten about this weekend. It's important to Mitchell that you be there."

There was a note of anxiety in her voice that always seemed to creep in when his brother was mentioned.

"You can't think I'd actually go to their wedding," Evan said mildly. And the only important thing to Mitchell was that Evan be there to see his triumph.

His mother made a disapproving sound. "I know it won't be easy for you, Evan. But don't you think you should forgive him? It's obvious he and Bettina belong together. It would be so nice to have the whole family back together again."

"Easy? It won't be easy *or* difficult, Mom. I don't care, and frankly they're welcome to each other. I simply don't have the time or the desire to attend."

"Would you do it for me?" she begged. "Please. I want just one time to see my sons in the same room."

Evan sank onto the edge of the bed and pinched the bridge of his nose between two fingers. If his dad had called, he would have had no problem refusing. If Mitchell had called, Evan nearly laughed at that idea. Mitchell wouldn't be calling him for anything after Evan had told him to go to hell and take his faithless fiancée with him.

But this was his mother, whom he harbored real affection for. His mother, who was always caught in the middle of the tension that existed between him and his father and between him and Mitchell.

"All right, Mom. I'll come. But I'll be bringing someone with me. I hope you don't mind."

He could practically see her beam right through the phone.

"Why, Evan, you didn't tell me you were seeing someone new! Of course you're welcome to bring her. I'll very much look forward to meeting her."

"Can you forward all the details to my assistant so she can make arrangements?"

His mom sighed. "How did I know you wouldn't have kept the original e-mail?"

Because he'd immediately sent it to the trash folder? Of course he wouldn't tell her that.

"Send it to Vickie and I'll see you on Friday. I love you," he said after a short pause.

"I love you too, son. I'm so very glad you're coming."

He ended the call and stared down at his BlackBerry. Friday. Hell. Friday was when he was meeting Celia. Finally meeting Celia.

He'd planned meticulously, not wanting to seem overanxious. He'd flirted, exchanged long, seeking glances and had spent a lot of damn time in the shower. He was surprised he hadn't come down with hypothermia.

And now he was going to have to cancel because his mother thought that he should go see the woman he was supposed to have married instead marry his younger brother.

He needed to find a date. Preferably one who would convince his mother he wasn't secretly pining over Bettina. He wasn't. He'd gotten over her the moment she'd dumped him for his brother when Mitchell was appointed the CEO position in their family jewelry business.

She preferred the glitz-and-glamour facade of the jewelry world over the sweaty, athletic image of his company. It was just as well she wasn't bright enough to have done any research. If she had, she would have known that Evan's company's earnings far exceeded those of his father's jewelry business. And it had only taken him a few years to accomplish it.

His mother wouldn't believe it but Evan was grateful to his

brother for being a selfish pinhead. Mitchell wanted Bettina because Evan had her. Thanks to that deep need for one-upmanship, Evan had narrowly escaped a huge mistake.

But it didn't mean he wanted to spend quality time with his controlling father and his spoiled, self-indulgent sibling. He'd agreed, however, and now he needed a date.

With a shake of his head, he began scrolling through his address book in his BlackBerry. He had narrowed his options to three women, when the solution came to him.

It was brilliant, really. He was an idiot for not having thought of it immediately. It certainly solved *all* his problems.

Finally he had a way of luring Celia to him. It would be business, of course, but if the setting happened to be intimate and she was for all practical purposes stranded with him on Catalina Island for three days…

A satisfied smile raised the corners of his mouth. Maybe the wedding wouldn't be such a bad thing after all.

Two

When Celia pulled into her father's driveway, she was relieved to see Noah's Mercedes parked beside their father's pickup. She pulled her black BMW on the other side of the truck and grinned at how the two expensive cars flanked the beat-up old piece of family history.

As she got out, she heard the roar of another engine and turned to see Dalton pull in behind her. To her utter shock, Adam climbed out of the passenger seat.

"Adam!" she exclaimed, and ran straight for him.

He grinned just before she launched herself into his arms. She hit his chest and as she'd known he would, he caught her and whirled her around. Just like he'd done when she'd been five years old and every year since.

"How come I never get greetings like that?" Dalton grumbled as he climbed from behind the wheel.

"I'm so glad to see you," she whispered fiercely.

His big arms surrounded her in a hug that nearly squeezed the breath out of her. Adam always gave the best hugs.

"It's good to see you too, Cece. I missed you. Took you long enough to come back home."

She slid down until her feet met the ground again, and she briefly looked away.

"Hey," he chided as he nudged her chin until she looked at him again. "None of that. It's all in the past, and it's a good damn thing it is otherwise your brothers would hop the first plane to New York and beat the crap out of your former boss."

"Hey, hello, I'm here, too," Dalton said, waving a hand between them.

She held Adam's gaze for a moment longer and then smiled her thanks. Her brothers were overbearing. They were loud, protective and they certainly had their faults. Like not believing she needed to do anything more in life than look pretty and let them support her. But God love them, they were fierce in their loyalty to her, and she adored them for it.

Finally she turned to Dalton. "You I saw two weekends ago. Adam I haven't seen in forever." She glanced back at Adam. "Why is that anyway?"

He grimaced. "Sorry. Busy time of the year."

She nodded. Adam, her oldest brother, owned a successful landscaping business and spring was always a hectic time. They rarely saw him until the fall when business started to slow.

Dalton slung an arm over Celia's shoulders and planted an affectionate kiss on her cheek. "I see Mr. Baseball is here. Must have caught a break before the season starts."

"You guys going to the season opener?" she asked.

"Wouldn't miss it," Adam said.

"I have a favor to ask then."

Both brothers looked curiously at her.

"I'm bringing a client and I'd like to keep my relationship to Noah on the down low."

Curiosity gleamed in their eyes. She knew they wanted

to ask, but when she didn't volunteer her reasons why, they didn't pursue the matter.

"Okay. Not a problem," Adam finally said.

"Are you three going to stand out there all day or are you coming in to eat?"

Her father's voice boomed from the front porch, and they turned to see him leaning against the doorframe, impatience evident in his stance.

Celia grinned. "We better go in before he starts muttering threats."

Adam ruffled her hair then tucked his arm over her neck so he had her in a headlock. He started toward the house, dragging her with him.

When they got to the porch, she laughingly stumbled from Adam's hold and gave her dad a quick hug. He squeezed her and dropped a kiss on the top of her head.

"Where's Noah?" she asked.

"Where he always is. Parked in front of the big screen, watching baseball."

She slipped past her father while he greeted his sons and entered the home she'd grown up in. When she got to the living room, she saw Noah sprawled in the recliner, remote in hand as he flipped through footage of past baseball games.

"Hey," she called.

He looked up, his eyes warming in welcome. As he got up, he smiled broadly at her then held out his arms.

She hugged him then made a show of feeling his ribs.

"They don't feed you in training camp?"

He laughed. "You know damn well that all I ever do is eat. I think my tapeworms have tapeworms."

She glanced back to make sure they were still alone and then lowered her voice.

"Are you going to hang around later or do you have to be somewhere?"

His eyes narrowed, and he lost the smile.

"I don't have to be anywhere today. Why do you ask?"

"I need to talk to you about something. I have a favor to ask, and I'd rather not get into it in front of everyone."

He frowned now. "Is everything okay, Cece? You in some kind of trouble? Do I need to kill anyone?"

She rolled her eyes. "You're too valuable to go to prison. You'd have Dalton do it anyway."

Noah smirked. "The pretty boy would be popular in prison."

"You're a sick puppy. And no, nothing's wrong. Promise. Just want to run something by you that could be beneficial to us both."

"Okay, if you're going to be all mysterious on me. I guess I can wait until later. You want to go back to your place for a while? I'd invite you to mine but the maid quit on me last week and it's not a pretty sight. You do have food, right?"

She shook her head. "Yes, I have food, and yes, we can go back to my place. For God's sake, Noah, how hard is it to pick up after yourself? Or if you can't do that, at least pick up the phone and get another maid service?"

"I've sort of been blackballed," he mumbled. "I have to find an agency where my reputation hasn't preceded me."

"I feel so sorry for the woman you marry. She'll be in ten kinds of hell."

"You don't have to worry because that's not going to happen."

"Sure. Okay. I believe you."

They both looked up when the others spilled into the living room. Noah gave her arm a light squeeze and mouthed "later."

"Food'll be on the table in fifteen minutes," her father announced.

Her mouth watered. She didn't even know what her dad had cooked. It didn't matter. The man was a culinary genius.

Lunch was a rambunctious affair. Her brothers bickered and joked endlessly while her father looked on indulgently. She'd missed all of this during her years in New York. Though she loathed the circumstances that brought her home, she was glad to be back in the comforting circle of her family. Even if they were all just a generation from knuckles-dragging-on-the-ground cavemen.

After the table had been cleared, the argument started over what channel the television landed on. Noah didn't know anything but ESPN or the Food Network existed, Dalton liked anything that was mindless, particularly if explosions were involved, and Adam liked to torment his brothers by forcing them to watch gardening shows.

Celia settled back to enjoy the sights and sounds of home. Her father sat on the couch next to her and shook his head over his sons' antics.

It was the truth, she'd fled the hovering overprotectiveness of her family. She'd been determined to make her mark on the world while they wanted her to stay home, where they could support her and look out for her.

She wasn't a vain woman, but she knew men found her attractive. She was probably considered beautiful by most, but her looks had been the cause of a lot of problems in her life.

Because of her delicate looks, her brothers and even her father thought her job was just to look pretty and let them provide for her. She hadn't been encouraged to go to college—she'd done all of that on her own—and they certainly hadn't wanted her to have a career in something as demanding as advertising.

She'd ignored their objections. She'd gotten her degree and after graduation, she'd taken a job in New York City. After a couple of years, she'd taken a position with a large, prestigious firm. She was on her way up. A promotion had just cemented her triumph. And then it had all come crashing down like a bridge in an earthquake.

Adam rising from his chair shook her from her angry thoughts. She forced her fingers to relax and winced at the marks she'd left on her palms.

"Leaving already?" she asked.

Adam pulled her up into a bear hug. "Yeah. I need to check on a job. I'll see you at the season opener, though."

She kissed his cheek and patted his shoulder affectionately. "Of course."

She turned to Dalton. "I guess you'll be going, too, since you brought him over."

"Yep. I have a date I've got to get ready for anyway."

No one seemed surprised by that announcement.

"I'll walk you guys out. I need to run, too. I have a pitch to prepare for."

Her father grimaced, and she steeled herself for another gruff lecture about how she worked too hard. An interesting statement since Adam worked harder than all of them, and no one ever lectured him.

To her surprise, he remained silent. She regarded him with a raised eyebrow and wondered if he'd burst at the seams, but his lips remained in a firm line. He rose from the couch to hug her and then gruffly reminded her to be sure and get enough rest.

They all walked out together, and her father reminded them all of lunch next Sunday. Celia waved to Adam and Dalton before climbing into her car. Noah stood, saying his goodbyes to their father, and she drove down the driveway. Noah would be along shortly and she needed to make sure her pantry would survive the assault.

Celia had just done a cursory examination of her stock of food—cursing the fact she hadn't been to the market in far too long—when the door buzzer sounded.

She strode across to the call box and mashed the button. "That you, Noah?"

"Yep, buzz me in?"

A few seconds later, Noah walked in, and she smiled her welcome.

"I know that smile," he said suspiciously. "That's a smile

that says you lured me here under false pretenses. You don't have any food, do you?"

"Weeeell, no. But I did just order pizza."

"You're forgiven, but I refuse to have a reasonable discussion until it gets here."

She laughed and punched him on the arm when he flopped on the sofa next to her. "If I didn't need a favor from you, I'd make you pay for it."

His expression grew serious. "So what is this favor, anyway?"

"Oh, no. I'm not asking you for anything until you have a full stomach. Again, since you ate not even three hours ago."

He grunted but didn't offer any argument. His stomach was too important.

He reached for the remote and flipped on the TV. A few seconds later, the sports recap was on, and he settled back against the couch.

The pizza didn't take long—thanks to the bistro right around the corner offering delivery service. Soon the decadent smells of a completely loaded pizza filled her apartment. Despite all she'd eaten at lunch, her stomach growled in anticipation. She eyed the gooey dripping cheese and grimaced. It might taste good, but it would go straight to her hips. Then again, that's what the treadmill was for.

She dropped the box on the coffee table in front of Noah, not bothering with plates. He eyed the mountain of toppings with something akin to bliss.

She waited until he'd grabbed the first piece before she carefully took a slice and nibbled on the end. It was, in a word, sheer heaven. She leaned back and waited for Noah to down the first slice. When he was on his second, he turned and said around a mouthful of pizza, "So what's this favor you need?"

She sat forward, putting half the slice down on a napkin.

"I have this client...well he's a client I want to land. Evan Reese."

Noah stopped chewing. "The guy who sells athletic wear?"

She nodded. "Yeah. He fired his last agency and has yet to sign with a new one. I want him. Maddox Communications wants him."

"Okay. So where do I fit into the picture?"

For a moment her nerve deserted her, and then she mentally slapped herself upside the head. In her profession there was no room for the spineless. She hadn't worked her way into the confidence of Brock Maddox acting like a jellyfish.

"I want you to agree to front his new line of athletic wear."

Noah blinked then he frowned, and finally he put down his half-eaten slice. For a moment he was quiet. She waited, fully expecting him to say no or to launch into all the reasons why he didn't take endorsement deals. She knew them all. But he did none of those things. Instead he studied her carefully, his gaze sliding over her features as though he was reaching right into her head and pulling out her every thought.

He wouldn't ask why him. He was a huge name in baseball, and he was more sought after than any other professional athlete mainly because of his refusal to take endorsement deals. Instead of deterring companies, it made them all the more determined to be the first to lure Noah Hart to their brand.

She could beg. She could hurry through a prepared explanation as to why she needed him, but she wasn't going to wheedle and cajole.

Noah was still frowning as he studied her. "This is important to you."

She nodded. "Evan is a big client. My boss is trusting me to land the account. Don't get me wrong, I'll get him with or without you, but you'd be the nail in his coffin. Plus it would be huge for you. Reese will pay a lot to have you be the spokesman for his sportswear."

Noah sighed. "I wish you'd just quit this job. You don't have to work, and you know it. You don't have to prove yourself to anyone, Cece. Certainly not to your family. Adam, Dalton and I make more than enough money to support you. It would make Dad happy if you didn't have such a stressful job. He's convinced you'll have an ulcer before you're thirty."

She smiled faintly. "I am thirty."

He shot her an impatient look.

"Look, Noah, would you quit baseball just because your brothers make enough money to support you? They do, you know."

A derisive, strangling sound rose from his throat. He licked his lips as if to rid himself of a really bad taste.

"It's different."

"I know, I know. You're a man, and I'm a woman." Her lips curled in disgust. "Noah, I love you dearly. You're the best brother a girl could ask for. But you're a chauvinist to your toes."

He huffed but didn't dispute her accusation. Then his expression grew thoughtful again. "I assume you've done your research on this man and his company."

Celia nodded before he'd even finished. On the surface, Noah looked and acted laissez-faire. He had all the appearances of a golden-boy jock whose only concern might be fast cars and faster women. But beneath that illusion lay a man who had a deep social conscience.

His refusal of endorsement deals had gained him a reputation of eccentricity from some. Others regarded him incredulously as a fool to pass on the opportunity to make millions by doing nothing more than lend his name to countless companies willing to part with their dollars for his endorsement. But the simple fact was that Noah did meticulous research on all the corporations that approached him, and so far none had passed muster with him.

"E-mail it all to me. I'll take a look. If it checks out, I'm willing to listen to his offer."

She leaned over and kissed his cheek. "Thanks, Noah. You're the best."

"I don't suppose you'll be so grateful that you'll volunteer to clean my apartment?"

She snorted and picked up her slice of pizza again. "Put it this way. I'd rather quit my job and let you and Adam support me than clean your place."

He winced. "Well, damn. No need to be so mean about it."

"Poor baby. Oh, hey, I need one more favor."

His eyes narrowed, and he glared at her. "You just turn down my request for you to play cleaning lady and you insult me in the process and then have the cheek to want another favor?"

"How about I find you a replacement cleaning service? Then both of us are happy."

He got a hopeful puppy dog look that would probably make mush of most women. Thankfully she was his sister and completely immune to any adorableness on his part.

"Okay, you find me someone to clear a path in my apartment and whatever this other favor of yours is I'll do it."

"Wow—and you don't even know what it is."

"Should tell you how desperate I am," he muttered.

She laughed and punched him in the arm. "All I need are two very cushy seats behind home plate for the season opener. I'll be taking Evan. Hopefully."

"Anyone ever tell you how expensive you are?"

"Hey, wait a second. A minute ago, you were trying to convince me to quit my job so you could support me."

His expression went from teasing to serious with one blink. "I just worry about you, Cece. That's all. What happened in New York would have never occurred if—"

She stiffened and held her hand, halting him in mid-sentence. "I don't want to talk about New York."

Regret flashed in his eyes. "Sorry. Consider it dropped."

She waited for her pulse to settle and then she forced a smile. "So you'll take a look at the research I've compiled? You'll like Reese. He's a veritable Boy Scout. His employees love him. He has a cracking health-insurance plan. He's had no layoffs since his business started and he's not shipping jobs or production overseas. Let's see. What else? He's a regular contributor to a half dozen pet charities—"

Noah held up his hands in surrender. "Okay, okay, he's a saint. I get it. How do other men ever measure up?"

"Cut the sarcasm."

He checked his watch and let out a sigh. "Sorry to break this up so early, especially since I haven't finished the pizza. *Somebody* talked too much. Very distracting. E-mail me the stuff. I'll take a look. And the tickets will be waiting for you at the box office."

"You always were my favorite sibling," she said affectionately.

He dropped a kiss on top of her head then stood and stretched lazily.

"I'll give you a call when I'm through reading everything."

Three

Evan walked into the suite of offices he leased for the times he was in San Francisco. It wasn't home, and though Union Square was a sumptuous neighborhood that catered to upscale businesses, he preferred the funky modern feel of Seattle.

He nodded a good morning to his receptionist but halted when she came out of her seat, a concerned expression on her face.

"You shouldn't go in there," Tanya said in a hushed whisper.

He raised an eyebrow when he realized she was gesturing toward his office.

"Why the devil not?" he demanded.

She put one hand up to shield her mouth and then she tapped her finger against her palm—in the direction of his office.

"Because *she's* in there."

Evan turned to stare down the hall toward his office, but the door was closed. Damn, but he didn't have time for this. He looked back at Tanya and tried to stifle his growing impatience. The girl was highly efficient if a little eccentric. But he liked unconventional, and while she'd probably fit in better with his Seattle staff with her colored hair, multiple piercings and vintage 1930s clothing, he found she brought a sort of vibrancy to an otherwise stuffy office here.

"Okay, Tanya. First of all, who the hell is 'she' and where is Vickie?"

It wasn't like Vickie not to meet him as he got off the elevator. His longtime assistant traveled with him everywhere. She had an apartment here and in Seattle. She had an uncanny knack for knowing precisely when he'd show up, and as a result she was always there, ready to pelt him with the day's obligations.

Tanya's face fell. "Oh, sir, did you not get your message? I left you two. Vickie's granddaughter was rushed to the hospital early this morning. They suspect appendicitis. She's in surgery now."

Evan frowned. "No, I didn't get any such message. Keep me updated. I want to know the minute she's out of surgery. Send flowers and make sure Vickie has everything she might need. On second thought, send over food for the family. Hospital food is terrible. And arrange for a hospitality suite. If there is a hotel close to the hospital, have a block of rooms set aside for any of the family members."

Tanya blinked then hurriedly picked up a notepad and began scribbling.

Evan waited a moment then sighed. "Tanya?"

She looked up, blinking, as if surprised to still see him standing there.

"Who is the 'she' waiting in my office?"

Tanya's nose curled in distaste. "It's Miss Hammond, sir. I couldn't stop her. She was quite imperious. Told me she'd wait for you."

It was all Evan could do not to look heavenward and ask "why me?" He glanced down the hall and briefly considered leaving. He had no patience for Bettina today, and after his mother had extracted his promise to attend this weekend's debacle, he couldn't imagine anything Bettina could have to say to him.

"Keep me posted on Vickie's granddaughter," he said as he turned to go down to his office.

He opened the door and swept in, his gaze immediately finding Bettina. She was sitting on one of the sofas lining the window that overlooked the outdoor cafés lining the sidewalk below.

"Bettina," he said as he tossed his briefcase onto his desk. "What brings you here?"

Bettina rose, her hands going down to smooth her dress. The motion directed attention to her legs—her self-admitted favorite personal attribute. The dress stopped almost at mid-thigh, which meant quite a lot of those legs were on display.

Evan wouldn't lie. He'd enjoyed those legs. It was just too bad they were attached to the rest of her.

Her expression creased into one of fake pain. She crossed the room, holding her hands dramatically in front of her to grasp his.

"I wanted to thank you for agreeing to come to the wedding. It means the world to Mitchell and your mom and dad. I know how painful it must be. I can't imagine how difficult it was for you to agree to go after I broke your heart."

Evan just stared at her. Part of him wanted to ask her what planet she existed on, but he already knew the answer to that. It was planet Bettina, where everything revolved around her. Did she honestly believe he was still pining for her?

"Cut the theatrics, Bettina. Why are you really here? You don't care if I show up or not, so why pretend otherwise? In fact, I'd be willing to admit you hoped I wouldn't."

She blinked, and for a moment he saw bitterness in her eyes.

"Lucy said you were bringing a…date. It was clever of you, really. But you don't fool me, Evan. Everyone knows you haven't been serious about anyone since me. Who is she? Someone you've met socially? Do you know anything about her? Does she know she's going as an accessory? God knows that's all I ever was to you."

"You can't have it both ways, Bettina. Either I was serious about you or you were an accessory," he drawled. "Which is it?"

She flushed angrily. "I only meant that you haven't dated any woman more than once since I broke things off with you."

He made an exaggerated expression of surprise. "You flatter me. I had no idea you were so interested in who I date. I would have thought my brother kept you too occupied to monitor my love life."

"Bring your date, Evan. But you know and I know she isn't me. She'll never be me. Don't think you'll take anything away from my wedding day."

With that she stalked out of his office, leaving Evan to shake his head. He really ought to call his brother and thank him profusely.

He sank into his chair and opened his day planner. Vickie kept meticulous records of all appointments for just such rare occasions that she was out of pocket. He frowned when he saw his calendar was full. Except for one forty-five-minute window for lunch.

His mind immediately went to Celia. Celia, whose office was just two blocks from his. He'd planned to call her, but a proposition such as he had in mind was really better delivered in person. He wouldn't have a lot of time, and he doubted she had much free time, either, but he knew without arrogance that if he asked her to lunch, she wouldn't refuse. She wanted his business too badly.

He hit the button to call Vickie then quickly remembered she wasn't there. He connected to Tanya instead.

"Yes, sir?"

"Tanya, I need Celia Taylor of Maddox Communications on the phone."

Celia stepped out of the elevator and was met with a cheerful hello from Shelby, the receptionist for Maddox Communications. Shelby was young and friendly. She also had superb organization skills and a memory like a steel trap. Which made her a perfect asset. But more importantly, she knew everything about everyone at Maddox. There wasn't a piece of juicy gossip floating around that Shelby didn't know, and she didn't mind sharing it. Celia found it useful to keep in the know. Never again would she be caught off guard like she'd been in her last job.

"Good morning, Shelby," Celia returned as she paused in front of Shelby's desk. "Any messages for me?"

Shelby's eyes twinkled and she leaned forward to whisper conspiratorially. "Latest rumors that have surfaced are about the boss man and his assistant."

Celia frowned. "You mean, him and Elle?"

Elle didn't seem like the type to indulge in a torrid office affair and definitely not with her boss. Celia felt compelled to warn Elle about the potential pitfalls of even having such a rumor circulate, but it was just a rumor, and Elle might not appreciate Celia broaching the subject.

Shelby shrugged. "Well, they do seem to spend a lot of time together."

"Of course they do. She's his assistant," Celia pointed out.

"I just repeat what others are saying."

Celia gripped her briefcase a little tighter. It wouldn't do her any good to get involved. Brock and Elle were adults. She just hoped Elle wasn't hurt by the idle gossip.

"Hey, Shelby," Celia began as she remembered why she'd stopped to begin with. "I need you to look up a cleaning service." She dug around in her briefcase then pulled out a sheet of paper that had all the names of the agencies Noah had already contacted. She handed it over the counter to Shelby. "These are the ones marked off the list of possibilities. I need you to make it clear this is a demanding client and that he's a slob through and through. Money is no object but whoever the poor soul is who takes the job will definitely earn their paycheck."

Shelby's eyes widened. "Noah Hart. *The* Noah Hart? He needs a housekeeper? I'm available. I mean, I can totally quit here, right?"

Celia shot her a "get real" look. "Let me know if you find someone. Oh, and I'm expecting a call from Evan Reese's assistant. I don't care what I'm doing or who I'm with, make sure I get that call."

As she walked away, Shelby called out to her. "Hey, wait. How do you know Noah Hart? He's not a client of Maddox."

Celia smiled and kept walking toward her office. Normally she'd stop in on some of her coworkers, say hello, get a feel for what the day's events were, but she was already running late, thanks to a breakfast meeting going well into the brunch hour. She needed to play catch-up on phone messages and e-mails before a full afternoon of client calls and a staff meeting to close out the day.

She'd made a sizeable dent in the backlog of messages when her interoffice intercom buzzed.

"Celia, Mr. Reese is on line two."

Celia frowned. "Mr. Reese himself or Mr. Reese's assistant?"

"Mr. Reese."

"Put him through," she said crisply.

She wiped her hand on her skirt then shook her head. What did she have to be nervous about? As soon as the phone rang, she picked it up.

"Celia Taylor."

"Celia, how are you?"

Even his voice sent a bolt of awareness through her body. When would she stop acting like a teenage girl in the throes of her first sexual awakening? It was ridiculous. It wasn't professional.

"I'm good, Evan. And you?"

"I don't have a lot of time. I wanted to meet for lunch today. That is, if your schedule permits?"

There was a note of confidence in his voice. He knew damn well she wouldn't say no. Hastily, she checked the clock.

"What time?"

"Now."

Panic scuttled around her stomach. Now? She wasn't prepared to meet him now. Surely he didn't want to reschedule their informal pitch session from Friday to now?

"I thought we had a lunch date on Friday?"

She was stalling as her brain scrambled to catch up.

"I want to discuss Friday today. There's been a change of plans."

Her heart sank. There was no way she could have her act together right now.

"I only have forty-five minutes," he continued. "We're two blocks apart. Shall we meet in the middle? Our choices are French, Italian or good ole American."

"I'm up for anything," she said faintly.

She propped the phone between her shoulder and her ear and began frantically digging for her notes on his account. She stuffed everything into a folder and reached for her briefcase.

"Great. Shall we meet in say five minutes? I'll start out now."

"Sure, meet you there."

He hung up and for a moment she stood there like a moron, the phone still stuck to her ear. Then she slammed it down, took in a deep steadying breath and declared battle.

She could do this in her sleep.

Slinging the bag over her shoulder, she all but jogged out of her office and down the hallway.

She passed Ash Williams, Maddox's CFO, who held up a finger and opened his mouth to say something to her.

"Not now, Ash, she called as she hustled by. "Late for an important lunch date."

She didn't even look to see his reaction.

She ran past Shelby and hollered back as she punched the button for the elevator.

"If Brock asks, I'm having lunch with Mr. Reese. Just tell him Friday got moved up. If anyone else asks, just tell them I'll return this afternoon."

The elevator opened and she ducked in. As she turned around, she saw Shelby's look of befuddlement just as the doors slid shut again.

When she reached the lobby, she stopped in the bathroom long enough to check her appearance. She wouldn't stop traffic for sure, but at least she didn't look as frazzled as she felt.

The heels she'd chosen to complete her outfit were fabulous—as long as she didn't have to actually walk in them. A trek down the block on uneven cement sidewalks wasn't what she had in mind. She kept tennis shoes in her office for just such occasions, but five minutes notice on the most important lunch date of her career didn't give her time to worry over footwear. She'd just suck it up.

When she crossed the street to the next block, she realized she never had gotten where they were supposed to meet. Italian, French or American. Her gaze scanned the bright umbrellas scattered along the sidewalk cafés, first on her side of the street and then across.

A vacuum formed, sucking all the oxygen right out of her lungs the moment she laid eyes on him. He stood in the sunlight, one hand shoved into the pocket of his slacks, the other holding a phone to his ear.

Power. There was an aura of power that surrounded him, and it drew her like a magnet. For a moment, she just stood

watching him in absolute girly delight. He was simply…
delicious looking.

Then he turned slightly and found her. How, she wasn't
sure given how busy the street was, but he locked onto her
immediately almost as if he'd sensed her perusal.

She straightened and started forward, embarrassed to have
been caught staring.

She crossed the street, hugging her briefcase between her
arm and her side. Evan watched her approach, lean hunger
gleaming in his eyes. His features relaxed into a smile as she
drew abreast of him.

"Right on time."

She nodded, not wanting to betray how out of breath she
was from her flight from her office.

"I chose good ole American," he said as he gestured toward
a nearby table. "I hope that was all right."

"Of course."

He held out his arm for her to precede him to the table at
the end of the row. She sat, grateful to be off her feet, and
placed her briefcase beside her.

He took his seat across from her and motioned for the
waiter.

"Would you like wine?" Evan asked Celia when the waiter
approached.

"Whatever you're having is fine."

Evan relayed his request and then looked over at Celia. "I
asked you to lunch because I'm afraid something has come
up and we won't be able to make our lunch date on Friday."

She nodded then reached down for her briefcase. "That's
all right. I brought along the information I wanted to
present—"

He reached over and circled her wrist with his fingers.
"That isn't why I invited you to lunch."

She blinked and let go of her briefcase.

"I'd still like to keep our appointment…I'd just like to
change the location."

She was royally confused now, and it must have shown. Amusement twinkled in his eyes and he smiled.

"I don't have a lot of time today, so let me come straight to the point."

His fingers were still around her wrist, though they'd loosened, and his thumb moved idly over her pulse point. She was sure her pulse was racing. It probably felt like a train under his fingers. She didn't move. Didn't even breathe. She didn't want to lose the marvelous sensation of his touch. Did he have any idea just how devastating his effect on her was?

"I have a wedding this weekend." She could swear his lips curled in distaste. "A family wedding. My brother is getting married on Catalina Island. I'm to be there Thursday evening, hence the reason I can't make our Friday meeting."

"I understand," she said. "We can reschedule at your convenience."

"I'd like you to go with me."

Before she could call back the reaction, her eyes widened and she pulled her hand from his. She put it in her lap and cupped her other hand over it, wanting to preserve the sensation of his fingers over hers.

He put up his hand in an impatient gesture then lowered it and fiddled with the napkin on the table. He seemed almost uneasy. She cocked her head, curious now as to what he would say next.

"My schedule is quite busy. I need to move on this new campaign. I can't spare weeks searching for a new agency. If you went with me, I could listen to your ideas. I realize a wedding isn't ideal. I'd rather be just about any other place myself."

Though it certainly wasn't voiced as a threat, it was certainly implied. If she went with him, he'd listen to her pitch. If she didn't he might not have time for her when he returned.

Worry knotted her stomach. Tagging along to a family wedding seemed entirely too personal even if the purpose was solely business. Not to mention it was hard enough to battle her attraction for him in a business setting. But something as intimate as a wedding?

"How long would we be…away?"

The question came out more as a squeak than a concise, professional query. She sounded like a scared little girl facing the big bad wolf. Oh, but Evan made such a yummy wolf.

It was all she could do not to put her head on the table and bang a few times.

"We'd fly out Thursday evening. Rehearsal and dinner on Friday, wedding Saturday with reception to follow and since it will likely go well into the night, we'd return Sunday."

It would only require one missed day of work. No one but Brock would even need to know, and he certainly wouldn't spill the beans.

She didn't know why she hadn't immediately agreed. She couldn't afford to say no. He had her over a barrel and he damn well knew it. Still, she hesitated—if for no other reason than to let him know he didn't call all the shots.

Okay, so maybe he did, but it didn't hurt him to think otherwise. For two seconds.

"All right," she said in as level a voice as she could manage.

Did he expect her to attend the festivities? It certainly sounded as though he did by the way he outlined the events. She supposed it would be rude to tag along and lurk in the shadows waiting for her appointed time. Or maybe he envisioned having her follow him around everywhere so he could fit in snatches of conversation when possible.

"I'd be happy to purchase any items you may need for the trip," he said.

Startled, she glanced up. "No, I mean…no. Of course not. I can manage just fine. You'll need to tell me the appropriate dress code of course."

He managed a wry smile. "I'm sure anything to do with Bettina will be formal. Quite formal with lots of glitter and fanfare."

His gaze slid sensuously over her features and then lower until her neck heated with a blush.

"I think anything you wear will be stunning. The dress you wore the other night was perfection on you."

The blush climbed higher and she prayed her cheeks didn't look like twin torches.

"I'm sure I can find something glitzy and glamorous," she said lightly. "We girls do like the opportunity to play dress up."

Interest sparked in his eyes. "I can't wait."

The waiter returned with the wine, and Celia latched gratefully onto the glass. Her hands shook. She was sure if she stood, she'd go down like a brick. She'd break an ankle trying to stay up on these ridiculous heels.

Note to self: Don't pack gorgeous, sexy shoes for the weekend. Around him, she'd be a disaster on stilts. He'd spend his entire time picking her up off the floor, that is if she didn't end up in the hospital in traction.

"I'll call you later in the week with the flight arrangements. We'll be taking my private jet."

She swallowed and nodded, then realizing he'd need her number—her cell number and not her office number—she reached down into her briefcase to retrieve a business card.

She frowned, fumbled some more then pulled the bag into her lap. With a groan she realized her business-card holder must have fallen out. Impatiently she tore a piece of paper off a notepad and took out her pen.

Dropping the bag again, she put the paper on the table and hastily scribbled her home and cell number then passed it across the table to Evan.

He took it, studied it a moment then carefully folded it and tucked it away in the breast pocket of his jacket. The waiter approached with menus and Evan looked to her for her order.

"Just the lunch salad," she said. What she really wanted was a really greasy burger with onion rings, but she didn't want to appall Evan. Her brothers gave her all sorts of hell for her indelicate tastes, but then they were to blame for them.

Evan ordered a steak, medium, and after the waiter was gone, Evan stared over at her, his gaze inquisitive.

She cocked her head, prepared for him to ask her a question, but he didn't say anything. He just seemed to study her as if he wanted to uncover all her deep, dark secrets.

Finally he sat back with a satisfied smile. His eyes glinted with triumph.

"I think this wedding is going to turn out to be enjoyable after all."

Four

Celia stepped off the elevator and walked by Shelby, who held her hand up to get Celia's attention.

"Later, Shelby," she called as she headed for Brock's office.

When she got to his door, she was nearly run over as Ash came out. He sidestepped her and kept on walking, his forehead wrinkled as if he were lost in thought. She wasn't even sure he'd seen her.

She stuck her head in Brock's door and breathed a sigh of relief when she found him alone. He glanced up and motioned her in.

"What's with him?" she asked, jerking her head over her shoulder in Ash's direction. "He's been weird lately."

Brock gave her one of those puzzled male looks that suggested he didn't have a clue what she was talking about. She rolled her eyes. Ash had been walking around in a fog, which wasn't typical. He was usually on top of everything and everyone. Celia had overheard Shelby talking about a falling out with a girlfriend, but then she hadn't even known Ash had been seeing anyone. Not that he would have confided in her.

She didn't bother sitting. She had too much to do, and this wouldn't take long.

"I have to go out of town Thursday afternoon."

Brock stared back at her for a moment and then his brows drew together. He frowned and dropped the pen he'd been fiddling with.

"Is this some kind of emergency? You're supposed to meet with Evan Reese on Friday."

His tone suggested someone better be dying. He opened his mouth to say more but before he got off on the tangent she knew was coming, she held up her hand.

"I just had lunch with Evan. There's been a change in plans. He has to be at some family wedding this weekend in Catalina so he couldn't make it on Friday. He said he wants to move on this campaign and he doesn't have a lot of time to spend in the selection process."

Brock swore, his face going red. He picked the pen back up and flung it across his desk. "Dammit, is he even going to listen to our pitch?"

She sucked in a breath. "He wants me to go to Catalina with him. We'd leave Thursday afternoon. It's the only time he can spare me and he's promised to listen to my ideas while we're there."

Brock's brow furrowed further and he studied her intently. "I see."

Forgetting about all she needed to do and that she didn't want to be stuck here in Brock's office forever, she sank down into one of the chairs and stared glumly at her boss.

"I told him I'd go. I didn't see that I had a choice. While he didn't come out and say it, he implied that if I didn't, he was prepared to go with another agency."

"I agree you should go. Does that make me an ass?"

Celia laughed, some of the tension leaving her shoulders.

"No, it doesn't make you an ass. I guess I just worry about the fallout. It's stupid. I shouldn't care. I never would have before, but I know what will be said if it gets out and how things will be twisted."

"You have my support, Celia, and you have the support of the agency. Don't ever doubt that."

She rose and smiled gratefully at him. "Thank you, Brock."

He grunted. "Get me the damn account. That's all the thanks I need."

She stopped on her way out, put her hand on the door frame and looked back. "I'll need someone to cover for me on Friday. I have two client appointments, one in the morning and one in the afternoon."

"Jason will cover for you. You just worry about knocking Evan Reese's socks off."

"I will," Celia murmured. "I will."

On her way down the hall, her BlackBerry rang and she dug into the pocket of her briefcase for it. Seeing Noah's number on the LCD, she mashed the answer button and stuck the phone to her ear as she walked into her office.

"I'm working on the maid service," she said in lieu of hello.

Noah chuckled. "Great, I nearly killed myself getting out of bed this morning. You'd be amazed how dangerous a pair of dirty underwear can be."

Her nose wrinkled in disgust. "Would you at least try not to send the maid screaming from your house on her first day? That's just gross."

He made a derisive sound. "So I read through the info you sent. I also had my agent do some checking. I might add that my agent is orgasmic that I'm considering this endorsement deal."

"Tell him I expect a nice Christmas gift as thank you," Celia said.

"Oh, please. He doesn't even give his mother presents."

Usually she wouldn't mind chatting mindlessly with her siblings, but she had a hundred things to do before Thursday, including figure out how she was going to survive a weekend on an island with a man who made mincemeat of her willpower.

"So does this mean you'll consider it?"

There was a pause, and she found herself holding her breath.

"Yeah. He checks out. He seems as solid as you said he was. I'll talk to him if nothing else."

She did a double-fist pump and dropped her bag on the floor by her desk.

"Have his people call my people," Noah said airily.

Celia laughed. "I am his people. Or at least I will be."

"Hey, you going to be at Dad's this weekend?"

She winced when she remembered that she'd told their father she would indeed be there for Sunday dinner again.

"Afraid not. Something's come up."

Noah made a disapproving sound. "Don't you ever take off? It's Sunday, for Pete's sake."

"How do you know it's work?" she defended. "Maybe I have a hot date."

He snorted. "When was the last time you went on a hot date? It's always work with you."

Knowing they were about to get into lecture territory again, Celia cut him off before he got carried away.

"Hey, I have to run, Noah. Have a meeting in five minutes. I'll call you later, okay?"

Before he could call her a liar, she hung up and plopped into her chair. She blew out a long sigh of relief and closed her eyes.

It was all coming together. Not without a few potholes, but it was within reach. All she had to do was hold it together and get through the weekend and the account would be hers.

"Knock, knock."

Celia opened her eyes to see Jason Reagart standing in her doorway.

"Brock told me I needed to cover for you on Friday, so I stopped by so you could get me up to speed on what I need to know."

"Yeah, have a seat. Give me a minute. Been running all morning. I'll dig out my notes."

Jason eased into a chair, his long legs eating up most of the space between it and her desk. Celia picked up her beleaguered briefcase and opened it on her desk.

"So how is Lauren?"

She hated idle conversation, but the silence was more awkward and she hadn't planned on having to turn over the two meetings to anyone, so her notes were haphazard at best.

"Pregnant. Grumpy. You know, typical pregnant woman."

Celia scowled at him over the top of her briefcase. "Like you wouldn't be if you had to deal with water retention, hormones and arrogant men?"

Jason laughed. "Hey, I spoil her rotten."

"As you should. Ah, here we go."

She pulled out a folder and tossed it to Jason.

"Everything you need to know for the morning meeting is on pages one through three. This isn't a big deal. They just need a little hand holding and a little ego stroking. Bowl them over with how Maddox is going to make them look good while increasing their exposure by three hundred percent and they'll be fine."

Jason flipped through the pages, his brow creased in concentration. She felt comfortable leaving her clients in his very capable hands. He took his job very seriously and moreover, he was damn good at what he did. Maddox had landed a huge account thanks to him, and if Celia had her way, she was going to top that by landing Evan Reese.

"And the afternoon meeting?" Jason asked.

"Hopefully you can read my notes. I have the PowerPoint

presentation ready to go. They need to view it and sign off or suggest any changes so we can move it into the production stage. Impress upon them that this is their last chance to see it before it goes nationwide so make sure they're happy with it."

He nodded and straightened the papers before closing the folder. "Don't worry. I'll take care of it. Brock said you were going to be out of town. Hope everything is all right."

There was a subtle question there, and she knew he hoped she'd expound on her reasons for not being there on Friday. She was just grateful Brock hadn't told him where she was going and why.

She smiled. "Everything's fine, and thank you again for stepping in on such short notice. I owe you one. Send Lauren my love. I'll have to remember to buy her a gift certificate from my favorite spa. I can't think of a pregnant woman alive who wouldn't appreciate a massage."

Jason sent her a disgruntled look. "I don't want some beef-cake putting his hands on my wife."

Celia rolled her eyes. "The poor woman can't see her feet and is probably miserable, and you're going to be picky about who gives her some relief?"

"Damn right I am!"

Celia made a shooing motion with her hands. "Out. I have work to do."

And she made a mental note to call her salon and make an appointment for Lauren. She'd ask for the hunkiest massage therapist they had.

Five

The car that Evan had sent to collect Celia pulled up to the plane parked on the paved landing area that led to the single runway and stopped just a few feet from where the door to the jet lay open.

Celia looked out the window to see Evan standing a short distance away. He was waiting for her.

The driver opened her door, and she stepped into the afternoon sun. She blinked a few times then pulled her shades from her head over her eyes. Maybe then it wouldn't be so obvious how she ate Evan up with her gaze.

He was dressed casually. Jeans, polo shirt and loafers. She'd only ever seen him in suits, and she hadn't imagined he could look better. She was wrong. So, so wrong.

The jeans cupped him in all the right places. They clung to his thighs, rounded his butt and molded to his groin. They weren't new, starchy-looking jeans, either. They were faded and worn, just like a good pair of jeans should be.

"Celia," he said with a nod as she approached. "If you're ready, we can be on our way."

"I just need to get my luggage..."

She turned to see that the driver was handing her luggage to a uniformed man.

"Okay then, I'm ready," she said cheerfully.

He smiled and motioned for her to precede him onto the plane. She mounted the steps and ducked inside.

Her eyes widened at the luxurious interior. It was simple and understated, but she recognized it for what it was. Very expensive comfort. She shoved her shades up so she could get a better look.

There was nothing gaudy about any of the furnishings. It looked very masculine. It even smelled masculine. Leather and suede. Earth tones.

Beyond the three rows of seats, there was a small sitting area with a couch and one chair with a coffee table and a television. To her left between the seats and the cockpit was a small galley area complete with a steward.

The older man smiled at her and welcomed her on board.

As she and Evan took their seats, the steward introduced himself as William and asked her if she wanted a drink.

She glanced at Evan then back at William. "Do you have wine?"

William smiled. "But of course. Mr. Reese keeps the airplane stocked with all the necessities."

She'd agree that wine was very necessary.

A few moments later, William returned with two glasses of wine.

"The pilot wished me to tell you he is ready for takeoff at your convenience."

Evan took the glasses and offered one to Celia.

"Tell him I'm ready."

"Very good, sir. I'll close the doors and we'll take off shortly."

"Comfortable?" Evan asked Celia.

She settled back into her seat and sipped at her wine. "Mmm, very. Nice jet."

She should have sat across the aisle from him, but that would be rude since he'd chosen the seat next to her. His nearness was killing her, though. His scent drifted enticingly across her nostrils and she could *feel* his heat. When he moved, his arm brushed against hers, and short of shifting in her seat—which would be terribly obvious—there was no escaping him. Furthermore, she didn't really want to.

It was on the tip of her tongue to suggest they use the time on the flight to go over her ideas, but she couldn't bring herself to have business intrude.

She mentally shook herself. Intrude on what? This wasn't some romantic getaway. It *was* business. Only business and nothing else.

It was unfair that she should be attracted to someone who was a solid no in her rule book. She'd never broken that unspoken rule. She had never been tempted to get involved with someone she worked with, or worse—a client. It didn't matter, though, because she'd carry the stigma of someone who advanced her career by bestowing sexual favors.

The memory sent rage curdling through her veins. She had to work at keeping her fingers relaxed. She'd worked damn hard to go beyond her family's expectations. And to have it all taken away by someone in a position of power over her made her head explode.

The advertising community was small, and gossip was rampant. She was under no illusion that fleeing New York made it possible for her to leave what happened behind. It hadn't been private. It had been very, very public.

She knew speculation ran wide. She knew people talked. Knew her coworkers probably whispered behind her back and pondered the possibility that she'd slept with Brock or Flynn Maddox to secure her position in the agency and to be granted the opportunity to land Evan Reese's account. They probably thought she'd do whatever it took to persuade Evan.

The only person she'd bothered to defend herself to was Brock, and she figured she owed him that much if he was going to hire her. Only he knew the truth about what really happened at her former agency. And when he'd assured her that she'd suffer no such situation here, she'd believed him. It might make her unbelievably naive after her last run-in with her boss, but Brock struck her as a deeply honorable man, and more importantly, someone who kept his word.

"Is everything all right?"

Evan's softly spoken question jarred her from her thoughts. His hand had gone to hers, and he carefully uncurled her fingers that were wound so tightly that the tips were white.

"Do you have a fear of flying?"

She shook her head. "Sorry. I was thinking about something else."

He studied her intently, his gaze stroking her cheeks and then her mouth.

"Seems a shame to waste time on such unpleasant thoughts."

The urge to deny that her thoughts had been unpleasant lasted all of about two seconds. She wrinkled her nose and grinned ruefully.

"Busted."

He chuckled. "I like an honest woman."

It was then she realized that they were already in the air. Wow, she really must have been intensely lost in thought to have missed the takeoff.

"Relax. There'll be plenty of time to discuss business during our stay. Let's begin the trip by enjoying the short flight."

Either she was exceedingly transparent or he'd just anticipated her jumping into things right away. Either way, she was perfectly willing to delay their discussion until she felt a little more on equal footing. Sitting here in such close proximity on his jet, drinking his wine…it was more than a little overwhelming.

His hand remained on hers, his thumb sliding idly over

her knuckles in a soothing pattern. She liked it. She liked it too much.

Survive, Celia. Survive this weekend. Be a professional. After this weekend you'll only have to see him in a business environment.

She swallowed and let calm descend. There was no way she'd screw this opportunity up just because she couldn't get all her girly hormones in check.

The flight went quickly, and oddly, after the first awkward moments, Celia sat back and enjoyed the casual conversation with Evan. William had kept a steady presence to refill their wineglasses and offer a variety of finger foods. By the time they landed at the Airport in the Sky, Celia was limber and completely relaxed. Probably due to the wine.

They were met by a hotel representative and were quickly whisked into a waiting shuttle. It only took a few minutes to arrive at the gorgeous beachfront resort. It was so beautiful, it took her breath away.

The sunset over the water gave the place a decidedly romantic feel, but then they were here for a wedding, so Celia supposed it was only appropriate that romance positively danced on the air.

Evan escorted Celia through the glass doors into the lobby. A bellhop followed behind with a rolling cart that held their luggage.

"Wait right here," Evan murmured. "Take a seat if you like. I'll get our room keys so we can go up."

Before he could go, a feminine voice rent the air.

"Evan! Oh, Evan, you're here!"

Evan stiffened against Celia. He went positively rigid, and Celia could swear she heard him curse under his breath. Celia turned in the direction of the call and saw a regally dressed older woman hurrying across the lobby, her heels tapping delicately on the polished floor.

Behind her, a grim faced older gentleman flanked by a

younger woman and a man who looked slightly younger than Evan, walked slower but with no less purpose in Evan's direction.

To her surprise, Evan took her left hand in his and held it close to his side. He fumbled with her fingers even as he looked up with a welcoming smile. It looked completely forced to Celia, but the woman didn't seem put off.

The woman threw her arms around Evan, and still, he didn't let go of Celia's hand. He returned her embrace with his free arm and said, "Hello, Mom. I told you I was coming."

"I know, but after Bettina told me she'd been to see you and when she told me that…"

She broke off and looked curiously at Celia, whose hand was still securely held in Evan's.

Then his mom looked back at Bettina, confusion clear in her eyes.

"But my dear, you told me that Evan wasn't seeing anyone, that he just told me that to ease my concern."

"Did she?" Evan asked in an even tone. He pinned Bettina with a stare that would have had Celia fidgeting.

His mom nudged him impatiently. "Well, introduce us, Evan."

"Yes, do introduce us," Bettina said in a chilly voice.

About the time she felt Evan's grip on her hand tighten and the cool metal slide over her finger, Celia regretted having agreed to come. She tried to look down, wondering what Evan had done to her finger, but he kept his hand over hers. Awkward didn't begin to cover it. She felt as if she'd just entered a minefield.

"Mom. Dad. Bettina. Mitchell." His lips curled when he said the last and Celia zeroed in on the man in question. He had to be Evan's brother. The similarity was striking. "I'd like you to meet—" His entire body tensed and he gripped her hand almost painfully. It was like he was sending her a silent message. "I'd like you to meet my fiancée, Celia Taylor."

Six

Celia froze. There was a horrible buzz in her ears, and she stared in horror at Evan. She hadn't heard him right. What kind of idiotic thing had he just done?

She wasn't sure who was more stunned. Her or his family. Bettina looked as if she just swallowed a lemon. Mitchell looked annoyed, while Evan's father simply frowned. His mom was the only person who actually seemed happy about the bomb.

"Oh, Evan, that's wonderful!"

Celia found herself in the older woman's arms and was hugged so tight that she was in danger of passing out.

"I'm so glad to meet you, my dear."

She held Celia out at arm's length and beamed at her. Then she proceeded to kiss her on both cheeks and if that wasn't enough, she yanked her into another long hug.

This was insane. Evan was insane. His entire family was nuts. She opened her mouth to blast Evan with both barrels and ask him what the hell kind of stunt he was trying to pull when Evan's father put his hand on Evan's shoulder to steer him away from the women.

"Come with me and we'll get you checked in and get your keys. Then you can take Celia up to the room."

Evan looked a little reluctant to leave her. She could well imagine why.

It was then that she remembered her finger. He'd put something on her finger.

She looked down. Holy cow! He'd slipped a huge diamond engagement ring on her finger while he'd held her hand. Fury simmered in her veins. She mentally counted to ten just so she didn't explode on the spot. The bastard had planned this all along. No one carried around a rock like this for the hell of it.

"You two go on ahead and be seated. Order our drinks. Marshall and I will be along in just a moment. I want the chance to speak to Celia for a moment."

Celia regarded Evan's mom warily as she shooed Mitchell and Bettina on toward the hotel restaurant.

When they'd disappeared, only after Bettina had glared enough holes in Celia to rival a hunk of Swiss cheese, Evan's mom seized Celia's hands and squeezed affectionately.

"Oh, my dear, I'm so thrilled to meet you. I can't tell you how fantastic your news is. I was so worried about Evan. He didn't take Bettina's defection very well, but look at you! Even more gorgeous than Bettina. I can see why Evan was so taken with you."

Celia opened her mouth and halted. What on earth could she say? With every word that poured out of the other woman's mouth, the more furious Celia became and the more sickened she was by Evan's deception.

This was some huge soap opera. Things like this didn't happen in real life. Even in really wealthy people's lives, surely.

"By the way, I don't think I introduced myself…well, other than as Evan's mother. I'm Lucy. Please do call me Lucy. Mrs.

Reese just sounds so formal and we're going to be family after all."

Celia's heart sank. Lucy obviously was a really wonderful lady and super kindhearted, which only made her angrier that Evan had just lied to her. What the hell had he been thinking?

But then Lucy's other statement came back to her. The part about Bettina's defection, and suddenly it all made sense.

"Bettina and Evan were involved?" Celia asked.

Lucy colored slightly and looked abashed. "Oh, heavens, I've said too much. I always do have a problem with just prattling on. Do forgive me."

Celia smiled. "It's all right. Truly. It is one of those things women like to know. Men are so thick when it comes to these things, but if any awkwardness can be avoided, I would like to know."

And she could go straight to hell for lying, too. She'd just make sure Evan got there first for his role in this debacle.

"It's all in the past. Rest assured."

"Naturally," Celia said drily.

"Evan and Bettina were engaged. It was a long engagement. The truth of the matter is, I'm just not sure how much of Evan's affections were engaged. Bettina and Mitchell fell in love, and well, it's obvious to anyone that those two were meant for each other. Evan didn't take it well, though, and if I hadn't begged him to come to the wedding, I have no doubt he wouldn't be here."

Lucy smiled and reached out to touch Celia's arm. "Bettina led me to believe that Evan was just going on about being involved because he wasn't over her yet and didn't want to worry me, but I can see that isn't the case. You're even more beautiful than Bettina. I can tell by the way he looks at you that he's besotted. He never looked at Bettina that way."

You are such a sucker, Celia. There should be a law about being so stupid when it came to men. But then she'd spend a lot of time behind bars if that were the case.

She felt Evan's approach. It was hard to miss all that tension. Celia glanced up and met his gaze, and she didn't at all try to disguise her fury. Let him stew. He was damn lucky she liked his mom so much or she would have denounced him in front of the entire hotel lobby.

The poor woman didn't deserve to be humiliated just because her son was a first-rate ass.

Evan regarded her warily even as he turned to his mom. "We'll catch up tomorrow, Mom, okay? Celia and I have had a long day and we'd like to go up and have dinner in the room."

Lucy patted Evan on the cheek and then leaned up on tiptoe to kiss him. "Of course, dear. I'll see you both tomorrow for rehearsal."

She reached back and squeezed Celia's hand. "It was so nice meeting you, Celia."

She walked toward Evan's father and the two went in the direction of the restaurant, leaving Celia and Evan standing in the middle of the lobby.

"We're on the top level," Evan said evenly. He gestured toward the elevator and Celia strode in that direction.

They rode up in silence, the tension so thick Celia felt like the entire elevator would explode before it stopped. It was all she could not to tap her foot in agitation as she waited for the doors to open.

When they finally did, Celia stepped out, glanced down the hall and then back at Evan.

"My key," she said pointedly. "What room am I in?"

Evan sighed and pointed at the end. "We're in the two-bedroom suite on the end."

Her mouth fell open. She reached forward and snatched the key card from his grasp. Then she spun on her heel and stalked down the hall. The hell she'd share a room with him. He could go find other accommodations or he could bunk with his brother. They'd probably have a lot to talk about. Maybe they could compare notes on Bettina.

She jammed the card into the lock, listened for the snick and then shoved it open. She stepped inside and slammed the door in Evan's face.

Her feet were killing her, she was angry as hell and she was hungry. And she needed to figure out how to get off this damn island.

She kicked off her shoes and then sat on the edge of the couch next to the table with the hotel directory and a telephone. Surely the front desk could make arrangements for her departure.

The sound of the door opening had her on her feet again, and she glared indignantly as Evan walked in and shut the door behind him. He held up another key card in explanation.

He looked tired and resigned.

"Look, I know you're angry."

She held up a hand. "Don't you dare patronize me. You have no idea how furious I am. Angry doesn't even begin to cover it."

He blew out his breath and ran a hand through his hair. He tossed his suit coat onto the arm of the couch.

She pointed to the door with a shaking finger. "Out. I won't share a suite with you. I don't care how many bedrooms it has."

"I need a drink," Evan muttered.

The man wouldn't even fight with her, and by God she wanted a fight.

"You never had any intention of listening to my ideas, did you?"

He stopped on his way over to the liquor cabinet and turned back around to stare at her. He had the audacity to look puzzled.

"I've been such an idiot. I can't believe I fell for this crap. How this was the only time you could fit me in. Blah, blah, blah. How naive does that make me? How stupid does it make me?"

He held up a hand and took a step in her direction.
"Celia…"

"Don't Celia me," she whispered furiously. It galled her
that she could feel the prick of tears. He would not make her
cry. She was through letting men make her cry.

She needed to pull it together and be professional. A
really nasty, vivid curse word, one that she'd learned from
her brothers burst into her mind. It was certainly appropriate
under the circumstances.

Screw professional.

"I have had it with men who manipulate me because of my
looks. Here's a clue. I can't help the way I look and it doesn't
give you the license to use me or make assumptions about my
character. And it damn sure doesn't give you the right to use
me to lie to your mother because your fiancée humiliated you
by dumping you for your brother. Here's another clue. Crap
happens. It happens all the time. Get over it."

Evan's hands closed over her shoulders. She tried to flinch
away, but he held tight. There was honest regret in his eyes,
but there was also determination. Stubborn determination.

"Sit down, Celia," he ordered in a low voice.

She gaped at him.

"Please."

It was the please that did it. Or maybe it was how tired and
resigned he sounded. Or maybe it was the bleak light that
entered his eyes. Or maybe she was just a flaming idiot who
deserved everything she got for being sucked into this in the
first place.

She sank onto the sofa, her entire body trembling as he
took a seat beside her.

"I'm sorry," he said. "I don't expect you to believe I didn't
do this maliciously or to hurt you. I swear, I didn't."

She cast a sideways glance at him.

He sighed. "Someone really did a number on you, didn't
they?"

She turned away, refusing to give him confirmation.

"Celia, look at me."

He waited, and she stared ahead. Still, he waited. Finally, she gave in and turned to look at him.

"I completely and utterly messed this up. I freely admit it. I expected to have time to discuss this with you before we ran into my family."

She struggled to control her temper. He obviously wanted a reasonable discussion when she was feeling anything but reasonable. What she really wanted was to crack his skull on the coffee table and leave, but then she'd be without a room, and if anyone was sleeping in the hallway, it wasn't going to be her.

"First, this has nothing—and I mean nothing—to do with you landing my account. You're going to have to do that on your business and advertising savvy. I'm not putting my entire company in the hands of a woman based on her looks or anything else. Can we at least be clear on that?"

She swallowed. "That's not how it looks to me, Evan. It looks to me like I got played for the fool and that you led me here on the premise of listening to my pitch when you never had any intention of this being about business. Tell me this much, have you already signed with Golden Gate? You owe me that much honesty at least."

Evan gripped a handful of his hair and closed his eyes. "You're pissed. I get it. You have every right to be, but will you please listen to my explanation. If afterward you want me to take a flying leap, I'll be more than happy to accommodate you. You'll never hear from me again."

"I think you know I don't have any other choice," she said helplessly.

"I'll try to make this as short and as concise as possible."

She nodded.

"I didn't have any intention of coming to this damn wedding. I couldn't care less if they live happily ever after and I have even less interest in being here to wish them well along that path to happily ever after.

"Then my mother called and she begged me to come. She was worried that I wasn't over Bettina and that's why I wouldn't come. The woman has a heart of gold, but she obviously knows nothing about me or she'd realize that Bettina was nothing to me the moment she left me for what she perceived to be the better catch."

"Harsh," Celia murmured.

"Is it? I'm only speaking the truth. Bettina was calculating. She hedged her bets and went with Mitchell as soon as he was named my father's successor in the family jewelry business. To her it seemed a more glamorous life. I'd like to be a fly on the wall when she realizes how wrong she is."

Celia's lips curled in amusement. "Not feeling a wee bit vindictive, are you?"

He gave a short laugh. "I may not harbor any love for the woman, and I may not be a bit sorry that she's out of my life, but she is a manipulative cat, and I won't be sorry to see her suffer for the choice she made."

"So your mom doesn't think you're over Bettina. That has what to do with me and this hoax you're perpetuating? Which I really resent by the way because your mom is nice. I feel like pond scum for deceiving her."

"I'm getting there. Just bear with me. When I got off the phone with Mom, I was angry because I let her talk me into going and I said as a last-minute thing that I was bringing someone. I fully intended to look up someone I'd seen casually in the past. Then I remembered that Friday I was supposed to be meeting you and that this meeting was extremely important to me. It seemed logical to combine the two and bring you out with me. I didn't lie about needing to move on this fast. I've wasted weeks listening to pitches. I'm ready to move."

"I'm still seeing a *but* here," she muttered.

"The but occurred when Bettina herself came to see me. She was steamed that I had the audacity to bring someone to her wedding. She felt like it was a poke in the eye at her, and if you can believe, she honestly thinks I'm still pining over her. She basically accused me of being a fraud and of trying to upstage her at her own wedding."

Celia burst out laughing. God, he didn't even see it. How typical a clueless male was he.

"What's so damn funny?" he demanded.

"She accused you of doing exactly what you're doing! The audacity. You crack me up."

He blinked and then looked a little sheepish. "Okay, I get it. I'm an immature, egotistical man. The male ego is obviously a fragile creature. I think we can agree on that. Yes, it occurred to me to get a little of mine back on her by showing up with a gorgeous, stunning woman. Sue me. I even hatched the whole engagement scheme complete with the ring because I figured it was the best way to get them all off my back."

Her shoulders shook and she closed her eyes. The man was nothing if not honest. She had to give him that much.

"Celia, look at me, please."

His entreating tone had her turning once more to stare into those intense green eyes. He looked earnest, and he looked... worried.

"I didn't do any of this to hurt you, I swear. I thought if I just came out and asked you to do me this favor, you'd have never agreed to come with me, even with the promise of listening to your pitch."

"So you lured me here and ambushed me instead," she said drily.

"It didn't go exactly as I'd planned. I'd hoped to have a nice dinner together in our suite and I was going to ask you to do me a personal favor then. I was going to outline the entire charade and ask you to play along. Just for the time we're here. But that all went to hell when we immediately ran into my parents."

His hand crept over hers, and she didn't pull away. She should. She should already be on her way back to San Francisco, and she should be calling Brock to tell him that there was no way in hell she was delivering Evan Reese on a platter to Maddox Communications.

She pressed her lips together and tried to collect her scattered thoughts. "So you want me to pretend to be your fiancée." She lifted her hand to angle the huge diamond in the light. "Complete with a really gorgeous ring. What happens after the wedding?"

Evan shrugged. "We break up quietly later. They'll never know the difference. We don't see each other that often. One day Mom will call and I'll say 'oh, by the way, Celia and I broke things off.' And that will be that."

She shook her head. "All of this because you couldn't stand the thought of your fiancée thinking you weren't over her?"

Evan scowled. "It's not that simple. There are other factors. Besides, we've already established the fact that I'm an egotistical, immature male. We don't have to go back into that territory."

"Poor baby." She patted his arm and then laughed at his disgruntled look. "I can't believe I'm even considering this."

His eyes glinted predatorily. "But you are."

"Yes, dammit, I am. I'm a sucker for immature, egotistical males. But we need to establish a few ground rules."

"Of course," he said solemnly.

"My reputation is everything to me, Evan," she said quietly. "I won't have any notion of impropriety attached to this account. I won't have it bandied around that I got the account because I slept with you."

Something that looked an awful lot like lust gleamed in his eyes a second before he blinked and adopted a more serious expression.

"This favor is separate. If I don't like your ideas, you'll go home without my business. It's that simple. Agreeing to be my fake fiancée doesn't buy you anything but my gratitude. It won't land you Reese Enterprises. Are we clear on that?"

"Crystal," she said. "Tell me something, Evan. If I refuse

to play the part of your lover, are you still going to hear my pitch? Are you even going to consider Maddox?"

"Well, I do have a fragile ego, remember?"

"Will you be serious?"

A grin worked at the corners of her mouth. She should be mad as hell at this man, not entertained by his self-effacing wit. And she definitely shouldn't be attracted to his boyish charm or his straightforward handling of this entire ridiculous affair.

"I tell you what, Celia. The plan was always to have a quiet dinner in tonight where I could explain my plan and beg you to go along. Then tomorrow morning we were going to have our business meeting, again, in the privacy of our hotel suite. Afterward we would perpetuate my silly hoax on my brother and his grasping, manipulative bride-to-be. See? Completely separate."

"You are completely irreverent, and I'm disgusted that I like it so much."

He smiled, and his eyes twinkled with amusement. "You're as diabolical as I am, face it."

"I could have used some of your evilness in the past. That's for sure. I'm a little envious of how you don't mind poking your finger in the eyes of those who have screwed you over. I need to learn how to do that."

He cocked his head to the side. "What happened to you, Celia?"

She flushed and turned away. "It's nothing. Definitely in the past and that's where I want it to stay."

"Okay. Fair enough. But I hope one day you'll tell me."

"We don't have that kind of relationship," she said lightly.

"No," he murmured. "We don't. Not yet."

Her gaze lifted but his expression didn't betray his thoughts. She swallowed the knot in her throat and hoped she wasn't making a huge, huge mistake. So much could go wrong with this.

"You're so worried about the position I've placed you in," he said. "But the truth is, if I don't like your ideas tomorrow morning, what's to say that you don't leave me to face the festivities on my own? I'd say that gives you all the power and none to me."

"Or you could just say you like my ideas to keep me on the line long enough to get through the wedding," she pointed out. "Nothing to say that you don't dump me the minute we get back to San Francisco."

He nodded. "True. All of it is true. Looks like we both have some trusting to do."

She looked down at her hand that was still underneath his. His thumb pressed into her palm, and his fingers lay still over hers, but the warmth of his touch spread up her entire arm and into her chest.

She liked this man. Genuinely liked him, stupid ambush aside. He hadn't sugarcoated any of it. And above all else, she liked honesty. He hadn't shied away from how the entire situation made him look. It certainly didn't make him appear very noble, but she couldn't get beyond thinking he was just that. Noble and honest.

The ring on her finger sparkled and glinted in the light. For just one moment, she allowed herself to imagine what it would be like if it were all real. Two seconds later she mentally slapped herself silly and told herself to get over her foolishness.

She had a job to do. She had to impress this man with her brains and her creativity, her drive and her determination. She could do all that. And if it meant she had to go beyond the call of duty to do a personal favor for him, then she needed to suck it up and just get the job done. Too many people were counting on her.

It was silly. She felt like an idiot and she was sure Evan didn't feel any better, but it wasn't up to her to question his motives. For whatever reason, he didn't want his brother and his fiancée to see him bleed. She could understand that. She would have died rather than let her old boss and his scheming wife know how much they'd destroyed her.

"All right, Evan. I'll do it."

Triumph mixed with relief flared to life in his eyes.

"Thank you for not bashing my skull in and leaving, but more than that, thank you for not reacting in front of my family. It was more than I deserved given how I sprang it on you. I swear, that was not the way I wanted to approach you with my proposition."

"If we're done with all that, can we eat? I'm starving. You can tell me all I need to know about your family and also tell me how it was we met and when you proposed, but not until I get something to eat."

He leaned forward, caught her jaw in his hand and turned her toward him. Their lips were so close that his breath blew warm over her mouth. She swallowed nervously, wondering if he would kiss her. And then she wondered if she'd let him. Or if she would kiss him instead.

"Thank you," he murmured.

Slowly, he withdrew, and to her chagrin, disappointment washed over her.

Seven

Evan watched as Celia sat sideways on the couch, her back against the arm and her knees doubled in front of her. She looked comfortable and completely relaxed, which was more than he could have hoped for given how stupidly he'd sprung the whole engagement thing on her.

After her initial fury, though, she'd calmed down and had taken it well. Damn, but he liked this woman. Oh, he was definitely attracted to her sexually, but beyond that, he genuinely liked spending time with her.

If he was smart, he'd take that as a huge warning sign to stay away and not become involved, but he'd never claimed brilliance.

She'd changed into nothing more glamorous than a pair of sweatpants and a San Francisco Tide jersey. Odd, but she hadn't struck him as a baseball fan.

Her shoes had long since been shed, and her toenails, painted a delicate shade of pink, teased him. Hell, he was even attracted to her feet. Small and dainty.

He was officially losing his mind. Never before had he lusted after a woman's feet.

She forked another bite into her mouth then sighed and made a low sound of agony before putting her plate down on the coffee table.

"That was fabulous. I've eaten so much that I won't fit into that sparkly dress I brought for the wedding."

That statement brought a whole host of splendid ideas to mind. Namely that they could both skip the wedding and stay in bed where clothing was entirely optional.

He shifted in his seat and wondered for the sixth time why he was so bent on torturing himself.

"So tell me something, Evan," she said as she leaned farther into the sofa cushions. Her eyelids lowered and she tucked those pink toes underneath a throw pillow. "What made you walk away from your family's business and start your own in a field that was so different from the jewelry trade?"

It didn't surprise him that she knew so much about his background. She would have researched him tirelessly. Still, he debated how much to tell her.

Their gazes locked, and he saw only simple curiosity. No ulterior motive, just interest.

"There were several reasons," he finally said. "Emotion has no place in business and yet I find myself making emotional decisions."

Her eyebrows rose. "I'm surprised you'd admit that. Doesn't jive with your big, bad, ruthless businessman persona."

He smiled ruefully. "Okay, so part of it was emotion based. I didn't agree with my father's style of management. The fact is his company is in trouble. I saw it coming years ago and he was in flat denial. He saw no reason to change the way he ran things since it had worked for decades before.

"The other reason was I don't exactly get along that well with him and Mitchell."

"You don't say," she said drily.

He chuckled. "Yeah, I know, hard to believe. Mitchell…

there are lots of more appropriate words for him, but I'll go with the fact that he's a lazy, unmotivated brown noser. All his life, because he was the baby, he's never had to actually work for anything. He's been handed everything since he was a child. As a result, his sense of entitlement is huge. I would work for something and he would want what I had worked for. Dad would give it to him."

"Ah, I think I'm beginning to understand the fiancée thing more now."

He nodded. "Yes, I don't harbor any illusion that Mitchell and Bettina are some great love match. I had Bettina, so Mitchell decided he wanted her. Bettina saw Mitchell's appointment to CEO as her ride into a life of glamour."

"And were you and Bettina? A love match, I mean?" she asked gently.

He pursed his lips and blew out a long breath. "This is where I look like the jerk."

Celia chuckled. "Jerk? You? Surely you jest."

"All right, don't rub it in," he grumbled. "I've admitted my shortcomings."

"Do continue. I'm dying to hear all about what a toad you are."

Her eyes sparkled with mischief and amusement. He'd never wanted to kiss her more than he did right now. Instead he found himself telling her stuff he'd never tell a woman he planned to take to bed.

"Bettina didn't pose a challenge. That sounds bad but when I met her, I was devoting all my time to making my business a success. It was exciting and exhilarating. I exceeded even my wildest expectations. Everything was falling into place at the speed of light. All that was missing in my mind to complete the image of perfection I had built up was a wife and a family. Perfect house in the suburbs. I'd come home after a hectic day and she'd have dinner waiting. The kids would all be bathed and well behaved. Even the dog would be the epitome of good behavior. I wanted—still want—a woman who'll put me first."

Celia snorted, covered her mouth and then dissolved into hoots of laughter.

He regarded her dubiously. "I do believe you're mocking me."

"Mocking you?" She wheezed between words and tears gathered in the corners of her eyes. "Oh my, Evan. You do dream big, don't you?"

"Well, it was a good fantasy while it lasted," he grumbled. "I looked around and there was Bettina. I didn't have time to figure out what my ideal woman was. I wanted my perfect life then and I didn't want to wait. So I asked her to marry me, she said yes, I gave her a ring and that was that."

"And yet here you are. With me. The fake fiancée."

He scowled ferociously at her only for her to dissolve into laughter again.

"Okay, so what happened? Other than Mitchell stepping in and being an overindulged twit."

He liked this woman. She was good for his ego even when she was tearing it down.

"Bettina wanted to set an immediate date. She had a grand wedding planned. Even had the honeymoon destination picked out. She littered my office with brochures. Hell, she even had our children's names picked out."

"I would have thought given your fantasy that you would have eaten that up with a spoon," she pointed out.

"Yeah, so did I. Only I found myself backing off. I kept making excuses to extend the engagement. I was busy. This deal had to take priority. That deal needed immediate attention. Before I knew it, we had been engaged a year with a wedding scheduled another year beyond that. And moreover I was content with that."

"Did you never love her?" Celia asked quietly.

"No. No, I didn't. Which is why I can't really blame her for wanting out. Our marriage would have been a disaster just as soon as I figured out the reality didn't live up to the fantasy I'd created in my mind. I just didn't think she'd dump me for Mitchell or that Mitchell would have been poaching on my territory."

Celia winced. "Yeah, I can understand that."

"I found them in bed, you know. How clichéd is that? The sad thing is, when I found them together in my bed, I just laughed, because to me it was just the next step in an already farcical relationship. I tossed them out of my apartment and washed my hands of them both."

Celia's expression grew thoughtful. "Hmm, so you don't necessarily object to the fact that she found someone else. Or that she cheated on you. Just who she indulged herself with."

Evan nodded and rubbed the back of his neck to ease some of the tension and fatigue. Just talking about it raised his ire all over again.

"Yeah, it's stupid I know. I mean, she could have cheated on me with my business partner, or my vice president or, hell, even my driver. I wouldn't have cared. I might have even given the man a raise. But my brother. My spoiled, overindulged brother. No, that was the one thing I couldn't forgive."

"Well, if their relationship is based on all you say, then I'd imagine they'll suffer enough in the long run without you wishing them ill."

He regarded her for a long moment. "You're not going to lecture me about harboring childish grudges?"

She smiled, and those gorgeous green eyes cut right through him. She took his breath away until he was helpless to do anything but stare back.

"Nope. Not a word. Considering I have my own grudges and I don't plan on forgetting them in this lifetime, I could hardly chastise you for the same."

"Oh, do tell. You sound so…vicious. I like it," he teased.

Her expression grew serious. Pain flickered in her eyes, and she turned away, her mouth drawn into a tight line. He was immediately sorry that the light mood had dissolved. As much as he wanted to know her secrets, he wanted to see her laughing and smiling even more.

To cover the sudden heaviness in the air, he got up to pour a glass of wine. Without a word, he offered one to her, and she took it, gratitude easing some of the tightness around her eyes.

He wanted to touch her so badly. Wanted to ease the strain and the unhappy tilt to her lips. He wanted to kiss her plump mouth until he owned her very breath.

He forced himself to return to his chair. The remains of their dinner was scattered across the coffee table. Some had fallen to the floor, but he wasn't inclined to clean it up. They sat there sipping their wine as evening fell all around them.

Finally he could remain silent no more.

He leaned forward to set his glass on the table. For a moment he looked down at his hands and imagined her flesh beneath his fingertips. Then he glanced back up to see her studying him with the same keen interest flashing in her eyes. She wasn't immune. He wasn't the only one who felt the magnetic pull between them.

"What are we going to do, Celia?" he murmured.

He saw her swallow nervously. She hadn't misunderstood, but neither did she respond.

"I want you so damn much I hurt. I've hurt for weeks. Every time I look at you, I get so many knots that I can't function. I've thought of all the ways I can explain to you that our business relationship has nothing to do with the desire I feel for you. But the simple truth is I don't give a damn. I want you in my bed, and I don't care what has to be done to make that happen."

Her eyes went wide and frightened. He hated that. He didn't want her to be afraid of him.

"You feel it, too. Don't deny me that much."

Slowly she nodded. Her fingers went to her forehead and she dug them into her hair. Still, he could see them shaking, and she swallowed again, her slim neck working with the effort.

"Please," she whispered. "I can't do this, Evan. It's the one thing I can't do. Don't ask it of me. If you want me to admit it, fine. I want you. More than I've ever wanted another man."

Savage satisfaction gripped him. Didn't just grip him but lunged for him and wrapped a hand around his throat and his groin. His entire body reacted to that simple statement. She wanted him more than she'd ever wanted anyone else.

She turned on the couch until she faced forward and her feet met the floor. She looked in turns miserable and scared. Her eyes closed in what looked to him like self-condemnation. He swore, startling her with the force of his curses.

"Whatever you're thinking, I don't like it," he said flatly. "I have no idea what the hell kind of blame you're placing on yourself, but I can guarantee that you didn't use your feminine wiles to seduce me into signing with your agency. I wanted you from the first moment I saw you. Want to know when that was, Celia? Go ahead, ask me."

He stared at her in blatant challenge, waiting, wanting her to take it up.

Her eyes went wide with shock, and her face was pale and drawn. "W-when?"

"At the Sutherland's reception. You were there with one of your clients. Copeland, if I remember correctly. The grocery-store giant."

Her mouth fell open. "But you were still with Rencom."

He nodded. "Precisely. I looked across the room, and you took my breath away. Want to know another of my sins, Celia? I was still engaged to Bettina. It was a week before I found her in bed with Mitchell. I didn't care. I wanted you so much. Now tell me how big of a bastard that makes me. Try to tell me this has anything to do with your pitch."

In the course of their conversation, he'd moved to the couch. He moved closer still, stalking her like prey. Her scent lured him, and he inhaled the delicate, feminine smell that he'd come to associate with only her.

Her eyes were flush with awareness and caution. There was confusion in her deep green pools, but something else, too. Desire. Matching desire. She wanted him. Maybe as much as he wanted her. It didn't matter because he would have her.

"Want to know something else?" he murmured. "I almost didn't consider Maddox for the account. Want to know why? Because I didn't want it to interfere with my pursuit of you."

He was close now. So close he could feel every little puff of breath that came from her lips. He could see the tiny little nervous swallows that worked her throat up and down. And her mouth. Her luscious, sweet mouth. He wanted to taste it, devour it like candy.

"W-what changed your mind?" she whispered.

"I'm perfectly capable of separating business from pleasure," he said evenly.

"Evan, we can't."

She put her hand on his chest. Big mistake. A current of electricity singed him. They both jumped, but before she could withdraw, he caught her fingers and trapped her hand between his and his chest.

"Just one kiss, Celia. Just one. I have to kiss you. It's all I'll demand for now. I can wait for more until we have this account settled."

Without waiting her consent, he swept his mouth over hers. Finally. Her sweetness exploded onto his tongue the moment he licked over her lips. Her mouth parted in a gasp, and he took full advantage, delving deep into her moist heat.

She made the sweetest sounds. He swallowed them up as he devoured every inch of her mouth. He was transfixed by her full bottom lip. He nipped lightly at it, teasing it to fullness and then he sucked it between his teeth.

Her tongue stroked tentatively over his, just light brushes

with the tip and then she grew bolder, taking a more active part in the kiss.

His hands delved into her hair. He loved her hair. Long and glorious, the color like a russet sunset over the desert. The temptation was too great. He'd fantasized about it for too long.

He fumbled with the clip and released its hold on her hair. It tumbled down her back, over his hands like a wave. He gathered the strands between his fingers, mesmerized by their silky smoothness.

He drank deeply, not wanting the moment to end. He could spend hours kissing her, but he wanted more. He wanted to work his mouth down the curve of her jaw to her neck. He wanted to peel every layer of clothing from her body and then run his tongue over her soft skin.

He wondered what her breasts would feel like in his hands and what her nipples would taste like, how they'd feel as he sucked them into his mouth.

Oh, yes, he'd spent a lot of time wondering about her breasts. She never wore clothing that could be deemed too provocative. She was fashionable, yes, but he secretly wished she'd wear something a little more revealing. It was killing him not to get a hint of her full, ripe breasts.

Soon. Soon, he'd unwrap all of her. He'd possess her. She'd be his.

He needed air and he broke away only long enough to pull oxygen into his starving lungs. She gasped along with him, and then he started at the corner of her mouth and licked and kissed his way across to the other corner.

Her small hands slid up his chest. It was like a heating element sliding over his skin. She left a blazing trail of fierce need in her wake. His entire body came alive, and all she'd done was touch him. Innocently.

They wound up around his neck and then her fingertips just delved into the hair at his nape. He shuddered, and it was all he could do to retain his tight hold on his control.

His body screamed at him to haul her over his shoulder and drag her caveman-style to the bedroom. He'd rip off her clothes and spend the night taking her over and over until they both succumbed to exhaustion.

His mind yelled at him to be careful. To take it slow. Not to push her so far away that she never returned.

It was that fear of driving her away permanently that finally pulled him back from the brink of insanity.

With great reluctance, he pulled back. His hands were still tangled up in her hair, and he carefully extricated them from the heavy coil that lay over her shoulders.

Her eyes were cloudy, a gorgeous mix of confusion and desire that had him wanting to throw caution to the wind and continue his seduction.

"That," he whispered, "is what I've been wanting to do ever since I saw you across a crowded room six months ago. Now you tell me this has anything to do with Maddox Communications and Reese Enterprises."

Her hand fluttered to her mouth and she stared at him with shocked awareness.

"Oh, God, Evan. What are we going to do?"

He smiled gently and slowly pulled her hand away from her swollen lips.

"What we're going to do is get your pitch out of the way tomorrow morning. Whatever happens afterward, we take it as it comes."

Eight

There was no need for Celia to set her alarm. She never went to sleep. She lay in bed, staring at the ceiling, her senses completely shattered by something as simple as a kiss.

No. That kiss could never ever be called simple.

She'd thought to go over her pitch. Mentally replay everything she wanted to say until it flowed seamlessly through her mind. But all she'd been able to do was lay there and wonder how she was going to manage to keep things with Evan on a strictly professional level.

He kissed like a dream.

He'd make love like a dream.

And the sick thing was she'd never find out.

She rolled over and buried her face in her pillow.

Celia, Celia.

The admonishment burned like acid on her tongue. She was walking a very tight, very dangerous line. It was bad enough that she was here with Evan. Sharing a suite with Evan. Her groan was swallowed up by the pillow.

The least she could have done was insisted on a separate room, but that wouldn't have gone far in convincing his family that they were happily engaged.

Friendship. Okay, she could handle a friendship with Evan. She liked him. He asked her to consider this a personal favor. As a friend. And she'd forget the kiss. Forget that he had made his intention to make love to her abundantly clear.

All she had to do was get through her presentation, go to a rehearsal dinner, wedding and reception with Evan—as his fiancée—and then she could go home and put him firmly back in his neat, tidy little corner.

She struggled out of bed, knowing it would take her the better part of an hour to erase the look of someone who hadn't slept. Evan had ordered room service to be brought up at eight, and she wanted plenty of time to go over her notes again.

She purposely toned down her looks, choosing subtle makeup. She did nothing to highlight her eyes, which were her best feature. And she pulled her hair back into a tight knot and used hairspray to keep the wispy tendrils from escaping. She wanted no distractions. No sizzling looks. No temptation to do something utterly stupid.

To her immense relief, when she walked out of her bedroom, Evan was in total business mode. He didn't stare at her like he was set to devour her. He gave her a cursory glance and motioned for her to sit across from him at the dining table where breakfast had already been served.

"We can eat and talk, or we can eat and then talk. Strictly up to you," he said when she took her seat.

"We can eat and talk," she said. "I'm not using props or anything, and I planned it to be more conversational than a formal presentation."

He nodded approvingly. "Great. Let's dig in and get started then."

There was a moment of transition where they ate in silence before Celia shut off everything but the task at hand. This was her career and she knew she was damn good at it. She hadn't gotten to where she was and survived the pitfalls without the ability to put her game face on in the face of adversity.

"I studied your last ad campaign, and I believe you're missing a huge segment of your target audience."

He blinked, set his fork down and stared across at her. "Okay, you have my attention."

"Perhaps I should put it another way. I think you're not targeting the right audience. You're missing a huge opportunity."

She paused for effect and then segued into her spiel.

"Right now you appeal to the sports crowd. The guy who jogs. The woman who goes to the gym. The person who cares about staying in shape. You're all about functionality. The kids who play sports. The guys who play racquetball at the club. The casual basketball game on the weekends."

Evan nodded.

"Then there are the people, like me, who are allergic to physical activity."

He snorted and sent an appraising look over her body.

She ignored him and continued on.

"These are the people who watch sports. They're tuned in to every game. The players. The teams. They run the gambit from the fanatic to the casual observer. They're the people who will buy your sportswear not because they're going to worry over the functionality. They don't care. They want to look cool. They want to immerse themselves in the aura of the sports world. You're a brand, a label. It's a status symbol."

Her excitement mounted with every word. He was listening intently. She had him.

"So you do dual marketing. You go after the die-hard fitness enthusiast with the sweaty workout commercials. The driven athlete who's going to be the best and wearing your brand the entire time."

Again she paused to gauge his reaction, and he was leaning forward, his brow creased in concentration.

"Then you go after the men and the women and the kids

who want your clothing and your shoes because they look good. Because they make them feel athletic without ever lifting a finger. You show them someone looking cool and sophisticated in your clothing. You show them it's hip to have Reese Wear. They can be average, everyday Joes and still know what it feels like to be a star."

Then she went for the kill shot. Her excitement mounted because she knew he was interested. This had nothing to do with personal attraction. He was all business right now and his eyes gleamed with enthusiasm.

"And the person you show to both of these groups, the man you have doing the sweaty, driven shoots and the cool, suave commercials is Noah Hart."

Evan's eyes widened a fraction, and then he sat back in his seat. "Wait a minute."

She waited, trying valiantly to hide her smug grin. This would be the fun part.

"You're telling me you can get me Noah Hart?" He didn't even wait for her to reply. "Companies have been after Noah Hart ever since he entered the major leagues."

"Before," she said airily. "They wanted him out of college."

"Whatever. The point is, the man has never agreed to an endorsement deal. What makes you think you can change his mind?"

"And if I told you he's willing to talk to you?"

"No way," Evan breathed.

"It'll cost you."

"Hell, it would be worth it!" His eyes narrowed again. "He'll talk to me. You've already been in contact with him?"

"I might have mentioned the possibility of you doing a new ad campaign."

"And he's interested?"

"He'll talk to you. I provided him research, which means you passed the first round of scrutiny with him. He's a hard guy. You land him and it'll be huge. Not only will you have a kick-ass ad campaign, but you'll also be the guy who signed Noah Hart."

"I'd want exclusivity," Evan said quickly.

"You'd have to be prepared to pay for that privilege," Celia pointed out. She wasn't about to tell Evan that exclusivity or not, the chances of Noah agreeing to do another deal with someone else was slim to none. The man simply wasn't motivated by money.

"Okay, let's forget Noah Hart for the moment. I like your ideas, Celia. I mean, the average Joe has never escaped my notice, but you're right. I've never gone after him in marketing. My commercials are always about the drive to succeed. I talk to the athlete in all of us."

"Which I've just pointed out doesn't exist in everyone," she said drily.

"Yes, you're right. Completely. The junior-high kid trying to look cool. Huge market there that I've yet to tap."

"Most of my ideas are about how to structure television commercials, Internet advertising and print media to target all segments of the population from the die-hard sports and fitness enthusiast to Suzy Homemaker who just wants a comfortable pair of tennis shoes. We'd speak separately to teens, young adults all the way up to the retired folks."

Evan nodded. "I'm interested. Definitely interested. When can you have a presentation put together for me? As I said before, I'm ready to move on this. I don't mind taking a little extra time if I can be guaranteed better results."

"You tell me when you can meet with us at Maddox and I'll arrange it," she said evenly.

"And Noah Hart?"

"I'll arrange it as soon as we get back."

"Then I'd say you've got your pitch appointment, Celia. I'm very impressed with what you've had to say. If your presentation delivers on the promise of your ideas, it's something my company will be very excited about."

Though she had every confidence in her ability to win him

over, his enthusiasm gave her a wicked thrill. She was forced to play it cool and smile politely as she thanked him, but on the inside she was doing an insane victory dance.

She had phone calls to make. Brock would need to know so they could start preparing. They'd want to do mock-ups of the advertising and have it prominently displayed on the television monitors in the Maddox reception area. On the day she'd give Evan her presentation, Maddox Communications would be all about Reese Enterprises. No one else would exist in the timeframe Evan was present in their offices.

"You have to tell me how you managed to get Noah Hart to agree to talk to me," Evan said as he pushed his plate aside.

A small smile flirted at the edges of her mouth and she suppressed the urge to grin broadly.

"I can't reveal all my secrets."

"You pull this off and you'll be legendary," Evan said. "The man has never so much as been tempted to take a deal."

Okay, now she felt a little like a fraud. Legendary indeed. While she did love having an ace up her sleeve, she felt a little squeamish over Evan's praise. Noah Hart was her big brother, and the truth was, there wasn't much he wouldn't do for his little sister. Never mind that she'd never asked him for any such favor before. She was this time, and it was the only reason Noah was contemplating breaking his long-held policy.

"Don't fawn yet," she murmured. "He might prove to be too expensive for you."

Evan's eyes glinted with a predatory gleam. He had the look of a man sure of himself and all things.

"I've not found many things in life that proved to be too expensive. I may not always want to pay the price, but rarely have I found them out of my range."

She smiled. "I sensed that about you, which is why I thought you might be the one Noah would come to terms with. I think the two of you are probably a lot alike."

Evan cocked his head to the side. "Just how well do you know him?"

Her lips lifted again, but she didn't answer. Evan's BlackBerry rang and provided much needed distraction. She wasn't ready to tell Evan about her relationship with Noah. Not yet.

She tuned into Evan's conversation when he said her name. He was obviously talking to his mom.

"We'll be there this afternoon. Four o'clock. Yes, I know. I won't miss it. Dinner afterward. Celia and I are having lunch together down by the marina. We'll meet you back at the hotel in time for rehearsal. You have my word."

He hung up and let out a sigh as he tucked the phone back into his pocket.

"The woman is convinced I'll flake on the wedding. I wonder how on earth she got that idea?"

It was said so innocently that Celia burst into laughter. Evan joined her and business was effectively put back out of the way once more.

Nine

The nice lunch by the harbor never happened. As Evan and Celia were leaving the hotel, they ran into Evan's parents and Mitchell and Bettina.

Lucy was thrilled, since they were on their way to lunch, as well, and she suggested they eat together before they gathered on the terrace for the very informal rehearsal.

It amused Celia that there would even be an actual rehearsal of the ceremony since it wasn't a big affair and the bride and groom only had two attendants each. Still, it was evidently important to keep up appearances because they were going all out with a full-blown rehearsal and a dinner and party afterward.

Bettina acted less than thrilled that Celia and Evan would be joining them for lunch. Mitchell was visibly uncomfortable. When they were seated, as luck would have it, Evan and Celia were placed across the table from Bettina and Mitchell while Lucy and Marshall sat on the ends.

As a result, Celia was treated to Bettina's malevolent stare.

The woman wasn't even subtle about it. She picked Celia apart like a bug under a microscope.

Evan reached for her hand under the table and gave her a squeeze. She couldn't figure out if it was a gesture of support, sympathy or a thank-you.

She turned and gave him a smile. For a long moment their gazes locked and he smiled back.

"Tell me, Celia, what is it that you do? Evan tells me you live in San Francisco. Will you be moving once you and Evan are married?"

Celia turned to Lucy in surprise. The questions were natural for a mother to ask, but Celia hadn't been prepared for them. Who was she kidding? She hadn't been prepared for any of this.

"Celia is a crack advertising executive," Evan smoothly inserted. "We haven't discussed where we'll live after we're married. Her career is very important to her. I'd never expect her to give it up."

Oh, the man was good. If she was getting married, she'd want the guy she was marrying to say exactly what Evan had said, and she'd want him to mean every word.

Bettina sniffed. "But don't you feel a woman's place is at home with the children? You do plan on having children don't you?"

Celia frowned as she stared at the other woman. Was she for real? Granted she was young. Celia guessed she was in her early twenties. What the hell had Evan been thinking when he'd hooked up with her in the first place? She was practically an infant and Evan had to be pushing forty.

"I don't see that it's any of your concern whether I want children or not and as for where my place is, it's wherever I'm the happiest," Celia said. "I fail to see how I could possibly be the best wife and mother by staying at home and being miserable."

Bettina looked genuinely confused. "I feel it's important for a woman not to overshadow her husband. A husband's job is to provide for his family. I'd never take that away from him."

Celia snorted. "You keep telling yourself that, honey. Call me up when your provider husband has decided he no longer wants that job and is going to leave you and the children to go find himself. Then tell me how important it was for you to depend solely on him for your support, and then tell me how easy it is to go find a job making enough money to support yourself and your children when the sole job experience on your resume is changing diapers and cooking dinner."

Evan choked on his laughter while Lucy's eyes widened in shock. Mitchell looked a little green while Bettina's mouth hung open. Marshall cleared his throat and actually looked at Celia with something akin to respect.

"Well said, young lady. A woman should never put the welfare of herself and her children solely in her husband's hands no matter how solid the relationship."

"Marshall!"

Lucy sounded positively scandalized.

Evan sat back and looked at his dad. "You see why I'm so determined to marry her. If my company ever goes bankrupt, I can stay at home and let her support me."

The two men burst into laughter and Evan squeezed her hand harder.

"Have you two set a date yet?" Mitchell asked, entering the conversation for the first time.

He'd been strangely silent, and he'd studied her and Evan until Celia squirmed under his scrutiny.

Not wanting Evan to do all the talking, even if this was his charade and not hers, she smiled and looked back at Mitchell.

"He's only just convinced me to marry him. I did make him wait, and he had to ask me several times."

Evan squeezed again only this time it was a definite retaliation squeeze. She grinned and plunged ahead.

"I finally put him out of his misery and said yes. He wants a short engagement." Some little evil imp made her poke Bettina a little with that statement since Evan had kept prolonging their engagement. "He wanted to elope to Las Vegas, but I want to take our time and really get to know each other before we tie the knot."

Evan made a strangled noise and promptly took a long drink of his wine. Celia kept a perfectly straight face as she took in the reactions of Evan's family.

Lucy looked wary. Bettina looked murderous. Mitchell had a strange look that could only be interpreted as a cross between regret and sadness while Marshall nodded approvingly. He reached over to slap his son on the back.

"You've got yourself a winner here, son. I heartily approve. This one will keep you on your toes well into your old age. I like her."

Greaaat. She had the approval of her fake father-in-law to be. She looked over at Evan as guilt swamped her. She'd gotten carried away and hadn't been able to resist the opportunity to needle Evan a bit. Though he deserved it, she still felt bad about carrying things so far.

To her surprise, he was staring thoughtfully at her, his eyes warm with something she was afraid to analyze.

"I absolutely agree," Evan murmured. "I'm a very lucky man."

Evan kept a possessive arm wrapped around Celia's waist as they navigated the small field of people in the ballroom where everyone had gathered after the rehearsal dinner.

A band played, and already several couples were dancing, his mom and dad included.

He knew the closeness between him and Celia was all for show, but the primitive part of him recognized his desire to publicly brand her as his woman. She'd probably knee him right in the groin if she had any inkling what his thoughts were. The image made him wince and chuckle all at the same time.

Every time he looked at Bettina, he was gripped by such gratitude and relief that it staggered him. How close he'd come to an unmitigated disaster.

All the things he had thought he wanted were ludicrous in hindsight. A woman like Bettina would never hold his attention for long. She didn't challenge him.

He wanted someone intelligent, as driven as he was, someone he could consider a partner.

Someone like Celia.

His lips tightened. Thanks to his decision to go with Maddox—he hadn't told Celia yet—a relationship between them was impossible. Not that he'd give a rat's ass that she worked for him indirectly, but Celia would never agree.

"If you hold me any tighter, someone's going to call the police on us," Celia murmured.

He loosened his hold on her waist and uttered a low apology.

"Let's dance," she suggested. "You're way too tense. No one's ever going to believe we're newly engaged and head over heels in loooove with you scowling like that."

"You're right. Sorry. Got distracted."

"I'll try not to take that personally," she teased.

He relaxed immediately and let her pull him onto the dance floor. The music was slow and seductive and gave him the perfect opportunity to do what he'd been wanting to do all damn day. Hold her flush against his body so he could feel every one of her soft, delectable curves.

They fit perfectly and he tucked her as close as she would go. His cheek rested against her temple as he slowly whirled her around the floor. Her hips swayed, brushing her belly across his groin. He let one hand trail down her spine and over the curve of one hip.

She tensed a moment, and he wondered if she'd tell him to back off but then she relaxed with a sigh and melted into his arms once more.

"You were fantastic at lunch today," he said against her ear.

"I never thought my father would become such a fan. He's typically a stodgy, conservative chauvinist."

Her shoulders shook with laughter. "He'd fit in quite well with my family then. My father and brothers think my sole ambition in life should be to look pretty and let them take care of me."

"I'm going to admit something," he said gravely.

She turned her face up, her eyes sparkling with amusement. "Oh, do tell. Is this where you divulge your deepest, darkest secrets?"

"You could try to express an appropriate amount of appreciation for my confiding in you," he huffed.

"Very well. Let me just bat my eyelashes in adoration, but be quick or I'll mess up my mascara."

He shook his head as helpless laughter escaped. "What I was going to admit was that while I truly appreciate and agree with everything you had to say, there is a caveman lurking underneath my civilized exterior. I can see why your family wants to protect and take care of you. I think if you were mine, I'd feel much the same way."

Her lips parted, and she stared at him with the oddest expression. There was no anger or condemnation. Interest and something else gleamed in her emerald eyes.

"And sometimes I think if you were mine, I just might let you," she said huskily.

His entire body tightened. His hand raced up her spine and he curled his fingers gently at her nape. Their eyes were locked together and all he had to do was lean down. Just a bit. He could taste her already.

His head lowered. Her eyes narrowed to slits and she let out a breathy, feminine sigh of anticipation.

"Evan, you've monopolized her long enough."

His father's voice boomed in his ears and Evan jumped, sending Celia away from him for a brief moment.

Marshall stood there expectantly. "Going to let me cut in?"

Evan slipped Celia's hand into his father's. "Of course. Just don't keep her for long."

Marshall chuckled as he spirited Celia away. "One dance won't kill you, son."

Evan watched his dad whirl Celia across the floor. In a word, she was magnificent. She laughed at something he said and her smile lit up the entire room. She sparkled.

"Quite a woman," Mitchell drawled.

Evan stiffened and turned to see his brother standing there, drink in hand.

"Where's the bride-to-be?" Evan asked. "Didn't figure she'd let you out of her sight until the vows are spoken."

Mitchell shrugged. "She's over with Mom, talking about the honeymoon arrangements." He looked again at Celia and their father. "You're marrying her for real?"

"Is there some reason I shouldn't?" Evan asked mildly.

"Doesn't seem your type."

Evan regarded his brother with curiosity. "And what is my type?"

"Someone like Bettina. You seemed pretty hung up on her."

"I think it's safe to say I'm not hung up on Bettina."

"I can see why you're attracted to her," Mitchell said.

"Who?" Evan demanded sharply.

"Celia."

Both men stared across the room to where Celia danced with Marshall.

"She's a beautiful woman. I bet she's awesome in bed."

Evan rounded furiously on his brother. "You shut the hell up. Don't even breathe her name again. You got it?"

Mitchell smiled and backed away, holding his hands up in surrender. "Okay, okay, I get it. You're awfully touchy about her. Funny, you weren't that pissed when you found out about Bettina."

Mitchell sauntered off and Evan turned away, angry that he'd let his brother goad him.

"Evan, there you are."

He sighed when his mom latched on to his arm and dragged him over to introduce him to people he had zero interest in and would never see again in his life. After several minutes of pleasantries, Evan grew restless. The song ended, and he turned in search of Celia.

His father was making his way through the crowd toward Evan and Lucy, but Celia was nowhere to be seen. Frowning, Evan scanned the room until finally he found her.

She was dancing with Mitchell. She didn't look altogether thrilled, but Mitchell was smiling as he held Celia close.

Irrational anger exploded over Evan. All he could see was that it was Bettina all over again, only this time it mattered. This was Celia. His Celia.

His brother was a slimy predator. Never mind that Celia was perfectly capable of fending off any advances. He didn't even imagine she'd ever be receptive to an overture on Mitchell's part. But the fact that his brother would behave this way at his own wedding celebration enraged Evan.

His woman. He let Bettina go because she was never his. Celia was his even if she hadn't recognized that little fact.

Not stopping to think how it would look to others, he cut a path through the crowd that had people exclaiming on either side of him. When he got to Mitchell and Celia, he reached for his brother's arm and spun him around.

"What the—" Mitchell began.

His eyes narrowed angrily, but Evan stopped him with a look.

"You'll excuse us, Mitchell. I find I've spent entirely too much time away from my fiancée."

Celia stared at both brothers in shock but didn't utter a single protest when Evan all but dragged her out of the ballroom and into the hallway.

The predator had been unleashed. No way he'd stand by and watch his brother move in on what he considered his.

He stalked toward the elevator, his only thought to get Celia as far away from everyone else as possible. He punched the button and hauled her inside. As soon as the door closed, he slammed her against the back wall and angled his mouth over hers.

It was like a fuse igniting. Desire sizzled down his spine, frying every nerve ending in its path. He wasn't gentle. He wasn't sure he had it in him. He devoured her. Claimed her.

She gasped for breath, and he stole it as soon as she could gain it back.

"Evan, what on earth…"

The question ended on a moan as his mouth slid down her jaw to her neck. He sucked hungrily at the soft skin just below her ear.

Behind him the doors opened and without taking his mouth from her skin, he maneuvered them down the hall toward their suite.

He was on fire. He had no rational thought. His only instinct was to take her. To make her understand she belonged to him. Only to him.

Her eyes were dazed when he leaned her against the wall next to the door. His hands shook as he rummaged in his pocket for the key. It took two times before he inserted it correctly and as soon as the lock released, he threw open the door, held it with his foot and reached for her again.

This time she did her share of grabbing. Amid the turmoil of his jumbled, raging lust, relief hit him hard. She was with him. She wanted him every bit as much as he wanted her.

He tore at her clothing. Then he tore at his. Shoes and shirts hit the floor, leaving a trail across the floor to his bedroom.

By the time the backs of her knees hit the edge of his bed, she was down to just her bra and panties. Not just underwear. Pink, delicate, frothy confections that accentuated every curve and swell. Her breasts bulged and plumped upward over the cups. He could see a hint of her aureole and it was driving him crazy.

His fingers fumbled with his pants. Her hands tangled with his as they both shoved downward.

"God, Celia." He couldn't catch his breath long enough to say what he wanted. "I always swore when I made love to you I'd savor you for hours. I told myself I'd take my time touching and kissing every inch of your body. But I swear, if I don't get inside you soon, I'm going to explode."

"Fast is good," she panted. "We can do slow later."

"Thank God."

He fell forward, taking her with him. They both hit the bed, and she absorbed the shock of his body melding to hers.

"I'll savor you next time," he promised between kisses.

"Savor is good. We can definitely savor. But, God, Evan, make love to me now. Please."

He chuckled and captured her mouth with his. "Sweet. So sweet. I'm going to take you, Celia. I'm going to take everything you have to offer. If you don't want this, tell me now. I'll stop. It'll kill me, but I'll stop."

She pulled away and stared up at him with glowing, brilliant eyes. Her hands traced a line from his temples over his face and to his jaw.

"Take me then," she whispered.

Ten

Celia lay underneath Evan's big body. Every part of her was covered by him. His heat penetrated her, seeped into her flesh and whispered seductively through her veins.

She wanted him. God, she wanted this man. Her need for him frightened and exhilarated her in equal parts. She knew she shouldn't—that she mustn't—and yet she also knew she wouldn't tell him no.

There would be no recriminations later. There would be no regret. She knew the potential pitfalls of making love with Evan, and she would face them with full acceptance.

"What are you thinking?" he asked.

She raised her gaze to meet his. He was propped on his arms, his body still flush with hers and their noses were mere inches apart.

His eyes were warm with desire, liquid with want, and her heart fluttered in response.

His voice was so tender and understanding. He stared down

at her like she was the only woman he'd ever made love to. A mixture of awe and wonder that humbled her.

"I was thinking we shouldn't do this," she admitted.

"But? There's definitely a but in that sentence."

He sounded so hopeful that she smiled and once again traced the lean lines of his face with a fingertip.

"But I don't care. I should care. I should be on my way back to San Francisco. I should have never agreed to stay."

"But," he murmured again, his voice husky and so very predatory.

"But I'm here, in your arms, and I want you so much that I'm willing to take the biggest risk of my life. I won't lie, I don't like that about myself. I don't like that I'm allowing infatuation and sexual desire to mess with my head. It's stupid and irresponsible and…"

He shushed her with one finger and then followed it down with his lips. He nibbled playfully at the corner of her mouth and then licked the spot where he nipped.

"Trust me, Celia."

She went completely still and stared up at him, the intensity that burned so bright in his gaze.

"Trust me to take care of you. I won't let this hurt you. We can make it work."

"What are you saying?" she whispered.

"Let's take it slow. Well, after we go really fast this time." He grinned crookedly and shifted so she could feel his straining erection against her groin. "We can do this, Celia. We're adults in charge of our own destiny. There's no problem we can't solve together. Trust me."

Peace descended, enveloping her in its sweet, soothing grasp. In response, she wrapped her arms around his neck and tugged him down into a long, passionate kiss.

Trust him.

He made it sound so simple, and maybe it was.

She slid her mouth up his jaw to his ear. As she nibbled on it, she said softly, "Make love to me, Evan."

With a groan, he rolled until their positions were reversed and she was sprawled atop him. His fingers fumbled with the clasp of her bra and a second later, it flew across the room, hitting the drawn curtains over the window.

She felt his sudden inhalation. He stilled and then his hand skimmed up her back and around to her breasts. His fingertips brushed over the swells and to her nipples.

Each stroke, each touch no matter how light, ignited a fire deep inside that threatened to overtake her. Her urgency matched his own. Her impatience was his.

And then he leaned up and took one sensitive nipple in his mouth and she was lost. Her head fell back. Her eyes closed as sweet, sharp pleasure radiated in waves through her body.

Despite his impatience, his lips and tongue were exquisitely tender as he suckled first one breast and then the other.

His hands spanned her waist and then moved lower until his fingers caught in the band of her panties. He yanked, and she heard them rip.

"I'll buy you more," he rasped as he rolled again, putting her underneath him once more.

"Buy me what?"

"Panties."

"Highly overrated," she murmured.

He laughed against her mouth. "I totally agree."

"Speaking of…underwear. You're still wearing yours."

He reared up between her knees, yanked his briefs off, and she stared shamelessly at his distended length. He followed her gaze down then looked back up at her, a cocky grin making him adorable.

"You like?"

She reached for him, enfolding him in her hands. "Oh, yes, I like."

He clamped a hand over her arm and squeezed. "Celia, you can't. I'm too close. This will never work. I have to get inside you or it's going to be over way too soon."

She rose up, curling one hand around his neck even as she slid her fingers suggestively up and down his erection.

"Savor later. Remember?"

"Condom," he bit out.

She let him go long enough for him to fumble through his discarded pants. Seconds later, he started to roll the latex on, but she reached for it, snagging it from his grasp.

"Come here."

"Oh, yes, ma'am," he breathed.

She lay back and he straddled her hips. He loomed over her, big and strong. She felt entirely too small, too at his mercy, but as her hands slid over his manhood, he closed his eyes and a shudder rippled through his massive body, and the power shifted significantly in her direction.

Then he fell forward, planting his hands on either side of her head. "I can't wait."

"Savor later," she reminded.

His smile was brilliant. He leaned down to kiss her just as he reached down to part her thighs. With one hand, he pulled one leg away from the other. His mouth never left hers. His weight was supported by his left arm. He angled to the side as he gently explored her swollen, feminine folds.

"Evan, please," she begged. "You're killing me here. If you don't hurry, I'm so leaving you behind."

He eased one finger inside and evidently satisfied that she was ready for him, he shifted over her and settled between her thighs. His erection prodded carefully at first, then he found her heat and thrust hard and deep.

She arched, bowing her back off the mattress. She grasped desperately at his shoulders, her fingers curling into his skin until she was sure she drew blood.

It was too much. It was absolutely magnificent. He filled her. She'd never felt so alive, so splendid, so tuned in to her own pleasure.

"Hold on to me," he ordered in a thick, hazy voice.

It was a needless command. She couldn't do anything but hold him as he drove into her over and over.

"Oh," she gasped. "Evan, please, I need…"

She didn't even know what she was asking for, only that she'd die if she didn't get it. Her body was near to breaking point. All she needed was…

He reached down and his fingers slid between them.

"That. Oh my God, that."

Her cry echoed sharply over the room. It was the single most exquisite pleasure and pain all in one she'd experienced in her life. The tension was so sharp, so unbearable and then finally she exploded.

The room darkened around her. She blinked but everything was fuzzy. All she was aware of was Evan stroking into her and the wonderful melting sensation as she went liquid around him.

He growled her name and then he gathered her in his arms, holding her so tight she couldn't breathe. His hips jerked against her before finally he collapsed onto her, his chest heaving with exertion.

Her hands relaxed on his shoulders and went from punishing grip to soothing caresses. His skin was damp, and all that could be heard were his harsh breaths against her neck.

She held him as tight as he held her, determined to offer him all of herself. No barriers. No defenses. Just two people connecting in a way that overwhelmed her senses.

"You undo me, Celia," he said, his voice muffled against her neck.

She smiled and continued to stroke his back, enjoying the feel of his flesh beneath her fingers.

He finally rolled away to discard the condom and then came back and pulled her into his arms so they faced each other.

"That was…amazing."

She touched his lips, still fascinated with the feel of him, the rougher textures and the softness of his mouth.

"I felt pretty savored."

He smiled and kissed her, just one light smooch that sent a giddy little thrill down her back.

"I have this fantasy. It's pretty vivid, actually."

"This I gotta hear."

He smacked her lightly on her behind. "Listen up, woman. Pay attention when your man bears his soul."

She laughed and he continued.

"It didn't quite go according to plan because I was supposed to savor you first. I planned to take a couple of hours and make love to you until you were mindless. Then I was going to take you hard and fast."

"Screwed that one up."

He smacked her again and shook his head.

"So now I have this fantasy where we have fast and furious sex. Then I savor you for…okay maybe an hour. And then we have fast, furious sex again. Then you get on top and have your wicked way with me. And then you get on your hands and knees…"

Celia put her hand over his mouth and burst out laughing. "Okay, okay, I get the picture. You're an insatiable, horny male."

"Only for you," he said seriously. "You seem to regularly star in my most-vivid fantasies. I could probably be arrested for some of them. They might not be legal in all states."

"Lucky for you, California is so progressive," she murmured.

Her heart fluttered helplessly. His words…God, his words. How could she even respond to what he'd said? He sounded so…sincere. How had they gotten to this point? It scared the living hell out of her.

"So what about you? Have any interesting fantasies about me?"

He sounded so hopeful that she had to laugh again. She leaned forward and brushed her mouth against the muscled wall of his chest.

"I'm liking the savor part a lot."

"Me, too," he murmured as he reached down to tug her chin high enough that he could kiss her again.

He was a man of his word. He spent every bit of the next hour driving her mindless with his hands and his mouth. His tongue. Have mercy, his tongue.

There wasn't an inch of her he left untouched. He put his stamp on her. She felt branded. Possessed.

His tongue circled her most sensitive point nestled among the soft folds of her femininity. He worked her to the very brink of orgasm, until she quivered uncontrollably. She shivered when he pulled away and then finally he slid into her, long and slow. Hot and so tender. So very tender.

She squeezed her eyes shut but then he pressed gentle kisses to her lids until she opened them again. He stared down at her with such intensity she forgot to breathe. His eyes burned a fiery trail over her face, stroking and caressing her cheeks and her mouth.

He was dangerous. Oh, yes, so dangerous. She had no protection from him, and worse, she didn't want any. He could easily find his way into her heart.

Maybe he already had.

That should scare her to death, but instead, a warm, comfortable feeling settled over her. Contentment.

She stared into his eyes and saw herself. Saw them. Together.

He rocked over her, taking his time as he stoked the fire inside her higher and higher.

The strain was evident on his face. He held himself in check as he drove her relentlessly toward release. He wasn't going to let go of his own until she reached hers.

She twined her body tightly with his, loving the sensation of being so connected, so intrinsically linked.

"Evan," she whispered against his mouth.

He kissed her. Hard. "Give it to me. Let go."

The breathless words unlocked something deep inside

her. She arched into him, giving herself unreservedly. Wave after wave of the most beautiful pleasure rolled through her, fanning out and rippling.

He groaned and followed until she wasn't sure whose pleasure was whose and where hers began and ended.

He eased down, and she welcomed him into her arms. She pillowed his head on her chest, his mouth a breath away from her nipple. He kissed the plump swell of her breast but didn't move. Their hearts thudded against each other and neither did anything to break the silence.

What could be said? She knew she didn't have words. She didn't want to dissect the moment. Words would only ruin the euphoric aftermath of an experience she was at a loss to describe anyway.

She ran her hand idly through his mussed hair. At his nape the crisp hairs were slightly damp with sweat. She inhaled, savoring the uniquely masculine smell of sex and sweat. It was intoxicating and erotic.

"Does it make me a bastard that I'm already fantasizing about the part where you climb on top of me and have your wicked way?" he mumbled against her chest.

She smiled. "As soon as I regain the feeling in my legs, I'll see what I can do about that particular fantasy."

Eleven

Waking in bed with Evan didn't bring about the immediate what-the-hell-have-I-done feeling she would have thought. No, when her eyes opened, she registered a fantastic male body wrapped around hers, and instead of shoving him over and wailing on about how dumb she was, she snuggled deeper into his embrace and soaked up every minute of the lazy morning.

"Good morning," Evan murmured against her temple.

"Mmm."

He chuckled softly and rolled away for a moment.

"Damn."

"I don't like that damn," she grumbled. "Bad things are going to happen after that word."

He sighed in regret. "Sorry. Yeah, we have to get up."

"What time is it?"

"Noon."

Her eyes popped open and she scrambled up to look over his body at the clock.

"Noon? I've never slept until noon in my life!"

He grinned and tugged her down onto his chest. "Glad I could contribute to your downfall then."

"So arrogant," she said. "Now let me go, otherwise I'll look like a bag lady for your brother's wedding."

"I like bag ladies."

She snorted. "Ladies carrying Hermes Berkin bags maybe."

He gave her a puzzled look that suggested he didn't have a clue what she was talking about. She rolled her eyes and then pried herself out of his arms.

"Come on, get up," she coaxed. "The sooner we get it over with, the sooner you can see your brother and his new wife on their way, and we can go home."

He threw off the covers, and she nearly squeaked as he got up from the bed, stark naked. Then she realized that she wasn't any more clothed, and she fled for the bathroom, his laughter ringing in her ears.

Two hours later, dressed appropriately, they made their way to the terrace where the lovebirds would exchange their vows. As they reached the door leading out, Evan slipped an arm around her waist and pulled her close to his side.

Warmth spread through her cheeks until she remembered that this was all for show. She'd been stupid to forget that even for a moment.

When navigating the chairs and the people mingling became too difficult, he loosened his hold on her waist and tucked her hand in his instead. His fingers laced with hers and his thumb rubbed her palm as he smiled and said his hellos.

The preceremony was a bit of a madhouse and was without structure. Everyone just gathered on the terrace overlooking the cozy inlet, talking and visiting until finally Evan's father stood close to the floral arch and raised his hands for attention.

"If everyone will take their seats, I believe we're ready to begin."

Evan led Celia to the front row where they sat beside Lucy and Marshall. Evan kept a firm hold on her hand until Bettina made her appearance.

Despite his seeming indifference, Evan's demeanor changed as soon as the ceremony began. His fingers loosened from hers until she drew her hand away to rest in her own lap. He made no move to prevent the action.

His gaze was locked on Bettina and his brother, and he wasn't smiling as the rest of the attendees were. He looked like a stone pillar. No emotion.

What made it worse was when Lucy started sending sidelong glances at Evan. She'd obviously picked up on his coldness.

It begged the question as to whether Evan was as unaffected as he'd reported. Did he still love Bettina? If he was to be believed, he never had, but then did a man like Evan fall in love?

His association with Bettina could hardly be deemed romantic. He'd formed a shopping list for a prospective bride and he hadn't looked far. The first suitable candidate he'd found he put a ring on her finger and that was that.

Celia glanced down at the diamond gleaming on her third finger and winced.

Oh, Celia, tell me you haven't gotten caught up in this nonsense. You're too practical.

She almost snorted. When it came to Evan, practicality didn't crop up first. Or second or even third. She'd lusted after forbidden fruit from the moment she'd seen him.

A tiny, unwelcome thought niggled at her consciousness. Would she have begged so hard to be the one to pitch to Evan if she hadn't been so fascinated with him? Another derisive sound had to be stifled. Fascination was a very tame word to describe her fixation with Evan. Attracted. That wasn't a very descriptive word, either. It seemed no matter the word, it didn't do justice to the overwhelming barrage of sensations she experienced in his presence.

Thank God the weekend was almost over and she could hopefully gain some objectivity again. This ruse of theirs was a dangerous fantasy for her. If she didn't remove herself from it immediately, she was going to fall complete victim to it.

She could just see trying to explain that to her boss. The boss who had put his company's fate in her hands.

And then the ceremony was over and suddenly Evan was smiling down at her once more. She promptly forgot all about her worries and reservations.

Once again he was attentive. He touched her frequently as if he couldn't keep his hands off her. It made her nuts the way her body leaped to life under his attention, but she couldn't control it.

As they waited behind the line of people going back inside, Evan leaned down and nuzzled her ear.

"Let's go have some fun at the reception," he murmured. "You, me, a little dirty dancing…"

She laughed as the tightness left her chest. It was hard to remember all the reasons she shouldn't become involved with this man when he charmed her to her toes.

She tucked her hand willingly in his, and this time she curled her fingers around his as he led her into the hotel. No, logically she shouldn't immerse herself in this charade. But then attraction was anything but logical. She had only a few more hours before she would be jolted back to reality. She planned to enjoy every single one of them.

They danced. Slow, sensual songs and even the more upbeat tunes. Evan was astonishingly adept as he spun her around the room. Somehow she hadn't seen him as the type to do more than a staid waltz or just a slow cuddle type dance in the middle of the floor.

She should have known. The man was a study in athletic grace.

They took a quick break and Evan left Celia to go get drinks for them both. Celia turned to see Lucy approaching through the crowd, her face lit up like a Christmas tree.

"Celia! I'm so glad I got over to you before Evan spirits you away again."

Celia smiled warmly back at Evan's mother.

Lucy reached out to squeeze Celia's hand. "I can't thank you enough for coming. It's so obvious that the two or you are in love."

It took everything Celia had not to react to that statement. Obvious? How could it be? In lust, yes, but love? Evan would be horrified that his farce had worked a little too well. Nothing like a rumor of being in love to scare off the opposite sex. A man like Evan probably had more women than he could shake a stick at.

But he didn't take any of them to the wedding. He'd taken her.

Business, Celia reminded herself. It was convenient and business had been at the forefront of his mind.

"The two of you make such a lovely couple," Lucy said wistfully. "I do hope you'll agree to a wedding date soon. Don't make him wait, even though I'm sure he deserves it. I want him to be happy."

"I'm sure the both of us will come up with a mutually satisfactory date," Celia said diplomatically.

Lucy squeezed again and then suddenly Celia found herself enveloped in the older woman's arms.

"It was a joy to have you here, Celia. I can't wait to see you again."

Lucy drew away, beaming at Celia the entire time, and Celia felt like the lowest form of pond scum for her part in deceiving this woman.

"Oh, look, there's Evan with your drink. I'll disappear now and let you two get back to your fun."

Lucy blew a kiss in Evan's direction and melted back into the crowd.

"What was that all about?" Evan asked as he approached.

He handed her a wineglass and stepped in close, their bodies touching.

Celia grimaced. "She was telling me how wonderful she thought it was that we're getting married."

"Ah, well, that would explain the look of torture in your eyes."

He slid his arm around her waist and pulled her close. He stared down into her eyes, and then he simply kissed her.

Stunned that he would be so public, even when perpetuating a hoax, she stood there in the circle of his arms while he kissed her senseless.

Desire unfurled and spread rapid fire through her belly. All he had to do was kiss her and she was helpless to do anything more than respond.

"You know, we have late check-out," he murmured against her lips. "Very late check-out. My jet can leave at my ready. What do you say we go back to the room?"

No. They needed to return home. She needed the weekend to be over so she could recover her sanity. But instead of no, she opened her mouth and whispered, "yes."

The predatory gleam was back in his eyes. He put both their glasses down on a nearby table and then he took her hand and all but dragged her from the reception. They ran down the hallway to the elevator like two hormonally imbalanced teenagers.

When they reached the room, he threw open the door, swung her into his arms and carried her straight to the bedroom. He plopped her down on the bed and stood back as he tore out of his clothes.

She leaned up on one elbow to stare appreciatively at his physique.

"You know," she said coyly. "There is one of your fantasies we haven't played out yet."

His eyebrows shot up and then he crawled onto the bed until he loomed menacingly over her.

"Oh, really. Which one?"

She circled her arms around his neck and pulled him down into a kiss. Then she slid her mouth to his ear to whisper in shocking detail exactly which fantasy she was talking about.

Evan's plane landed in San Francisco close to midnight. He helped her down the steps onto the tarmac and stood next to her as they waited for his car to pull forward.

He touched her cheek, pushing aside a stray strand of hair. In truth, she looked and felt disheveled from head to toe. What had started as a quick interlude had turned into an afternoon of wanton, hedonistic pleasure. They'd made love more times than she could count.

They'd stumbled out of the hotel looking like a pair of illicit lovers hurrying back to their spouses after a hot weekend affair.

She shook her head to clear that notion. There was nothing dishonorable about her liaison with Evan. It was separate from business, she asserted firmly. Separate.

"Are you sure you won't let me escort you home?" Evan asked.

He glanced between her and the car that was now parked a few feet away, and his lips were drawn into a fine line.

She shook her head. "No, you still have to fly back to Seattle, and it's already past midnight. I'll be fine. Your driver will take good care of me."

He looked as if he was going to press the point when she raised her hand. The diamond caught the glare from the headlights. Slowly she removed the thin band from her finger and pressed the ring into Evan's palm.

"I won't be needing this anymore," she said lightly.

He frowned as he stared down at the delicate piece of jewelry lying in his hand.

It was ridiculous that this felt like a real break-up. Her heart seized and she had the absurd urge to snatch the ring back out of his hand and put it back on her finger.

She leaned up on tiptoe and brushed her lips across his cheek. "Goodbye, Evan. Have a safe trip home."

She turned and allowed the driver to usher her into the backseat. As they pulled away, she saw Evan standing in the same place she'd left him, his hand closed around the ring. They stared at each other through the window until the car got too far away for her to see him any longer.

Twelve

Evan tucked his hand into his pocket to touch the diamond engagement ring Celia had given back to him the night before. His finger ran over the edges, took it out and let it lay in his palm to catch the light.

For a long while, he stared down at it before closing his hand over it. As his driver pulled to the curb in front of Maddox Communications, he shoved the ring back into his pocket.

Celia wouldn't be expecting him. Hell, he wasn't expecting him. To be here, that is. He was supposed to have flown back to Seattle. He had any number of issues to deal with including talking to his team about Noah Hart. They needed to come big with an offer, and they needed to make sure any offer they made was tied up neatly with a big bow.

Yet, here he was, getting out at Celia's building because he wanted to see her again. And business had nothing to do with it.

He instructed his driver to find suitable parking and to

swing back around when he phoned to say he was ready. Then he headed into the stately building to take the elevator up to the sixth floor.

When he stepped off, he was immediately impressed with the very modern, "in touch" feel of Maddox Communications. There was a lot of attention given to comfort, and it worked, because he felt relaxed.

Two large-screen plasma televisions were positioned on either side of the large reception desk, and Maddox's latest ad campaigns were predominately displayed in a series of commercials.

Behind the desk, a cheerful looking younger woman smiled a warm welcome as he approached.

"Good morning and welcome to Maddox Communications."

He returned her smile. "Can you tell Celia Taylor that Evan Reese is here to see her?"

The sudden awareness in the receptionist's eyes told him she knew well who he was. She recovered quickly, though. With brisk efficiency, she rounded the corner of her desk and gestured toward the set of couches in the waiting area.

"If you'll have a seat, I'll get her at once. Would you care for some coffee?"

"No, thank you."

She turned to stride down the hallway, leaving Evan standing there. He walked to the window to look down on the street instead of sitting. If he had his way, he wouldn't be here for long anyway.

A few moments later, he heard the tap tap of heels and turned to see Celia approaching, a confused, wary look in her eyes.

"Evan," she greeted. "I wasn't expecting to see you. I thought you were going back to Seattle. Is anything wrong?"

She'd put her impersonal business face on the moment he looked up. It annoyed him that she was pushing him away, already distancing herself from the weekend they'd shared. It should be him doing the pushing. He should have gotten her out of his system after making love to her more times than he could count.

But he hadn't, which was why he found himself standing here, trying to come up with an excuse to see her again.

"Nothing's wrong. My plans changed. I thought we could have lunch. If you're free, that is."

She checked her watch, a quick, nervous motion that told him she was merely stalling—and trying to think of an excuse why she couldn't.

"I would very much like to have lunch with you, Celia."

Her forehead wrinkled in indecision. She nibbled at her bottom lip. He took advantage of that moment to move closer until he crowded her. Before she could take a step back, he grasped her arm.

Alarm flared in her eyes, and she broke the contact, stepping hastily away as she stared wildly in all directions.

"For God's sake, Evan, not here," she hissed.

Her hand trembled as she raised one to smooth her hair. Instead of repairing the knot, she only managed to work more strands free. They fell down her neck, calling attention to the slim column. He was reminded of all the time he'd spent nibbling at that sweet flesh.

He raised an eyebrow at her vehemence but kept his distance.

"Lunch?"

"All right. Let me get my purse. I'll meet you downstairs."

Her dismissal rankled him. He was used to calling the shots when it came to women and relationships.

Hell, now he was thinking of her in terms of a relationship? The only thing he should be thinking was how quickly he could get her back into bed so that hopefully this time he'd get rid of the burning ache he felt when she crossed his mind.

Crossed. What a funny word, one that denoted an occasional, unintentional meeting. She lived in his mind. He didn't like it, didn't particularly care for the implication, but he was powerless to rid himself of her assault on his senses.

He stared at her for a long moment, and only because he was convinced she was ready to bolt, did he acquiesce.

"All right. I'll call my driver around. Oh, and Celia. I don't like to be kept waiting."

Celia spun around before she exploded. She wished she could blame it all on her anger and his arrogance, but she'd been flabbergasted when Shelby had rushed into her office to tell her Evan Reese was here and he wanted to see her.

The giddy thrill that sizzled down her spine annoyed her. And then his arrogant presumption that she'd drop everything to have lunch with him. He didn't like to be kept waiting. Who did he think he was?

She sighed as she collected her purse. Where to even begin? He was an important client. The most important client of her career. And then there was the fact she'd acted as his fake fiancée, and oh yeah, she'd slept with him. Repeatedly.

A hot blush shot up her neck and nearly burned her cheeks off as she remembered just how often they'd had sex. They'd re-enacted all his fantasies and some of hers, too.

They'd been insatiable.

Hell and damnation but she'd expected several days to recover from the weekend before she had to see him again. In her utter befuddlement and not to mention being blown over by the sex, she hadn't even mentioned the season opener to Evan.

It was as good an excuse as any to accompany him to lunch. At least then she could pretend it was all about business.

After a quick wave to Shelby, she rode the elevator down to the first floor. She passed the busy American cuisine restaurant with the lunch crowd lined up at the door and exited the building.

Evan was standing at the curb, one hand resting on the open door to the backseat of his car, the other shoved into his pocket. He looked positively arrogant. Like he not only belonged in the world but owned it.

He nodded as she approached and motioned her inside the car. Then he slid in beside her and shut the door.

"I thought we could eat at this restaurant I know across town. It's small and not so well-known, but the food is excellent and it affords privacy."

He looked at her almost like the last was a challenge.

She tilted her chin up and stared coolly at him. She hoped that she looked as unruffled as she wanted to portray.

"Is this business, Evan? Why did you come to my office today?"

His mouth tightened briefly before he relaxed and eyed her with thinly veiled amusement.

"We slept together, Celia. I don't think lunch is that scandalous given that fact."

She curled her fingers into tight fists. She wanted to close her eyes and moan her dismay. No, she doubted he'd understand why it was so important to her that there be no hint of impropriety between them. He was the type who'd never let what others thought rule his life. She hated that evidently she was the type. Hated it but couldn't change it.

"Evan."

She stopped when her voice cracked. She felt like the worst sort of idiot. Around others she had no problem being blunt—and forceful when the occasion called for it. But with Evan, she was ridiculously tongue-tied.

"Yes?" he prompted.

He wore a curious smile, almost as if he found her and the situation amusing. It made her angry.

"We can't do this. We simply can't. This weekend was a huge mistake. I don't want to be one of these women who say no, no, no, and then yes, yes, yes and then spend the next week castigating myself for my weakness. I shouldn't have slept with you. I swear, I left my brain behind when we went to Catalina. I knew what I was getting into. Don't get me wrong. I don't blame you or think you manipulated me into having sex with you. I'm a big girl and I knew full well what I was doing. It doesn't make me any less stupid, mind you."

Evan simply hauled her into his arms and stifled her tirade with a kiss. Not just any kiss. He devoured her whole. She melted—positively melted—in his arms. She went limp against him.

Yep, she was one of those silly women at the mercy of her hormones.

She placed both hands on his chest and shoved until they sat apart, both breathing raggedly. She probably looked demented sitting there, hair askew, chest heaving up and down as if she'd run a marathon.

"Stop kissing me!"

He smiled again, a lazy, sensual smile of a lion standing over its prey. She was lunch apparently.

"But I like kissing you and I try never to deny myself life's little pleasures."

She rolled her eyes then caught herself before she laughed.

"Dammit, Evan. Be serious for one minute. I mean it. Stop kissing me and stop touching me."

He held his hands up in surrender. "Okay, okay. I won't touch you."

She crossed her arms protectively over her chest and moved as far over in the seat as she could. Why had she agreed to lunch with him? Why?

Because you're a masochist and you can't resist him.

There was that.

She's always thought it was a myth. The out-of-control hormones that made an otherwise intelligent woman make waste of her brain cells every time she came into contact with the one.

She was certainly proving the waste of brain cells to be true.

The rest of the journey was spent in brooding silence. Evan

was silent and Celia brooded. When they finally pulled up to a restaurant that boasted the best seafood on the west coast, she raised a skeptical eyebrow.

"Try it first and then tell me if you disagree," Evan said in amusement.

He was becoming way too adept at reading her and it annoyed her to no end, especially since she had no idea what went on in his head. She was afraid to find out.

When she stepped out and glanced around, she had to hand it to him. For a man who didn't seemingly care if they were seen together or not and certainly didn't have the objections she had, he'd chosen a restaurant where they weren't likely to be seen by anyone who knew them.

Evan guided her in to the rustic cedar building with its quasi-southern charm mixed with California décor. It was an odd blend that, to her surprise, worked well.

The two sat in the far corner where the lighting so was so dim a small kerosene lantern sat in the middle of the table to offer ambience.

"I feel like I'm on a first date," she said ruefully after Evan had ordered the wine.

He smiled and waggled his eyebrows suggestively. "Would it make me less of a jerk to be up front about the fact I plan to have you in my bed tonight?"

She sucked in her breath until she felt curiously lightheaded. She suspected of course, but to hear him say it outright was way sexier than it should have been.

"I have to go back to work," she murmured.

He nodded. "Of course. I didn't intend to spirit you away for an afternoon tryst, though the idea has merit. I wonder if your coworkers would call the police?"

She glared at him—determined not to laugh. But even her scowl twitched. Irreverent bastard.

The waiter appeared with food, and she blinked because

she hadn't remembered ordering. She glanced at the half-empty wineglass and couldn't for the life of her remember drinking so much as a sip. Evan was bad, bad for her brain. He was as bad as some wasting disease. She wouldn't survive, either.

"Evan," she began again, and promptly shut up when it came out more as a plaintive wail than a protest.

"I'll send a car for you, Celia. No one needs to see you getting into a vehicle with me. I'll have my driver pick you up from work, or if you prefer, you can drive your car to your apartment and I'll have him pick you up there. And I'll have him take you home in time for you to prepare for work."

Why wasn't she immediately shutting him down? Instead of telling him that in no uncertain terms would she agree to such a thing, she found herself contemplating how decadent it would be to dash off to an elicit rendezvous with her lover.

She shivered at the word *lover*. Evan was a superb specimen of a man. He was fantastic in bed and insatiable to boot. He knew how to pleasure a woman and was as unselfish a lover as she'd ever had. The mere idea of spending the night with him had her tied in so many knots it would take a team of massage therapists to work them out.

She chewed absently at the food, not registering the taste or even what she ate. Her throat was as dry as the desert and her tongue was swollen and clumsy.

"You act as though it's a crime for us to make love," he said in an oddly tender voice.

If it had been coaxing or wheedling, she could have been cold to him. But she could swear he was reassuring her and attempting to allay her fears.

She licked her lips and raised her gaze to meet his. Awareness hit her square in the chest. In his eyes she saw undulating bodies. Hers and his. In perfect rhythm. So beautiful and so pleasurable that she closed her eyes to further immerse herself in the memory.

"Say yes."

His voice stroked her as surely as his fingers had done. A prickle of goose bumps spread rapidly over her shoulders and down her chest until her nipples tightened into two painful knots.

"Celia," he prompted.

Finally she opened her eyes and fixed him with her unfocused gaze.

"Yes," she whispered.

Thirteen

Celia entered her office with a heightened sense of anticipation. She already knew she'd be clock watching until it was quitting time and then she'd race home so she could change and look her best for her naughty escape to Evan's.

Her mouth curved into a naughty smile to match the naughtiness of her and Evan's plan. It was wicked, forbidden, and she was so turned on that she was ready to fidget right out of her shoes.

With a sigh, she sank into her chair behind her desk, kicked off her shoes and logged on to catch up on e-mail. She hadn't planned to go out for lunch at all and had, in fact, brought food from home, planning to eat at her desk. After missing Friday, she'd spent the morning getting a report from Jason on her client meetings he covered and then she'd gone through messages.

She groaned as her in-box stacked up with e-mail after e-mail. She started at the bottom and worked up, deleting several after cursory glances. Those requiring a lengthy response she flagged to respond to later and the ones she could just do a one-line response to she typed furiously and sent on their way.

She was nearly to the end when her gaze flickered over the name Lucy Reese. She did a double take. Evan's mom? Why would she e-mail and how had she gotten Celia's address?

Her stomach fluttered a bit, and guilt crept over her all over again. Lucy was nice and Celia hated lying to her. She hated lying as a rule for any reason but especially not for such a frivolous endeavor.

She braced herself and clicked on the message. It began as cheerfully as Lucy herself was in person. She said again how thrilled she was that Celia and Evan had found each other.

Talk about another shot to the gut.

She expressed her desire to see Celia again and hoped Evan would bring her to Seattle for a visit.

Could this get any worse?

Her message ended with a short note that she'd attached some pictures from the wedding that she thought Celia would enjoy.

Celia opened the attached JPEGS and couldn't help but smile. The pictures were of her and Evan at the wedding reception. They looked happy and…in love.

There was one of them dancing, another of Evan looking down with a tender expression and the last was when Evan had kissed her. Celia's hand rested on his chest and the glitter of the ring contrasted with the black of Evan's tuxedo. Their mouths were fused together, and it was obvious to anyone looking at the picture that they were in danger of combusting right there in the middle of a crowded reception.

For several minutes, she debated whether or not to reply to Lucy's e-mail. It seemed rude not to, but it was also a terrible thing to prolong the charade.

Finally, she settled for a brief thank you and that she'd enjoyed meeting Lucy, as well. It was true and didn't delve into any part of her nonexistent relationship with Evan.

Stealing over to the man's hotel room after work hours certainly couldn't be considered a relationship.

Her intercom beeped, startling her from her thoughts.

"Celia, I have a cleaning service willing to take over Noah Hart's house."

"Brave," Celia muttered.

"What was that?"

"Nothing. Do you have details on when they'll start? Can you e-mail me that and the agency name and contact info so I can forward it?"

"Sure."

There was a distinct pause and then Shelby's hesitant voice filtered through the intercom.

"Sooo, are you going to give me the dirt on Noah Hart? Like how you know him and why you're arranging his maid service?"

"No," Celia said shortly.

She punched the button to end the conversation and hoped Shelby would get the hint. True, Shelby liked to gossip but she wasn't overtly intrusive. She backed off when people wanted her to.

She checked her e-mail and then forwarded the information to Noah. After closing her e-mail program, she stared at her phone and sighed. Noah was a disaster when it came to e-mails. The man just didn't care about advanced methods of communication. If it couldn't be said on the phone or person, he wasn't much interested. It drove his agent nuts. Simon Blackstone much preferred the impersonal methods of e-mail and text messages to actual conversations, but if he wanted to talk to Noah, he had to pick up the phone. Celia was convinced Noah did it just to torque his agent's jaw.

At any rate, she'd better call and leave a message on Noah's cell or God knows what the cleaning lady would come across when she went to his house.

She'd hit the end button after leaving him a nagging, sisterly message when it hit her square in the face that she had neglected to mention the game to Evan.

How could she be so stupid? With everything else that had gone on in the weekend, the game had slipped her mind. Even when she'd done the pitch and specifically dangled the Noah carrot in front of Evan's nose, she'd flaked on the season opener.

He was probably already booked solid, if he was even going to be in town. The game was the night before her scheduled pitch session and he'd probably just fly in on the morning of their meeting.

"Stupid, stupid, stupid," she muttered.

Would it be crass to mention it tonight? During their little sex getaway? If she wanted to get him in front of Noah in a casual setting, then she was going to have to move fast and hope he hadn't locked up his week already with other obligations.

She looked up when a knock sounded at her door. Brock stood against the door frame, a smile easing the newly developed lines at his eyes and mouth.

"Hey, we wanted to get together at Rosa after work today. You're the star and we want to toast with copious amounts of alcohol. It will be a good pep rally for the presentation on Friday."

Her stomach rolled into a tight ball. The last thing she wanted was a raucous night at Rosa with the work gang. Usually she'd be all over it. The Maddox employees regularly hung out at the upscale martini bar just a block away. It's where they met to celebrate, commiserate or just take a break from a hellish workday.

The last celebration they'd staged there had been for Jason after he'd landed the Prentice account. Now Brock was lining up the chorus for her.

Her cheeks tightened in pleasure even as her heart sank at the idea of ditching Evan after agreeing to meet him. He'd think her the worst sort of coward even if it was the smart thing to do.

"I'd love to, Brock, but I already have plans for the evening. Important plans," she added after a pause. "Besides, I'd rather not jinx myself before going into the presentation. It's not in the bag—yet—but I certainly plan to perform a slam dunk on Friday."

He nodded. "Yeah, I understand. We'll go and just call it a pre-planning session. It's as good an excuse as any to throw back a few. But if you land this, just be prepared for a victory celebration to end all victory celebrations."

She grinned. "Oh, you know it. I can't wait. I'll totally hold you to it."

"Okay, take care and see you tomorrow." He turned to go but stopped and turned back once more. "Oh, and, Celia, if I haven't already said it, thank you. You did a magnificent job. I doubted your approach at first, but you came through in spades."

Her heart sped up and she curled her fingers until her nails dug into her palms. It was all she could do not to stand up and throw her arms in the air complete with an obnoxious yell.

"Thank you for your trust," she said as calmly as possible.

With a short salute, he disappeared down the hallway, leaving Celia grinning like a loon.

Promptly at a quarter to five, Celia headed down the elevator—fifteen minutes before quitting time so she'd miss the majority of her coworkers. She didn't want to explain why she wasn't joining them at Rosa.

Her apartment wasn't far, and usually she'd enjoy driving her Beamer with the top down—it really was a sassy, smooth handling dream machine—but today she was just impatient to be home, and the traffic was driving her mad.

When she reached her apartment, she recognized the car out front and the driver standing on the curb beside it. With a groan, she slowed to a stop on the street and rolled down her window.

"I'll only be a moment," she called.

The driver smiled, tipped his hat and said, "No hurry, Miss Taylor. Take your time."

She maneuvered into her parking spot and dashed inside, ready to do battle. She hadn't missed Evan's reaction to her sexy, feminine lingerie. It was her one indulgence or what she deemed a silly indulgence since her sex life was so staid in the last few years that no one but her had a prayer of ever seeing what her underwear looked like.

Hopping on one foot as she stepped out of her clothing, she went over to her drawer to find the most sinful set of lingerie she owned. She settled on pink. What was more feminine or soft looking than pink? Even growing up with a hoard of boys hadn't erased the girly from her. And since she was a redhead, wearing pink clothing wasn't an option. But pink underwear she could do.

Unsure of whether she'd return to her apartment before going to work the next day—and she did like to be prepared for anything—she threw an outfit into an overnight bag along with her toiletries and a lavender bra and panties.

She did a quick check of her messages and then did something she never did. She turned off her BlackBerry and tucked it into her overnight bag. Tonight was hers. She needed no reminders from the business world. If she was going to indulge in fantasy, she was going whole hog.

She locked up and hurried out her door to the street where the driver waited. He ushered her into the backseat and they drove away into traffic.

It amused her how exciting she found the whole experience. She could be a mistress at the beck and call of her über-wealthy benefactor, discreetly bundled into a private car and rushed to meet him at an undisclosed location.

"Get it together, Celia," she muttered.

Lord, but she did lose all her brain cells when it came

to this man. If she wasn't careful, she'd throw away all her independence and start greeting him at the door every evening, wearing a kitchen apron with oven mitts and a piping-hot casserole dish.

Oddly but the image wasn't all that distasteful. For the first few seconds anyway. She laughed outright and it had the effect of someone popping her thought bubble with a sharp pin.

The driver looked up in the rearview mirror, and she valiantly tried to look back with a straight face. If he only knew the absurd thoughts she was processing.

If she was truly the naughty girl of her fantasies, she would have ridden over with only a trench coat covering her sexy lingerie. Then when she walked into Evan's room, she could discard the coat and watch his reaction.

The idea certainly had merit, and if she ever received another invitation such as tonight, she'd give it serious consideration.

A few minutes later, the driver pulled up to the sumptuous hotel Evan resided in when he was in town, bypassed the main entrance and stopped at the second pull in where her door was immediately opened by one of the hotel staff.

Maybe Evan had his own entrance. The thought amused her, but then he had so much money, it wouldn't surprise her.

She was immediately met by concierge and was handed a keycard.

"Mr. Reese wishes for you to go right up," the older man said.

She blushed from head to toe. She knew well what it looked like. Like she was some hooker or mistress—precisely what she'd imagined on her way over—all set to have a clandestine meeting.

She took the key card, murmured her thanks, and shot past the doorman and into the small hallway leading directly to the elevators. Thankfully she bypassed the lobby entirely. It seemed like everyone in the world knew what she was here for.

In the elevator, she inserted her key and punched the button for the top floor. She was whisked to the top in no time at all and stepped into the eerily quiet hallway. There were only a few doors. The rooms must be huge because she only counted four doors total. Evan's was on the very end, and she took a deep breath before inserting the key into the slot.

When she opened the door and stepped inside, she immediately saw Evan standing across the room, drink in hand, his eyes fixed on her. He'd been waiting. She could sense his impatience and see the triumph in his expression when she closed the door behind her.

She stood there, unmoving, as he put his drink aside and crossed the room in just a few, long strides.

"You came," he murmured.

He swept her into his arms and kissed her. He wasn't gentle or even particularly careful. Their bodies came together in a clash she felt all the way to her bones.

"Did you think I wouldn't?" she asked when she was finally able to draw a breath.

His eyes glittered, and his throat worked up and down as if he was trying to hold on to his control.

"If you hadn't, I was prepared to go and drag you out of your apartment."

All her concerns fell away. Nothing else mattered but the intense need they felt for each other.

"Next time I won't come. I have my own set of caveman fantasies wherein the Neanderthal drags me off to his cave."

He growled low in his throat and before she could react, he had her in his arms and was striding toward the bedroom.

Fourteen

They made it as far as the dresser. Evan slid her onto the polished surface of the wood and leaned in until she straddled his hips.

"I swore this time I'd savor first," he said against her mouth. "Dammit, but when I see you, all reason flies out the door."

She hooked her legs around his back and pulled him into the V of her groin.

"Has anyone ever told you that you talk too much?"

"Never a woman," he murmured as he swept hungrily over her mouth.

Her excitement mounted as Evan ripped at her shirt. He shoved it down over her shoulders, trapping her arms to her sides. His hands smoothed up her bare skin to her shoulders. He gripped her so hard, she knew she'd wear his prints.

His breath blew hot over her chin and then her jaw. He kissed a line to her ear then sucked the lobe between his teeth.

Shivers overtook her. Delicate little goose bumps dotted her flesh until she trembled uncontrollably.

He stepped back, his hands falling to the waistband of her pants. His fingers hung in the snap and he stood there staring at her heaving chest.

"You're so beautiful."

He raised one finger to hook in the strap of her bra. He ran it up then down, and he grazed the tip over the swell of her breast.

"I love the lingerie."

She leaned back on the dresser, resting her palms on the top to give him a better glimpse of her cleavage.

"You're absolutely merciless, aren't you?" he murmured.

She smiled and arched invitingly until the barest hint of her nipples peeked at him over the lace cups of her bra.

He wrapped both arms around her waist and lowered his mouth to the valley between her breasts. He kissed and nibbled at the plump swells until she gasped and struggled for each breath.

The straps had loosened and tumbled down her shoulders. He slid his palms up her body, hooked his thumbs in the straps and dragged them back down.

He tugged until finally one cup slipped down and freed her breast. He licked the nipple until it puckered and strained outward. Then he closed his mouth ever so gently around the tip.

"Evan," she whispered as her hands tangled in his hair.

He sucked softly and then with more pressure until her entire focus was the streaks of pleasure radiating from her nipple.

Clumsily, he yanked and fumbled with the clasp of her bra until it fell completely free. He shoved it aside and focused on unbuttoning her pants, his mouth never leaving her breast.

He lifted her hips. She hoisted herself up, giving him room to pull her pants down. They fell to the floor and he took a step back and ran his gaze up and down her body.

She felt beautiful and desirable. Even irresistible. He ate her with his eyes. Appreciation didn't adequately describe what she saw in his gaze. This was a man who saw only her. There were no other women.

"I can't say I ever fantasized about having sex with a woman on top of a dresser, but I'm re-evaluating. I can see the appeal."

She wiggled a little closer to him so that she was perched on the edge. Right now she wanted him so much, even the short distance to the bed seemed too much.

He tucked his finger underneath the lace of her panties and ran it along the edge until he delved into her hot, liquid heat. She leaned back, closed her eyes and moaned as he grew bolder with his exploration.

The sensation of his hands rasping lightly over her behind as he cupped her and began to slide her underwear off was enough to drive her beyond endurance. She had to have him. Her nerve endings were fried.

And then she was naked under his seeking gaze and inquisitive fingers. He stroked and caressed until she was a mass of gasping, breathless anticipation.

"No fair," she panted. "You still have clothes on."

He gave her a faint smile before quickly shedding his clothing. Then he dropped to his knees in front of the dresser. His hands slid sensuously up her legs, setting fire with the barest of touches.

Her breath caught and held when he parted her thighs and pressed his mouth to her most intimate flesh.

"Oh…"

It was all she could manage. Everything went fuzzy around her. Swimming. She was swimming in the most exquisite, mind-numbing waters she'd ever navigated.

The man was talented. He was generous. Even when he was pushed to his limits, he brought her to the brink of ecstasy before satisfying his own needs.

"Evan, please!"

He rose up, gripped her knees and yanked her forward until she perched precariously on the edge of the dresser again. There was savage menace in his expression, the look of a man pushed too far too fast and struggling to hold on with everything he had.

He paused only long enough to roll on a condom and then he found her center and plunged deep.

His hands slid under her bottom, gripped tight and pulled her to meet his thrusts. He was deep and she felt him in every part of her soul. She ended, he began. He was a part of her, taking, giving and sharing.

He leaned forward to bury his face in her neck as he rocked against her. Lightning sizzled down her spine as he nuzzled her sensitive skin and suckled the column of her neck.

She wrapped her arms and legs around him until there wasn't an inch of space between them. Still buried tightly inside her, he lifted her up and backed toward the bed. He fell, her on top, and they landed with a jolt.

"Ride me," he said in a strained voice.

His pupils dilated and his brow constricted. Tight lines were etched into his forehead, and his hands gripped her hips so tightly that she could do nothing more than squeeze her inner muscles around his erection.

"Sweat heaven," he groaned.

She wasn't going to last, and she was helpless to do anything about it. She needed to move. She had to move.

Placing her palms flat on his chest, she wiggled free of his grasp and began to move up and down, taking him, releasing him, then taking him again.

Sweat beaded his brow. His eyes were narrow slits, and he never took his gaze from hers. He urged her closer so he could cup her breasts. They filled both palms and he rubbed the pad of his thumb over the painfully erect nubs.

"I can't hold on," she whispered.

"Then let's go together," he urged.

His hands left her breasts and he gripped her hips, lifting

her and pulling her down in time with his upward thrusts. The
burn spread. Tension mounted. She wound tighter and tighter
until it was all she could do to hang on.

She threw her head back, her mouth open in an endless cry
of agony. The sweetest, most breathtaking agony of her life.

His hands left her hips to tangle in her hair. He rose up,
pulling her harshly to meet his kiss. Frantically, his hands
moved up and down her back, into her hair, through her hair,
over her face as if he couldn't get enough and wanted to
memorize every feature.

And then it was as if the world went silent. The wave rolled,
crashed and then broke into a million tiny ripples, each feeding the other.

She was no longer cognizant of holding on to him. She was
riding high and fast.

She had no idea how long she lay sprawled over Evan, her
heart beating so frantically that she literally felt each thud.
His arms were wrapped around her, and their legs were all
tangled up. He was still buried inside her, and she could feel
the remnants of his orgasm. Each little pulse sent a tiny shock
of aftermath flooding through her body.

Slowly she became aware that he was stroking her back
and her hair. He murmured little sweet words in her ear but
nothing seemed to make sense. She was completely befuddled
by this man, by her reaction to him.

"I think I blew it again."

She smiled and snuggled a little closer, tucking her head
under his chin and nuzzling his chest.

"You blew, all right. But I think I blew first."

His chest heaved as he chuckled. "You're such a naughty
girl."

Summoning energy she sorely lacked, she raised her head
and propped up on his chest so she could stare down into his
eyes. What she saw sent a pang of longing straight through
her heart.

He looked content. Sated, but not just in a sexual way. He

looked at home, like they'd been together forever. Oh, she had an overactive imagination. She was sure of that. But when he looked at her like that, with the world in his eyes, a world where only she existed, it was hard not to get caught up in the fantasy they'd created between them.

He ran a gentle finger over her mouth. "What are you thinking?"

"I'm fairly certain a man should never ask a woman what she's thinking right after sex," she said lightly.

"I'm fairly certain all women like to talk after sex. Well, talk and cuddle, or some girly thing like that."

She grinned and leaned down to kiss him. "I like the cuddle part."

He gathered her in his arms and rolled until they lay on their sides. "Not a talker, huh?"

She reached down and carefully rolled the condom off him. He put his hand down to stop her.

"No, I'll do that. You don't have to mess with it."

But she already had it off. She kissed him again then scooted off the bed to discard it. When she looked back, he was propped on one hand, watching her intently.

His naked body was a gorgeous sight. Even in a relaxed state, his proportions were generous to say the least.

"If you keep looking at me like that, it's not going to stay down," he growled.

"You only have one condom?" she asked in mock horror.

He reached over, grabbed her arm and yanked her back down beside him. "I'll have you know, I had a case delivered."

She snorted with laughter. "A case? Are you planning an orgy?"

"I may have exaggerated...slightly. But only slightly," he said with a sly grin.

"That's good to know. I'd hate to think I was under that kind of pressure."

He tweaked her nose then followed up with a kiss. "Somehow I think you could hold up quite well."

She cuddled deeper into his embrace. She hadn't lied about the cuddling part or the talking part. Well, maybe about the talking part. In truth, she'd love to bare her soul, learn all his secrets, tell him all hers. Tell him how much she loved…

She froze. For a moment she simply couldn't breathe. It wasn't as if she'd just fallen in love with the man. No, it had probably been coming for a while now. But she hadn't admitted it. Hadn't even thought it much less said it aloud.

Yeah, it was there in the background just waiting for the time when she let it slip in. She'd been so good—or so she thought—about keeping her emotional distance.

She loved this man. Her heart seized. It was a painful admission. Wasn't figuring out you were in love supposed to be accompanied by fireworks, a fanfare, a giddy thrill? Wasn't it supposed to be the most wonderful thing in the world?

Why then did she have the sudden urge to run to the bathroom and throw up?

"We have options," Evan said.

She blinked and focused her attention back on the here and now and the fact she was in bed after hot, sweaty sex with the man she…loved.

It was all she could do not to groan.

"What options?" she asked huskily.

"I can feed you. I can make mad, passionate love to you again. Or we can take a short nap and then do either option one or two. Or both. See? I'm easy."

She smiled and squeezed him. She did love him. It scared her to death just how much she loved him, and now that she'd admitted it, she was flooded by so much emotion. It was all she could do not to blurt it out like some teenage girl with her first crush.

"Am I staying over?" she asked. She hadn't wanted to assume, but she needed to know before she started choosing options.

He leaned up and cradled her so he looked down at her. "Of course. That is, if you want to. If you didn't bring clothes to go to work in, I can have my driver take you home."

She swallowed. "I did bring clothes. But if he takes me to work, I'm without a car. It would probably be best if he did take me home early enough for me to get my car. I can dress here."

He looked for a moment like he'd say something but then evidently he thought better of it and didn't push. She wondered what he'd wanted to say, but like him, she didn't push.

"All right. I'll make sure we get an early enough wake-up call for you to shower and get ready here before he takes you home to get your car."

Unable to resist, she kissed him. It wasn't a playful little peck this time, but a warm, deep kiss that showed without words the depth of her feelings.

When she finally drew away, his eyes were glazed with passion, but there was also contentment that she didn't want to speculate about.

"In that case, I vote we go with eat, mad passionate love and then sleep," she murmured.

"Sold."

A half hour later, they sat cross-legged on the bed, devouring the room service Evan had ordered. She was swallowed up by one of his robes, and he was wearing a pair of boxer shorts.

She ate indelicately, with her fingers, foregoing the utensils. It was finger food anyway, and it was too scrumptious to be all highbrow about eating it.

They were nearly done when it hit her that she still hadn't broached the subject of the baseball game. Where before she'd felt a little awkward about bringing it up during what was obviously an illicit rendezvous, here with Evan, she was completely at ease.

"Tell me your plans for the rest of the week. Are you returning to Seattle until our presentation on Friday?"

He cocked his head and studied her intently. "That depends, I suppose."

"On what?"

"On whether I have a reason to stay."

Her cheeks warmed. His meaning couldn't have been more clear. Her mouth suddenly went dry and she gulped a mouthful of water.

"I meant to invite you to the Tide season opener. I have tickets. Good tickets. Are you interested?"

He looked a little surprised, and for a moment she wondered if she'd overstepped her boundries. But then he smiled. A genuine, warm smile that told her he was pleased with her invitation.

"I'd love to go. It's Thursday night, isn't it?"

She nodded. "I could pick you up and drive us over."

His eyes gleamed, and for a moment she could swear he looked victorious. Over what, she hadn't a clue.

"Just tell me what time, and I'll be waiting with bells on."

"It starts at seven, so I'll be here around five-thirty."

"I'm looking forward to it already."

She relaxed. Things were shaping up perfectly. She'd take him to the game and introduce him to Noah afterward. Then she'd wow him the next morning with a kick-ass presentation. The deal was hers. In the bag. She couldn't contemplate any other outcome.

Golden Gate and Athos Koteas might be coming on strong, but they didn't have Noah Hart, and they damn sure didn't have her ideas. Ideas she knew were perfect for Evan and his company.

This was hers.

Evan reached out to wipe a smudge from the corner of her mouth. She glanced down to see his food gone and most of hers, as well. And the way he was looking at her, she had a good idea what was for dessert.

"Give me two seconds to clear this away and roll the cart

out into the hall and we'll get on with option two, although I'm thinking that option three should be significantly delayed."

She raised an eyebrow and her heart started tripping double time.

"Oh? How delayed?"

"Very delayed," he said silkily. "I'm thinking option two could be divided into options three, four, five…"

In response, she untied her robe and tugged it away until she sat naked on the bed.

Fifteen

Celia pulled into one of the reserved parking spaces at the stadium and cut the engine. She glanced over at Evan. "Ready?"

He looked out the windshield at the proximity of their space and the stadium entrance and whistled in appreciation.

"These must be some tickets you have."

She smiled. "I told you they're good."

They got out and Celia led the way. Normally she would have gone in through the players' entrance, but she didn't want to tip her hand just yet, so they headed through the main gate just as everyone else did.

Evan waited for her while she went through security and had her bag screened and then they had their tickets scanned and walked in the direction of the field.

Since she'd handled the tickets, she knew he hadn't seen them and she couldn't wait to get his reaction to the behind the home plate VIP tickets she'd scored from Noah.

Several minutes later, and after navigating two entrances,

they entered the field above the home plate. She flashed her tickets and an usher led them down the steps to a box of seats directly behind the batter's box.

He motioned them into the row and Celia settled in the seat four rows up from the bottom.

"Wow," Ethan said as he took his seat beside her. "I mean, wow. How the hell did you get these tickets? They must have cost a fortune. Not to mention they've been sold out. I know because I've tried to get them."

"I know people," she said smugly.

He eyed her curiously. "I'm beginning to get the impression you do."

They caught the tail end of batting practice and then settled back as the field was watered and prepared for the start of the game.

Evan relaxed in his seat and knocked his shades down over his eyes. It was exceptionally sunny today and there was absolutely no cloud or fog cover. It was a perfect day for baseball.

In typical business-geek style, his gaze roved over the fans, looking for those who wore Reese designs. If Celia had her way, a lot more normal, everyday people would want to wear his line of sportswear.

He turned when he heard Celia talking to a hot dog vendor. She twisted to look at Evan. "You want something?"

"Whatever you're having," he replied.

He dug into his wallet to pay the vendor, but the older man smiled and waved him off.

"Our Cece is taken care of. No charge for her."

Evan watched the banter between Celia and the vendor in utter bemusement. They chattered about batting averages, who to watch in the coming season and the travesty that had occurred the previous season when the Tide had finished one game back from the division leader.

"They'll win the pennant this year," Celia consoled. "Noah is in top form. He was only warming up his bat last year."

The vendor nodded enthusiastically. "I believe you're right, Miss Cece. He got hot and the season ended."

Celia turned and made an expression like she'd forgotten something.

"Oh, my manners are horrible. Please forgive me. Evan, this is Henry Dockett. He's worked here since the stadium was built thirty years ago. He knows everything there is to know about everything around here. Henry, this is Evan Reese."

Evan extended his hand to shake the older man's and Henry's face lit up.

"You're the Evan Reese from Reese Enterprises?"

Evan smiled. "One and the same."

Henry nodded approvingly. "Good place for you to be then. Miss Cece will show you a good time."

Someone else signaled for Henry and he nodded at Evan and Celia. "I'll be back later on to check on you, Miss Cece."

She smiled and patted Henry on the arm and thanked him for the hot dogs.

When she turned back in her seat, Evan leaned over to take his hot dog from her lap.

"Do you have everyone eating out of your hand, *Miss Cece?*"

She actually blushed and ducked her head.

"Henry is an old friend."

Evan chuckled, delighted at the rosy bloom of her cheeks.

"Do you have any other surprises in store for me today?"

"Maybe," she mumbled around a bite of hot dog.

The Tide took the field, and the very first batter walked. Celia groaned her dismay along with the rest of the crowd.

"Our pitching has been what's let us down in the past," she whispered to Evan.

He didn't have the heart to tell her that not only did he know, but he could quote the stats for every one of the Tide's pitching roster.

"This year should be better," Evan consoled.

She nodded. "Soren is our best. He usually starts cold, though. If we can get out of the first inning, he's awesome."

Again Evan grinned and sat back to watch. Celia bolted from her seat when the second batter grounded to second and Noah scooped, tossed to the shortstop who turned the double play to first.

Evan could swear that Noah looked straight at Celia and winked. He looked between the two and finally shook off the absurd notion.

Soren struck out the next batter and the Tide was up to bat. Celia clutched her hands like an anxious mother. Todd Cameron, the lead off, looked up at Celia as he headed to the plate, grinned and waved. Celia waved and blew him a kiss.

Evan stared but didn't say anything. Things just got stranger and stranger. He was willing to put the first off as a fluke, but when the third batter came up and gave Celia a thumbs-up, he wondered what the hell he was missing.

After the batter flied out to center field, advancing the two runners on a sacrifice, Evan leaned over, intending to ask Celia exactly what he was missing out on, but she put her hand on his arm and squeezed hard.

"Just a minute. Noah's up!"

Her fingers dug into his arm like little daggers, but he didn't pry her away. He was too interested to see what would happen when Hart came up. And, too, he was interested to get a close up glimpse of what he hoped would be his company's golden PR boy.

Noah's face was drawn in concentration as he began the walk to the plate. He swung the bat a few times then stopped, two inches out of the box. He turned and glanced first to the right of Evan and Celia and dipped his head in acknowledgment. Then he turned and scanned behind home plate until his gaze lighted on Celia.

He lost the look of intense concentration, and his face relaxed into a smile. He gave her an exaggerated wink and then held up his fist.

Evan's mouth fell open as he glanced between the two. Celia's hand tightened further on his arm when Noah took the first strike.

"Come on, come on," she whispered.

The next two were balls. Then he swung at the second strike. If he didn't hit soon, Evan was going to lose the feeling in his arm.

The next pitch, Noah fouled back. The next was a ball, making it a full count.

"I can't watch," Celia whispered.

The pitcher wound up, threw a fastball and Noah swung. The bat connected with a sweet crack that to anyone listening signaled a smash hit. The ball sailed over the center-field wall into the upper deck. Three-run homer to start the game.

Celia lunged to her feet and screamed at the top of her lungs. "Did you see?" she yelled at Evan. "Did you see?"

"I saw, I saw!"

He laughed as she continued to bounce up and down. Noah rounded the bases, taking high fives from the first- and third-base coaches. He met his teammates at the plate, where the group jumped up and down and pounded on Noah.

Noah looked up at Celia and pointed. She leaped to her feet again and pointed back, her smile so wide Evan was sure she'd hurt something.

Then she glanced over in the direction that Noah had first looked when he'd come up to the plate and then back down at Evan.

"I'll be right back, okay? I'll just be a second."

She hurried up the row of seats and then cut over to the section that adjoined the home-plate area. Evan watched as she hugged two younger looking men and an older guy. They glanced over in Evan's direction once but then didn't look back as they chatted with Celia.

A few minutes later, she returned and took her seat beside Evan again. He was beginning to think he'd been dropped in an alternate reality. Was there anyone here she didn't know?

When she'd offered Noah to him on a virtual silver platter, he'd only assumed that she'd contacted him through his agent and offered him a deal he couldn't refuse. He hadn't considered that she had such a connection to his team. And what connection that was had Evan insanely curious.

He leaned over so she'd hear over the still insanely celebrating crowd. "What am I missing here?"

She smiled. "I'll explain later. Just enjoy the game."

Mysterious little wench. He'd make her pay later when he had her alone.

The rest of the game followed a similar pattern. Celia seemed to know every damn person on the team. He began to have uncomfortable thoughts, like whether or not Celia was involved with Noah Hart. It would certainly explain how she'd been able to get him to agree to the endorsement deal.

But it also brought up a lot of questions. Like whether she was using Evan to further her career. He glanced sideways at her. No way. It would take someone pretty diabolical to have a man like Noah Hart on the line and then sleep with Evan to secure his business. Why would she even need it if she was involved with Hart? The man made a lot of money, even without the million-dollar endorsement deals. He was one of the highest-paid baseball players in the league.

Before he could get carried away with thoughts that would only enrage him, he made himself back down and quit speculating. He'd find out before the end of the day. One way or another. And then he'd decide what to do about Celia. And his account.

When the game ended after the visiting team failed to score the necessary runs to overtake the Tide in the ninth inning, Celia stood, her cheeks flush with excitement.

"We're going to have an awesome season. I just know it!"

He stood beside her unsure of what would happen now. Nothing had gone the way he'd anticipated.

Sure enough, she grabbed his hand and began pulling him toward the exit. "Come on," she said.

But they didn't leave the stadium. Instead they went down to a restricted area, where Celia flashed a pass he hadn't seen up to this point. He shouldn't be surprised. But when they stopped outside the players' locker room, he was.

They waited a good while. Several members of the press came and went. Finally one of the players stuck his head out the door, looked up and down and then his eyes brightened when he saw Celia. Evan was a little starstruck. It was the Tide's catcher, Chris Davies. He was a veritable legend in baseball, and it was rumored this would be his last year before he retired.

"Cece! You should have just come on in. Noah got held up by an interview, but he wanted you to come on back."

Celia walked over and gave the catcher a big hug and a kiss on the cheek. "Good game, Chris. You're looking as awesome as ever."

The big man actually blushed. He glanced up at Evan, and Evan was convinced the guy scowled at him.

"Oh, Chris, this is Evan Reese. Evan, this is Chris Davies, the Tide's star catcher."

"Yes, I'm well aware," Evan said. "Great game. I've watched you a lot of years."

"You Evan Reese who makes the sportswear?" Chris asked.

Evan nodded.

"Cool. You two come on back. Noah should be done by now."

Despite his wealth and position, Evan couldn't control the incredible rush of walking into the Tide's locker room. It was every little boy's dream. It was why he'd gone into the business he had. He loved sports, and he was as in awe of the big dream as any other kid out there who loved sports.

Several players stopped Celia for a quick hug and a kiss.

Some ruffled her hair and she gave them affectionate pats in return.

"Cece! There you are."

Evan looked up to see Noah barreling his way through a crowd of people. The next thing he knew, he had Celia in a giant bear hug, swinging her around in a circle.

Evan watched, his irritation growing more with each passing second.

Finally Noah put her down.

"Hey, did you see? Fantastic hit, wasn't it?"

Celia smiled broadly at the other man and her affection for him was obvious. A fact that made Evan even grumpier. Endorsement or not, he was ready to deck the star right in the jaw.

"I saw, of course. You were awesome as always."

"Hey, I need to get a quick shower. You two can wait for me over there," he said, gesturing toward a sitting area that was removed from the chaos of the open locker room. "I won't be long."

Celia kissed his cheek. "We'll be there. Take your time."

Noah ruffled her hair affectionately and loped off toward the showers.

Evan opened his mouth to ask but then shook his head. He'd wait. This had to be worth the price of admission.

Celia led him into the adjoining room and sat on one of the leather couches.

"This is usually reserved for coaches and their families," she said when he sat down in one of the chairs across from her. "None of the press or players will come in here."

"You know I have a hundred questions, *Cece*," he said drily.

She flushed a little guiltily. "Okay, so maybe I'm guilty of wanting to watch you experience everything firsthand. I mean I could have warned you but that wouldn't have been any fun."

He raised an eyebrow. "The only question I want answered right now is whether you're involved with Noah Hart."

He watched her eyes go wide in shock. Her mouth fell open, and he knew in that moment, whatever he might have assumed—even with good reason—he was dead wrong.

"It was a sensible assumption," he defended before she could speak.

"Evan, Noah is my—"

They were interrupted when the three men Celia had gone to visit in the stands came through the door.

"Cece, love," the older man said when his gaze lighted on her. He smiled big and held out his arms. Celia went into his embrace and endured a painful-looking bear hug.

The other two men regarded Evan with what could only be considered as suspicion.

"Going to introduce us, Cece?" the bigger man asked.

"Of course," she said as she curled her arm around the older man's.

"Evan, I want you to meet my family. This is my father, Carl, and these two are my brothers, Adam and Dalton. Guys, this is Evan Reese. He owns Reese Enterprises. I brought him back to talk to Noah."

Evan could swear she said the last pointedly. He relaxed and shook the hands of each man and endured a painful grip from each. Typical measuring stick of a man. See if you could make the other wince. He squeezed back with as much force and endured grudging looks of respect from her family.

Interesting that they were all back in the players area and that they'd sat in different areas for the game, although Celia had said she'd gotten the tickets particularly for him.

"Very glad to meet you, sir," he directed at Celia's father.

"Are you the man responsible for my Cece working so many long hours?"

Evan lifted one eyebrow then glanced between Celia and her father. Celia closed her eyes in despair and shook her head helplessly at Evan. He remembered her saying that according to her father and brothers, her only requirement was to look pretty and let them support her. Apparently they weren't on board with her having a career.

"I'm afraid I am, sir. I wish I could say it was something I regret, but Celia is one of the brightest minds I've encountered. She's going to single handedly turn my advertising efforts around. I think in a year or two, Reese Enterprises won't simply be one of the leaders in athletic apparel, but the *undisputed* leader when it comes to sportswear.

Her two brothers eyed Celia with renewed interested while Celia stared at Evan, her eyes wide with shock. He could almost swear she looked a little teary. He smiled at her and reached for her hand. To his surprise she accepted without complaint and curled her fingers tight around his.

"If you're meeting Noah about business, we'll just scoot on out," her father said. "You going to make Sunday dinner this time or will you be busy again?"

"No, I'll make it," she said as she leaned up on tiptoe to kiss his cheek. "Sorry about last weekend. Something came up."

Evan realized that he was what came up when he'd finessed Celia away for the weekend. While he was sorry she'd missed what was evidently an important family gathering, he couldn't summon any regret for the way their weekend in Catalina had come together.

"It was nice meeting you all," Evan said sincerely.

The other men nodded and shook his hand again before departing the room.

"Interesting family," he said when they'd gone.

Celia sighed. "I love them dearly, but they're pretty insufferable."

"It's obvious they love you a lot."

She smiled. "Yeah, and I love them to pieces, too. Warts and all."

A moment later, Noah Hart ambled into the room and once

gain gave Celia a bone-crushing hug. Then he turned to Evan
nd looked back at Celia.

"So, is this the man?"

"I'd say you're the man if you agree to front my new line
f athletic wear," Evan said, taking charge of the meeting.

"Evan, I'd like to you to meet my brother. Noah Hart,"
Celia said as she stepped forward. "Noah, this is Evan Reese,
wner of Reese Enterprises."

Evan eyed them skeptically. Her brother? Everything made
a hell of lot more sense with that revelation. And what was
with the different last name? To his knowledge, Celia hadn't
married, or was this one more thing she'd kept him in the dark
over?

His question must have been obvious even to Noah, because
he grinned and slung an arm over Celia's shoulder.

"Cece had a different father—well, different mother, too.
Kind of a long story but my father married Celia's mother
when Cece was just a baby. We helped raise her, especially
when her mom died when Cece was so young. Hence the
reason her last name is Taylor."

Evan cleared his throat. Here he'd been granted a once-
in-a-lifetime opportunity, and he was more concerned with
finding out Celia's secrets than securing a deal with Noah
Hart.

"I thought it might be best if you and Evan went to dinner
and talked about the deal Evan is offering," Celia inserted.

"What about you?" Evan asked sharply. He hadn't counted
on Celia leaving him and Noah. Hell, he hadn't even realized
he'd be meeting Noah so soon. Suddenly his plans for a night
of making love to Celia didn't seem so realistic.

"I have other plans," she said lightly. "Besides, I really have
nothing to do with this part. You and Noah need to discuss
the possibilities. I'd just be in the way."

Noah shrugged then looked at Evan. "You like barbeque?"

"Love it."

"Good. I know this great place just a few blocks from here. We can grab dinner and talk."

"I drove him here, Noah, so you'll need to give him a ride back to his place. That okay?" Celia asked. She turned to Evan. "I'll see you tomorrow morning. Nine o'clock at the Maddox."

"I can have my driver meet me," Evan said. "It's not a problem." He glared at Celia as he said it. The woman was ditching him. What he'd thought was finally an effort to see him outside of a business setting had, in fact, just been a business meeting in disguise. He'd deal with her later, though. Right now he had a sports superstar to woo, and he'd be damned if he let his irritation with Celia interfere.

Sixteen

Celia paced the Maddox conference room. Her nerves were wound tight, and she'd meticulously gone over every little detail of her presentation. The televisions out front had mock-ups created by the media folks. An endless stream of Reese Enterprise promotion ran on the video monitors and the art department had framed several print-ad options and displayed them in the conference room.

With fifteen minutes to go time, the other members of her team had assembled. Tension was high but so was excitement. Ash had congratulated her on landing the biggest client for Maddox thus far, but he'd acted distracted and distant. Celia wondered if he was indeed having issues with the rumored girlfriend.

The others had all been quick to add their congratulations. No contract had been signed, but they all seemed convinced that after this morning, Reese Enterprises would be in the bag. She hoped they were right.

Noah had called last night after an extended dinner with

Evan. Apparently after barbeque the two had gone for beers and spent the evening like old college buddies.

Evan had extended an extremely cushy offer, one that had surprised even a very jaded Noah. The two were meeting later with their respective lawyers to iron out the details, but Noah said he'd agreed.

"Okay, we've got five minutes," Celia said. "Let's take our places and get ready to knock his socks off."

They took their seats along the conference table. Brock smiled at Celia and gave her a thumbs-up before taking a seat next to Elle. Jason took the seat next to Ash, who frowned and reached into his pocket for his phone.

"Excuse me for a minute," he said as he rose from his seat. He crossed the room out of earshot to take a phone call.

The intercom buzzed and Shelby announced that Evan had arrived. "Shall I show him back?" she asked.

Celia took a deep breath, looked at her coworkers lining the conference table all ready to do their part, and said, "Show him back, Shelby."

As Celia ended the conversation, Ash returned to the table.

"Sorry, but I have to go," he announced. "And I'm not sure when I'll be back. Hopefully no more than a few days. I'll let you know when I have more details."

He turned and strode out of the room, leaving Celia and the others to stare after him in astonishment. Celia glanced over at Brock and raised an eyebrow. Brock shrugged and gestured for her to continue on. Whatever was up with Ash would have to wait. This meeting was too important to all of them.

Seconds after Ash's abrupt departure, Evan entered behind Shelby. Celia crossed the room and extended a hand to Evan. Instead of shaking it as she'd intended, he slid his fingers over her palm and held it far too long for her liking. She snatched it away and turned to introduce him down the row.

Her presentation went off without a hitch. Each part of her

team executed their part flawlessly, and through it all, Brock sat back with a very satisfied expression on his face.

By the time she was done, she was as convinced as everyone else that Evan would sign with Maddox. He'd be a fool not to.

The lights went back up after her last video clip.

"This concludes our presentation," she said to Evan. "I hope we've convinced you of our commitment to you and your company."

He took his time responding. For a moment he studied her, his hands in a V in front of him. Then he simply nodded.

"I'm very impressed. My question is, how soon can we move on this?"

Rosa was packed with the after-work crowd, but the entire back room was filled with Maddox employees, all celebrating their biggest coup to date—Reese Enterprises.

Celia was high on her achievement, but she couldn't shake the anxiety over her relationship with Evan. She'd avoided him last night when she'd all but dumped him on Noah. She'd avoided him after her presentation when he'd wanted to take her to lunch to celebrate.

Brock passed out champagne to every one then called for a toast. He saluted Celia with his glass and the room erupted into cheers.

She smiled her pleasure, but all she could think was that she'd rather be with Evan. And that was a very big problem.

"For a girl who's the toast of Madcom, you don't look very happy."

Celia turned to see Elle standing beside her, drink in hand. She tried to smile but then gave up with a sigh. "Am I that obvious?"

Elle shrugged. "Probably not. I doubt others are paying too much attention to you. You looked…distracted."

"I'm in a mess, Elle," Celia admitted. "I don't know what to do."

Elle wrapped a comforting arm around her. "Surely it can' be that bad?"

"I'm involved with Evan Reese. Intimately."

Elle stiffened. "Oh. Maybe you're right."

Celia couldn't help but notice the way Elle's gaze drifted to Brock, who stood across the room talking with Jason Reagart Brock turned and caught Elle's gaze, and what Celia saw there made her pause. Possession.

"I didn't intend for it to happen," Celia said. "I know better Me of all people should know better. I've kept it secret, and it's driving me insane. I worry over who'll see us together and whether they'll draw the wrong conclusion. I'm so tired of sneaking around. The worst part is I'm in love with him."

Elle made a sound of sympathy and pulled Celia away from the others until they stood in a dark corner.

"You need to be honest and open about this, Celia. If you don't, it'll tear you apart," Elle said earnestly.

Elle was so sincere and her words were so heartfelt that Celia wondered if she was speaking from personal experience. Was it possible that Elle was having a secret fling with Brock? If the looks between the two were any clue, there was some serious chemistry there.

It was on the tip of her tongue to ask, but she didn't want to hurt Elle, especially if she didn't want anyone to know.

Instead she squeezed Elle's hand. "Thank you, Elle. I know you're right. I just have to figure out how to handle this. It's giving me a headache."

"First thing you should do is enjoy your moment in the sun," Elle returned. "This is your night to shine. You worked hard for this, Celia. Go have some fun."

"Okay, okay, Mom," Celia teased. "I'm up for another drink if you are."

Elle smiled and the two women headed for the bar for another round. Celia endured another series of toasts, backslaps and loudly yelled congratulations. Elle was right. This was her night. It was the culmination of weeks of hard work and long hours. Damn if she wouldn't enjoy every minute of it.

Celia's cab pulled up to her apartment, and she pulled out several bills to pay the driver. While she was far from toasted, she hadn't wanted to chance driving home, so she'd left her Beamer at work and taken a cab from Rosa.

It was late, but not ungodly so, and she was still riding high from the celebration.

The cab pulled away and across the street she saw Evan leaning against his car, watching her. He started forward, and she stood there like a statue, watching him approach.

"Out celebrating?" Evan asked with a slight smile.

She nodded. "After-work thing. Took a cab back so I didn't have to drive."

"You should have called me. I would have had my driver take you home."

"I don't think that would have looked good if the man whose account I just landed sent a car to take me home after my celebration party."

He regarded her with no expression. Then he asked, "Going to invite me in?"

As if she'd tell him no.

He fell into step beside her as they walked to her door. He waited while she unlocked the door and then followed her inside. As soon she as she locked up behind them, he had her in his arms.

Not again. She couldn't lose all control of her senses the moment he touched her. It wasn't normal.

"Do you have any idea how turned on I was watching you take control of that presentation this morning?" he said between kisses. "You were glowing and you were such a hardass. I wanted so bad to drag you into a closet and have wild, crazy sex."

He always knew exactly what to say to melt any resistance on her part. He was a seducer with words.

He had her clothes off before they got to her bedroom. How he knew where it was, she didn't know. Maybe all men had a natural instinct for where to find the nearest bed.

They went hard and fast. No matter what their intentions, that first time was always desperate, like it was their last. She gripped him, he cradled her, she kissed him, he thrust into her.

It was crazy, irrational, it was the most erotic, bone-melting sex of her life.

And she loved him beyond all reason and sanity.

She lay under him, holding him close as he panted against her neck. She was positively weak, and thank God they were on the bed, because she wasn't moving. It wasn't possible.

Finally Evan rolled away and threw his arm across the bed with a groan.

"Every time, I swear, I'm going to take it slow, make love to you with all the finesse I'm capable of. Then I see you and the teenage hormones start revving out of control, and I become some seventeen-year-old on steroids."

Celia died laughing and then moaned when she moved too much. "I would have liked a seventeen-year-old on steroids with your sexual know-how when I was seventeen. All the boys I knew thought a kiss and quick grope was all the foreplay necessary before penetration."

"I'd say what morons they are if I hadn't just practically done the same thing to you," he said in a pained voice.

She rolled into the crook of his arm and laid her head on his chest.

"You don't hear me complaining, do you? I haven't thrown you out for being an inconsiderate toad."

He kissed the top of her head. "And for that I'm extremely grateful."

She snuggled into his arms. "Are you going back to Seattle for the weekend?"

He went still and then tightened his arm around her. His hand lay possessively on her hip.

"There's no reason we can't go public with our relationship now, Celia. It's all over. You have the account."

She sucked in her breath.

"But, yes, I do need to go back to Seattle and tie up some things. I plan to spend a lot more time in San Francisco over the next few months and I need to make arrangements."

Her heart sped up. Did he mean he was staying in San Francisco to be near her? She hated guessing, but she hated assuming even more.

She was still uneasy about the timing of them seeing each other. It was too close to when he'd signed on with Maddox.

"I'll be back Monday afternoon. I want to spend the evening with you. Dinner. Dancing. You can stay over at the hotel and my driver will take you into work on Tuesday."

She loved it when he got all demanding. She was a sucker for someone who planned in detail, and he'd certainly planned their evening down to her staying over for what would undeniably be amazing sex.

"When do you leave?" she asked quietly.

"First thing in the morning."

She leaned up on her elbow so she could look him in the face. "Then what are you doing here?"

He rolled her into his arms and under him again. "I can sleep on the short flight home."

She made a show of checking her nonexistent watch. "You have six hours left. What do you plan to do with them?"

"I'm going to show you just how good I am at time management," he murmured as he swept down and hungrily devoured her lips.

Seventeen

After a Sunday of fielding curious questions from her brothers about Evan, Celia was relieved to go into work on Monday. She wasn't ready to admit to even her family that she and Evan were anything more than business associates. They knew what had happened in New York and that it was complete nonsense. She loved them for their undying loyalty and their absolute faith in her. Which was why she was reluctant to confess to a relationship with Evan. It would only muddy the waters even though she and Evan both knew the truth.

She was late, thanks to a traffic snarl that lasted an entire hour and an already late start from her apartment. By the time she made it off the elevator, it was closing in on noon, and her mood was in the toilet.

When she saw Shelby, she knew something was wrong. The usually cheerful receptionist eyed Celia with something that looked suspiciously like pity, and she refused to hold Celia's gaze for long.

Not even wanting to know what that was all about, Celia

bypassed her usual meet and greet with Shelby and headed for the sanctuary of her office. To her surprise, Elle was waiting for her.

"Hello, Elle," Celia said as she came in and tossed her briefcase onto her desk.

Elle's face was drawn, and she looked like she was dreading talking to Celia. In her hands was a folded newspaper or magazine. Celia couldn't tell.

"Celia, there's something you need to see. Everyone else has already read it. I tried to call you but couldn't reach you at home or on your cell."

Celia's stomach sank. She didn't like the look on Elle's face or the way she was coming at her with that paper.

Elle plopped the newspaper on Celia's desk and it was then that Celia saw it was a gossip rag. Her nose wrinkled in disgust.

"Elle, what are you doing reading that crap?"

"Look at it, Celia."

Elle jabbed her finger at the photo spread and the headline. Celia looked down and all the blood drained from her face. She had to grip the edge of the desk to keep her knees from giving way.

There were pictures of her and Evan at Mitchell's wedding. The same pictures she'd received via e-mail from Evan's mother. One was of them dancing and her laughing up at him. The other was of Evan kissing her. Her hand was splayed over his chest and there was no mistaking the huge rock on her third finger.

The headline blurred in front of her, but she got the gist. It was all about Evan and his new fiancée and was it coincidence that Evan had allegedly signed a contract with Maddox Communications, the agency where his fiancée worked.

She scanned the article, but she was too furious to continue past the insinuation that Celia had spent the last several weeks doing whatever was necessary to land Evan's business.

"That's not all," Elle said grimly.

She walked around Celia's desk and jostled the mouse so that her screen came up. She typed in a URL and navigated to an advertising community site that hosted a blog and a message board, mostly used by advertising professionals. There in the latest blog post was the picture of Evan kissing her along with the announcement of Evan going with Maddox Communications. The subtitle was short and to the point, and made no bones about the way they thought Celia landed the account.

Celia sank into her chair, stunned. Absolutely and completely stunned by what she'd read.

"My God, Elle, what do I do?" she whispered.

Elle squeezed her shoulder in sympathy, but her eyes told Celia she was at as big a loss as Celia was as to how to handle it.

"Does everyone in the office know?" Celia asked painfully. "Have they all seen it? And what do they think?"

"Well, Ash hasn't been back in, so I don't know if he's seen it. I know Brock and Jason saw it because I was in Brock's office with both of them. Jason didn't have much to say but Brock was pissed."

"At me?"

Elle shook her head. "I don't know, to be honest. I doubt it. He's not the type to get angry before he hears your side. Besides, you got the account. It shouldn't matter to him how you did it."

"That's true, I guess. It only matters to *me*."

"I'm sorry, Celia. Really sorry."

Celia put her hands over her face. "I was stupid, Elle. I was stupid, and now I have to pay the price."

The sound of someone clearing their throat had Celia looking up toward the door. Brock stood there, an indecipherable expression on his face.

"Elle," he said. "Would you leave me and Celia for a moment?"

"Of course," Elle murmured as she hurried away.

Tears burned Celia's eyes. She was holding on by a sheer thread.

"Want to talk?" Brock asked.

It was that question that did it for Celia. If he'd been angry or if he'd been indifferent, she could have handled it, but the simply worded request broke her down.

Her shoulders shook, and she lowered her head as a sob welled from her throat. It appalled her that she'd cry in front of her boss. But there was no holding back the release of the crushing pressure that had been building over the course of the last few weeks.

Brock didn't say or do anything. He just stood there while she gathered herself together again. When she looked up, he sat in one of the chairs in front of her desk and waited for her to speak.

"It's not how it looks," she said as she wiped tears from her cheeks.

He glanced at the spread out paper on her desk. "Well, it looks like you were wearing his ring, but you're not now."

With a sigh, she explained the whole sorry tale about her trip to Catalina with Evan and how she hadn't felt like she could refuse when he was short on time and ready to move on his campaign.

She left out the mushy details she'd shared with Elle. Brock was, after all, A. her boss and B. a man. He didn't need to know that she'd stupidly fallen in love with a man she'd be working with for a long time to come. It made things entirely too messy. What if they broke up? Would Evan feel weird about continuing the relationship with Maddox or would he take his business elsewhere?

There were a million reasons why she should have never ever gotten involved with Evan, and yet, she hadn't heeded any of the warning signs.

"I overheard what Elle said about how it shouldn't matter to me how you got the account. I won't lie. It doesn't. Furthermore, it's none of my business unless you broke the law or did something to damage the reputation of Maddox. I don't think this qualifies. My concern is for you. I know how devastated you were by what happened in New York.

"I meant what I said when I told you that you had my support. That hasn't changed. I'll make sure to put an end to any speculation going on in the office, but I can't control what people think or say outside the work area. I don't imagine this is going to be easy for you to deal with in the next little while, but Maddox Communications stands behind you."

"Thank you, Brock," she said in a shaky voice. "That means a lot to me."

"Any idea who would have done this?" Brock asked.

She frowned and stared down at the pictures. Then she looked back up at Brock.

"These pictures were on my company computer. Evan's mom sent them here. They've only been here. I don't imagine Evan's ex has any love for me, but she and Mitchell left immediately on their honeymoon. They haven't even seen the photos yet. So other than me, and maybe Evan if his mom showed them to him, the only other person who's seen them is his mom. These weren't taken by the professional photographer. Evan's mom shot these with her digital camera, and I don't believe for a minute she'd go to these lengths to discredit me. She was too damn excited over our supposed engagement."

Brock swore long and hard. "Are you sure this is the only place you had them?"

Celia stared back at him. "You don't think…surely not. No one here would do something like that."

"I don't know, but I'll find out," he snapped.

He rose and stalked to the door. Then he paused and turned back for a moment. "Don't let this get you down, Celia. I have a feeling that whoever did this intended just that. You did a damn good job on this account. No one can take that away from you unless you let them."

Then he was gone, leaving Celia sitting there like a deflated balloon.

She was supposed to meet Evan in just a few hours. Their evening was already planned, complete with the sleepover at his hotel and his driver taking her to work in the morning. She'd already had reservations about it all, but now the idea made the knot in her stomach grow even larger.

Who the hell had released those pictures? It made her furious. Why would anyone even care or go to such lengths to discredit her?

She wouldn't put it past Athos Koteas. He'd made it a point to tar Maddox Communications any way possible, but how would he have gotten his hands on those pictures?

The idea that one of her coworkers was responsible made her want to puke. She couldn't believe it and work here another minute. She had to push that possibility out of her mind or go insane.

How sick was it that she didn't even want to venture out of her office now? She couldn't face everyone knowing that they'd seen that damn article.

She laid her head on her desk and tried to ignore the painful ache that had developed around her temples.

She knew what she had to do, and it hurt far more than those damn pictures. But she hadn't worked this hard to re-build her reputation and her career to have it go down the toilet over one torrid affair.

The rest of the day was spent sequestered in her office. She only spoke to Shelby to tell her she wasn't accepting any calls and the rest of the time she spent in brooding silence.

At five, she stared out the window, watching as her co-workers left the building. She purposely waited until everyone else had left before she locked up her office for the night.

Though it was well past seven, she dragged herself down six flights of stairs just on the off chance any stragglers were in the elevator. She was pathetic and spineless but she didn't care. She'd face them all when she had some semblance of control over her emotions.

She drove to her apartment with her fingers curled tightly around the wheel. She battled bouts of fury and the impulse to break down into tears. By the time she reached home, she was mentally exhausted.

To make matters worse, Evan was waiting for her by the door. He wore a deep frown, and his brow was creased with concern.

"Where the hell have you been?" he demanded. "I was worried. We were supposed to meet here an hour and a half ago."

She couldn't even meet his gaze as she jammed her key into the lock. She shoved the door open, and went inside, allowing the dark to swallow her up.

"Hey, Celia, what's wrong?"

He flipped on the light, and she winced. He was in front of her immediately. He grasped her arm and tilted her chin up with his other hand.

"What the hell? Have you been crying?"

She closed her eyes and tried to pull away, but he held tight.

"Talk to me, dammit."

"We can't see each other for a while," she blurted out. "Okay? We need to cool it. Things are crazy. My life is crazy."

Her words did what she hadn't been able to do. He let go of her arm and took a step back.

"Want to run that by me again? In a way that I understand?"

There was a wary look in his eye that warned her this wouldn't be easy. But then he didn't give a damn about what people thought. He wasn't ruled by the opinions of others. As she had so many times before, she wished she could be like him.

Instead of answering him, she rummaged in her bag for

the stupid gossip rag and then she thrust it at him as if it was self-explanatory. And it was in a way.

He glanced over the paper and then looked back up at her. "So? What's the problem?"

She knew he'd react that way. Positively knew it, and it drove her crazy. She wanted to scream and rail at him, but she'd come across as some hysterical banshee, and then he'd never take her concerns seriously.

"That's not all," she said stiffly. "It's all over the Internet. An advertising community site has it on their blog along with some snotty little line about how I got the account after the announcement of you signing with Maddox."

He looked blankly at her. "I fail to see what the big deal is, and I damn sure don't see why it's any cause for us not to see each other anymore."

She gritted her teeth. "You fail to see. Well, I don't, Evan. This is my career we're talking about. My reputation. Which I might add is in shreds now. Everyone in my office saw that. Everyone in the advertising community saw it. Everyone knows, or thinks they know, just how I got you to sign with Maddox. It doesn't matter if it's true. It's what everyone thinks. Our announcement of our agreement will be posted in *Advertising Media*. Right on the heels of those pictures. Do you know how that looks?"

She stopped and swallowed back the damning sob that welled up in her throat.

"How am I supposed to go out on my next client call? What if the client is male and what if he expects the same favors I granted you? Or maybe he'll agree to sign with Maddox if I sleep with him."

"I'll kick his ass," Evan growled.

"You can't be there to kick everyone's ass, Evan. That's what I'm trying to tell you. The best thing you can do for me is to back off until the smoke clears."

He blinked and then his eyes went cold and hard. "Is that what you want, Celia? What you really want?"

She was afraid to answer, afraid to confirm after that terrible look that had come over him. But she wouldn't lie.

"Yes," she whispered.

His lip curled in derision. "I won't be anyone's dirty little secret, Celia. I'm tired of running around like two people having an affair behind their spouses' backs. I made the mistake of settling once. I'll never do it again."

"Evan, please, it's not like that. I just need some time," she pleaded.

"It is like that, Celia. It's very much like that. It's apparent to me that I'm definitely not first on your list of priorities. Or even second or third. There's a hell of a lot of things that rank higher than me. I don't give a damn who knows that we're sleeping together. And I damn sure won't continue to sleep with someone who does."

He turned and stalked toward the door. He flung it open and caught it with one hand, turning as he stepped out.

"If you change your mind, don't bother to come crawling back. I think you've made it abundantly clear what I'm good for."

The door slammed, and Celia's heart shattered into tiny little pieces. She stared numbly, hoping, expecting that he'd come back and tell her they could work things out, that he'd wait.

Minutes passed, and the sickening realization hit her that he wasn't coming back. Not only had she lost her reputation, and possibly her career, but she'd lost the one man she loved enough to have risked it all in the first place.

Eighteen

Tuesday morning, Celia took the coward's way out and called Brock to schedule vacation time for the rest of the week. He didn't like that she was hiding. It was no way to face the issue, but after hearing how horrible she sounded, he didn't argue the matter further.

The rest of the day she spent moping around her apartment, alternating between anger and fits of upset.

Wednesday, she packed a bag and headed for the one place she knew she could lick her wounds in safety. Her dad's house.

He took one look at her and held out his arms for a giant bear hug. She needed it. Never had the comfort of home felt so good to her than now.

He sat her down and cooked her a huge breakfast, because in his book, there wasn't anything that couldn't be cured by a big, home-cooked breakfast.

All the time she ate, he sat beside her, eating his own food in silence. He didn't pry or demand answers. It was what she loved most about him. He never intruded into his children's lives. No, he didn't have to. He just waited for them to come to him, and then he'd move heaven and earth to make everything right again.

Only this time he couldn't fix it.

She spent the afternoon on the couch, watching television with him. He babied her endlessly, fixing her a snack in the afternoon and even baking her favorite cookies. Chocolate chip with no nuts.

By the time evening rolled around, it was obvious her father had spent the afternoon on the phone with her brothers. They arrived, one at a time, and made it a point to shower her with lots of hugs and endless pampering. Or at least Adam and Dalton did.

When Noah showed up, he took one look at her and demanded to know what the hell had happened. She burst into tears which prompted Adam, Dalton and her dad to threaten to dismember him for upsetting her.

"Well hell, Dad, I didn't upset her. It's obvious that someone did, but it sure as hell wasn't me!" Noah protested. "Hasn't anyone asked her what's wrong yet?"

"We were waiting," her father said gruffly.

"Waiting for what?" Noah asked in exasperation. "For her to cry?"

Celia wiped at her eyes and tried to stop the sniffling. She knew her brothers hated it when she cried. Especially Noah.

Noah turned to her, his eyes softening at the signs of her distress. Then he sat down on the couch next to her.

"This doesn't have anything to do with Evan Reese, does it?"

Despite her vow to cease and desist, his question spurred another round of tears.

"Good going, bonehead," Adam growled.

"Anyone ever tell you that your skill with the opposite sex sucks?" Dalton asked.

Noah put an arm around her and squeezed comfortingly. "What happened, Cece?"

"Oh God, Noah, it was awful. The paper printed these horrible pictures and this blog said horrible things. My career is shot to hell. My reputation is in shambles and Evan doesn't want to see me anymore because I asked him to back off until the smoke cleared. He thinks I think he's my dirty little secret, and he hates it. And me."

She dug her palms into her eyes and rubbed until it felt like she was scraping her eyelids across sandpaper every time she blinked.

"Whoa," Adam said. "Did any of that make sense to the rest of you?"

Dalton and her father exchanged helpless looks.

Noah sighed. "Maybe you should back up and start with what the newspaper printed and what the blog said and why your career and reputation have been dragged through the mud."

"It's a long story," she muttered.

"We've got all night," Dalton offered.

She sighed and once again poured out the whole story from start to finish, not leaving a single detail out. Except for the sex. Her brothers had a hard time seeing their baby sister as anything other than their baby sister, and telling them about her sex life would only make them turn a sick shade of green. And then they'd probably go after Evan with one of Noah's baseball bats.

"That's crazy," Adam huffed.

Dalton nodded his agreement. Noah, who was a lot more tuned in to just what bad press could do to a career and reputation, was a lot more subdued. Concern flared in his eyes when she got to the explanation of the article and blog.

"That sucks," Noah said.

Celia nodded. "Tell me about it."

"So where does this Evan person fit in?" her dad asked. "I mean, there seems to be a big piece missing here. You were pretending to be his fiancée and this paper prints stuff about you, and you said he's angry because he thinks you think he' your dirty little secret. Am I missing something?"

She sighed. "I'm in love with him, Dad. And now he hate me."

All four men's mouths rounded into Os.

There was marked silence, and she regretted having blurted out that fact. Love was girly stuff, and none of the men looked like they had a clue what to say or do next.

"Look, I appreciate you guys. I love you all to pieces. don't know what I would do without you. I don't expect you to fix this for me. I'm thirty years old. Not a little girl anymore The days of me coming to you with my scrapes and boo-boos should be well behind me. I'll figure out something. I jus needed a place to lick my wounds and regroup."

Adam frowned. "Now, you wait just one damn minute You're family, Cece. I don't care how old you are."

Even Dalton scowled and nodded his agreement. Noah merely squeezed her hand and told her bluntly to shut up.

"You'll always be my little girl and their little sister," he dad said in his soft, gravelly voice. "That don't change because you go away to college, get a fancy degree and get a job tha beats you down every chance it gets."

She winced at the direction this was heading.

"We love you and we'll always be here for you to come running to. You got that?"

"Yeah, Dad, I do."

"Now come here and give your old man a hug. Sounds like you've had one hell of a week."

She scrambled up from the couch and threw herself into his beefy embrace. She squeezed for all she was worth and inhaled his scent.

"Love you, Dad," she muffled out against his shirt.

"I love you, too, Cece. Don't you forget it, either. Now back up and tell me more about this Evan fellow and if I need to round up your brothers to go beat him up."

* * *

Evan's office staff was avoiding him. Not that he could blame them. He'd arrived back on Tuesday, acting like a bear with a sore paw. He'd briefly touched base with his assistant, long enough to tell her not to hurry back in to work and to remain with her granddaughter as long as she was needed.

He'd gone over his last conversation with Celia until it rolled like video footage through his head. No matter how hard he tried, he couldn't get it to turn off.

It was his own fault for pursuing Celia so relentlessly. She'd been hesitant from the start, and he'd ignored all the warning signs. He'd never become serious about a woman who didn't put him first. And he damn sure wouldn't be involved with a woman who put more importance on what the world around her thought about her than on her relationship with him.

He scowled when a knock sounded at his door. One of the secretaries poked her head in and held up an envelope like a shield.

"This just came for you, sir."

"Bring it over," he said, waving her in.

She hurried over and all but threw the envelope at him before beating a hasty retreat out of his office. He shook his head. He hadn't been that bad since he'd returned two days ago.

Okay maybe he had.

With a sigh, he glanced at the envelope. It was an overnight package with the name of some corporation from San Francisco he'd never heard of before. It was marked extremely urgent.

He opened it and to his surprise it only held a folded newspaper. Nothing else. No letter, no explanation. He pulled it out and it fell open on his desk. It was turned to a specific page, and when he looked down, he saw Celia's picture, only it wasn't one he was familiar with. She looked different. Maybe younger? And she looked terrified in the picture. She had one hand up like she was trying to avoid the camera.

Frowning, he scanned the article. He was so pissed by the time he got to the end that he had to go back and read it more carefully.

The photo was indeed of a younger Celia when she lived and worked in New York. She'd landed a position with a prestigious advertising firm one year out of college. She'd done impressive work and then she'd been promoted to senior executive—above several other junior executives who'd been there longer.

A relationship with the CEO had been quickly revealed, and Celia had been named in the divorce proceedings between the CEO and his wife. Celia had fled New York in disgrace to return home to San Francisco, where she took a job with the smaller, on-the-rise Maddox Communications.

Only last week, intimate photographs of Celia Taylor with billionaire Evan Reese had appeared in another article the day after Reese had reportedly signed a multimillion-dollar advertising contract with Maddox.

Blah, blah, it went on and on, vilifying Celia and along with her, Maddox Communications. His stomach churned, and he felt the urge to go vomit.

His gaze caught the latest issue of *Advertising Media*. Fresh off the press and delivered just this morning. It was just as Celia had said. The announcement was there for the world to see, but it was tainted by those photos.

He picked up the paper and stared at it again. There was no way. No way in hell she'd done what they accused her of. He hadn't known Celia for long, but he damn well knew she wouldn't have done something like this. If she did have a relationship with this bastard, it wasn't so she'd get a promotion.

He wanted to go kill someone. Preferably whoever had started this smear campaign. No one messed with the woman he loved and got away with it.

All the air left his lungs in a painful jolt.

Loved?

He liked Celia. Liked her a damn lot. She was beautiful, vibrant, sexy as hell. She was a great lover and partner. He had fun with her. He loved her company. But did he love her?

The knot in his stomach grew. How could he be so stupid about his own personal life? Surely it would have occurred to him before now if he was in love with someone.

He stopped and let his thoughts catch up with the breathless, panicky feeling in his chest.

How had he gone thirty-eight years with never having fallen in love? He'd never even contemplated the idea until now. He wasn't at all sure he liked it, either.

Love was such a messy emotion. It was bound to be inconvenient. You sure couldn't put it on a schedule and love never played by the rules. He liked rules. And schedules.

Ah, hell, he was absolutely in love with her.

It was why he was sitting here in such a terrible mood that his usually easygoing office staff wouldn't come near him for fear of being decapitated.

He looked again at the article, and his chest utterly caved in. Celia. God, he'd been such an idiot. A complete and utter, madly-in-love moron.

He'd reacted just like a petulant child, furious that his favorite toy was being taken away. In this case, Celia had wanted to put their relationship on hold and all he could see was that she was pushing him away. He'd panicked. He'd been a total ass.

She needed him. Needed his support. And he'd told her to take a hike. Worse, he'd arrogantly told her not to bother changing her mind and come crawling back.

He winced. Holy hell in a bucket but he'd said some horrible things. If there was any crawling to do, it would be him doing it. In the mud. Over broken glass.

Her tear-stained face came painfully to mind. The hell she must have endured. Her coworkers had seen the photos. Everyone in her profession had likely seen them. They'd all probably come to some very inaccurate conclusions.

He'd been selfish and demanding from the start. He hadn't given one moment's consideration to how their relationship would reflect on her. It had all been about him. His wants and needs. He didn't care if anyone knew about them, but she had. And with good reason.

He should have been standing with her. He should have supported her. Now it looked as if the world had turned on her, and where was he? Off licking his wounds while she faced the world alone.

To hell with that.

He had a woman to win back.

Nineteen

Celia sipped her hot chocolate and stared over her dad's backyard to the ocean in the distance. She'd always loved the view here. His house was perched on a cliff, though it was situated a good distance from the drop-off.

As a child, after reading about mudslides, she'd been convinced that they'd fall into the ocean. Her brothers had told her it was far more likely they'd fall off in an earthquake. She shook her head at the memory of how they liked to torment her.

It was peaceful here, and not for the first time, she wondered why she'd been so anxious to move away. True, her family could be overbearing at times, but they loved her. They were loyal and they'd do anything in the world for her. That wasn't something to run away from. It was something to hold on to and never let go.

No, she wouldn't leave again. She was through discovering the world. Her world was here. Home. Where her family lived.

The sliding-glass doors opened and Noah stepped out. She turned all the way around in her chair to greet him, but stopped when she saw the expression on his face.

"I was about to say good morning," she said as he came over and plopped down beside her.

He sighed and held out another newspaper. "I thought about not showing you this, but I knew if something was being said about me, I'd want to know about it so I wouldn't be blindsided."

Dread began low in her stomach. She stared fearfully at the extended paper. Then her disgust overcame her apprehension and she plucked it from his hand.

There in black and white for the entire Bay area to see was a detailed account of all that had happened in New York. Oh, it was a *blatant* smear campaign. It was written in the guise of an article announcing the deal brokered between Reese Enterprises and Maddox Communications.

It detailed her job history, colorful as it was, to the present and hinted broadly about there being a relationship between her and Evan.

Nothing was left to the imagination. Everything she'd worked so hard to overcome had been splashed in excruciating detail.

She should be angry. Furious even. But what she felt was... resignation.

She looked up into the worried eyes of her brother as the realization hit her.

It would always be something. Evan was right to be angry that she'd placed more importance on what others thought of her than she did what *he* thought of her.

As long as the people she loved knew the truth, it shouldn't matter what some stranger thought. Brock believed in her and her abilities. She had the backing of her agency. Her family loved her unconditionally. Evan evidently didn't care who knew they were involved, so why should she?

For the first time in a long while, she looked at her life

with a sense of deep gratitude. For so long she'd been shaped
by external forces. Her desire to shed the protective grasp of
her family. Her need to escape from the scandal in New York
and prove herself to everyone around her.

The only person she'd been proving anything to was herself.
Everyone else had known all along what kind of person she
was.

"Oh, Noah, I've been so stupid," she whispered.

He cocked his head in confusion. She responded by throwing her arms around his neck and hugging him fiercely. Then
she drew away and kissed him on the cheek.

"Thank you."

He still looked supremely puzzled. "For what?"

"For opening my eyes. I've been so very blind to what was
in front of me all along."

He grinned crookedly. "Well, okay. Do me a favor and the
next time Adam and Dalton start riding my ass, you remind
them that I opened your eyes. Whatever that means."

She smiled back. "What it means is that I'm through trying
to please others. I'm through caring what they think about
me. The only people in this world who matter to me already
believe the best of me. What more do I need?"

"Don't let these bastards get you down, Cece. You're right.
We love you to pieces and nothing anyone ever insinuates is
going to change that. Furthermore, I know good and damn
well that the girl I helped raise isn't a manipulative, calculating
bitch who doesn't care who she hurts on her way up the corporate ladder."

She hugged him again. "Thank you, Noah. You have no
idea what that means to me."

He leaned away, still holding her arms. "So what about
Evan?"

She pressed her lips together. "He told me not to bother
crawling back if I changed my mind. Well, too bad. I made a
mistake. It's not the end of the world. We all make them. I'm
sure he's made his share. He was angry and I'm sure he didn't

mean half of what he said. I'm going to make him listen to me. Then I'm going to take the leap and tell him I love him and hope like hell that doesn't make him run for cover."

Noah touched her cheek in a tender gesture. "If he does, he's a fool who doesn't deserve you. Remember that, okay?"

She glanced down at her rumpled appearance. She shuddered to think what her hair looked like. She's spent the last three days moping.

"I need to go jump in the shower and then I have some apologizing to do in person."

Noah got up, leaned over and kissed her on the forehead. "Good luck."

He held his hand out to help her up. She hurried inside, determined not to waste another minute without telling Evan she was sorry and that she loved him.

She took a while in the shower mainly because she was working out just what she wanted to say to Evan. Simple vanity also made her want to look her absolute best. I mean, who went and groveled when they looked like a hag with a hangover?

She pulled on a robe and twisted a towel around her hair. Then she walked through her bedroom and into the hall on her way to the kitchen. She needed something to eat, and she needed to tell her dad she'd be leaving in the next hour.

When she rounded the corner into the living room, she looked up and nearly fell over in shock. There, sitting on her father's couch, was Evan. Noah and her father were nowhere to be found.

"Oh, no," she whispered. "No, no, no." This wasn't supposed to be the way she confronted him.

She turned, intending to make a mad dash for her bedroom and shut the door until she could make herself presentable. He caught her before she'd gone three steps.

He grabbed her arm and pulled her into his arms. "No, Celia, don't go. Please."

She moaned in frustration. "Dammit, Evan. You've ruined everything. I was going to look nice when I came to apologize. Now I'm in my bathrobe and my hair is all wet and in a towel. I don't even have any makeup on."

Then it hit her. What was he doing here? At her dad's? How had he even known where to find her and, moreover, why would he care?

He chuckled and pulled her even closer. "I don't give a damn what you look like. I need to talk to you. Personally I don't think you've ever looked better to me."

She narrowed her eyes at him. "What are you doing here, Evan? How did you know where to find me? I was about to leave to go find you."

"Then it's good we found each other," he said softly.

He tugged her back into the living room. "Come sit with me, Celia. Please. There's so much I need to say to you."

"Ditto," she murmured.

She let him pull her down beside him on the couch, even if she was still horrified by the fact she was wearing a robe, with nothing on underneath, and she was wearing a wet towel on her head, for God's sake.

But when she looked at him, she promptly forgot all that. All she knew was that she loved this man, and she'd do anything to make things right between them.

"I'm sorry," she said in a low, shaky voice.

He pressed a finger to her lips. "Shh. I don't want to hear that word cross your lips. It's me who is sorry. I was an ass. I said despicable things to you."

Her eyes widened, and she felt the ridiculous urge to cry again, as if she hadn't done enough of that in the last few days.

"First, I want to talk about this," he said as he drew out the dreaded newspaper clipping from his pocket.

She froze, her stomach seizing with dread.

"Don't look like that. I don't believe a word of it. But it's obviously an important part of your past. It hurt you and it's affected a good portion of our relationship. I want you to tell me what really happened."

Her lips trembled and she twisted her hands nervously in her lap. "I got out of college, intending to rule the world. I moved to New York. I loved it there. Such a big, busy city, and I was away from home, away from my family. At the time that was important to me. I was stupid."

"I think we all go through the desperate need to get away from our family," Evan said.

She shrugged. "So there I was, out to take on the world. I landed a job with a prestigious agency and I worked my butt off to advance as rapidly as possible. I was good and I knew it. So when I got promoted, it wasn't a surprise to me. There were people who'd been there longer who were pissed, but I knew I deserved it. I felt like I deserved it.

"And then one day my boss called me in his office to congratulate me, and he let me know at the same time what he expected in return for the favor he'd granted me."

"Son of a bitch," Evan growled.

"I was horrified. And a bit naive because I honestly hadn't seen it coming. I didn't even know what to do at first, other than turn him down flat. I was stupid enough to think that would be the end of it."

Evan scowled and reached over to take her hand.

"I buried myself in work, convinced that if I worked harder, landed more accounts, that he'd just go away. One night I was working late and he dropped in to see how I was doing."

She made a derisive sound deep in her throat. The memory strangled her. She hated that helpless feeling.

"He came onto me hard and didn't intend to take no for an answer. He probably would have raped me if his wife hadn't burst in. I think she knew what was going on, but she didn't care. She had her way out of the marriage and a way to make him pay for everything he'd ever done wrong to her in their marriage.

"I was named the other woman. Everyone knew what

happened. I had no defense. Suddenly I was a woman who'd slept her way to the top and then destroyed my boss's marriage. Believe me when I say no one was lining up to do business with me. So I quit and came home. Brock gave me a shot with his agency and the rest, as they say, is history."

Evan closed his eyes and let out a sound of disgust. "I was so unfair to you, Celia. You tried to tell me so many times how our relationship might affect you and your career, but I wouldn't listen. I was selfish and egotistical. I was determined that I should be enough for you. What a jerk I was. I wasn't even here when all hell broke loose. I should have been beside you, shouting to the world that you were my woman and I was damned proud of it. Instead I slunk off like a sulking two-year-old when I didn't get my way, and I can only imagine how it looked."

He gathered both her hands in his and brought one to his lips. He kissed each finger. "I'm so sorry. I hope you'll let me make it up to you. I wish you would have told me all this sooner. Maybe I would have understood you better. But I also know I gave you no reason to trust me. That's going to change. I want you in my life. I'll do whatever it takes to make that happen."

She stared at him in utter bewilderment. "What are you saying?"

"I'm saying I love you. That I'm sorry. That I want another chance and that it's me who's crawling back on hands and knees, begging for your forgiveness. You'll never lack for my support again, Celia. You'll always have me to lean on. And I'll personally throttle anyone who so much as whispers an ill word about you."

Her throat closed in. Her mouth went dry. The world tilted a little crazily around her.

"But I was going to you to apologize," she whispered. "I was wrong, Evan. I did put too much importance on what others thought. As long as I have the support of those who love and respect me, it doesn't matter what the rest of the world thinks. I should have to crawl back. I was *horrible* to you."

"No, no, my love," he said as he hugged her tighter to him. "Never crawl. *Never.* Forget I said it, please. You weren't horrible. You were upset. Your world had been upended, and I should have been the one person you could come to and who would support you and understand. I didn't even try to understand. I got angry and stormed away. I love you. Please forgive me."

"Oh, Evan, I love you, too. So much. I do forgive you as long as you'll forgive me, too."

His entire face lit up. He looked almost boyish as he stared at her in wonder. "You love me? You're not just saying it?"

She smiled and kissed him. She wrapped her arms around his neck and put every ounce of her love into her kiss. He lifted her up until their mouths were even and their noses bumped.

"How did you find me?" she asked.

Evan sobered and he let her slide back down until her feet touched the floor. He cast her a sheepish look. "I might have stormed into Maddox Communications, threatening death and destruction if someone didn't tell me where the hell you were. I'd already tried your apartment, your cell phone. I even called Noah's agent because I couldn't reach Noah, either."

Celia giggled. "Death and destruction? Noah's agent?"

"Well, maybe not death and destruction but I did threaten to pull my contract if I didn't get some answers. Let's just say that the entire Maddox team developed a sudden interest in your whereabouts. Someone found Adam's business number, had him paged and then waited an eternity for him to call back. He told us you were here and I came right over."

She shook her head, but her grin was so big she couldn't hide it.

"Did you mean it?" he asked softly. "Do you love me? Enough to put up with my ogre ways and my demanding personality? Enough to marry me?"

She sucked in her breath as tears flooded her eyes.

"I think I can tolerate you," she said teasingly. "If you can tolerate the fact that I can't cook worth a darn. I'll probably never meet you at the door wearing an apron, and the thought of having children scares the bejesus out of me."

A slow grin spread across his face. "I think I can handle all that. So will you? Marry me? Put me out of my misery?"

"You don't mind me keeping my job? I've fought too hard and have spent too long coming to grips with my issues regarding public opinion. There's no way I'd want to quit now."

He cupped her chin and smoothed a thumb over her cheek. "You can't quit. You're handling all my advertising. I'd be broke inside of a year without you. Besides, I'm way too damned proud of you to ever want to clip your wings."

"I love you," she said fiercely. "And, yes, I'll marry you."

He lowered his head to hers and kissed her long and sweet. "I love you, too," he whispered.

He reached down into his pocket and pulled out the same ring he'd given her before. He grasped her hand in his and slid it back on her finger.

"I've kept this in my pocket ever since you gave it back. I can't tell you how wrong it felt when you handed it back to me that night. Promise me you'll never take it off again."

She glanced down at the glittery diamond, tears blurring her vision. Then she glanced back up at the man staring at her with so much love in his eyes that her knees threatened to buckle.

"Never. This time our engagement is for real."

* * * * *

This Week in Advertising…

The Adman:
Ash Williams

His New Campaign:
Truth serum. When you have to discover what's real … by whatever means necessary.

We've been wondering what's been going on with Ash Williams. Maddox Communications' CFO has always been controlled and on his game. But lately he's become very distracted, almost as if he were missing something. Could it have been a woman? Perhaps the very same woman who is now living in Ash's home? His fiancée…?

How is it possible that one of the most eligible bachelors in San Francisco is engaged and no one suspected a thing? We've all seen how Ash has discarded one woman after another, never willing to be "shackled" for long. So why is this mystery woman now wearing his ring, having no memory of how or why the millionaire proposed?

MONEY MAN'S FIANCÉE NEGOTIATION

BY
MICHELLE CELMER

All the characters in this book have no existence outside the imagination of
the author, and have no relation whatsoever to anyone bearing the same name
or names. They are not even distantly inspired by any individual known or
unknown to the author, and all the incidents are pure invention.

Published in Great Britain 2011
Harlequin Mills & Boon Limited,
Eton House, 18-24 Paradise Road, Richmond, Surrey TW9 1SR

MONEY MAN'S FIANCÉE NEGOTIATION © 2010 by Michelle Celmer

Special thanks and acknowledgment to Michelle Celmer for her contribution
to the KINGS OF THE BOARDROOM series.

ISBN: 978 0 263 88092 2

51-0211

Printed and bound in Spain
by Litografia Rosés S.A., Barcelona

To the ladies of Sister Night:
Karen, Janet, Susie, Toni and Cora.

Bestselling author **Michelle Celmer** lives in southeastern Michigan with her husband, their three children, two dogs and two cats. When she's not writing or busy being a mum, you can find her in the garden or curled up with a romance. And if you twist her arm really hard you can usually persuade her into a day of power shopping.

Michelle loves to hear from readers. Visit her website, www.michellecelmer.com, or write her at P.O. Box 300, Clawson, MI 48017.

Dear Reader,

Welcome to book four of the *Kings Of The Boardroom* series, the story of CFO Ash Williams and his mistress, Melody Trent. Or is she his fiancée? I guess you'll just have to read to find out!

There is nothing more lethal than a man with power who is out for revenge. Especially one who is too stubborn to consider that he might be wrong. Ash is determined to make Melody pay for betraying him. But it's tough to be angry with someone recovering from a nearly critical brain injury. And even harder to hold her responsible for things she can't remember doing. She's not the person she was before the accident. He has to wonder if he's finally seeing the real Melody, not the carbon-copy mistress she thought he wanted her to be.

She nearly died, and she spent weeks in a coma, but Melody Trent refuses to let her guard down and play the victim, and she's wary of this steamy man who claims to be her fiancé. His story checks out, and he's playing the part of the devoted companion convincingly, but she can't shake the feeling he's hiding something. What was she doing in Texas without him, and why was she carrying four thousand dollars in her purse?

Melody wants answers, but Ash is determined to keep their past a secret. Now that he's let himself fall for her, her memories are the one thing that could tear them apart.

Writing their story was exhilarating and heartbreaking and sometimes downright confusing! But their journey was a rewarding one.

I hope you enjoy it!

Best,

Michelle

Prologue

Melody Trent shoved clothes into a suitcase feeling a sense of urgency that was totally without merit. Ash wouldn't be back until late. He'd been working longer and longer hours lately. Spending less and less time with her. Honestly, she would be surprised if it didn't take a few days before he even noticed she was gone.

Emotion welled up in her throat and tears stung her eyes. She bit down hard on the inside of her cheek and took a deep, calming breath. It had to be hormones because she had never been a crier.

She would love to be able to blame her mother and her revolving bedroom door for this. She would like to think that she'd stayed with Ash for three years because her mother's longest marriage—and there were five in total— barely lasted nine months. She wanted to be different from her mother, better than her, and look at the mess it had gotten her into.

She looked over at the photo on the dresser of her and her mother. It was the only one Mel had of them together. She was thirteen, with the body of a ten-year-old. Scrawny, skinny and awkward, standing next to her voluptuous, beautiful mother. No wonder she'd felt so insignificant, so invisible. It wasn't until college, when she shared an apartment with another student who worked part-time as a personal fitness trainer, that she finally started looking like a woman. It took vigorous daily workouts and relentless weight training, but she finally had curves to speak of, and within a year men began noticing her and asking her out.

Her body was the bait, and sex the addiction that kept them coming around, that kept them interested, because what other reason would a man have to be with someone like her? She was smart, but in her own opinion not very pretty. She was content to sit at home and study, or read a good novel, when her peers only wanted to party.

That was why she and Ash had always worked so well. She was able to go to law school, and do all the other things she enjoyed, and never worry about how the rent would get paid, or where she would find money for her next meal. He took care of her financially, and in return all she had to do was take care of everything else. And the truth was, she didn't mind the cooking and cleaning and laundry. She'd been doing it nearly her whole life, as her mother had never taken an interest in anything domestic—God forbid she break a nail.

And of course part of the package was keeping him sexually satisfied, and at that she was a master. Only lately, the past six months or so, she could feel him pulling away from her. When they made love she felt as though his mind was somewhere else. No matter what she did, however kinky and adventurous to hold his attention, she could feel him slipping away.

When she missed her period she was sure it was a fluke. Ash had been pretty clear about the fact that he was sterile. And though their relationship had never been about love, it was mutually exclusive, so for almost three years they had never so much as used a condom.

But then her breasts started to feel tender, and her appetite suddenly became insatiable. She knew even before she took the pregnancy test that it would be positive. And of course it was. Ash had made it clear on more than one occasion that he didn't want to be tied down. But he was a good man, and she knew he would do the right thing. The question was, did she want to be stuck in a relationship with a man who didn't want her or her child?

If she left Ash, she would have to quit law school, though honestly, she'd lost her interest in the law a while ago. She just hadn't had the heart to tell Ash. He had invested so much in her education. How could she tell him it was all for nothing?

She had been in the shower, debating her next move, when Ash came in with the video camera. She felt exhausted, and depressed, and in no mood to play the vixen, and really saw no point. She had already pretty much decided what she had to do. There was no need to keep trying to impress him. Three years of playing the role of the perfect woman had left her utterly exhausted. But when he stepped in the shower and started touching her, started kissing her, more tenderly than he ever had before, she melted. And when he made love to her, she could swear that for the first time he actually saw her. The *real* her. She let herself believe that somewhere deep down maybe he loved her.

For two weeks she agonized over what to do. She let herself hope that he would be happy about the baby. Then he came home from work in a foul mood, ranting about Jason Reagart being forced to marry and have a child he hadn't planned or expected. He said how lucky he was to have a woman who respected his boundaries. She knew then that her fantasy about her, Ash and the baby was never going to happen.

That was last night. Today she was leaving.

She stuffed the rest of her things in her case, leaving the cocktail dresses and sexy lingerie behind. She wouldn't be needing them where she was going. They wouldn't fit in a few months anyway. She zipped it up and hauled both pieces of luggage off the bed. Her entire life in two suitcases and an overstuffed duffel bag. She was twenty-four with hardly anything to show for it. But that was going to change. She was going to have a child to love, and maybe someday she might meet a man who appreciated her for who she really was.

She lugged the bags to the front door then grabbed her purse from the kitchen counter. She checked to make sure the six thousand was safely tucked inside. It was money she had been gradually accumulating over the past three years and saving for a rainy day.

When it rained it poured.

Next to the stack of credit cards Ash had given her, Mel set a notepad and pen out so she could write Ash a letter, but the truth was, she didn't have a clue what to say. She could thank him for all he'd done for her, but hadn't she thanked him enough already? She could tell him she was sorry, but honestly, she wasn't. She was giving him his freedom. Wasn't that enough?

She didn't doubt he would find someone to replace her, and in a few weeks she would be just a distant memory.

She grabbed her bags and opened the door, took one last look around, then left that life behind for good.

One

Asher Williams was not a patient man by nature. When he wanted something, he didn't like to wait, and truth be told, he rarely had to. However, he was warned, when he enlisted the services of a private investigator, that finding a missing person could take time. Particularly if the person they were looking for didn't want to be found. That being the case, he was surprised when he received a call from him a mere two days later.

Ash was in a meeting with several of his colleagues and wouldn't normally answer his cell phone, but when he saw the P.I.'s number on the screen, he made an exception. He suspected it was either very good news, or very bad.

"Excuse me for just a minute," he told his colleagues. He rose from his chair and walked across the room, out of earshot. "You have news?" he asked, then heard the three words he had been hoping for.

"I found her."

In that instant he felt a confusing and disturbing combination of relief and bitterness. "Where is she?"

"She's been staying in Abilene, Texas."

What the hell was she doing in *Texas?*

That wasn't important now. What mattered was bringing her back home where she belonged. And the only way to do that was to go and get her. He was sure, with some convincing, he could make her see that he knew what was best for her, that leaving him had been a mistake. "I'm in a meeting. I'll call you back in five minutes."

He hung up the phone and turned to his colleagues.

"Sorry, but I have to go," he told them. "And I'm not sure when I'll be back. Hopefully no more than a few days. I'll let you know when I have more details."

The look of stunned confusion on their faces as he walked from the room was mildly amusing, and not at all unexpected. In all his time as CFO of Maddox Communications, Ash had never missed a meeting or taken a sick day. He had never been so much as five minutes late for work, and he honestly couldn't recall the last time he'd taken a vacation—much less one with two minutes' notice.

On his way into his office Ash asked his secretary, Rachel, to hold all his calls. "And cancel any appointments I have for the next week, just to be safe."

Her eyes went wide. "A *week?*"

He closed his office door and settled behind his desk, his mind racing a million miles an hour with all that he needed to do before he left as he dialed the P.I.'s number. He answered on the first ring.

"You told me it could take months to find her," Ash said. "Are you sure you have the right Melody Trent?"

"I'm positive it's her. Your girlfriend was in an auto accident. It's how I found her so quickly."

Melody Trent wasn't his girlfriend. By definition, she was his mistress—a warm body to come home to after a long day at work. He paid her law school tuition and living expenses and she offered companionship with no strings attached. Just the way he liked it. But it was no time to split hairs.

"Was she injured?" he asked, expecting, at worst, a few bumps and bruises. He truly was not prepared for what the P.I. said next.

"According to the police report, the driver, your girlfriend, was pretty banged up and there was one fatality."

Ash's stomach bottomed out and his mouth went dry. "How banged up?"

"She's been in the hospital for a couple of weeks."

"You said there was a fatality. What happened exactly?" He rose from his chair, began pacing as the P.I. gave him what few details he had about the crash. And it was bad. Worse than Ash could have ever imagined. "Is Melody being held responsible?"

"Fortunately, no. The police filed it as an accident. That doesn't mean there won't be a civil suit, though."

They would deal with that when and if the time came. "How is Melody? Do you have any details on her condition?"

"All the hospital would say is that she's stable. They'll only give details to family. When I asked to talk to her, they said she wasn't taking phone calls. That usually means that for whatever reason, the patient is unable to speak. My best guess would be she's unconscious."

Since Melody left him, Ash had been counting the hours

until she came crawling back to ask forgiveness, to say that she'd made a mistake. At least now he knew why she hadn't. Although that wasn't much of a consolation. And he would be damned if anyone was going to stop him from learning the truth. "I guess I'll just have to be family."

"You going to say she's your long-lost sister or something?" the P.I. asked.

"Of course not." He needed something a bit more believable. Something he could easily prove.

Melody was his fiancée.

The next morning Ash caught the earliest flight to the Dallas/Fort Worth airport, then rented a car and made the two-and-a-half-hour drive to Abilene. He had called ahead the afternoon before, setting up a meeting with the doctor in charge of her care. They told him that Melody was conscious and out of the woods, but that was the most they would say over the phone.

Once he got to the hospital he strode right past the registration desk. He'd learned a long time ago that if he looked as though he belonged somewhere, showed he was in charge, people naturally followed along, and no one tried to stop him as he stepped onto the elevator. He got off on the third floor, surprised to realize that he was actually nervous. What if Melody didn't want to come back to him?

Of course she would, he assured himself. Her leaving had obviously been a great error in judgment, and it would have only been a matter of time before she realized how much she missed him. Besides, where else would she go while she healed from her injuries? She needed him.

He stopped at the nurses' station and they paged a Dr. Nelson. He appeared less than five minutes later.

"Mr. Williams?" he said, shaking Ash's hand. The

department on his name badge was neurology, which likely meant that Melody had suffered some sort of brain injury. Which explained why she would have been unconscious. But did it mean her injuries were even more serious than he could have imagined? What if she never made a full recovery?

"Where is my fiancée?" Ash asked, surprised by the note of panic in his voice. He needed to hold it together. Barging in and making demands would only make this more difficult. Especially if Melody told them he actually wasn't her fiancé. He took a second to collect himself and asked, in a much calmer tone, "Can I see her?"

"Of course, but why don't we have a talk first."

He wanted to see Melody now, but he followed the doctor to a small family waiting room by the elevator. The room was empty, but for a television in the corner playing some daytime game show. He sat and gestured for Ash to join him.

"How much do you know about the accident?" the doctor asked.

"I was told that the car rolled, and there was one fatality."

"Your fiancée is a very lucky woman, Mr. Williams. She was driving on a back road when the crash occurred and it was several hours before someone drove past and discovered her there. She was airlifted here for treatment, but if the local EMS team hadn't worked so quickly, you would be having this conversation with the coroner."

A knot twisted his insides. It was surreal to imagine that he had come so close to losing Melody for good, and the thought of her lying trapped and alone, not knowing if she would live or die, made him sick to his stomach. He may have been angry that she left him, but he still cared deeply for her. "What was the extent of her injuries?"

"She suffered a subdural hematoma."

"A brain injury?"

He nodded. "Until two days ago she's been in a drug-induced coma."

"But she'll recover?"

"We expect her to make a full recovery."

Ash's relief was so intense, his body went limp. If he hadn't already been sitting, he was sure his legs would have given out from under him.

"Although," the doctor added, his expression darkening, "there were a few...complications."

Ash frowned. "What complications?"

"I'm sorry to have to tell you that she lost the baby."

"Baby?" he asked, the doctor's words not making any sense. Melody wasn't having a baby.

The doctor blinked. "I'm sorry, I just assumed you knew that she was pregnant."

Why would Ash even suspect such a thing when the radiation from childhood cancer had rendered him sterile? It had to be a mistake. "You're *sure?*"

"Absolutely."

The only explanation, Ash realized, was that Melody had been cheating on him. The knot in his gut twisted tighter, making it difficult to take a full breath. Is that where Melody had been going when she left him? To be with her lover? The father of her child?

And like a love-sick fool Ash had been chasing after her, prepared to convince her to come home. She had betrayed him, after all that he had done for her, and he hadn't suspected a damned thing.

His first reaction was to get up, walk out of the hospital and never look back, but his body refused to cooperate. He needed to see her, just one last time. He needed to know why the hell she would do this to him, when he had given her everything she had ever asked for, everything she could have ever needed. She could have at least had the decency, and the courage, to be honest with him.

He could see that the doctor was curious to know why, as her fiancé, Ash hadn't known about the pregnancy, but Ash didn't feel he owed him or anyone else an explanation. "How far along was she?" he asked.

"Around fourteen weeks, we think."

"You think? Didn't she say?"

"We haven't mentioned the miscarriage. We think it would be too upsetting at this point in her recovery."

"So she believes she's still pregnant?"

"She has no idea that she was pregnant when she was in the accident."

Ash frowned. That made no sense. "How could she not know?"

"I'm sorry to have to tell you, Mr. Williams, but your fiancée has amnesia."

The gripping fingers of a relentless headache squeezed Melody's brain. A dull, insistent throb, as though a vice was being cranked tighter and tighter against her skull.

"Time for your pain meds," her nurse chirped, materializing at the side of the bed as though Melody had summoned her by sheer will.

Or had she hit the call button? She honestly couldn't remember. Things were still a bit fuzzy, but the doctor told her that was perfectly normal. She just needed time for the anesthesia to leave her system.

The nurse held out a small plastic cup of pills and a glass of water. "Can you swallow these for me, hon?"

Yes, she could, she thought, swallowing gingerly, the cool water feeling good on her scratchy throat. She knew how to swallow pills, and brush her teeth, and control the television remote. She could use a fork and a knife and she'd had no trouble reading the gossip rags the nurse had brought for her.

So why, she wondered, did she not recognize her own name?

She couldn't recall a single thing about her life, not even the auto accident that was apparently responsible for her current condition. As for her life before the accident, it was as if someone had reached inside her head and wiped her memory slate clean.

Post-traumatic amnesia, the neurologist called it, and when she'd asked how long it would last, his answer hadn't been encouraging.

"The brain is a mysterious organ. One we still know so little about," he'd told her. "Your condition could last a week, or a month. Or there's a possibility that it could be permanent. We'll just have to wait and see."

She didn't want to wait. She wanted answers *now*. Everyone kept telling her how lucky she'd been. Other than the head injury, she had escaped the accident relatively unscathed. A few bumps and bruises mostly. No broken bones or serious lacerations. No permanent physical scars. However, as she flipped through the television channels, knowing she must have favorite programs but seeing only unfamiliar faces, or as she picked at the food on her meal tray, clueless as to her likes and dislikes, she didn't feel very lucky. In fact, she felt cursed. As though God was punishing her for some horrible thing that she couldn't even remember doing.

The nurse checked her IV, jotted something on her chart, then told Melody, "Just buzz if you need anything."

Answers, Melody thought as the nurse disappeared into the hall. All she wanted was answers.

She reached up and felt the inch-long row of stitches

above her left ear where they had drilled a nickel-size hole to reduce the swelling on her brain, relieving the pressure that would have otherwise squeezed her damaged brain literally to death.

They had snatched her back from the brink of death, only now she wondered what kind of life they had snatched her back to. According to the social worker who had been in to see her, Melody had no living relatives. No siblings, no children, and no record of ever having been married. If she had friends or colleagues, she had no memory of them, and not a single person had come to visit her.

Had she always been this...alone?

Her address was listed as San Francisco, California—wherever that was—some sixteen hundred miles from the site of the accident. It perplexed her how she could still recognize words and numbers, while photos of the city she had supposedly lived in for three years drew a complete blank. She was also curious to know what she had been doing so far from home. A vacation maybe? Was she visiting friends? If so, wouldn't they have been concerned when she never showed up?

Or was it something more sinister?

After waking from the coma, she'd dumped the contents of her purse on the bed, hoping something might spark a memory. She was stunned when, along with a wallet, nail file, hairbrush and a few tubes of lip gloss, a stack of cash an inch thick tumbled out from under the bottom lining. She quickly shoved it back in the bag before anyone could see, and later that night, when the halls had gone quiet, she counted it. There had been over four thousand dollars in various denominations.

Was she on the run? Had she done something illegal? Maybe knocked off a convenience station on the way out of town? If so, wouldn't the police have arrested her by now?

She was sure there was some perfectly logical explanation. But just in case, for now anyway, she was keeping her discovery to herself. She kept the bag in bed with her at all times, the strap looped firmly around her wrist.

Just in case.

Melody heard voices in the hallway outside her room and craned her neck to see who was there. Two men stood just outside her door. Dr. Nelson, her neurologist, and a second man she didn't recognize. Which wasn't unusual seeing as how she didn't recognize anyone.

Could he be another doctor maybe? God knew she had seen her share in the past couple of days. But something about him, the way he carried himself, even though she only saw him in profile, told her he wasn't a part of the hospital staff. This man was someone…important. Someone of a higher authority.

The first thing that came to mind of course was a police detective, and her heart did a somersault with a triple twist. Maybe the police had seen the money in her purse and they sent someone to question her. Then she realized that no one on a public servant's pay could afford such an expensive suit. She didn't even know how she knew that it was expensive, but she did. Somewhere deep down she instinctively knew she should recognize the clothes designer, yet the name refused to surface. And it didn't escape her attention how well the man inside the suit wore it. She didn't doubt it was tailored to fit him exclusively.

The man listened intently as the doctor spoke, nodding occasionally. Who could he be? Did he know her? He must, or why else would they be standing in her doorway?

The man turned in her direction, caught her blatantly staring, and when his eyes met hers, her heart did that weird flippy thing again. The only way to describe him was…intense. His eyes were clear and intelligent, his build long and lean, his features sharp and angular. And he was ridiculously attractive. Like someone straight off the television or the pages of her gossip mags.

He said a few words to the doctor, his eyes never straying from hers, then entered her room, walking to the bed, no hesitation or reserve, that air of authority preceding him like a living, breathing entity.

Whoever this man was, he knew exactly what he wanted, and she didn't doubt he would go to any lengths to get it.

"You have a visitor, Melody." Only when Dr. Nelson spoke did she realize he'd walked in, too.

The man stood silently beside her bed, watching her with eyes that were a striking combination of green and brown flecks rimmed in deep amber—as unique and intense as the rest of him.

He looked as though he expected her to say something. She wasn't sure what though.

Dr. Nelson walked around to stand at the opposite side of her bed, his presence a comfort as she felt herself begin to wither under the stranger's scrutiny. Why did he look at her that way? Almost as though he was angry with her.

"Does he look familiar to you?" Dr. Nelson asked.

He was undeniably easy on the eyes, but she couldn't say that she'd ever seen him before. Melody shook her head. "Should he?"

The men exchanged a look, and for some reason her heart sank.

"Melody," Dr. Nelson said, in a soothing and patient voice. "This Asher Williams. Your fiancé."

Two

Melody shook her head, unwilling to accept what the doctor was telling her. She didn't even know why. It just didn't feel right. Maybe it was the way he was looking at her, as if her being in an accident had somehow been a slight against him. Shouldn't he be relieved that she was alive?

So where were his tears of joy? Why didn't he gather her up and hold her?

"No, he isn't," she said.

The doctor frowned, and her so-called fiancé looked taken aback.

"You remember?" Dr. Nelson asked.

"No. But I just know. That man can't be my fiancé."

Tension hung like a foul odor in the room. No one seemed to know what to do or say next.

"Would you excuse us, Doctor?" her imposter fiancé said, and Melody felt a quick and sharp stab of panic. She didn't want to be alone with him. Something about his presence was just so disconcerting.

"I'd like him to stay," she said.

"Actually, I do have patients I need to see." He flashed Melody an encouraging smile and gave her arm a gentle pat. "The nurse is just down the hall if you need anything."

That wasn't very reassuring. What did they even know about this man? Did they check out his story at all, or take him on his word? He could be a rapist or an ax murderer. A criminal who preyed on innocent women with amnesia. Or even worse, maybe he was the person she had taken that cash from. Maybe he was here for revenge.

She tucked her purse closer to her side under the covers, until she was practically sitting on it.

The phrase *never show fear* popped into her head, although from where, she didn't have a clue. But it was smart advice, so she lifted her chin as he grabbed a chair and pulled it up to the side of her bed. He removed his jacket and draped it over the back before he sat down. He wasn't a big man, more lean than muscular, so why did she feel this nervous energy? This instinct to run?

He eased the chair closer to her side and she instinctively jerked upright. So much for not showing fear. Even in repose the man had an assuming presence.

"You don't have to be afraid of me," he said.

"Do you honestly expect me to just take your word that we're engaged?" she asked. "You could be...*anyone*."

"Do you have your driver's license?"

"Why?"

He reached into his back pants pocket and she tensed again. "Relax. I'm just grabbing my wallet. Look at the address on my driver's license." He handed his wallet to her.

The first thing she noticed, as she flipped it open, was

that there were no photos, nothing of a personal nature, and the second thing was the thick stack of cash tucked inside. And yes, the address on his license was the same as hers. She knew without checking her own license because she had read it over and over about a thousand times yesterday, hoping it would trigger some sort of memory. A visual representation of the place she'd lived.

Of course, it hadn't.

She handed his wallet back to him, and he stuck it in his pocket. "That doesn't prove anything. If we're really engaged, where is my ring?" She held up her hand, so he could see her naked finger. A man of his obvious wealth would have bought the woman he planned to marry a huge rock.

He reached into his shirt pocket and produced a ring box. He snapped it open and inside was a diamond ring with a stone so enormous and sparkly it nearly took her breath away. "One of the prongs came loose and it was at the jeweler's being repaired."

He handed it to her, but she shook her head. She still wasn't ready to accept this. Although, what man would offer what must have been a ridiculously expensive ring to a woman who wasn't his fiancée?

Of course, one quick thwack with the ax and it would easily be his again.

She cringed and chastised herself for the gruesome thought.

"Maybe you should hang on to it for now, just to be safe," she told him.

"No. I don't care if you believe me or not." He rose from his chair and reached for her hand, and it took everything in her not to flinch. "This belongs to you."

The ring slid with ease on her finger. A perfect fit. Could

it just be a coincidence? It was becoming increasingly difficult not to believe him.

"I have these, too," he said, leaning down to take a stack of photos from the inside of his jacket. He gave them to her, then sat back down.

The pictures were indeed of her and this Asher person. She skimmed them, and in each and every one they were either smiling or laughing or…*oh, my*…some were rather racy in nature.

Her cheeks blushed brightly and a grin quirked up the corner of his mouth. "I included a few from our *personal* collection, so there wouldn't be any doubt."

In one of the shots Asher wore nothing but a pair of boxer briefs and the sight of all that lean muscle and smooth skin caused an unexpected jab of longing that she felt deep inside her belly. A memory, maybe, or just a natural female reaction to the sight of an attractive man.

"I have video, as well," he said. She was going to ask what kind of video, but his expression said it all. The look in his eyes was so steamy it nearly melted her. "Due to their scandalous nature, I felt it best to leave them at home," he added.

Melody couldn't imagine she was the type of woman who would let herself be photographed, or even worse videotaped, in a compromising position with a man she didn't trust completely.

Maybe Asher Williams really was her fiancé.

Ash's first suspicion, when the doctor told him Melody had amnesia, was that she was faking it. But then he asked himself, why would she? What logical reason did she have to pretend that she didn't know him? Besides, he doubted that anyone in her physical condition could convincingly fabricate the look of bewildered shock she wore when the doctor told her Ash was her fiancé.

Of course, she had managed to keep the baby she was carrying a secret, and the affair she'd been having. After the initial shock of her betrayal had worn off, he'd felt nothing but seething, bone-deep anger. After all he had done for her—paying her living expenses and college tuition, giving her credit cards to purchase everything her greedy heart had desired, taking care of her for *three* years—how could she so callously betray him?

Coincidentally, just like his ex-wife. He hadn't had a clue then either. One would think he'd have learned his lesson the first time. And though his first instinct had been to walk out the door and never look back, he'd had an even better idea.

This time he would get revenge.

He would keep up the ruse of their engagement and take Melody home. He would make her fall in love with him, depend on him, then he would betray her, just as cold-heartedly and callously as she had him. And he wouldn't lose a single night's sleep over it.

"What was I doing in Texas alone?" Melody asked him, still not totally convinced.

Ash had anticipated this question and had an answer already prepared. "A research trip."

"Research for what?"

"A paper you were working on for school."

She looked puzzled. "I go to school?"

"You're in law school."

"I am?" she asked, looking stunned.

"You have a year to go before you take the bar exam."

Her brow furrowed and she reached up to rub her temple. "Not if I can't remember anything I've learned."

"I don't care what the doctors say," he told her, taking her hand, and this time she didn't flinch. "You'll get your memory back."

Her grateful smile almost filled him with guilt. Almost.

"So you just let me go on this trip, no questions asked?"

He gave her hand a squeeze. "I trust you, Mel."

The comment hit its mark, and the really pathetic thing was that it used to be true. He never would have guessed that Melody would do something like this to him.

"How long was I gone?"

"A few weeks," he lied. "I began to worry when you stopped answering your phone. I tried to find you myself, but that went nowhere fast. I was beside myself with worry, Mel. I thought something terrible had happened. I thought…I thought that you were dead. That I would never see you again." The fabricated emotion in his voice sounded genuine, even to his own ears, and Melody was eating it up. "The police were no help, so I hired a private detective."

"And here you are."

He nodded. "Here I am. And I would really like to hold my fiancée. If she would let me."

Melody bit her lip, and with gratitude in her eyes, held her arms out. She bought his bull—hook, line and sinker. This was almost too easy.

Ash rose from his chair and sat on the edge of her bed, and when he took her in his arms and she melted against him, soft and warm and a little fragile, he had a flash of something that felt like relief, or maybe satisfaction, then he reminded himself exactly what it was that brought them to this place. How deeply she had betrayed him. His first instinct was to push her away, but he had to play the role of the loving fiancé.

She let her head rest on his shoulder and her arms slipped around his back. The contour of her body felt so familiar to him, and he couldn't help wondering what it must have been like for her, holding a stranger. Some deep place inside him wanted to feel sympathy, but she had brought this on herself. If she hadn't cheated on him, hadn't stolen away like a criminal, she never would have been in the accident and everything would be normal.

As her arms tightened around him, he did notice that she felt frailer than before, as though not only had she lost pounds, but muscle mass. Their building had an exercise room and as long as Ash had known her, Melody had been almost fanatical about staying in shape. He wondered if this would be a blow to her ego.

But how could it be if she didn't even remember she *had* an ego? Or maybe that was something that was inborn.

Under the circumstances Ash didn't expect the embrace to last long, and he kept waiting for her to pull away. Instead she moved closer, held him tighter, and after a moment he realized that she was trembling.

"Are you okay?" he asked, lifting a hand to stroke her hair.

"I'm scared," she said, her voice small and soft. Melody wasn't a crier—in three years together he could recall only two times he'd even seen the sheen of moisture in her eyes—but he could swear that now he heard tears in her voice.

"What are you scared of?" he asked, stroking her hair and her back, pretending to comfort her, when in reality he felt that she was getting exactly what she deserved.

"Everything," she said. "I'm afraid of all I don't know,

and everything I need to learn. What if I'm never…" She shook her head against his chest.

He held her away from him, so he could see her face. Melody was a fighter. Much like himself, when she wanted something, she went after it with all pistons firing. It was what had drawn him to her in the first place. But right now, he couldn't recall ever seeing her look more pale and distraught, and he actually had to harden his heart to keep from feeling sorry for her.

She had brought this on herself.

"If you never what?" he asked.

Her eyes were full of uncertainty. "What if I can't be the person I was before? What if the accident changed me? What will I do with my life? Who will I be?"

Not the heartless betrayer she had been before the accident. Not if he had anything to do with it. He would break her spirit, so no other man would have to suffer the same humiliation he had.

A tear spilled over onto her cheek and he wiped it away with his thumb, cradling her cheek in his palm. "Why don't you concentrate on getting better? Everything will work out. I promise."

Looking as though she desperately wanted to believe him, she leaned her head back down and sighed against his shoulder. And maybe she did believe him, because she was no longer shaking.

"I'm getting sleepy," she said.

"I'm not surprised. You've had an eventful morning. Why don't you lie down?"

He helped her lie back against the pillows. She did look exhausted. Mentally and physically.

He pulled the covers up and tucked them around her, much the way his mother had for him when he was a boy. When he'd been sick, and weakened by the radiation, she'd somehow managed to be there every evening to kiss him goodnight, despite working two, and sometimes three jobs at a time to keep their heads above water. Until she'd literally worked herself to death.

Though Ash was declared cancer free by his thirteenth birthday, the medical bills had mounted. His father had been too lazy and most times too drunk to hold down a job, so the responsibility of taking care of them had fallen solely on his mother. And due to their debt, annual trips to the doctor for preventative care that wasn't covered by their insurance had been a luxury she couldn't afford. By the time she'd begun getting symptoms and the cancer was discovered, it had already metastasized and spread to most of her major organs. The news had sent his father into a downward spiral, and it was left up to Ash to take care of her.

Eight months later, and barely a week after Ash graduated from high school, she was gone. For years, he felt partially responsible for her death. Had it not been for his own cancer, they might have caught hers sooner, when it was still treatable.

The day of his mother's funeral was the day Ash had written his father out of his life for good. His aunt had contacted him several years later to let him know that his father had passed away. Advanced liver cirrhosis. Ash didn't go to the funeral.

By then Ash was living in California, and going to school. Like his mother, he worked two and three jobs to make ends meet. Despite that, he'd somehow managed to maintain a near-perfect GPA. After graduation he'd married his college sweetheart and landed a job with Maddox Communications, convinced he was living the American dream. Unfortunately things had not been what they seemed.

The day he was offered the position of CFO, what should have been one of the best days of his life, he'd learned that his wife was having an affair. She'd claimed she did it because she was lonely. He'd worked such long hours he was never there for her. She sure hadn't minded spending the money he earned working those long hours, though. Not to mention, when he *had* been home, the "I have a headache" excuse was a regular. The irony of it would have been laughable had he not been so completely devastated.

Granted, theirs had never been a particularly passionate marriage, but he'd thought they were relatively happy. Apparently not. And the worst part had been that he hadn't suspected a thing.

Ash had thought he was through with women for good, but only a few months after the divorce was final he met Melody. She was young and beautiful and bright, and he was fascinated by her spunk and enthusiasm. Probably because he saw much of himself mirrored back in her eyes.

They had come from similar humble beginnings, and, like him, she was determined to succeed. They'd started dating in early April. The last week of May when the sublet on her apartment expired, he'd suggested she stay with him until she found another place, and she just never left.

Since then they seemed to have an unwritten understanding. She made herself accessible to him in any capacity necessary with no strings attached. There were no sentiments of love or talk of marriage, no questions or accusations when he worked late or cancelled a date. In return he provided financial security.

At times, he couldn't help thinking he was getting the better end of the deal. Not only did he have a willing mistress at his disposal 24/7, he also had the satisfaction of knowing that he was helping her make something of her life. If his mother had someone like that, someone to take care of her, she might still be alive.

Helping Melody had, in his own way, been a tribute to his mother. An homage to her strength and character, and as far as he was concerned, Melody had betrayed her, too.

He gazed down at Melody and realized she was sound asleep. For several minutes he just watched her, wondering what could have driven her to be unfaithful to him. When had she changed her mind, and decided that she wanted more than what they had? And why hadn't she just told him the truth? If she'd truly wanted out, he would have respected that. He wouldn't have liked it, and he would have tried to talk her out of leaving, but he would have eventually let her go. No strings attached.

Instead she had thrown back in his face everything he had ever done for her.

"How is she?" someone asked, and Ash turned to see Dr. Nelson standing in the doorway.

"Sleeping."

"I just wanted to stop back in once more before I left."

"I'm glad you did. We never discussed when I could take her home. I'd like to make travel arrangements."

He gestured Ash into the hall. "If she continues to improve, I would say a week to ten days."

"That long? She seems to be doing so well."

"She suffered a severe brain injury. You can't necessarily see the damage, but believe me, it's there." He paused then added, "When you say home, I assume you mean California."

"Of course."

"You should know that flying will be out of the question."

"Not even in my company's private jet?"

"She had a brain bleed. The change in pressure could very literally kill her. Frankly, I'm not crazy about the idea of her being on the road for that long either, but I guess there aren't any other options."

Sixteen hundred miles trapped in a car together. Not his idea of fun. Besides, he wanted to get her home and settled before she remembered something. If she ever did.

"I was wondering," Ash said. "If she does regain her memory, how long will it take?"

"There's no definitive answer that I can give you, Mr. Williams. If she does regain any memories, it can be a slow and sometimes traumatic process. Just be thankful that she's doing as well as she is. It will just take time and patience."

Unfortunately he had little of either.

"Even if she doesn't regain her memories," he added, "there's no reason to expect that you two won't live a long and happy life together regardless."

Actually, there was one damned good reason. Whether she remembered it or not, Melody had crossed him. It was time she got a taste of her own medicine.

But to make this work, Ash had a bit of cleaning up to do first.

Three

When Melody opened her eyes again, Ash wasn't in the room. She had the sudden, terrifying sensation that everything that had happened earlier was a dream or a hallucination. Then she lifted her hand, saw the diamond on her ring finger and relief washed over her.

It was real.

But where did Ash go? She pushed herself up on her elbows to look around and saw the note he'd left on the tray beside her:

> Went to get your things. Back later to see you.
> XOXO
> Ash

She wondered where he was going to get them, then realized she must have been staying in a hotel when she'd had her accident. But that was more than two weeks ago.

Wouldn't they have discarded her things by now? Did hotels hang on to the items abandoned by their customers?

She hoped so. Maybe there was something among her things that would spark a memory, and she was interested to see this so-called research Ash had been talking about. Not that she didn't believe him. It was just that something about this whole scenario was...off.

If what he said was true, and she was only here for school, what was she doing with four thousand dollars hidden in the lining of her purse? Was she trying to bribe someone, or buy information? Had she gotten herself into something illegal that she had been afraid to tell him? What if her accident hadn't been an accident after all?

And even worse, what if the person she was trying to get away from was Ash?

She realized just how ridiculous that sounded and that she was letting her imagination run away from her. She'd seen the photos; they were obviously very happy together. She was sure that the expression she'd mistaken for anger when he'd first entered her room was just his reaction to learning that she didn't remember him. After all, how would she feel if the man she had planned to spend the rest of her life with forgot who she was? Then insisted that he supply proof of their relationship? That would be devastating.

There were other things that disturbed her, as well. It seemed as though the news that she was in law school would evoke some sort of emotion. If not excitement, then maybe mild curiosity. Instead she'd just felt...disconnected. As though he were talking about another woman's life. One she had little interest in. And in a way maybe she was.

She was sure that once she got home and back into a regular routine, things would come back to her. She would be more interested in things like her career and her hobbies. If she had any hobbies. She hadn't even thought to ask him. There were all sorts of things he could tell her about her life.

She heard footsteps in the hall, her spirits lifting when she thought it might be Ash, but it was only the nurse.

"I see you're awake," she said with her usual cheery disposition. "How are you feeling?"

"Better," she said, and it was true. She still had a million questions, but at least now she knew that when she was discharged from the hospital, she would have somewhere to go. There was someone out there who loved and cared about her.

"I saw your fiancé," the nurse said as she checked Melody's IV. "He's very handsome. But that just stands to reason, I guess."

"Why?"

"Well, because you're so pretty."

"I am?"

The nurse laughed. "Well, of course you are."

She made it sound so obvious, but when Melody had seen her reflection the other day, the only thing she noticed was that a stranger's eyes stared back at her. She didn't stop to consider whether she was attractive. It just didn't seem important at the time.

"I hear that you're in law school," the nurse said, jotting something down on Melody's chart. "I never would have guessed."

"Why is that?"

She shrugged. "Oh, I don't know. I guess you just don't seem the type. I think of lawyers as pushy and overbearing. You're not like that at all."

She wondered what she *was* like, but she was a little afraid to ask.

The nurse closed her chart and asked, "Is there anything you need?"

She shook her head.

"Okay, well, you ring if you need me."

When she was gone Melody considered what she said. What if she really wasn't cut out to be a lawyer? Would she be throwing all those years of school down the toilet?

But honestly, what did the nurse know of her? She was not going to plan the rest of her life around a comment made by someone who had known her for less than three days. And not at her best, obviously. Maybe when she was back on her feet and feeling like her old self she would be lawyer material again. A real shark.

Or, as she had considered earlier, maybe the accident had changed her.

There was really no point in worrying about it now. Like the doctor said, she needed to concentrate on healing. It was sage advice, because the sooner she got back to her life, the sooner she would get her memory back. And in the meantime she was sure, with a fiancé like Ash to take care of her, everything was going to be okay.

Ash stood in the impound lot at the Abilene police station, heart in the pit of his stomach, knees weak, looking at what was left of Melody's Audi Roadster. Suddenly he understood why everyone kept saying that she was lucky to be alive.

Not only was it totaled, it was barely recognizable. He knew it was a rollover accident, he just hadn't realized how *far* it had rolled, and the momentum it had gained by the time it hit the tree that had ultimately stopped it. The passenger's side was pretty much gone, completely crushed inward.

Had she hit the tree on the driver's side, there was no

doubt she wouldn't have survived. Also, Mel always drove with the top down, but apparently it had been raining, so when she flipped over there was at least something there to keep her from snapping her neck. Although just barely, because the top, too, was crushed, and at some point had come loose and was hanging by a single bolt.

He hated Melody for what she had done to him, but he wouldn't wish an accident like this on his worst enemy.

According to the police, she'd tried to swerve out of the way when she saw the bike. Unfortunately it had been too late.

He walked over and peered in the driver's side, immediately seeing what he was looking for. He tried the door but it was hopelessly jammed. With one hand he pushed the top out of the way then reached around the steering wheel and grabbed the keys from the ignition. He hit the release for the trunk, but it didn't budge, and he had no better luck with the key. If there was anything in there, she was going to have to live without it.

He turned to walk back to the entrance, then as an afterthought, walked back and snapped some pictures with his phone. The matter had already been reported to his insurance company, but it never hurt to be thorough and keep a record for his own reference.

When he was back in his rental car, he punched the address the P.I. had given him into the GPS and followed the commands until he was parked in front of a house about fifteen minutes from the hospital.

The house itself was tiny but well-kept, although the neighborhood left a lot to be desired. How could she go from a penthouse condo to living in what was barely a step above a slum? To be with her lover? If so, the guy had to be a loser. Although if she had come here to be with her lover, why hadn't he been at the hospital with her?

Well, if there was someone else there, he was about to find out.

There were no cars in the driveway, and the curtains were drawn. He walked to the front door with purpose, slid the key in, and opened it. The first thing that hit him was a rush of cool air punctuated by the rancid stench of rotting food. At that point he knew it was safe to assume that she lived alone. No one would be able to stand the odor.

Covering his face with a handkerchief, he walked through a small living room with outdated, discount-store furniture, snapping on lights and opening windows as he made to the kitchen. He saw the culprit right away, an unopened package of ground beef on a faded, worn countertop, next to a stove that was probably older than him. She must have taken it out to thaw right before the accident.

He opened the kitchen window, then, for the landlord's sake he grabbed the package and tossed it in the freezer. He was sure the contents of the fridge were similarly frightening, but since neither he nor Mel would be returning, he didn't feel compelled to check.

There was nothing else remarkable about the room, so he moved on to explore the rest of the house.

The bathroom counter was covered with various toiletries that he didn't recognize—and why would he when they didn't share a bathroom—but everything was distinctly feminine. He checked the medicine chest and the cabinet below the sink but there was no evidence that a man had ever lived there.

He searched her bedroom next, finding more old and tacky furniture, and an unmade bed. Which was odd because back home she always kept things tidy and spotless. He found a lot of familiar-looking clothes in the closet and drawers, but again, nothing to suggest she'd had any male companionship. Not even a box of condoms in the bedside table. He and Melody had at one time kept them handy, but not for quite some time. They were monogamous, and he was sterile, so there really never seemed a point.

She had obviously had unprotected sex with someone, or she wouldn't have gotten pregnant. It hadn't even occurred to him earlier, but now he wondered if he should go get himself tested for STDs. Melody had callously put her own health and his in jeopardy. One more thing to hold against her.

He searched the entire room, top to bottom, but didn't find the one thing he was looking for. He was about to leave when, as an afterthought, Ash pulled back the comforter on the bed and hit pay dirt.

Melody's computer.

In the past he would have never betrayed her trust by looking through her computer. He respected her privacy, just as she respected his. But she had lost that particular privilege when she betrayed him. Besides, the information it contained might be the only clue as to who she was sleeping with. The only explanation as to why she left him. She owed him that much.

He wanted to look at it immediately but he honestly wasn't sure how much longer he could stand the stench and he still had to pack Melody's things. Most of her clothes he would ship home and have his secretary put away, keeping only a smaller bag in Texas, to make his two-week trip story more believable.

He looked at his watch and realized he was going to have to get moving if he was going to get back to the hospital before visiting hours were over. Though he was exhausted, and wanted nothing more that to go back to the hotel and take a hot shower, he had to play the role of the doting fiancé.

He crammed her things into the suitcases he found stored in her bedroom closet, shoved everything into the trunk of his rental car to sort later, then headed back to the hospital, but when he got there she was sleeping. Realizing that he hadn't eaten since that morning—and then only a hurried fast-food sandwich before his flight boarded—rather than eat an overpriced, sub-par meal in the cafeteria, he found a family diner a few blocks away. It wasn't the Ritz, but the food was decent, and he had the sneaking suspicion he would be eating there a lot in the next week to ten days. When he got back to Mel's room she was awake, sitting up and clearly relieved and excited to see him. "I was afraid you wouldn't make it back."

"I said in my note that I would be back. I just had a few things to take care of." He pulled up a chair but she patted the bed for him to sit beside her.

She looked a lot better than she had earlier. Her eyes were brighter and there was more color in her cheeks, and as he sat, he noticed that her hair was damp. As if reading his mind, she said, "They let me take a shower. It felt *so* wonderful. And tomorrow they want me to start walking, to get the strength back in my légs."

"That's good, right?"

"The nurse said the sooner I'm up and moving around on my own, the sooner they'll discharge me." She reached for his hand, and he had no choice but to take it. "I can hardly wait to go home. I'm sure that once I'm there, I'll start to remember things."

He hoped not. At least, not for a while. That could definitely complicate things. "I'm sure it will," he told her.

"Did the hotel still have my things?" she asked hopefully.

"Hotel?"

Her brow furrowed. "I just assumed I was staying at a hotel, while I did my research."

He cursed himself for letting his guard down. The last thing he wanted was to rouse her suspicions. He swiftly backpedaled.

"You were. I just thought for a second that you remembered something. And yes, they did. Your suitcase is in the trunk of my car. I'll keep it at my hotel until you're released."

"What about my research? Were there papers or files or anything?"

"Not that I saw," he said, realizing that the lies were coming easier now. "But your laptop was there."

Her eyes lit with excitement. "There might be something on it that will shake my memory!"

"I thought of that. I booted it up, but it's password protected, so unless you remember the password…." He watched as Melody's excitement fizzled away. "Tell you what," he said. "When we get back to San Francisco I'll have the tech people at work take a look at it. Maybe they can hack their way in."

"Okay," she agreed, looking a little less defeated, but he could see that she was disappointed.

In reality, he would be calling work at his soonest convenience and with any luck one of the tech guys could walk him through hacking the system himself. Only after he removed anything pertaining to the baby or the affair, or anything personal that might jog her memory, would he let her have it back.

It would be easier to have the hard drive reformatted, but that might look too suspicious. He'd thought of not mentioning the laptop at all, but it stood to reason that since she was a student, she would have one.

He could have lied and said it was destroyed in the accident, but unfortunately it was too late for that now.

"Can you do me a favor?" she asked.

"Sure."

"Can you tell me about myself?"

"Like what?"

"My family, my friends, where I'm from. Anything."

The truth was, despite living together for three years, he didn't know a heck of a lot about Melody. If she had friends at school, she didn't mention them, and when she wasn't in school, he really wasn't sure what she did with her time, other than cooking his dinners, cleaning their condo and of course shopping. She had always kept personal things pretty close to the vest. Either that or he had just never thought to ask.

But she looked so hopeful, he had to come up with something.

"Your mom died before I met you," he told her. "Ovarian cancer, I think. You told me that you never knew your real father, but you'd had something like five or six stepfathers growing up."

"Wow, that's a lot. Where did I grow up?"

He struggled to remember what she had told him when they first met. "All over, I think. You said that she moved you around a lot. I know you resented it."

Just as he had resented so many things from his own childhood. The cancer not even being the worst of it. But he was in no mood to dredge that up. Besides, she had no idea that he'd been sick. It just never came up. He and Mel knew each other, especially in the biblical sense, but they didn't really *know* each other.

He'd been so sure that was the way he'd wanted it, so jaded by his marriage, he never considered that he might want more. Not until it was too late.

Four

Melody had this look, like the playground bully had just stolen her candy. "Wow. It sounds like I had a pretty lousy childhood."

Ash felt a jab of guilt for painting such a grim picture.

"I'm sure there were good things," he told her. "You just never talked about it much."

"How did we meet?"

The memory brought a smile to his face. Now, this was something he remembered. "A company party. At Maddox Communications."

"That's where you work, right?"

He nodded. "You were there with some cocky junior rep. Brent somebody. A real jerk. But the instant I saw you standing by the bar, wearing this slinky little black number, I couldn't look away. Hell, every man in the room had their eye on you. He was droning on, probably thinking he was hot shit because he was with the sexiest woman at the party, and you had this look like you were counting the minutes until you could send him and his overinflated ego packing. You looked over and saw me watching you. You gave me a thorough once-over, then flashed me this sexy smile."

Her eyes went wide. "*I* did that?"

Her surprise made him laugh. "Yeah. At that point I had no choice but to rescue you. So I walked over and asked you to dance."

"How did my date feel about that?"

Ash grinned, recalling the shocked look on the kid's face, the indignant glare as Ash led Mel onto the dance floor and pulled her into his arms. "He didn't look very happy."

"What did he do?"

"What could he do? I was CFO, he was a lowly junior rep. I could have squashed him. Although, if memory serves, someone else eventually did. I don't think he lasted long with the firm."

"So we danced?" she said, a dreamy look on her face.

"All night." Ash had been the envy of every man at the party. At the time he'd still been reeling from his divorce and the ego boost was a welcome one. It wasn't until later that he realized just how thorough of a *boost* she intended to give him.

"Then what happened?" she asked.

"You asked if you could see my office, so I took you there. The instant the door closed we were all over each other."

She swallowed hard, looking as scandalized as she was intrigued. And maybe a little turned on, too. "Then what?"

"You really have to ask?"

"We had *sex* in your office?" she asked in a hushed voice, as if she worried someone would overhear. "Right after we met?"

This from the woman who had never hesitated to tell him exactly what she wanted, when she wanted it, in the bluntest of sexual terms. Language that would make a lot of women blush. Or blanch.

He grinned and nodded. "On the desk, on the sofa, in my chair. Up against the plate-glass window overlooking the bay."

Her cheeks flushed bright pink. "We did it against a *window?*"

"You've always had voyeuristic tendencies." He'd never met a woman more confident, more comfortable in her own skin, than Melody. Though he would never admit it aloud, her brazen nature could be the slightest bit intimidating at times.

But obviously now something had changed. There was a vulnerability in her eyes that he'd never seen before. A hesitance she had never shown. Truth be told, he kind of liked it. And maybe it softened him up just a little. He may have supported Mel for the past three years, but he would never make the mistake of thinking that she depended on him. Had she not met him, she would have managed just fine on her own.

He'd forgotten what it felt like to have someone need him.

"I can't believe I slept with you on the first date," she said. "I can't imagine what you must have thought of me."

"Actually, with my divorce barely final, it was exactly what I needed."

"You were married before?"

"For seven years."

"Why did you split up?"

"I guess you could say it was due to a total lack of appreciation."

"What do you mean?"

"She didn't appreciate the hours I worked, and I didn't appreciate her screwing her personal trainer in my bed."

She sucked in a surprised breath, clearly outraged on his behalf. "She *cheated* on you?"

"For quite some time as I understand it." He wondered how Melody would feel if she knew she had done the same thing? Although, as far as he knew, never in *his* bed. But that was just geography. Cheating was cheating.

Melody tightened her grip on his hand. He hadn't even realized she was holding it. It occurred to him suddenly how cozy this little scenario had become. Too cozy for his liking.

He pulled his hand free and looked at his watch. "It's late. I should let you get some sleep."

"Did I say something wrong?" she asked, looking troubled. "Because if it bothers you to talk about your ex, we can talk about something else."

Frankly, he was all talked out. He wasn't sure what else to say to her. And he wished she would stop being so… nice. Not that she hadn't been nice before, but she'd always had an edge. A sharp wit and a razor-edged tongue. Now she was being so sweet and understanding, she was making it tough for him to hold on to his anger. To be objective.

"You didn't say anything wrong. It's just, well, it's been a really long day. Maybe I'm the one who's tired."

"I'm sorry, I'm being selfish," she said, looking truly apologetic. "I didn't even take into consideration how hard this has been for you."

"It has been a long couple of weeks not knowing where

you were," he said, which only made her look more guilty. "I'm sure I'll feel better after a good night's sleep."

"Go," she said, making a shooing gesture. "Get some sleep."

"Are you sure? I can stay longer if you want me to."

"No. I'm tired anyway. I'll probably watch a few minutes of television then fall asleep."

He had the distinct feeling she was lying, because honestly, she didn't look the least bit tired. But he wasn't going to argue.

"I'll be back first thing tomorrow," he assured her, rising from the edge of the bed.

"Thank you," she said, her expression earnest.

"For what?"

"Telling me those things about myself. It makes me feel a little less…lost. Even if it wasn't quite what I expected."

"You're welcome," he said, and leaned down to brush a kiss across her forehead. "I'll see you tomorrow."

As he walked from the room he heard the television click on. He couldn't help feeling the slightest bit guilty for leaving her alone, but he had a charade to plan.

It turned out that Ash didn't need the help of the tech guys at Maddox Communications to hack into Melody's computer. After only five or six tries, he figured the password out all by himself. His birthday. The fact that it was something so simple surprised him a little, but he was grateful.

His first task was to remove evidence of Melody's affair from her computer, only she must have been very careful because he found nothing, not even a phone number or an entry in her calendar, that suggested she was sneaking around.

As for the baby, there were a few doctor appointments

listed on her calendar, and the history in her Internet browser showed visits to several children's furniture store sites and a site called Mom-to-be.com, where it appeared she had been tracking her pregnancy—she was fourteen weeks and four days on the day of the accident—and blogging on a page for single mothers.

Apparently she had every intention of doing this alone. Was it possible that the father of the baby was nothing more than a one-night stand? A glorified sperm donor?

He skimmed the entries she had written, hoping to find a clue as to who the man was, or the circumstances surrounding their relationship. But after more than an hour of reading, all he'd learned was that the baby's father was, in her words, *not involved*. He noted that some of the earlier posts dated back to the weeks before she left him. It was also clear, by the tone of her posts, that she was very excited to be a mother, which surprised him.

She had always been so independent and career focused, he didn't think she even wanted a family. Of course, that was never something they talked about. Maybe because she knew that if she wanted children, she wouldn't be having them with him. Not naturally anyway. Knowing that he couldn't father a child of his own, he'd resigned himself to the idea of not having them at all.

What he found even more disturbing than the information about the baby was a file folder with electronic copies of her report cards. They dated back the past four semesters. Whenever Ash asked her about school, which admittedly wasn't very often, Mel claimed things were going great. Which was hard to believe now that he saw that she had been clinging to a low C average, when he knew for a fact that in her first year she'd never scored anything lower than an A minus.

It was as if she had lost her interest in the law. But if that was the case, why hadn't she said anything? It was true that they didn't normally talk about those kinds of things, but going to school for a career she no longer wanted seemed worth mentioning. Especially when he was shelling out the money for her tuition.

The more Ash looked through her files and read her e-mails, the more he began to realize that after three years together, he barely knew Melody. She lived a life that, outside the bedroom, had little to do with him. And though that was the way he'd always wanted it, he couldn't help but feel…indignant. And maybe a little angry with himself for not taking the time to get to know her better.

He may have been there for her financially, but even he had to admit that emotionally, he'd been pretty much vacant.

Which was exactly what they had agreed to going into this relationship, so he had no absolutely no reason to feel as though he had wronged her somehow.

If that was true, why did he feel like such a jerk?

Maybe his ex was right. Maybe he'd been too cold and distant. Maybe he used work as an escape from dealing with the ups and downs of his personal relationships. And maybe, like his ex-wife, Melody had grown tired of the distance. Tired of being alone.

Regardless of what she felt, that was no excuse to be unfaithful. If she wanted more, she should have leveled with him. Although for the life of him, he wasn't sure what he would have told her. If she had given him an ultimatum—a real relationship or she would find someone new—would he have been able to just let her go? A real relationship just seemed like so much work. More than he had time for.

But he was here now, wasn't he? He had *made* the time for this. Didn't that tell him something?

Sure it did, he just wasn't sure what. But he knew that at some point he was going to have to figure it out. Maybe it was simply that being with Melody had been very easy, and he wasn't quite ready to give that up.

Unfortunately, remembering how good things had been made her betrayal sting that much more.

Just as he promised, Ash was back at the hospital as soon as visiting hours began the next morning. He was dressed casually this time, in slacks and a silk, button-down shirt. And she could tell, as he walked into the room, a sly grin on his face, that he was holding something behind his back. Probably flowers.

"Wow, you look great," he said, and she knew he wasn't just saying it to be nice because the nurse had said the same thing.

"I feel really good," she admitted, and she was pretty sure it had a lot to do with him. Before he came to see her yesterday she had felt so depressed and alone. As though she had nothing to look forward to, no reason to get better. Everything was different now. She was engaged to be married, and had a home to return to. A whole life to explore and relearn. What more could she ask for?

"I got my appetite back in a big way. I just finished breakfast and I'm already anxious for lunch. Although I have to say, the food here leaves a lot to be desired."

"There's a diner a few blocks from here that has decent food. Maybe I can pick you up something for lunch, if it's okay with your doctor."

"I'll make sure the nurse asks him. I could go for a big juicy burger and greasy French fries."

"I didn't know you liked burgers and fries."

"What do I usually eat?"

"Salads and chicken mostly. Occasionally you'll have

red meat, but not more than once a week. You've always been extremely health conscious."

"Well, I keep seeing these fast-food ads and every time they show a burger my mouth starts to water. I'll worry about being health conscious when I'm out of the hospital." Which was a completely backward way of looking at it, she realized, but she didn't even care. Eating like a rabbit wouldn't build her strength and get her the heck out of here.

"A burger and fries it is then," he said, and he was still hiding whatever it was he was holding behind his back.

"So, are you going to show me what you've got there, or make me guess?" she asked.

"You mean this?" he asked, his smile widening as he pulled a laptop from behind him.

"Is that mine?" she asked and he nodded. "I thought it was password protected. Did you talk to the guys at work already?"

He set it in her lap. "I didn't have to. I made a few educated guesses and figured it out for myself."

She squealed with excitement. "Oh, my gosh! You're my hero!"

He regarded her quizzically, as if she had just said something totally off the wall.

"What?" she asked. "Why are you looking at me like that?"

"Sorry. I just never imagined you as the kind of a woman who would have a hero. You're far too self-sufficient."

"Well, I do now," she said with a smile. "And it's you."

She opened the laptop and pressed the button to boot it up, relieved that at least she recalled how. When the password screen popped up, she looked to Ash.

"Type in one, one, nineteen, seventy-five."

"What is it?"

"My birthday."

I guess it made sense that she would use her fiancé's birthday as a password. Unless she didn't want him getting into her files, which obviously wasn't an issue. She typed the digits in and the system screen popped up. "It worked!"

"You remember how to use it?"

She nodded. Like so many other things, navigating the computer just seemed to come naturally. She only hoped that the information it contained would spark other memories. Personal memories.

"I'm going to head down to the gift store and see if they have a *Wall Street Journal*," Ash said, and Melody nodded, only half listening as she began opening files on her desktop. "If they don't, I might try to find one at the party store around the block."

"'Kay," she said. "Take your time."

She started with her e-mail, thinking saved messages would hold the most information, but there weren't many. And of the dozen or so, most were from Ash. It seemed a little strange, especially being in school, that she didn't have more, but it was always possible she kept them on an off-site server for safekeeping. Especially if they were for her supposed research, and were of a high security nature.

Or maybe her imagination was getting the best of her again.

She opened her calendar next, going back for several months, and found nothing but her school schedule, a few theater and party dates with Ash, and of course her research trip, which according to this should have ended a few days after her accident. She also found a recent appointment with a wedding planner that they had missed, and realized that not only were they engaged, but apparently they had already set a date. One they would probably be forced to postpone now.

She quit out of her calendar and opened her photo file, but either she kept her pictures online or on a disk, or she wasn't a very sentimental person, because there were very few. Shots of herself and Ash, mostly. None of friends or fellow students. And none of family, which was no surprise since she didn't have any.

She did have a vast music library, and while she liked the various songs she sampled, she didn't relate them to any specific memories or events.

She went through file after file, but not a single thing, not even her school papers, looked familiar to her. She tried to be logical about it. She had barely been out of her coma for four days and the doctor had said it would take time. *Logically* she knew this, and she was trying to heed his advice. Emotionally though, she felt like putting her fist through the nearest wall.

"I hope you're not doing schoolwork already!" the nurse said as she walked in to check Melody's IV. Which was kind of a ridiculous notion, since not only would Melody not have a clue what work had been assigned, but even if she did, she wouldn't have any idea how to do it. She didn't remember anything about the law. But she had to cut the nurse some slack. It probably wasn't often she dealt with amnesia patients.

"I'm just looking at photos and things," Melody told her. "I was hoping I would remember something."

"That's a great idea! How's it going?"

"Nothing so far."

She hung a fresh IV bag and tossed the empty one in the trash by the sink. "Dr. Nelson would like to see you up and moving around today. But only with assistance," she added sternly.

Melody wouldn't dare try it alone. When she'd taken her shower earlier the nurse had to help her, and she had to shower sitting down. Her legs felt like limp spaghetti noodles and she was so dizzy she was having trouble staying upright.

"We could take a few practice steps right now," the nurse suggested, a not-so-subtle nudge, but Melody wasn't quite ready to put her computer aside.

"Could we maybe do it after lunch?" she asked.

"All right, but don't put it off too long. You need to rebuild your strength."

Melody knew that better than everyone else. And though walking might still be a challenge, she could feel herself improving by leaps and bounds. She gave most of the credit to Ash.

He'd given her something to fight for.

Five

After the nurse left, Melody went back to the photo file on her computer and opened a few of herself and Ash. When she looked at herself, it was still a bit like looking at a stranger. It was her, but not exactly her.

Her clothes were obviously expensive and quite form-fitting. The healthy eating must have paid off because she was very trim and fit—although now, after being in the coma, she looked a little gaunt. She seemed to like to show off her cleavage, which admittedly she had a fair amount of. She peeked under her hospital gown at her breasts and decided that she must own some pretty amazing push-up bras.

In the photos her hair was always fixed in a sleek and chic style that she couldn't help thinking must have taken ages in front of the bathroom mirror to perfect. So unlike the casual, wavy locks she was sporting now. Also, she wore a considerable amount of makeup and it was always flawlessly applied. She looked very well put together.

Just the thought of the time it must have taken to get ready each morning left her feeling exhausted. Maybe, when she was up and around again, she would feel differently. Although she couldn't help thinking she looked a bit...*vain*. But she was sure these photos represented only a small segment of her life. Who didn't like to look good for pictures? And she couldn't deny that she and Ash made one heck of a good-looking couple.

How would he feel if she didn't go back to being that perfectly put together woman? Would he be disappointed? Or did he love her for the woman inside?

The latter, she hoped. If not, would he be here by her side while she healed?

"Still at it?" the man in question said, and she looked up to find him standing at the foot of the bed. Ash was holding a newspaper in one hand and a brown paper sack in the other.

"You're back already?" she asked.

"Already? I've been gone almost two hours."

"Has it really been that long?" She would have guessed twenty-five or thirty minutes.

"I had to make a few calls to work, and I figured you wouldn't mind the time alone. Which apparently you didn't." He nodded to her computer. "Any luck?"

She closed the computer and shook her head, trying not to let it discourage her, or to dwell on it. "I've looked at pretty much all of it and I don't recognize a thing." She gestured to the bag he was holding. "What's that?"

"I stopped at the nurses' station on my way out this morning, and they called the doctor, who said there's no reason to have you on a restricted diet, so..." He pulled a white foam restaurant container from the bag. "Your burger and fries, madam."

The scent of the food wafted her way and her mouth instantly started to water. Now she knew why she was marrying Ash. He was clearly the sweetest man in the world.

"You're wonderful!" she said as he set it on her tray. "I can see why I fell in love with you."

He gave her another one of those funny looks, as though the sentiment was totally unexpected or out of character.

"What? Don't tell me I've never said I love you."

"It's not that. I just..." He shook his head. "I just didn't expect to hear anything like that so soon. I guess I figured you would have to take the time to get to know me again."

"Well, I sure like what I've seen so far." She opened the container top, her taste buds going berserk in anticipation. Her stomach growled and, up until that instant, she didn't even realize she was hungry. She automatically grabbed a packet of ketchup, tore it open with her teeth, and drizzled it over her fries. Ash pulled out a similar container for himself and set it beside hers on the tray, but his was a BLT with coleslaw. He sat on the edge of the mattress near her to eat.

The fries were greasy and salty, and by far the best thing Melody had eaten in days. Or maybe *ever*. And when she took a bite of her burger it was pure nirvana.

"How did your calls to work go?" she asked. "Are they upset that you'll be gone for a while?"

He shrugged. "Doesn't matter how they feel. They don't have a say in the matter."

She frowned. "I would feel awful if I got you in trouble, or even worse, if you got fired because of me."

"Don't worry. They aren't going to fire me. I'm the

best damned CFO they've ever had. Besides, they know that if they did let me go, their competitor, Golden Gate Promotions, would probably snap me up. The owner, Athos Koteas, would do just about anything for an edge. And that would be very bad for Maddox."

"Not if your contract has a noncompete clause," she said, stuffing a fry in her mouth. "Working for a competitor would be a direct breach. They could sue the pants off you. And I'm sure they would."

When she glanced up, Ash had gone still with his sandwich halfway to his mouth, and he was giving her that "look" again. Why did he keep doing that? "*What?* Do I have ketchup on my face or something?"

"Mel, do you realize what you just said?"

She hit rewind and ran it through her head again, stunned when the meaning of her words sank in. "I was talking like a lawyer."

Ash nodded.

"Oh, my gosh! I didn't even think about it. It just… popped out." A huge smile crept across her face. "I remembered something!"

Granted it was nothing important, or personal, but it was *something.* She tried to dredge up some other legal jargon, but her mind went blank. Maybe that was just the way it was going to be. Maybe it would come back in little bits and pieces. At that rate she would have her full memory back by the time she and Ash retired, she thought wryly.

"For the record," he said, "I did have a noncompete clause and they removed it when I refused to sign."

Maybe it was her imagination, but she had the feeling Ash didn't share in her happiness. It was as if he thought her remembering something was a *bad* thing.

It was just one more little thing that seemed…off.

She shook the thought away. She was being ridiculous.

Of course he wanted her to remember things. Didn't he? What reason would he have not to?

That, she realized, was what she needed to find out.

That had been a close call, Ash thought as he and Mel ate lunch. In hindsight, bringing her computer might not have been the brightest idea he'd ever had, but doing it today, instead of waiting until they got back to San Francisco, had sort of been an accident. He'd grabbed it on his way out the door when he left for the hospital. He didn't like the idea of leaving it in the room, for fear that it might be stolen. But as he climbed into his rental, the interior, at nine in the morning, was already about a million degrees. Assuming he would be in the hospital most of the day, it didn't seem wise to leave the laptop in the car, in the blistering heat.

What choice did he have but to bring it into the hospital with him, and as a result, give it to Melody? What if it did spark a memory? Was he willing to jeopardize his plans? He'd been up half the night removing personal information, so it seemed unlikely anything would shake loose a memory.

To confuse her, and hopefully buy himself a little more time, he not only removed things from the computer, but *added* a few things, as well.

To give her the impression they attended social functions together—when in reality they rarely went out socially—he added a few entries for fictional theater dates and parties. He also included a meeting with a wedding planner, which he thought was a nice touch. One they had regretfully missed because Mel had been missing.

The most brilliant switch, in his opinion, was her music. He knew from experience that some songs evoked specific memories or feelings. Like the knot he got in his stomach whenever he heard "Hey Jude" by the Beatles, the song that was playing the day he drove home to break the good news about his promotion and found his ex in bed with her personal trainer.

So, he deleted Mel's entire music catalog and replaced it with his own music library. Mel had always preferred current pop music, while he listened to classic rock and jazz. There wasn't much chance that would be jogging any memories.

Now he was wondering if that hadn't been enough. Or maybe the memories were going to come back regardless. Either way, he didn't want to panic prematurely. Remembering something about the law was still a far cry from regaining her personal memories.

He looked over at Melody and realized she'd stopped eating with nearly half her burger and fries still left.

"Full already?" he asked.

"Is there something you're not telling me?" she asked. "Something you don't want me to know?"

The question came so far out of left field he was struck dumb for several seconds, and when his brain finally kicked back in he figured it would be in his best interest to *play* dumb. "What do you mean?"

She pushed her tray aside. "I just get this nagging feeling that you're hiding something from me."

He could play this one of two ways. He could act angry and indignant, but in his experience that just screamed *guilty*. So instead he went for the wounded angle.

He pasted on a baffled expression and said, "God, Mel, why would you think that? If I did or said something to hurt your feelings…" He shrugged helplessly.

The arrow hit its mark. Melody looked crushed.

"Of course you haven't. You've been wonderful." She reached out and put her hand on his forearm. "You've done so much for me and I'm acting completely ungrateful. Just forget I said anything."

He laid his hand over hers and gave it a squeeze. "You suffered a severe head injury. You were in a coma for two weeks." He flashed her a sympathetic smile. "I promise I won't hold it against you."

Her smile was a grateful one. And of course, he felt like slime for playing on her emotions. For using it to his advantage.

Remember what she did to you, he told himself. Although, one thing he couldn't deny was that Melody was not the woman she'd been before the accident. In the past, she *never* would have confronted him this way with her suspicions. Yet, at the same time, she was much softer and compassionate than she used to be. Not to mention uncharacteristically open with her emotions.

When she told him she loved him he'd felt...well, he honestly wasn't sure *what* he'd felt. It was just...unusual. No one had said that to him in a long time. He and his wife had stopped expressing sentiments of love long before the final meltdown. The pain of their breakup had been less about lost love than the humiliation of her deceit, and his own stupidity for not seeing her for what she really was.

In the long run he honestly believed she had done him a favor, although he could have done without seeing the proof with his own eyes.

Even if Melody thought she loved Ash, she obviously didn't mean it or she wouldn't have cheated on him in the first place. Besides, their relationship wasn't about love. It was more about mutual respect and convenience. She was only saying what she thought she was *supposed* to say. She probably just assumed that she would never be engaged to a man she didn't love. But that was all part of the plan, wasn't it? To make her believe that they were in love. And apparently it was working.

He couldn't deny that in her current condition, he was having a tough time keeping a grip on the anger he'd felt when he learned about her pregnancy. He was sure that once he got her back home and she started acting like her old self, the wounds would feel fresh again. He would approach the situation with a renewed sense of vengeance.

He was counting on it.

Six days after Ash arrived in Abilene, after showing what Dr. Nelson said was remarkable progress, Melody was finally released from the hospital. An orderly wheeled her down to the front entrance, her heart pounding in anticipation of finally being free, and as they exited the building, a wall of hot, dry air washed over her.

She hoped their place in San Francisco had a courtyard or a balcony, because after being cooped up in the hospital for so long, she wanted to spend lots of time outside. She closed her eyes and breathed in deep, felt the sun beat down hot on her face as she was wheeled from under the awning to the curb where Ash waited with his rental car. It was barely 10:00 a.m. and it had to be pushing ninety degrees. The sun was so bright, she had to raise a hand to shade her eyes. She wasn't sure of the make of the vehicle, but it looked expensive.

Ash had dressed casually for the trip, in jeans and a T-shirt, and Melody didn't miss the group of nurses following him with their eyes, practically drooling on their scrubs.

Look all you like ladies, but he's mine.

Not that Melody blamed them for gawking. He looked hot as hell dressed that way. The shirt accentuated the width of his shoulders and showed off the lean muscle in his arms, and the jeans hugged his behind in a way that gave her impure thoughts. She could hardly wait until she was feeling well enough to have sex again. Right now, if she did anything marginally taxing, her head began to pound.

As soon as they reached the car Ash opened the door. A rush of cool air cut through the heat as he helped her from the chair to the front seat. The interior was soft black leather, and it had what looked like a top-of-the-line sound and navigation system. Ash got her settled in and helped with her seat belt, and as he leaned over her to fasten it, he smelled so delicious she wanted to bury her face in the crook of his neck and take a nibble. When he seemed convinced she was securely fastened in, with her seat as far back as it would go—just in case the airbag deployed and bonked her head, rattling her already compromised brain—he walked around and got in the driver's side. "Are you ready?" he asked.

"I am *so* ready."

He turned the key and the engine hummed to life, and as he pulled from the curb and down the driveway toward the road, she had this odd feeling of urgency. She felt that if he didn't hurry, the staff members were going to change their minds and chase her down like a fugitive, or an escaped mental patient, and make her go back to that awful room.

It wasn't until he pulled out onto the main road and hit the gas, and the hospital finally disappeared out of sight, that she could breathe easy again. She was finally free. As long as she lived, she hoped she never had to stay in a hospital room again.

He glanced over at her. "You all right?"

"I am now."

"You're comfortable?" he asked.

"Very." He'd brought her suitcase to the hospital and she'd chosen a pair of jeans and a cotton shirt to start the trip. She'd tried to find a bra she liked, but either they were push-up and squeezed her breasts to within an inch of her life or they were made of itchy lace, so she'd opted not to wear one at all. As long as she didn't get cold, or pull her shirt taut, it was kind of hard to tell. Besides, it was just her and Ash and he'd seen her breasts plenty of times before.

The jeans were comfortable, and although at one point she was guessing they were pretty tight, now they hung off her. Despite her constant cravings for food, her eyes were bigger than her stomach, but Dr. Nelson assured her that her appetite would return.

She'd opted to wear flip-flops on her feet and toed them off the instant she was in the car, keeping them within reach should she happen to need them.

Other than the dull ache in her temples, she couldn't be more comfortable.

"If you need to stop for any reason just let me know," Ash told her. "And if the driving gets to be too much we'll stop and get a hotel room."

"I'm sure I'll be fine." If it were at all possible, she wished they could drive straight through until they got to San Francisco, but it was a twenty-four-hour trip and she knew Ash would have to sleep at some point. Still, she wanted to stay on the road as long as possible. The sooner they got home, the better. She was convinced that once she was there, surrounded by her own possessions, her memories would begin to return.

Ash turned onto the I-20 on-ramp, hit the gas and zoomed onto the freeway, shooting like a rocket into traffic.

"This is pretty nice for a rental," she told him.

"It's not a rental," he said as he maneuvered left into the fast lane. "This is my car."

His car? "I thought you flew here."

"I did, but I wanted you to be comfortable on the way home so I arranged to have my car brought to Texas. It arrived yesterday morning."

That couldn't have been cheap. She'd never asked Ash about their financial situation, but apparently CFOs at San Francisco ad agencies made decent money.

"It looks expensive," she said. "The car, I mean."

He shrugged. "I like nice cars."

"So I guess you do okay? Financially."

He flashed her a side glance, one of those funny looks that had become so familiar this past week. "Are you asking how much I make?"

"No! Of course not. It's just, well…you wear expensive clothes and drive an expensive car. So I'm assuming you make a decent living, that's all."

"I do okay," he said, a grin kicking up one corner of his mouth, as though the idea of her even asking amused him. And she knew that if she asked exactly how much he made, he would probably tell her. It just wasn't that important.

All that mattered to her was how wonderful he'd been this week. Other than running an occasional errand, or stepping out to pick up food, Ash hadn't left her side. He got there every morning after visiting hours started and didn't leave until they ended at ten. She had been off her feet for so long and her muscles had deteriorated so much that at first walking had been a challenge. Because she was determined to get out of there as soon as humanly possible, Melody had paced, back and forth, up and down the corridors for hours to build her strength. And Ash had been right there by her side.

At first, she'd literally needed him there to hang on to, or to lean on when her balance got hinky. It was frustrating, not being able to do something as simple as taking a few steps unassisted, but Ash kept pumping her full of encouragement and, after the second day, she could manage with only her IV pole to steady her. When they finally removed her IV, she'd been a little wary at first, but realized she was steady enough walking without it. Yesterday she had been chugging along at a pretty good pace when Dr. Nelson came by to let her know she would be released in the morning. He had already discussed her case with a neurologist in San Francisco—one of the best, he said—and Melody would go in to see him as soon as they were home.

Melody's lids started to feel droopy and she realized the pain pills the nurse had given her right before she was discharged were starting to kick in.

Ash must have noticed because he said, "Why don't you put your seat back? It's the lever on the right. And there's a pillow and blanket in the backseat if you need them."

The man thought of *everything*.

It was plenty warm in the car, even with the air on, but the pillow sounded good. She reclined her seat then grabbed the pillow from the back and tucked it under her head. She sighed and snuggled into the buttery-soft leather, sure that her hospital bed hadn't been half as comfortable. She wanted to stay awake, to keep Ash company, but her lids just didn't want to cooperate, so finally she stopped fighting it and let them close. It couldn't have been ten seconds before she slipped into a deep, dreamless sleep.

Six

Melody woke, disoriented and confused, expecting to be in her hospital bed. The she remembered she'd been set free and smiled, even though her head ached so hard she was sure that her eyeballs were going to pop from their sockets.

"Have a good nap?"

She looked over and saw Ash gazing down at her, a bottle of soda in his hand. Only then did she realize they were no longer moving. She rubbed her eyes, giving them a gentle push inward, just in case, and asked, "Why are we stopped?"

"Lunch break."

She looked up and saw that they were parked in a fast-food restaurant lot.

"I was just going in to grab a burger. Do you want anything?"

"No, I'm good. But my head is pounding. What time is it?"

"After three."

She'd been asleep for *five* hours?

"It's probably the elevation. Do you need a pain pill?"

She nodded, so he opened the glove box and pulled out the prescription they had filled at the hospital pharmacy. "One or two?"

One pill wouldn't put her to sleep, and she would be able to keep Ash company, but gauging the pain in her head, she needed two. "Two, I think."

He tapped them out of the bottle and offered his soda to wash them down. "I'm going in. You sure you don't want anything?"

"I'm sure."

While he was gone she lay back and closed her eyes. She must have drifted off again because when the car door opened, it startled her awake.

Ash was back with a bag of food. He unwrapped his burger in his lap and set his fries in the console cup holder. It wasn't until they were back on the highway, and the aroma permeated the interior, when her stomach started to rumble in protest.

Maybe she was hungry after all. Every time he took a bite her jaw tightened and her mouth watered.

After a while Ash asked, "Is there a reason you're watching me eat?"

She didn't realize how intently she'd been staring. "Um, no?"

"You wouldn't be hungry, would you?" he asked.

She was starving, but she couldn't very well ask him to turn around and go back. "I can wait until the next stop."

"Look in the bag," he told her.

She did, and found another burger and fries inside.

"I kind of figured once you saw me eating you would be hungry, too."

"Just one more reason why I love you," she said, diving into her food with gusto.

She was only able to eat about half, so Ash polished off the rest. When she was finished eating the painkillers had kicked in and she dozed off with her stomach pleasantly full. A few hours later she roused for a trip to the rest stop, and as soon as the car was moving again, promptly fell back to sleep. The next time she opened her eyes it was dark and they were parked in front of an economy hotel. She realized that Ash was standing outside the open passenger door, his hand was on her shoulder, and he was nudging her awake.

"What time is it?" she asked groggily.

"After eleven. We're stopping for the night," he said. "I got us a room."

Thirteen hours down, eleven to go, she thought. Maybe this time tomorrow they would be home.

He helped her out and across the parking lot. All the sleep should have energized her, but she was still exhausted, and her head hurt worse than it had before. Maybe this trip was harder on her system than she realized.

Their bags were already inside and sitting on the bed.

"They didn't have any doubles left and there isn't another hotel for miles," he said apologetically. "If you don't want to share, I can sack out on the floor."

They had shared a bed for *three* years. Of course, she had no memory of that. Maybe he was worried that she would feel strange sleeping with him until they got to know one another better. Which she had to admit was pretty sweet. It was a little unusual being with him this late at night, since he always left the hospital by ten. But actually, it was kind of nice.

"I don't mind sharing," she assured him.

"How's your head feel?"

She rubbed her left temple. "Like it's going to implode. Or explode. I'm not sure which."

He tapped two painkillers out and got her a glass of water. "Maybe a hot shower would help."

She swallowed them and said, "It probably would."

"You can use the bathroom first."

She stepped in the bathroom and closed the door, smiling when she saw that he'd set her toiletry bag on the edge of the sink. He seriously could not take better care of her.

She dropped her clothes on the mat and blasted the water as hot as she could stand then stepped under the spray. She soaped up, then washed and conditioned her hair, then she closed her eyes and leaned against the wall, letting the water beat down on her. When she felt herself listing to one side her eyes flew open and she jerked upright, realizing that she had actually drifted off to sleep.

She shut the water off and climbed out, wrapping herself in a towel that reeked of bleach. She combed her hair and brushed her teeth, grabbed her dirty clothes, and when she stepped out of the bathroom Ash was lying in bed with the television controller in one hand, watching a news program.

"Your turn," she said.

He glanced over at her, did a quick double take, then turned back to the TV screen. "I thought I was going to have to call in the national guard," he said. "You were in there a while."

"Sorry. I fell asleep in the shower."

"On or off?" he said, gesturing to the TV.

"Off. The second my head hits the pillow I'll be out cold."

He switched it off and rolled out of bed, grabbing the pajama bottoms he'd set out. "Out in a minute," he said as he stepped in the bathroom and shut the door. Less than ten seconds later she heard the shower turn on.

Barely able to keep her eyes open, Melody walked on wobbly legs to the bed. She'd forgotten to grab something to sleep in from her suitcase, and with her case on the floor across the room, it hardly seemed worth the effort. It wasn't as if he had never seen her naked before, and if she was okay with it, she was sure he would be, too.

She dropped her towel on the floor and climbed under the covers, her mind going soft and fuzzy as the painkillers started to do their job.

At some point she heard the bathroom door open and heard Ash moving around in the room, then she felt the covers shift, and she could swear she heard Ash curse under his breath. It seemed as though it was a long time before she felt the bed sink under his weight, or maybe it was just her mind playing tricks on her. But finally she felt him settle into bed, his arm not much more than an inch from her own, its heat radiating out to touch her.

She drifted back to sleep and woke in the darkness with something warm and smooth under her cheek. It took a second to realize that it was Ash's chest. He was flat on his back and she was lying draped across him. At some point she must have cuddled up to him. She wondered if they slept like this all the time. She hoped so, because she liked it. It felt nice to be so close to him.

The next time she woke up, she could see the hint of sunlight through a break in the curtains. She was still lying on Ash, her leg thrown over one of his, and his arm was looped around her, his hand resting on her bare hip.

The covers had slipped down just low enough for her to see the tent in his pajama bottoms. It looked…well…*big,* and for the first time since the accident she felt the honest-to-goodness tug of sexual arousal. She suddenly became ultra-aware of her body pressed against his. Her nipples pulled into two hard points and started to tingle, until it felt as though the only relief would come from rubbing them against his warm skin. In fact, she had the urge to rub her entire body all over his. She arched her back, drawing his leg deeper between her thighs, and as she did, her thigh brushed against his erection. He groaned in his sleep and sank his fingers into the flesh of her hip. Tingles of desire shivered straight through to her core.

It felt so good to be touched, and she wanted more; unfortunately, the more turned on she became, and the faster her blood raced through her veins, the more her head began to throb. She took a deep breath to calm her hammering heart. It was clear that it would be a while before she was ready to put her body through the stress of making love.

That didn't make her want Ash any less, and it didn't seem fair to make him keep waiting, after having already gone through months of abstinence, when there was no reason why she couldn't make him feel good.

Didn't she owe him for being so good to her? For sticking by her side?

Melody looked at the tent in his pajamas, imagined putting her hand inside, and was hit with a sudden and overwhelming urge to touch him, a need to please him that seemed to come from somewhere deep inside, almost like a shadowy memory, hazy and distant and just out of reach. It had never occurred to her before, but maybe being intimate with him would jog her memory.

She slid her hand down his taut and warm stomach,

under the waistband of his pajama bottoms. She felt the muscle just below the skin contract and harden under her touch. She moved lower still, tunneling her fingers through the wiry hair at the base. He was so warm there, as if all the heat in his body had trickled down to pool in that one spot.

She played there for just a few seconds, drawing her fingers back and forth through his hair, wondering what was going on in his head. Other than the tensing of his abdomen and the slight wrinkle between his brows, he appeared to be sleeping soundly.

When the anticipation became too much, she slid her hand up and wrapped it around his erection. The months without sex must have taken their toll because he was rock hard, and as she stroked her way upward, running her thumb along the tip, it was already wet and slippery.

She couldn't recall ever having done this before— though she was sure she had, probably more times than she could count—but she inherently seemed to know what to do, knew what he liked. She kept her grip firm and her pace slow and even, and Ash seemed to like it. She could see the blood pulsing at the base of his throat and his hips started to move in time with her strokes. She looked up, watching his face. She could tell he was beginning to wake up, and she wanted to see his expression when he did.

His breath was coming faster now and his head thrashed from one side to the other, then back again. She was sure that all he needed was one little push…

She turned her face toward his chest, took his nipple in her mouth, then bit down. Not hard enough to leave a mark, only to arouse, and it worked like a charm. A groan ripped from Ash's chest and his hips bucked upward, locking as his body let go. His fingers dug into her flesh, then he relaxed and went slack beneath her.

Mel looked up at him and found that he was looking back at her, drowsy and a little disoriented, as if he were still caught somewhere between asleep and awake. He looked down at her hand still gripping him inside his pajamas. She waited for the smile to curl his mouth, for him to tell her how good she made him feel, but instead he frowned and snapped, "Mel, what are you doing?"

Mel snatched her hand from inside Ash's pajamas, grabbed the sheet and yanked it up to cover herself. He couldn't tell if she was angry or hurt, or a little of both. But Melody didn't do angry. Not with him anyway. At least, she never *used* to.

"I think the appropriate thing to say at a time like this is thanks, that felt great," she snapped.

Yep, that was definitely anger.

"That did feel great. The part I was *awake* for." Which wasn't much.

He knew last night, when he'd pulled back the covers and discovered she was naked, that sleeping next to her would be a bad idea. When he woke in the middle of the night with her draped over him like a wet noodle, limp and soft and sleeping soundly, he knew that he should have rolled her over onto her own side of the bed, but he was too tired, and too comfortable to work up the will. And yeah, maybe it felt good, too. But he sure as hell hadn't expected to wake up this morning with her hand in his pants.

Before the accident it would have been par for the course. If he had a nickel for every time he'd roused in the morning in the middle of a hot dream to find Melody straddling him, or giving him head.

But now he almost felt…violated.

Looked as if he should have listened to his instincts and slept on the damned floor.

The worst thing about this was seeing her there barely covered with the sheet, one long, lithe leg peeking out from underneath, the luscious curve of her left breast exposed, her hair adorably mussed, and all he could think about was tossing her down on the mattress and having his way with her.

Sex with Melody had always been off-the-charts fantastic. *Always.* She had been willing to try anything at least once, and would go to practically any lengths to please him. In fact, there were times when she could be a little *too* adventurous and enthusiastic. Three years into their relationship they made love as often and as enthusiastically as their first time when it was all exciting and new—right up until the day she walked out on him.

But when it came to staying angry with her, seeing her in such a compromised condition and knowing that she had no recollection of cheating on him took some of the wind out of his sails. For now. When she got her memory back, that would be a whole other story.

But that did not mean he was ready to immediately hop back into bed with her. When, and *if,* he was ready to have sex with her, he would let her know. He was calling the shots this time.

"I don't get why you're so upset about this," she said, sounding indignant, and a little dejected.

"You could have woken me up and asked if it was okay."

"Well, seeing as how we're *engaged,* I really didn't think it would be a problem."

"You're not ready for sex."

"Which is why I don't expect anything from you. I was perfectly content just making you feel good. Most guys—"

"Most guys would not expect their fiancée, who just

suffered a serious head injury, to get them off. Especially
one who's still too fragile to have him return the favor. Did
you ever stop to think that I might feel guilty?"

Some of her anger fizzled away. "But it's been months
for you, and I just thought…it just didn't seem fair."

Fair? "Okay, so it's been months. So what? I'm not a sex
fiend. You may have noticed that my puny reptile brain
functions just fine without it."

That made her crack a smile. "It didn't seem right that
you had to suffer because of me. I just wanted to make
you happy."

Is that what she had been doing the past three years?
Making him happy? Had she believed that she needed to
constantly please him sexually to keep him interested? Did
she think that because he paid for her school, her room
and board, kept her living a lifestyle many women would
envy, that she was his…*sex slave?* And had he *ever* given
her a reason to believe otherwise?

For him, their relationship was as much about companionship as sex. Although, in three years, of all the
times she had offered herself so freely, not to mention
enthusiastically, had he ever once stopped her and said,
"Let's just talk instead?"

Was that why she cheated on him? Did she need
someone who treated her like an equal and not a sex
object?

If she felt that way, she should have said so. But since
they were stuck together for a while, he should at least set
the record straight.

"The thing is, Mel, I'm *not* suffering. And even if I was,
you don't owe me anything."

"You sure looked like you were this morning when I
woke up," she said.

"Mel, I'm a guy. I could be getting laid ten times a day

and I would still wake up with a hard-on. It's part of the outdoor plumbing package."

She smiled and he offered his hand for her to take. She had to let go of the sheet on one side and it dropped down, completely baring her left breast. It was firm and plump, her nipples small and rosy, and it took all the restraint he could muster not to lean forward and take her into his mouth. He realized he was staring and tore his gaze away to look in her eyes, but she'd seen, and he had the feeling she knew exactly what he'd been thinking.

"Not suffering, huh?" she said with a wry smile.

Well, not anymore. Not much anyway.

"I honestly believe that we need to take this slow," he said. "If you're not physically ready, we wait. *Both* of us."

"Okay," she agreed solemnly, giving his hand a squeeze. "You mind if I use the bathroom first, or do you want it?"

"Go ahead."

She rolled out of bed and he assumed she intended to take the sheet along to cover herself. Instead she let it fall and stood there in all her naked glory, thinner than she'd been, almost to point of looking a little bony, but still sexy and desirable as hell.

Instead of walking straight into the bathroom, she went the opposite way to her suitcase, her hair falling in mussed waves over her shoulders, the sway of her hips mesmerizing him. He expected her to lift her case and set it on the bed, but instead she bent at the waist to unzip her case right there. She stood not five feet away, her back to him, legs spread just far enough to give him a perfect view of her goods, and he damn near swallowed his own tongue. He saw two perfect globes of soft flesh that he was desperate to get his hands on, her thighs long and milky white, and what lay between them…damn. Doing him must have turned her on, too, because he could see traces of moisture glistening along her folds.

He had to fist the blankets to keep himself from reaching out and touching her. To stop himself from dropping to his knees and taking her into his mouth. He even caught himself licking his lips in anticipation.

She seemed to take an unnecessarily long time rifling through her clothes, choosing what to wear, then she straightened. He pulled the covers across his lap, so she wouldn't notice that conspicuous rise in his pajamas, but she didn't even look his way; then, as she stepped into the bathroom she tossed him a quick, wicked smile over her shoulder.

If that little display had been some sort of revenge for snapping at her earlier, she sure as hell knew how to hit where it stung.

Seven

They got back on the road late that morning—although it was Melody's own fault.

She'd already had a mild headache when she woke up, compounded by the sexual arousal, but bending over like that to open her case, and the pressure it had put on her head, had been a really bad move. The pain went from marginally cumbersome to oh-my-God-kill-me-now excruciating. But it had almost been worth it to see the look on Ash's face.

She popped two painkillers then got dressed, thinking she would lie down while Ash got ready then she would be fine. Unfortunately it was the kind of sick, throbbing pain that was nearly unbearable, and exacerbated by the tiniest movement.

Ash's first reaction was to drive her to the nearest hospital, but she convinced him that all she needed was a little quiet, and another hour or so of sleep. She urged him to go and get himself a nice breakfast, and wake her when he got back.

Instead, he let her sleep until almost eleven-thirty! It was nearly noon by the time they got on the road, and she realized, with a sinking heart, that they would never make it back to San Francisco that evening. On the bright side she managed to stay awake for most of the drive, and was able to enjoy the scenery as it passed. Ash played the radio and occasionally she would find herself singing along to songs she hadn't even realized she knew. But if she made a conscious effort to remember them, her stubborn brain refused to cooperate.

When they stopped for the night, this time it was in a much more populated area and he managed to find a higher-class hotel with two double beds. However, that didn't stop her from walking around naked and sleeping in the buff. The truth was, when it came to sleeping naked she wasn't really doing it to annoy Ash. She actually liked the feel of the sheets against her bare skin. The walking-around-naked part? That was just for fun.

Not that she didn't think Ash was right about waiting. When she'd invaded his pj's yesterday morning she really hadn't stopped to think that maybe he didn't want to, that he might feel guilty that it was one-sided. If she wanted to get technical, what she had done was tantamount to rape or molestation. Although, honestly, he hadn't seemed quite *that* scandalized.

Really, she should be thrilled that she was engaged to such a caring and sensitive man. And she supposed that if the burden of pent-up sexual energy became too much, he could just take care of matters himself. Although deep down she really hoped he would wait for her.

Despite wishing she was in Ash's bed, curled up against him, she got a decent night's sleep and woke feeling the best she had since this whole mess began. Her head hardly hurt and when they went to breakfast she ate every bite of her waffles and sausage. Maybe just knowing that in a few hours she would be home was all the medicine she needed for a full recovery.

Ash spent a lot of the drive on the phone with work, and though she wasn't sure exactly what was being discussed, the tone of the conversation suggested that they were relieved he was coming back. And he seemed happy to be going back.

They crossed the Bay Bridge shortly after one, and they were finally in San Francisco. Though the views were gorgeous, she couldn't say with any certainty that it looked the least bit familiar. They drove along the water, and after only a few minutes Ash pulled into the underground parking of a huge renovated warehouse that sat directly across the street from a busy pier.

He never said anything about them living on the water.

"Home sweet home," he said, zooming past a couple dozen cars that looked just as classy as his, then he whipped into a spot right next to the elevator.

She peered out the window. "So this is it?"

"This is the place." He opened his door and stuck one foot out.

"What floor do we live on?"

"The top."

"What floor is that?"

"Six." He paused a second and asked, "Would you like to go up?"

She did and she didn't. She had been anticipating this day for what felt like ages, but now that she was here, back to her old life, she was terrified. What if she didn't remember? What if the memories never resurfaced? Who would she be?

Stop being such a baby, she chastised herself. Like Dr. Nelson had reminded her the day she was discharged, it was just going to take time and she would have to be patient. No matter what happened up there, whether she remembered or not, it was going to be okay. She was a fighter.

She turned to Ash and flashed him a shaky smile. "I'm ready."

She got out and waited by the elevator while Ash collected their bags from the trunk. He pushed the button for the elevator and it immediately opened. They stepped inside and he slipped a key in a lock on the panel, then hit the button for the top floor.

"Does everyone need a key?" she asked.

He shook his head. "Only our floor."

She wondered why, and how many other condos were on the top floor. She was going to ask, but the movement of the elevator made her so dizzy it was all she could do to stay upright. Besides, as the elevator came to a stop and the doors slid open, she got her answer.

They stepped off the elevator not into a hallway, but in a small vestibule in front of a set of double doors. Doors that led directly into their condo! They weren't a condo on the sixth floor. They *were* the sixth floor, and what she saw inside when he unlocked the door literally took her breath away. The entire living area—kitchen, dining room and family room—was one huge open space with a ceiling two stories high, bordered by a wall of windows that overlooked the ocean.

The floors were mahogany, with a shine so deep she could see herself in it. The kitchen looked ultramodern and she was guessing it had every device and gadget on the market. The furniture looked trendy but comfortable, and everything, from the oriental rugs to light fixtures, screamed top-of-the-line.

For a second she just stood there frozen, wondering if, as some sick joke, he'd taken her to someone else's condo. If they really lived here, how could she *not* remember it?

Ash set the bags on the floor and dropped his keys on a trendy little drop-leaf table beside the door. He started to walk toward the kitchen, but when he realized she wasn't moving, he stopped and turned to her. "Are you coming in?"

"You told me you do okay," she said, and at his confused look she added, "financially. But you do *way* better than okay, don't you?"

He grinned and said, "A little bit better than okay."

Her fiancé was loaded. She lived in a loft condo over-looking the ocean. It was almost too much to take in all at once. "Why didn't you tell me?"

He shrugged. "It just didn't seem that important. And I didn't want to overwhelm you."

"Oh, awesome idea, because I'm not the least bit overwhelmed *now!*" She was so freaked out she was practically hyperventilating.

"I take it nothing looks familiar."

"Curiously, no. And you'd think I would have remembered *this*."

"Why don't I show you around?"

She nodded and followed him to the kitchen, looking out the bank of windows as they passed, and the view was so breathtaking she had to stop. She could see sailboats and ships on the water and they had a phenomenal view of the Bay Bridge.

Ash stepped up behind her. "Nice view, huh?"

"It's…*amazing*."

"That's why I bought this place. I always wanted a place by the water."

"How long have you lived here?"

"I bought it after the divorce was final. Right before we met. You've lived here almost as long as I have. You've always said that your favorite room is the kitchen."

She could see why. The cabinets had a mahogany base with frosted glass doors; the countertops were black granite. All the appliances, even the coffeemaker, were stainless steel and it looked as functional as it was aesthetically pleasing. "Do I cook?"

"You're an excellent cook."

She hoped that was one of those things that just came naturally.

There was a laundry room and half bath behind the kitchen, then they moved on to the bedrooms, which were sectioned off on the right side of the loft. Three huge rooms, each with its own full bath and an enormous walk-in closet. He used one as a home office, one was the master, and the third he told her was hers.

"We don't share?" she asked, trying hard to disguise her disappointment.

"Well, you've always used this as an office and kept your clothes and things in here. I just figured that until things settle down, maybe you should sleep here, too."

But what if she wanted to sleep with him?

He's only thinking of your health, she assured herself. She knew that if they slept in the same bed they would be tempted to do things that she just was not ready for. Look what had happened in the hotel. And last night she had wanted so badly to climb out of her own bed and slip into his.

She walked over to the closet and stepped inside, looking at all of her belongings. She ran her hands over the shirts and slacks and dresses, feeling the soft, expensive fabrics, disheartened by how unfamiliar it all was.

"Well?" Ash asked, leaning in the closet doorway, looking so casually sexy in faded jeans and an untucked, slightly rumpled polo shirt, his hair stilled mussed from driving with the windows down, that she had the bone-deep feeling that as long as they had each other, everything would be okay.

"They're nice clothes, but I don't recognize them."

"It'll come to you, just—"

"Be patient, I know. I'm trying."

"What are you planning to do now?"

"Look through my things, I guess. It's weird, but it feels almost like I'll be snooping."

"If it's okay with you," he said, "I'm going to go to the office for a while."

They'd barely been back ten minutes and already he was going to leave her alone? "But we just got here."

"I know, but I'll only be a couple of hours," he assured her. "You'll be fine. Why don't you relax and take some time familiarizing yourself with the condo. And you look like you could use a nap."

She didn't want him to go, but he had sacrificed so much already for her. It was selfish to think that he didn't deserve to get back to his life. And hadn't the doctor suggested she try to get back into her regular routine as soon as possible?

"You're right," she told Ash. "I'll be fine."

"Get some rest. Oh, and don't forget that you're supposed to make an appointment with that new doctor. The card is in your purse."

"I'll do it right away."

He leaned forward and kissed her on the forehead, a soft and lingering brush of his lips, then he turned to leave.

"Ash?"

He turned back. "Yeah?"

"Thank you. For everything. I probably haven't said that enough. I know it's been a rough week, and you've been wonderful."

"I'm just glad to have you home," he said. He flashed her one last sweet smile, then disappeared from sight. Not a minute later she heard the jingle of his car keys, then the sound of the door opening and closing, then silence.

As promised, the first thing she did was fish the doctor's card from her purse and called to make the appointment. It was scheduled for Friday of that week, three days away at nine in the morning. Ash would have to drive her of course, which would mean him taking even more time off work. Maybe he could just drop her off and pick her up. She wondered if it was close to his work. The receptionist spouted off cross streets and directions, none of which Melody recognized, but she dutifully jotted them down for Ash.

With that finished, she stepped back into her bedroom, wondering what she should investigate first. There was a desk and file cabinet on one side of the room, and a chest of drawers on the other. But as her eyes swept over the bed, she was overcome by a yawn so deep that tears welled in her eyes.

Maybe she should rest first, then investigate, she thought, already walking to the bed. She pulled down the covers and slipped between sheets so silky soft she longed to shed all of her clothes, but this was going to be a short rest, not a full-blown nap.

But the second her head hit the pillow she was sound asleep.

Despite how many times Ash reminded himself what Melody had done to him, she was starting to get under his skin. He was sure that going to work, getting back to his old routine, would put things in perspective. Instead, as he rode the elevator up to the sixth floor, his shoulders sagged with the weight of his guilt.

Maybe it was wrong to leave Melody alone so soon. Would it have really been so terrible waiting until tomorrow to return to work? But he'd felt as though he desperately needed time away, if only a few hours, to get her off his mind. Only now that he was gone, he felt so bad for leaving, she was all he could think about.

Damned if he did, damned if he didn't.

The halls were deserted as he stepped off the elevator, but when he entered his outer office his secretary, Rachel, who'd single-handedly held his professional life together this week, jumped from her chair to greet him.

"Mr. Williams! You're back! I thought we wouldn't see you until tomorrow." She walked around her desk to give him a warm hug. He wouldn't ordinarily get physically affectionate with his subordinates, especially a woman. But considering she was pushing sixty and happily married with three kids and half a dozen grandchildren, he wasn't worried. Besides, she was sometimes more of a mother figure than a secretary. She reminded him of his own mother in many ways, of what she might have been like if she'd lived. However, no matter how many times he'd asked, she refused to address him by his first name. She was very old-fashioned that way. She had been with Maddox *long* before he came along, and probably knew more about the business than most of the hotshots working there.

"I decided to come in for a few hours, to catch up on things," he told her.

Rachel backed away, holding him at arm's length. "You look tired."

"And you look gorgeous. Is that a new hairstyle?"

She rolled her eyes at his less-than-subtle dodge. He knew as well as she did that her hair hadn't changed in twenty years. "How is Melody?"

"On the mend. She should be back to her old self in no time."

"I'm so glad to hear that. Send her my best."

"I will." Rachel knew Melody had been in an accident, but not the severity of it, or that she had amnesia. There would be too many questions that Ash just didn't have the answers to.

It was best he kept Melody as far removed from his life as he could, so the inevitable breakup wouldn't cause more than a minor ripple.

When rumors of her leaving the first time had circulated, the compassionate smiles and looks of pity were excruciating. He didn't appreciate everyone sticking their noses in his personal life, when it was no one else's business.

Rachel looked him up and down, one brow raised. "Did someone make it casual day and forget to tell me?"

He chuckled. "Since I'm not officially here, I thought I could get away with it."

"I'll let it slide this one time." She patted his shoulder. "Now, you go sit down. Coffee?"

"That would be fantastic. Thanks." He was so zonked that if he were to put his head down on his desk he would go out like a light. He'd slept terrible last night, knowing that Mel was just a few feet away in the next bed, naked. It only made matters worse that she insisted on walking around the room naked beforehand.

While Rachel fetched his coffee, Ash walked into his office. It was pretty much the way he'd left it, except his inbox had multiplied exponentially in size. He was going to have to stay all weekend playing catch-up. Just as he settled into his chair Rachel returned with his coffee and a pastry.

"I know you prefer to avoid sweets, but you looked as if you could use the sugar."

"Thanks, Rachel." He'd been eating so terribly the past week that one little Danish wasn't going to make much difference. Kind of like throwing a deck chair off the Titanic. Thankfully the hotel in Abilene had had a fitness room, and he'd used it faithfully each morning before he left for the hospital.

"I there anything else?" she asked.

He sipped his coffee and shook his head. "I'm good."

"Buzz if you need me," she said, then left his office, shutting the door behind her.

Ash sighed, gazing around the room, feeling conflicted. He loved his job, and being here usually brought him solace, yet now he felt as if there were somewhere else he should be instead.

With Melody, of course. All the more reason not to go home.

Ash picked up the pastry and took a bite. Someone knocked on his door, then it opened and Flynn stuck his head in.

"I see our wandering CFO had finally returned to the flock. You got a minute?"

Ash's mouth was full so he gestured Flynn in. He swallowed and said, "I'm not officially back until tomorrow, so I'm not really here."

"Gotcha." He made himself comfortable in the chair opposite his desk. "So, after you left so abruptly last week I tried to pump Rachel for information but she clammed up on me. I even threatened to fire her if she didn't talk and she said this place would tank without her."

"It probably would," Ash agreed.

"Which is why she's still sitting out there and I'm in here asking you why you disappeared. I know your parents are dead, and you never mentioned any relatives, so it can't be that. I'm guessing it had something to do with Melody." He paused then said, "Of course you can tell me to go to hell and mind my own business."

He could, and it was tempting, but Ash figured he owed Flynn an explanation. Not only was Flynn his boss, he was a friend. However, he had to be careful to edit the content. Maddox had some very conservative clients. Conservative, *multimillion-dollar* clients. If rumors began to circulate that his mistress of three years left him because she was carrying another man's love-child, it would only be a matter of time before word made it to someone at Golden Gate Promotions, who wouldn't hesitate to use it against Maddox.

Not that he believed Flynn would deliberately do anything to jeopardize the success of the company his own father built from the ground up, but despite the best of intentions, things had a way of slipping out. Like the affair that Brock, Flynn's brother, was rumored to be having with his assistant. Brock and Elle probably never intended that to get out either.

It just wasn't worth the risk.

"I found her," Ash told Flynn.

"You told me you weren't even going to look."

"Yeah, well, after a few weeks, when she didn't come crawling back to me begging forgiveness, I got...concerned. So I hired a P.I."

"So where was she?"

"In a hospital in Abilene, Texas."

His brow dipped low over his eyes. "A hospital? Is she okay?"

Ash told him the whole story. The accident, the drug-induced coma, all the time he spent by her bedside, then having to drive home because she couldn't fly.

Flynn shook his head in disbelief. "I wish you would have said something. Maybe there was a way we could have helped."

"I appreciate it, but really, there was nothing you could have done. She just needs time to heal."

"Is she back home with you now?"

"Yeah, we got back today."

"So, does this mean you guys are…back together?"

"She's staying with me while she recovers. After that…" He shrugged. "We'll just have to wait and see."

"This is probably none of my business, but did she tell you why she left?"

"It's…complicated."

Flynn held up a hand. "I get it, back off. Just know that I'm here if you need to talk. And if you need anything, Ash, anything at all, just say the word. Extra vacation days, a leave of absence, you name it and it's yours. I want to do anything I can to help."

He wouldn't be taking Flynn up on that. The idea of spending another extended amount of time away from work, stuck in his condo, just him and Melody, made his chest feel tight. "Thanks, Flynn, I appreciate it. We both do."

After he was gone Ash sat at his desk replaying the conversation in his head. He hadn't lied to Flynn; he'd just left out a few facts. For Flynn's own good, and the good of the company.

His mom used to tell him that good intentions paved the way to hell, and Ash couldn't escape the feeling sometimes that maybe he was already there.

Eight

Melody's quick rest turned into an all-day affair. She roused at seven-thirty when Ash got back feeling more tired than before, with a blazing headache to boot. After feeling so good the day before, the backslide was discouraging. Ash assured her that it was probably just the lingering aftereffects of the barometer and temperature change going from Texas to California, and she hoped he was right.

She popped two painkillers then joined him at the dining-room table in her sleep-rumpled clothes and nibbled on a slice of the pizza he'd brought home with him. She had hoped they could spend a few hours together, but the pills seemed to hit her especially hard. Despite sleeping most of the day, she could barely hold her head up. At one point she closed her eyes, for what she thought was just a second, but the next thing she knew Ash was nudging her awake.

"Let's get you into bed," he said, and she realized that he had already cleared the table and put the pizza away.

Melody stood with his help and let him lead her to the bedroom. She crawled in bed, clothes and all, and only vaguely recalled feeling him pull the covers up over her and kiss her forehead.

When she woke the next morning she felt a million times better. Her head still hurt, but the pain was mild, and her stomach howled to be fed. Wearing the same clothes as yesterday, her hair a frightening mop that she twisted and fastened in place with a clip she found under the bathroom sink, she wandered out of her bedroom in search of Ash, but he had already left for work.

The coffee in the pot was still warm so she poured herself a cup and put it in the microwave to heat, finding that her fingers seemed to know exactly what buttons to push, even though she had no memory of doing it before. While she waited she fixed herself something to eat. She spent a good forty minutes on the couch, devouring cold pizza, sipping lukewarm coffee and watching an infomercial advertising some murderously uncomfortable looking contraption of spandex and wire that when worn over the bra was designed to enhance the breasts and improve posture. She couldn't imagine ever being so concerned about the perkiness of her boobs that she would subject herself to that kind of torture.

She also wondered, if she'd never gone to Texas, and the accident hadn't happened, what she would be doing right now? Would she be sprawled on the couch eating leftovers or out doing something glamorous like meeting with her personal trainer or getting her legs waxed?

Or would she be in class? It was only mid-April so the semester wouldn't be over yet. She wondered, when and if she got her memory back, if they would let her make up the time and work she'd missed or if she would have to go back and take the classes over again. If she even wanted to go back, that was. The law still held little interest, but that could change. And what if it didn't? What then?

Worrying about it was making her head hurt, so she pushed it out of her mind. She got up, put her dirty dishes in the dishwasher alongside Ash's coffee cup and cereal bowl, then went to take a long, hot shower. She dried off with a soft, oversize, fluffy blue towel, then stood naked in her closet trying to decide what to wear. Much like the bras she had packed for her trip, everything she owned seemed to be a push-up or made of itchy lace—or both. Didn't she own any no-nonsense, comfortable bras?

It gave her the inexplicable feeling that she was rummaging through someone else's wardrobe.

She found a drawer full of sport bras that would do until she could get to the store and put one on. Maybe she'd liked those other bras before, and maybe she would again someday, but for now they just seemed uncomfortable and impractical. The same went for all the thong, lace underwear. Thank goodness she had a few silk and spandex panties, too.

She was so used to lying around in a hospital gown that the designer-label clothes lining her closet seemed excessive when all she planned to do was hang out at home, but after some searching she found a pair of black cotton yoga pants and a Stanford University sweatshirt that had been washed and worn to within an inch of its life.

Since she was already in the closet, she decided that would be the place to start her search for memory-jogging paraphernalia. But around ten, when Ash called to check on her, nothing she'd found held any significance. Just the typical stuff you would find in any woman's closet. She wondered if she was trying too hard. If she stopped thinking about it, maybe it would just come to her. But the thought of sitting around doing nothing seemed totally counterproductive.

Refusing to let herself get frustrated, she searched her desk next. She found papers in her hand that she had no recollection of writing, and an envelope of photos of herself and Ash, most in social settings. She'd hoped maybe there would be letters or a diary but there were none.

In the file cabinet she found pages and pages of schoolwork and other school-related papers, but nothing having to do with any specific research she'd been working on. In the very back of the drawer she found an unmarked file with several DVDs inside. Most were unmarked, but one had a handwritten label marked *Ash's Birthday*. Video of a birthday party maybe? Home videos could jog a memory, right?

Full of excitement and hope, she grabbed the file and dashed out to the family room to the enormous flat-screen television. It took her a few minutes just to figure out how to turn everything on, and which remote went with which piece of equipment. When the disk was in and loaded she sat on the couch and hit Play…and discovered in the first two seconds that this was no ordinary birthday party. At least, not the kind they would invite other people to. For starters, they were in bed…and in their underwear. Those didn't stay on for long though.

This was obviously one of those videos that Ash had mentioned. Although, at the time, she had half believed he was joking. She felt like a voyeur, peeking through a window at another woman's private life. The things she was doing to him, the words coming out of her mouth, made her blush furiously, but she was too captivated to look away. Was this the kind of thing Ash was going to expect when they made love? Because she wasn't sure if she even knew how to be that woman anymore. She was so blatantly sexy and confident.

Melody hated her for it, and desperately wanted to *be* her.

When the DVD ended she grabbed one of the unmarked DVDs and put it in the player. It was similar to the first one, starting out with the two of them in bed together. But this time after a bit of foreplay she reached over somewhere out of the camera's view, and came back with four crimson silk scarves that she used to tie a very willing Ash to the head and footboard.

Watching this DVD she discovered just how flexible she actually was. Physically and sexually. It was sexy and adventurous, and in a lot of ways fun, but it occurred to her as it ended that she wasn't particularly turned on. More curious than aroused. Not that she didn't enjoy seeing Ash naked. His body was truly a work of art. Long and lean and perfect in every way. It was the sex itself that was, she hated to admit, a little…boring.

She grabbed a third disk and put it in, and as it began to play she could tell right away that it was different. This one was set in Ash's bathroom, and he was filming her through the clear glass shower door. She was soaping herself up, seemingly lost in thought. He said her name, and when she turned she looked genuinely surprised to see him standing there holding the camera. After that he must have put the camera on a tripod because he came from behind it, already beautifully naked, and climbed in the stall with her, leaving the door open.

The tone of this video was completely different from the others. They soaped each other up, touching and stroking, as if they had all the time in the world. And unlike the others there was a lot of kissing in this one. Deep, slow, tender kisses that had Melody's attention transfixed to screen, actually licking her lips, wishing she could taste Ash there.

Missing was the sense of urgency, as if it were a race to see who could get who off first. Instead they took their time exploring and caressing, their arousal gradually escalating, until they both seemed to lose themselves. It was like watching a totally different couple, and this was a woman she could definitely imagine being. A woman she *wanted* to be.

The first two DVDs had been sexy, but they were just sex. There didn't seem to be much emotion involved. In this one it was clear, by the way they touched, the way they looked in each other's eyes, that they had a deep emotional connection. She could *see* that they loved each other.

On the screen Ash lifted her off her feet and pressed her against the shower wall. Their eyes locked and held, and the ecstasy on their faces, the look of total rapture as he sank inside her made Melody shiver.

She *wanted* that. She wanted Ash to kiss her and touch her and make love to her. She was breathing heavily, feeling so warm and tingly between her thighs that she wished she could climb through the screen and take the other Melody's place. They were making love in the purest sense, and she couldn't help thinking that if he were here right now she would—

"This one is my favorite," someone said from behind her.

Melody shrieked in surprise and flew off the couch so fast that the remote went flying and landed with a sharp crack on the hardwood floor several feet away. She spun around and found Ash standing behind the couch, a couple of plastic grocery bags hanging from his fingers and a wry grin on his face.

"You scared me half to death!" she admonished, her

anger a flimsy veil to hide her embarrassment. But it was useless because her face was already turning twenty different shades of pink. He'd caught her watching porn. Porn that *he* was in. What could be more embarrassing? "You shouldn't sneak up on people."

"I wasn't sneaking. In fact, I wasn't being particularly quiet at all. You just didn't hear me. I guess I see why."

On the television her evil counterpart was moaning and panting as Ash rocked into her, water sluicing down their wet, soapy bodies. Melody scrambled for the remote, but it took her a few seconds of jabbing random buttons before the DVD stopped and the screen went black. When she looked back at Ash he was still wearing that wry smile.

"What are you doing home? It's only—" she looked at the clock and could hardly believe it was after three "—three-fifteen."

Had she really been watching sex videos for almost two hours?

He held up the bags. "There's nothing here to eat but pizza so I stopped at the store after a lunch meeting. So you wouldn't have to go out."

"Oh. Thank you."

She waited for a comment about her watching the video, waited for him to tease her, but instead he walked past her and carried the bags to the kitchen. It was the first time she had seen him in a suit since the day he showed up at the hospital to claim her, and, oh, man, did he look delicious. There was something undeniably sexy about an executive who shopped for groceries. Of course, as turned on as she was right now, he would look sexy in plaid polyester floods and a polka-dot argyle sweater.

"I found the DVDs in my file cabinet," she said, following him, even though he hadn't asked for an explanation, or even looked as though he expected or required one.

He set the bags on the island countertop and started unpacking them. It looked as though he had picked up the basics. Milk, eggs, bread, a gallon of orange juice, as well as two bags full of fresh fruits and vegetables.

"I didn't know what they were when I found them," she said, stepping around to put the perishables in the fridge. "I was pretty surprised when I put the first one in."

One brow rose. "The *first* one?"

God, she made it sound as if she had been sitting there watching them all day.

"The *only* one," she lied, but it was obvious he wasn't buying it. Probably because he'd seen the DVDs strewn out on the coffee table.

"Okay, maybe I watched two…"

Up the brow went again.

"…and a *half*. It would have been three if I'd finished the one I was watching when you walked in."

He seemed to find her discomfort amusing. "Mel, watch as many as you like."

She wondered if he really meant that. "It doesn't… *bother* you?"

"Why would it?" he asked, looking very *un*bothered.

"Because you're in them, and they're very… personal."

He gave her a weird look. "You're in them, too."

"Yeah, but…it doesn't *seem* like me. It's like I'm watching someone else do all those things."

"Take my word for it, it was definitely you." He emptied the last of the bags so she balled them up, shoving one inside the other, and tossed them in the recycling bin under the sink.

"So," she said, turning to him. "The shower one is your favorite?"

He grinned and nodded, and she wondered if she could talk him into re-creating it someday soon. It only seemed fair, seeing as how she could no longer remember doing it.

"It was mine, too," she said.

"Why do you suppose that is?"

"I guess because it seemed more…*real*."

That brow rose again. "Are you suggesting that in the others you were faking it?"

"No! Of course not," she said, but realized, maybe she had been. The first two had been lacking something. They seemed almost…*staged*. As if she had been putting on a show for the camera. And there was no denying that, now at least, the hot sex and dirty talk didn't do half as much for her as watching them make love.

Had she been faking it in those first two?

"You look as though you're working something through," Ash said. He was standing with his arms folded, hip wedged against the counter. He narrowed his eyes at her. "*Were* you faking it?"

She hoped not. What was the point of even having sex if she wasn't going to enjoy it? "Even if I was, I wouldn't remember. Would I?"

"That's awfully convenient."

She frowned. "No. It isn't. Not for me."

"Sorry." He reached out and touched her arm. "I didn't mean it like that."

She knew that. He was only teasing and she was being too touchy. She forced a smile. "I know you didn't. Don't worry about it." She grabbed the last of the items on the counter, opened the pantry and put them away.

Ask looked at his watch. "Damn, it's getting late, I have

to get back. Thanks for helping put away—" He frowned and said, "Wait a minute."

He walked to the fridge and opened it, scanning the inside, all the drawers and compartments, as if he'd forgotten something, then he closed the refrigerator door and looked in the cabinet under the kitchen sink. He did the same thing to the pantry, then he turned to her and asked, "Do you realize what you just did?"

Considering the look on his face, it couldn't have been good. "No. Did I put everything in the wrong place or something?"

"No. Mel, you put everything in the *right* place."

"I did?" She wanted to believe it was significant, but at the same time she didn't want to get her hopes up. "Maybe it was a coincidence?"

"I don't think so. When it comes to your kitchen you're almost fanatical about keeping things tidy and organized. Everything in there is on the correct shelf, or in the right drawer. You even put the bags in the recycling bin when we were done and I don't recall telling you it was even there."

He was right. She hadn't even thought about putting them there, she just did it. Just like the law stuff. It just came to her naturally, by doing and not thinking.

Her heart started to beat faster and happiness welled up, putting a huge lump in her throat. "You think I'm remembering?"

"I think you are."

She squealed and threw herself into his arms, hugging him tight, feeling so happy she could burst. She realized, especially after watching those DVDs, just how many things she *wanted* to remember.

She laid her head on his shoulder and closed her eyes, breathing in the scent of his aftershave. It felt so good to be close to him. Even if he wasn't hugging her back as hard as she was hugging him. "Do you think it was the DVDs? Maybe watching them made me remember the other things?"

"Maybe."

She smiled up at him. "Well, then, maybe the real thing would work even better."

He got that stern look and she quickly backpedaled. "I know, I know. I'm not ready. Yet. It was just...an observation. For when I *am* ready." Which she was thinking might be sooner than they both expected.

He smoothed her hair back from her face and pressed a kiss to her forehead. "I think, when your brain is ready to remember things, it will. I don't think you can rush it. Every time you've remembered something it's been when you weren't thinking about it. Right?"

She nodded.

"So just relax and let it happen naturally." He looked at his watch, gave her one last kiss on the forehead, and said, "Now I really have to go."

She was disappointed, but didn't let it show. "Thanks for bringing the groceries. I suppose I should think about making something for dinner."

"Don't worry about feeding me. I'll probably be home late. I have a lot of work to catch up on."

Which was her fault, so she couldn't exactly complain. She walked him to the elevator instead, watching until he stepped inside and the doors closed.

This time it was definitely not her imagination. Knowing that she was remembering things troubled him for some reason, and the only reason she could come up with was that there was something that he didn't *want* her to remember. But she had no clue why, or what it could be. She thought about the money that she'd stashed in the pocket of one of the jackets in her closet. Was that the key to all of this?

She decided that if she had any more epiphanies or memory breakthroughs it would be best, for the time being anyway, to keep them to herself.

Nine

Ash took Friday morning off so he could take Mel to her appointment with her new neurologist. She had offered to have Ash drop her off and pick her up when she was finished, so he wouldn't miss more work, but the truth was he wanted to be there to hear what the doctor had to say.

It had been eerie the other day, watching her put the groceries away, only to realize that, right before his eyes, she was becoming herself again. She was remembering, no matter how small and insignificant a memory it had been. The point was, it was happening, and he wasn't sure he was ready.

Although since then, she hadn't mentioned remembering anything new. Not that he'd been around to witness it himself. Work had kept him at the office until almost midnight the past three days so he and Mel had barely seen each other.

The doctor gave her a thorough neurological exam,

asked a couple dozen questions, and seemed impressed by her progress. He suggested that she slowly begin adding more physical activities back to her daily regimen. Mel glanced over at Ash, and he knew exactly the sort of *physical activities* she was thinking of. And he knew, the second she opened her mouth, what she was going to say.

"What about sex?" she asked.

The doctor looked down at the chart, a slight frown crinkling his brow, and for one terrifying instant Ash thought he was going to mention the miscarriage. Had Dr. Nelson warned him not to say anything? Finding out about the baby now would ruin everything.

"I see no reason why you shouldn't engage in sexual activity," he said, then added with a smile. "I would caution against anything too vigorous at first. Just take it slow and do what you're comfortable with. I also suggest walking."

"I've been doing that. We live right by the water so I've been taking walks on the shore."

"That's good. Just don't overdo it. Start at ten or fifteen minutes a day and gradually work your way up." He closed her file. "Well, everything looks good. If you have any problems, call me. Otherwise, I won't need to see you back for three months."

"That's it?" Mel asked. "We're really done?"

The doctor smiled. "At this point there isn't much I can do. But only because Dr. Nelson took very good care of you."

He shook hers and then Ash's hand, and then he left. From the time they stepped into the waiting room, the entire appointment hadn't taken more than twenty minutes.

"That sure was quick," Mel said as they walked to

the reception desk to make her next appointment. "I was expecting CAT scans and EEGs and all sorts of tests. I'd thought I'd be trapped here all day."

So had he. Now that it was out of the way he was anxious to get back to work.

He drove her home and went up with her to grab his briefcase. He planned to say a quick goodbye and head out, but he could see by her expression that she wanted to "talk" and he knew exactly what about. Honestly, he was surprised she hadn't brought it up the second they got out of the doctor's office.

"Okay, let's have it," he said, dropping his briefcase beside the couch and perching on the arm.

She smiled shyly, which was weird because Mel didn't have a shy bone in her body. Or didn't used to. He couldn't deny that he liked it a little. "So, you heard what the doctor said, about it being okay to make love."

"When you're ready," he added, hoping she didn't think they were going to throw down right here on the living-room rug. Not that he hadn't been thinking about it either, after walking in to find her watching their home movies.

She had been so transfixed by the image of the two of them in the shower that she hadn't heard him come in. He'd taken his keys from the lock and gave them an extra jingle to alert her to his presence. When that didn't work he'd shut the door with more force than necessary, but she hadn't even flinched. He'd tried rustling the plastic bags he was holding, and determined at that point that it was a lost cause. She had been so captivated, it was as if the rest of the world had ceased to exist. Then he'd stepped closer to the couch, seen the rapid rise and fall of her chest as she breathed, the blush of arousal in her cheeks. She'd clenched the edge of the couch, looking as though she were about to climb out of her own skin.

The last time he'd seen her that turned on was when they had made that DVD.

In that instant he knew he wanted her, and it was just a matter of time before he gave in and let her have her way with him. But he'd wanted to wait and make sure everything went all right with her doctor appointment. And now he'd been given a green light.

When she didn't say anything, he asked, "Do you feel like you're ready?"

She shrugged. "I don't know. I guess I won't be sure until I try."

He waited for her to suggest that they try right now, but she didn't. Instead she asked, "Are you working late again?"

"Until at least nine," he said. "Probably later."

She sighed. "I'll be really happy when you're caught up and we can actually see each other for more than ten minutes in the morning before you walk out the door. And maybe one of these days I'll actually get to make dinner for you."

"Soon," he said, not sure if that was a promise he could, or *wanted*, to keep. He needed to keep some distance between them.

He waited for her to bring up the subject of sex again, but surprisingly, she didn't. "Anything else before I go?" he asked.

She shook her head. "I don't think so."

Oookay. With affirmation from the doctor, he expected her to all but throw herself at him. Why was she acting so…timid?

He walked to the door and she followed him. "Call me later and I'll try to wait up for you," she said.

"I will." He leaned down to brush a kiss to her cheek, but this time she turned her head and it was her lips he touched instead. He had kissed Mel at least a million times before, but this time when their lips met he felt it like an electric charge. Her sudden sharp intake of breath told him that she'd felt it, too. They stood that way for several seconds, frozen, their lips barely touching. He waited for her to make her move, but after several seconds passed and she didn't move, didn't even breathe as far as he could tell, he took matters into his own hands. He leaned in first, pressing his lips to hers.

Her lips were warm and soft and familiar and she still tasted like toothpaste. He waited for her to launch herself at him, to dive in with her usual enthusiasm, to ravage him with the deep, searching, desperate kisses that sometimes made him feel as though she wanted to swallow him whole.

But she didn't. In fact it took several seconds before he felt her lips part, and she did it hesitantly, as if she was afraid to push too far too fast. Even when their tongues touched it wasn't more than a tentative taste.

He'd never kissed her this way before, so tender and sweet. She didn't dive in with gusto, in what he had to admit sometimes felt more like an oral assault than a kiss. Not that it wasn't hot as hell, but this was nice, too. In fact, he liked this a lot.

It was so different, so *not* Melody. Even though he'd sworn to himself that he'd take this slow, he let himself be drawn in. Let her drag him down into something warm and sexy and satisfying.

He realized something else was different, too. Melody always wore perfume or body spray. The same musky, sensual fragrance that at times could be a touch cloying. Now the only detectable scent was a hint of soap and shampoo intermingled with the natural essence of her skin and her hair. Honestly, it was sexier and more arousing than anything she could find in a bottle.

And he was aroused, he realized. He was erect to the point of discomfort and aching for release. If her labored breathing and soft whimpers were any indication, he wouldn't have to wait long.

He deepened the kiss and her tongue tangled with his, and she tasted so delicious, felt so good melting against him, he was the one who wanted to ravish her. He had promised himself that he would make her wait a little longer, draw out the anticipation for another day or two, until he really had her crawling out of her skin, but at that precise moment, he didn't give a damn what he'd promised himself. He wanted her *now*.

Just as he was ready to make the next move, take it to the next level, he felt Mel's hands on his chest applying gentle but steady pressure, and he realized that she was pushing him away.

He broke the kiss and reluctantly backed off. "What's wrong?"

Melody's cheeks were deep red and he could see her pulse fluttering wildly at the base of her neck. She smiled up at him and said, a little breathlessly, "That was amazing. But I think it's all I can handle right now."

All she could *handle?* Was she kidding? Once Mel got started she was unstoppable. Now she was actually stopping him?

Ash was so stunned by her sudden change of heart that he wasn't sure how to act or what to say to her. She had never told him no. In fact, since he met her, he couldn't recall a time when he'd even had to *ask* for sex. She was usually the aggressor, and she had an insatiable appetite. There were even times when he wished they could take a day or two off.

Now, for the first time in three years, he wanted something that he couldn't have.

It was a sobering realization.

"I'm sorry," she said, and he realized she was gazing up at him, looking apologetic. "I just don't want to rush things. I want to take it slow, just like you said."

For a second he had to wonder if this was some sort of twisted game. Get him all hot and bothered then say no. But the thought was fleeting because the Melody gazing up at him wasn't capable of that kind of behavior. He was the one who had all but scolded her for touching him in the hotel room, the one who kept saying that they should take it slowly.

If anyone was playing games, he was, and he was getting exactly what he deserved.

"Are you okay?" she asked, her mouth pulled into a frown. "Are you upset with me?"

He desperately wished she was the old Melody again, so he could use this opportunity to hurt her. But in his mind they had inexplicably split into two separate and distinct people. The good Mel, and the evil Mel. And he knew that he couldn't hurt this Melody.

Jesus, he was whipped. He'd gone and let her get under his skin. The *one* thing he swore he wouldn't do.

"No," he said, pulling her into his arms and holding her. "I'm not upset. Not at all."

May as well enjoy it while it lasted, he thought, as she snuggled against him, burying her face in the crook of his neck. He knew, with her memory slowly returning, it was only a matter of time before the evil Mel was back and the good Mel was lost forever.

It was inevitable, but damn, was he going to miss her.

Leaving Mel and going in to work had been tough, but not as tough as it would have been staying with her. Sex had been the furthest thing from his mind the past couple weeks, but now, after one damned kiss, it seemed it was all he could think about. As a result, he was having one hell of a time concentrating on work.

He took an early lunch, early being noon instead of two or three, and though he didn't normally drink during work hours, he made an exception and ordered a scotch on the rocks. It helped a little.

On his way back to his office he ran into Brock Maddox.

"I was just going to call you," Brock said. "Can I have a quick word?"

"Of course."

He gestured Ash to his office, and when they were inside he closed the door and said, "Flynn told me what happened with Melody. I wanted you to know how sorry I am."

"Thanks. But she's actually doing really well. She had an appointment with her neurologist today and everything looks good."

"I'm relieved to hear it."

"Was that all?" Ash asked, moving toward the door.

"There's one more thing. As you've probably heard, we didn't get the Brady account."

"I heard." Brady Enterprises was a fairly large account, and the fact that they didn't get it was unfortunate, but Ash wasn't sure if it warranted the grim look Brock was wearing. As CFO, Ash knew they were financially sound with or without Brady.

"They hired Golden Gate Promotions," Brock told him.

"I heard that, too." It was never fun to lose, especially to a direct competitor, especially one as cocky and arrogant as Athos Koteas, but obviously Golden Gate pitched them an idea, and a budget, they couldn't refuse.

"Did you hear that they low-balled us out of the deal?" Brock asked, and when Ash opened his mouth to respond, he added, "Using a pitch that was almost identical to ours."

"What?"

"That's more the reaction I was hoping for."

"Where did you hear this?"

"I have an acquaintance over at Brady and she clued me in. She said it was even suggested that Maddox was stealing pitch ideas."

"Are we?"

The question seemed to surprise Brock. "Hell, no! That was *our* idea."

"So, how did Golden Gate manage to pitch the same thing? Coincidence?"

"Highly unlikely. The only explanation is that someone here leaked it."

If that was true, they had a serious problem. "What does Flynn think of this?"

"I didn't tell him yet."

As vice president, Flynn should have been told about this immediately. "You don't think he needs to know?"

"I wanted to talk to you first."

"Why? As CFO, this really isn't my area of expertise."

"Look, Ash, I'm not sure how to say this, so I'm just going to say it. You know that I've always liked Melody, but is it possible that she could have had anything to do with this?"

The question was so jarring, so out-of-the-blue unexpected, it actually knocked Ash back a step or two. *"Melody?* What would she have to do with this?"

"It just seems coincidental that right around the time we started laying out the framework for the pitch, meetings you were in on, she disappeared. I would understand completely if maybe you went home and mentioned things to her, never suspecting that she would leak it to our competitor. Maybe they made her an offer she couldn't refuse."

Ash's hands curled into fists at his sides, and had he been standing within arm's reach, he might have actually slugged Brock. "The idea that you would accuse Melody of all people of corporate espionage is the most ridiculous, not to mention *insulting,* thing I've ever heard."

"Considering the way she took off, it just seemed a plausible scenario."

"Yeah, well, you are *way* off base," Ash said, taking a step toward him, all but daring him to disagree.

Brock put his hands up in a defensive posture and said, "Whoa, take it easy, Ash. I apologize for offending you, but put yourself in my position for a minute. Like I said, I *had* to ask. There's a rumor that she didn't leave on the best of terms, so I figured—"

"So we're listening to rumors now? So should I assume that you're screwing your assistant?"

Brock's brow dipped in anger and Ash had the distinct feeling he'd taken this argument a step too far, then Brock's attention shifted to the door.

"Mother, would it really be too much for you to knock before you enter a room?"

Ash turned to see Carol Maddox standing in the now-open doorway. Small and emaciated but a force to be reckoned with nonetheless. And oh, man, she didn't look pleased. Of course, as long as Ash had known her, disappointment and contempt were the only two expressions that had ever made it through the Botox. In fact, he couldn't recall a single incidence when he'd seen her smile. She was probably one of the unhappiest, nastiest people he'd ever met, and seemed hell-bent on taking everyone else down with her.

"I need to have a word with you, dear," she said through gritted teeth, or maybe the Botox had frozen her jaw. Either way, she looked royally pissed off and Ash was in no mood to get caught in the crosshairs.

"I take it we're finished here," he said, and Brock nodded curtly.

As Ash sidestepped around Mrs. Maddox to get to the door, he almost felt guilty. The remark about Brock sleeping with Elle didn't seem to go over well with good ol' mom. But that was what he got for accusing Melody of all people of leaking company secrets.

Even if Ash had told her about the campaign—which he definitely hadn't—she was not the type to go selling the information to Maddox's rival. And somewhere deep down he would always resent Brock for even suggesting that she would.

Wait a minute...

He gave himself a mental shake. Wasn't he being a touch hypocritical? Why was he so dead set on defending the honor of a woman he planned to use, then viciously dump? This was the evil Mel they were talking about, right?

Because, although she may have betrayed Ash's trust, it would be against everything he believed to castigate someone for something they didn't do. And for this, she was completely innocent.

When he reached his office Rachel greeted him anxiously. "Oh, *there* you are. I've been calling you. Miss Trent called."

"Sorry, I forgot my cell in my desk. What did she want?"

"She said she needed to talk to you and she sounded frantic. *Completely* unlike herself. She asked to have you call her immediately on her cell phone."

Melody *wasn't* the frantic type, and that alone alarmed him. "Did she say why?"

"No. But I'm worried. She acted as if she'd never spoken to me before."

That was because, as far as she knew, she never had. "I'll call her right away."

He stepped into his office, shut the door and dialed her cell. She answered before it even had time to ring on his end, and the stark fear in her voice made his heart drop.

"Ash?"

"It's me. What's wrong?"

"I need you to come get me," she said, her voice quivering so hard he could barely understand her. His first thought was that maybe something had happened and she needed to be taken to the hospital.

"Are you hurt? Did you hit your head?"

"No, I just need a ride," she said, then he heard the sound of traffic in the background and realized that she must not be at home. She'd said something about taking a walk when he left for work. Had she maybe walked too far and couldn't make it back on her own?

"Mel, where are you?"

"The Hyde Street Pier."

The Hyde Street Pier? That was *way* the hell across town from their condo. There was no way she could have walked that far. "How did you get over there?"

"Can you just come?" she asked, sounding desperate.

"Of course. I'm leaving right now. I'm ten minutes away."

"I'll be in front of the Maritime store right on the corner."

Ash hung up the phone, grabbed his keys from his desk drawer, and as he passed Rachel's desk he said, "I have to run out for a while. I'll try to make it back this afternoon."

"Is everything okay?" she asked, looking concerned.

"I'm not sure." But he was about to find out.

Ten

Melody didn't have to remember her past to know that she had never felt so stupid or humiliated in her *entire* life.

She sat in the passenger seat of Ash's car, wringing her hands in her lap, wishing she could make herself invisible. At least she'd stopped trembling, and now that her heart rate had slowed her head had stopped hurting, and she wasn't dizzy anymore either. That didn't stop her from feeling like a total idiot.

"Are you ready to tell me what happened?" Ash asked gently, looking away from the road for a second to slide her a sideways glance.

"You're going to think I'm stupid," she said.

"I won't think you're stupid." He reached over and pried one hand free and curled it under his. "I'm just glad you're okay. You scared me."

She bit her lip.

"Come on, Mel."

"I got lost," she said quickly, immediately wishing she could take it back. But he didn't chastise or make fun of her, not that she thought he would. It didn't make her feel any less like a dope though. And to his credit, he sat there silently waiting for her to elaborate, not pushing at all.

"Remember I said I was going to take a walk?"

He nodded.

"Well, I felt so good, so full of energy, I guess I over-estimated my endurance a bit. I got about a mile and a half from home—"

"A mile and a half?" His eyes went wide. *"Mel!"*

"I know, but it felt so good to be in the fresh air, and it was mostly downhill. But then I started to get *really* tired, and the way back was all *up*hill. I knew I wouldn't be able to make it back, so I got on a bus."

"You knew which bus to take?"

"I thought I did. Unfortunately it was the wrong bus. It took me in the opposite direction of home, and by the time I figured it out I was *really* far. So I got off at the next stop and got on a different bus, but that one was going the wrong direction, too. It was such a strange sensation, like I knew deep down that I should know which bus to take, but I kept picking the wrong one."

"Why didn't you ask someone for help?"

"I was too embarrassed. Besides, I felt like I needed to do it on my own."

"And they say men never ask for directions," he said, rolling his eyes, and she couldn't help but crack a smile.

"I rode around for a couple of hours," she continued, "and finally got off at the pier. I had absolutely no idea where I was. I could have been in China for all I knew. Nothing looked familiar. And I guess…I guess I just freaked out. My heart was racing and I had this tightness in my chest, like I was having a heart attack. Then my hands started going numb and I felt like I was going to pass out and that *really* scared me. That's when I called you."

"It sounds like you had a panic attack. I used to get the same thing when I was a kid, when I went in for my treatments."

"Treatments?" she asked.

He paused for a second, then said, "Radiation."

She frowned. "Radiation? What for?"

"Osteosarcoma," he said, then glanced over and added, "Bone cancer."

He had cancer? She'd had no idea. Well, she probably *did,* she just didn't remember. "I know I've probably asked you this before, but when?"

"I was twelve."

"Where was it?"

"My femur."

"How long were you—"

"Not long. Eight months, give or take. They caught it early at my annual physical. A round of radiation and chemo and I was fine."

She was pretty sure it hadn't been as simple as he made it sound. Especially if he had been having panic attacks. "Do you worry... I mean, could it...come back?"

"If it was going to come back it would have a long time ago." He glanced over at her. "If you're worried I'm going to get sick and die on you, I'm probably more likely to be hit by a bus."

"I didn't mean that. I just...I don't know what I meant. The question just popped out. I'm sorry."

He squeezed her hand. "It's okay."

She could see that it was a touchy subject and she didn't want to push it. She just hoped he didn't think that it would ever stop her from marrying him. She was in this for the long haul, until death do them part and all that. And speaking of marriage…

"I was wondering," she said. "Is there a reason you wouldn't tell people at work that we're engaged?"

His shot a glance her way. "Why do you ask?"

"Well, when I called your office, and your secretary asked who it was, I said Ash's fiancée, and she sounded really confused."

"What did she say?"

"She said, *Ash's what?* and I said, *Ash's fiancée, Melody.* I got the distinct impression that she had no idea we were engaged."

"We just haven't officially announced it," he said. "I asked right before you left on your trip, then you didn't come back…." He shrugged.

"So you didn't say anything to anyone."

"It was the last thing on my mind."

"Well, I guess that explains the pictures and the videos."

"What about them?"

"I noticed that I wasn't wearing my engagement ring in a single one. So now I know why."

Melody looked over at him and Ash had a strange look on his face, as if he felt sick to his stomach or something.

"Is it okay that I said something to her? I mean, we have no reason not to announce it now. Right?"

"I've just been so swamped since we've been back, with everything at work, and the doctor's office. The truth is, it completely slipped my mind."

"But it is okay."

He smiled and squeezed her hand again. "Of course."

"Oh, good," she said, feeling relieved. "Since I kind of

already did. To your secretary anyway. Do you think we should plan some sort of engagement party? Or at least call the wedding planner?"

"I think you shouldn't worry about it until you've had more time to heal. There's no rush. Look at what happened today when you got too stressed."

He was right. She knew he was. It was just that she felt this need to get on with her life. This deep-seated urgency to move forward.

Give it time, she told herself. *Eventually you'll be yourself again.*

When they got back to their building, instead of pulling into the underground lot he stopped at the front entrance.

"You have your key?" he asked.

She pulled it from her jacket pocket and jingled it in front of him. "You're not coming up?"

"I really need to get back. You're okay now, right?"

Sort of, but she wasn't exactly looking forward to being alone. But she couldn't be selfish. "I'm okay. Maybe I'll take a nap."

"I'll call you later." He leaned over and kissed her, but not on the cheek or forehead. This time he went straight for her lips. He brushed them softly with his, and she could swear her already shaky knees went a little bit weaker.

"I'll see you later." She got out and shut the door and watched him zip down the block and around the corner. Incidentally, she didn't see him later. Well, not for more than a few seconds when he roused her with a kiss and said good-night.

From the light in the hallway she could see that he was still in his suit, and he had that fresh-from-the-office smell clinging to his clothes, so she knew he had just gotten home. She peered at the clock and saw that it was after midnight.

At least tomorrow was Saturday. They could finally spend some quality time together. Maybe they could take a walk down by the water and have a picnic lunch at the park. She wondered if they had ever done that before. She drifted off to sleep making plans, and woke at eight feeling excited.

She got dressed and as she brushed her teeth she caught the distinct aroma of coffee. She had hoped to be up first, so she could surprise him with breakfast in bed. Looked as though he didn't sleep in on the weekends.

She expected to find him in the kitchen reading the financial section, but he wasn't there. He wasn't in his bedroom either. Where had he gone?

She grabbed her cell off the counter and dialed his cell. He answered on the third ring. "Where are you?" she asked.

"Just pulling into the lot at work. I thought I would get an early start."

"It's Saturday."

"And your point is?"

"I just…I thought we could spend some time together today."

"You know I have a lot of catching up to do."

"What about tomorrow?"

"Working."

He was working on *Sunday?*

Or was he? What if all these late nights and weekends, he was actually somewhere else?

"Ash…are you having an affair?" The words jumped out before she could stop them, and the second they did she wished them back.

And Ash responded just as she would have expected.

Bitterly. "That's really something coming from…" He suddenly went dead silent, and for a second she thought the call had cut out.

"Ash, are you there?"

"Yes, I'm here, and no, I'm not having an affair. I would *never* do that to you."

"I know. I'm sorry for even suggesting it. I'm just… I guess I'm feeling insecure, and lonely. I never see you."

"I missed more than a week of work."

Which was her fault, so she shouldn't complain. That was more or less what he was saying. "I know. You know what, forget I said anything."

"Tell you what, I'll try to make it home in time for dinner tonight, okay?"

"That would be nice."

"I'll call you later and let you know for sure."

"Okay. I—I love you, Ash."

There was a sight pause, then he said, "Me, too. Talk to you later."

She disconnected, feeling conflicted, asking herself the obvious question. *Me, too?* Given the situation, wouldn't the more appropriate response be, *I love you, too?* Shouldn't he be happy that, despite technically knowing him only a couple of weeks, she knew she loved him? Or maybe he thought she was just saying it because she was supposed to. Maybe that was his way of letting her know that it was okay not to say it if she wasn't ready.

Or maybe she was just losing her mind.

She groaned and dropped her forehead against the cool granite countertop, which she realized was a really dumb move when her head began to throb.

Maybe the problem was that she just needed a purpose outside of Ash. She needed to get back to her education, back to law school. She needed a life. Maybe then she wouldn't care how little time Ash had for her.

If he really needed to be at work, why did Ash feel like such a jackass?

Mel was just going to have to learn that this was the way things were. The way it had *always* been. They had always led very separate lives. She was there when he had time for her, and when he didn't she filled her days with school and shopping. And she had never had a problem with that before.

It made sense that being stuck at home would drive her a little nuts. What she needed was a car, and her credit cards back. That should make her happy.

He rode the elevator up to his floor, feeling better about the whole situation, and wasn't surprised to see Rachel sitting there as he approached his office. She always worked half a day on Saturdays. Sometimes longer if there was a critical pitch in the works.

"G'morning, beautiful," he said and she just rolled her eyes.

"Coffee?"

"Please."

He shrugged out of his jacket and had settled behind his desk by the time she returned.

"How is Melody today?" she asked, setting his coffee in front of him.

"Better." He'd given her a very vague explanation of yesterday's event. He said only that she was out, and wasn't feeling well, and didn't think she could get back home on her own. Rachel hadn't said a word to him about his and Melody's supposed engagement. He didn't doubt that she was simply biding her time.

"I'm a little surprised to see you here," she said.

"Why? I always work Saturday."

"Well, with Melody still recovering…"

"She's okay. It's good for her to do things on her own."

Rachel shrugged and said, "If you say so." And before he could tell her to mind her own business she was gone.

Melody was a big girl, and she had always been extremely independent. Once she had a car, and money to spend, she would stop giving him a hard time.

Instead of working he spent the better part of the morning on the phone with his regular car dealership, negotiating a deal. Because he was a regular and valued customer the salesman even offered to bring the model he was interested in over for a test drive. Unfortunately they didn't have one in stock with all the options he wanted and had to ship it in from a dealership in L.A., but delivery was promised on Monday.

With that taken care of, he called to reinstate all the credit cards he'd cancelled when she left. With expedited delivery they would arrive around the same time as the car. By the time Rachel popped in at noon to let him know she was leaving, he was finally ready to start working.

"Stay home tomorrow," Rachel told him. "Melody needs you just as much as these clowns do. Probably more."

"Thanks, Dr. Phil."

She rolled her eyes and walked out.

Not ten minutes later Brock rang him.

"I need you in the conference room now," he said sternly. Considering his tone, this wasn't going to be a friendly chat, and Ash was not in the mood to get chewed out again. He couldn't even imagine what he'd done. Had Brock found something else to pin on Melody?

Dragging himself up from his desk, he headed down

the hall. The normally clear glass walls of the conference room were opaque, which in itself was not a good sign.

The door was closed, so he knocked.

"Come in," Brock snapped.

Jesus, he so didn't need this today. Ash sighed and pushed the door open, ready to tell Brock to go screw himself, and was nearly knocked backward by a roomful of people shouting, "Surprise!" at the top of their lungs.

He must have looked the part because after a beat, everyone started to laugh. They were obviously celebrating something, but he had no idea what. Had he gotten a raise that no one told him about?

On the conference table was a cake, then he noticed the hand-drawn banner draped from the ceiling.

Congratulations, Mr. Melody Trent.

Eleven

People started milling over to Ash, shaking his hand and congratulating him on his engagement. Brock and Flynn and Jason Reagert. Gavin Spencer, Celia Taylor and Celia's fiancé, Evan Reese. There were even a few public relations people, several creatives and a large group of his financial people from the fifth floor.

Everyone knew.

Dammit. So much for it not being a big stink when he dumped Melody.

Between handshakes someone stuck a drink in his hand and he took a long swallow. "You guys really didn't have to do this," he said.

"When we heard the news we knew we had to have some sort of celebration," Flynn said. "We wanted to invite Melody, but Rachel didn't think she would be feeling up to it."

Jesus, what a nightmare that would have been.

Rachel, the person he assumed was responsible for this fiasco, was on the opposite side of the room so it took him a few minutes to make his way over. When he did, she gave him a huge smile and hugged him. "Congratulations, Mr. Williams."

"You are so fired," he said, hugging her back.

She knew it was an empty threat, so she just patted his arm and said, "You're welcome."

Celia approached and handed him another drink. "I figured you could use it. I know you hate big productions like this."

"Thank you." He accepted the glass and took a long drink.

"I can't tell you how thrilled I am for the two of you," she said. "I know how hard the past couple of months have been. I'm so glad everything worked out. Have you set a date?"

He took another slug of his drink. "Not yet."

"I hope you're not planning to elope, or get hitched in Vegas. You know everyone here is expecting an invitation."

Well, then, everyone here was going to be very disappointed.

He finished his drink and someone gave him another, then someone else handed him a slice of cake. As desperately as he wanted to get the hell out of there, he was more or less stuck until the party wound down around three. And though he could have easily drunk himself into a stupor, he stopped at five scotches—although two were doubles. He wasn't drunk by any means, but tipsy enough to know he shouldn't be driving.

When everyone but the executives had cleared out, Ash figured it was finally safe to get the hell out of there. He hadn't gotten squat done. Not work anyway, and he was in no condition to go back to his office.

"I'm going to call a cab and head home," he told everyone.

"We're heading out, too," Celia said. "Why don't you let us drive you? You don't mind, do you, Evan?"

Her fiancé shrugged. "Fine with me. If you want, Celia could take you home in your car and I can follow. That way you won't have to take a cab into work."

"That would be great," Ash said.

Feeling pleasantly buzzed, he said his goodbyes to everyone else, and the three of them headed down to the parking garage.

When he and Celia were alone in the car and on their way to his condo she told him, "There's something we need to talk about."

"Is something wrong?"

"No. Everything is actually going great. But it's clear that the long-distance relationship Evan and I have is going to get tedious."

"But things are okay with you two?"

"Yeah. Things are so good, I'm moving to Seattle at the end of the year."

Ash hated to see her go, but he wasn't exactly surprised. She had fallen pretty hard for Evan. He just wanted her to be happy. "I guess this means you're leaving Maddox?"

"Technically, no. I'll be handling all of the advertising for Reese Enterprises as a consultant for Maddox. I'll just be doing it from Seattle."

"Wow, that's great."

"I told Brock and Flynn I was thinking of leaving, and they didn't want to lose me."

"That's because you've made them a lot of money. They know a good thing when they see it."

"I'm excited, but I'm going to miss everyone here."

"Who's going to take your place?"

"His name is Logan Emerson, he's going to start working with me Monday. I'll train him for a couple of weeks, then I'll be exclusively on the Reese account. I'm sure I'll be doing a lot of traveling back and forth until I make the move."

"Well, we'll miss you, but it sounds like an awesome opportunity."

They reached Ash's building and he directed her down into the parking garage, then they walked up to the street where Evan was waiting.

"Thanks for the ride," he said.

Celia smiled. "No problem. See you Monday. And say congratulations to Melody for us. We should all get together for dinner sometime, when she's feeling better."

"Definitely," he said, knowing that would never happen.

Ash waved as they drove off, then he went upstairs. The condo was quiet so he figured Mel was probably out for a walk, but then he saw her key on the counter. He walked to her room and looked in but she wasn't in bed, then he heard water turn on in her bathroom. He crossed the room, and since the bathroom door was open, he looked in.

Hot damn. Melody was in the shower.

He wondered if she might be in the mood for company. After watching her watch that video the other day, he had the feeling it could get very interesting.

He shrugged out of his jacket and tossed it on the bed, then kicked off his shoes.

He stepped into the bathroom, not being particularly stealthy, but Mel was rinsing shampoo from her hair so her head was thrown back and her eyes were closed. Suds ran down her back and the curve of her behind, and all he could think about was soaping up his hands and rubbing them all over her.

He waited for her to open her eyes, so she would see him there, but when she finally did she turned with her back to him. She grabbed a bottle of soap and poured some out into her hand then turned away from the spray and began soaping herself up. He had a fantastic profile view as she rubbed suds into breasts and her stomach and down her arms. It was far from a sensual display, but he was so hot for her, she might as well have been giving him a lap dance.

She finished her arms then her hands moved back to her breasts. She cupped them in her hands, her eyes drifting shut as she swirled her thumbs over her nipples. They hardened into two rosy pink points, and he could swear he saw her shudder.

Goddamn.

God knew he'd seen Mel touch herself before. So many times that, honestly, the novelty had sort of worn off. But this was different. Maybe because she didn't know he was watching. Because she wasn't putting on a show for him. She was doing it because it felt good.

She did seem to be enjoying it, and he was so hard his slacks were barely containing him. He watched, loosening his tie as she caressed herself. He tossed it across the back of the toilet and started unbuttoning his shirt.

Melody's hands slipped down off her breasts, then moved slowly south, stroking her hips and her stomach and the tops of her thighs. It was obvious what her final destination would be and he thought, *oh, hell, yeah.* Unfortunately she chose that moment to open her eyes and see him standing there.

She shrieked so loud he was sure the people living beneath them heard it.

"You scared me half to death!" she admonished when she realized it was just him. He half expected her to try to cover herself, but she didn't. Her cheeks did flush though. "How long have you been standing there?"

"Long enough to enjoy what I was seeing."

He could see that she was embarrassed, which made it that much more arousing.

"You know it's rude to spy on people," she said, then her hands came up to cover her breasts. "Tell me you don't have a video camera out there."

He chuckled. "No camera," he assured her, unfastening the buttons at his wrists. "And I wasn't spying, I was watching."

"Same thing."

"You make it sound like I was looking through a peephole in the wall." He tugged the shirt off and dropped it on the floor.

Mel watched it fall, and when she saw the tent in his pants her eyes grew larger. "W-what are you doing?"

He pulled his undershirt over his head and dropped that on the floor, too. "Taking off my clothes."

Her eyes strayed to his chest. He didn't think she realized it, but she was licking her lips. "Um…why?"

"So I can take a shower." He tugged off his socks then unfastened his pants and shoved them and his boxers down.

"With me?" she said, her voice suddenly squeaky and high-pitched, as if she'd been sucking helium.

"Unless you have someone else in there with you."

He crossed the room and pulled the shower door open, his hard-on preceding him inside. If Mel's eyes opened any wider they would fall out of her head.

"I thought we were taking this slow," she said, backing against the far wall, looking worried.

"Don't worry, we are." He stepped under the spray, slicking his hair back. "We're just doing it naked."

If they didn't make love that was okay with him; he just needed to touch her, get his hands on *some* part of her body. If she let him get her off, fantastic, if she returned the favor, even better. He was going to let her set the pace.

Mel stood in the corner watching him, chewing her lip. "This is going to sound stupid, because we've done this before, but I'm really nervous."

"That's why we're taking it slow." And if the anticipation killed him, well, he would at least die with a smile on his face. "So, tell me what you're ready for. What can I do?"

She thought about it for several seconds, then swallowed hard and said, "I guess you could…kiss me."

The logical place to start. He didn't want to corner her, so he took her hand and pulled her to him, so they were both under the spray. But when he leaned in to kiss her, the head of his erection bumped against her stomach. She jumped with surprise, then laughed nervously.

"Outdoor plumbing," he said with a shrug.

"I know, I'm being ridiculous. I'm sorry."

The weird thing was, he liked it. He liked that she wasn't trying to take charge, that for once he could be the aggressor.

"You know what, I have a better idea. Turn around." He grabbed the soap and poured some in his hand.

"What are you going to do?"

"Wash your back." She cast him a wary look, and he said, "Just your back. I promise."

She turned and faced the wall, bracing her hands on the tile as he smoothed the soap across her shoulders and down her back.

"Hmm, that feels nice," she said, as he used both hands to massage her shoulders, and he felt her begin to relax. He worked his way down, but as he got closer to her behind, she tensed again.

"Relax," he said, sliding his hands back up. "This is supposed to be fun."

"I'm sorry. I don't know why I'm so nervous. I wasn't like this in the hotel."

"Maybe it's because you knew you weren't able to do anything then."

She shrugged, and said without much conviction, "Maybe."

His hands stilled. "Why do I get the feeling there's something you're not telling me?"

"It's stupid."

He turned her to face him and she looked so cute, water dripping from her hair, her brow crinkled with the weight of whatever it was that troubled her. "If something is bothering you it's not stupid. If you don't tell me what's really wrong, we can't fix it." And he would *never* get laid.

"It's those videos."

"The shower one?"

She shook her head, eyes on her feet. "The other two. I know it was me, but it's *not* me anymore. That woman… she was just so confident and sexy. I don't think I can do and say the things she did. I can't be her anymore."

He shrugged. "So what?"

Her eyes met his, so full of grief and conflict that he felt his scotch buzz wither away. "I'm *so* afraid I'm going to disappoint you, Ash."

This wasn't one of the silly sex games she used to play with him, or even a mild case of the pre-sex jitters. She was genuinely distraught. He'd never seen her this confused and vulnerable before. Not even in the hospital.

"Mel, you *won't* disappoint me. That's not even a possibility."

She didn't look as though she believed him. She lowered her eyes but he caught her chin in his palm and forced her to look at him. "Listen to me. I don't want the Melody who was in those videos. I want *you.*"

He realized it was probably the most honest thing he had ever said to her. He wanted her in a way that he'd never wanted the other Melody.

So why was he still expecting her to act like her? Did he think that, despite being nervous and wanting to go slow, she would just magically shed her inhibitions the instant he touched her?

He wanted her, God knew he did, but not if it was going to hurt or confuse her. It just wasn't worth it. Physically she may have been ready for him, but emotionally she just wasn't there yet. He was pushing too far too fast.

Jesus, when had he gone so soft?

He turned and shut off the water.

"What are you doing?" she asked, looking even more confused, not that he could blame her. First he said they should wait, then he all but molested her, then he put on the brakes again. At this rate he was going to give them both whiplash.

Just because he bought her a car, and planned to give her a couple of credit cards, was he back to thinking she owed him? She hadn't asked for anything.

"We're getting out," he told her.

"But—"

"You're not ready for this. And I'm really sorry that I pushed you. I feel like a total jerk." He didn't just feel like a jerk, he *was* one. He grabbed the towel she'd hung on the hook outside the shower and wrapped it around her, then he got out and fetched one for himself from the linen closet. He fastened it around his hips, and when he turned Melody was standing in the shower doorway, wrapped in her towel, watching him, her brow wrinkled.

"Everything okay?" he asked.

She nodded, but she didn't move.

"We should get dressed. And if the offer for dinner is still good I'd love it if you cooked for me. Or if you prefer we could go out. Your choice."

"Okay," she said, but didn't specify which one, dinner in or out. But before he could ask, she walked out of the bathroom.

He gathered his clothes from the floor and walked into her bedroom, expecting her to be getting dressed. Instead she was lying in bed, propped up on one elbow, the blankets draped about waist level.

She probably wasn't trying to look sexy, but damn it all, she did. At that moment he would swear on his life that she had the most beautiful breasts in the free world. And, God, did he ache to get his hands on them.

"Taking a nap?" he asked.

She shook her head, then she pulled back the covers on the opposite side of the bed and patted the mattress. "Get in."

Get in? Into bed?

Now he was the one who was confused. "Mel—"

"Get in," she said more firmly.

"But…I thought…I thought we were waiting."

"Me, too. Now come over here and get into bed."

Though he still wasn't sure what was going on, he walked to the bed, tossing his clothes in a pile on the floor. His skin was still damp and the sheets stuck to him as he slid between them.

Since he didn't know what she expected from him, he

lay beside her, mirroring her position. "Okay, I'm in. Now what?"

"Now you should kiss me. And this time don't worry about the plumbing. I want you to touch me."

Good, because he started getting hard the second he saw her lying there, and short of putting on pants, or lying on top of the covers while she stayed under them, there was going to be inevitable physical contact. The question was, how far was she willing to let this go?

"Just to be clear, so I don't cross any boundaries, are you saying that you want to make love?"

"Yes, I am. And I do. Right now."

Thank You, God.

She lay back against the pillows, gazing up at him, waiting for his kiss. He knew what the old Mel would expect. She would want it hard and fast and breathless. But this Mel didn't have a clue what she wanted, so he was free to do whatever he chose, like a painter with a clean canvas.

But maybe this time, it was a picture they could paint together.

Twelve

Ash leaned in to kiss her, his hand cupping her face so tenderly, and Melody knew she was safe with him. That she would always be safe.

She wasn't exactly sure what happened in the bathroom, but when Ash shut off the water and wrapped her in a towel, told her they were stopping, something inside her shifted. She knew in that second that she wanted him, that she was ready *now*. It was time to stop looking backward and focus on the future.

His lips brushed hers, so gentle and sweet, and whatever anxiety or fear remained dissolved with their mingling breath. It was the kind of perfect kiss that every girl dreamed about. And she had, she realized. She had been that girl. The memory was so near she could almost reach out and touch it. But she didn't want to think about anything right now, she just wanted to feel. And Ash was exceptional in that department.

His kisses roused her senses and his caresses trailed fire across her skin. It was as if he owned a road map to every erogenous zone on her body, and he explored each one until she felt crazy with want. He made her shudder and quake, taking her to the brink of mindless ecstasy then yanking her back the second before she could reach her peak.

He aroused her with such practiced skill it made her feel inept in her own efforts, but he never once gave the impression that her touch did anything but arouse him. And nothing could be more erotic for her than touching him all over. Learning him again. She discovered that his ears were exceptionally sensitive, because when she nibbled them he groaned and fisted his hands in her hair. And when she did the same to his nipple he dragged her face to his and kissed her so hard she felt breathless. What he seemed to like most though was when she straddled his thighs, took his erection in her hand, but instead of stroking, swirled her thumb in slow circles around the head.

"My God, that feels amazing," Ash said, his eyes rolling closed, his fingers curling into the sheets. It was unbelievably arousing, watching him struggle for control. Knowing she was making him feel that way.

"Did I used to do this to you before?"

He swallowed hard and shook his head. "I don't want to come yet, but if you keep that up I will."

"It's okay if you do." She wanted him to.

He shook his head and opened his eyes. They were glassy and unfocused. "Not yet. Not until I'm inside you."

Well, all he had to do was ask. She rose up on her knees and centered herself over him. When he realized what she intended to do, he asked, "Are you sure?"

She had never been so sure of anything in her life.

Her eyes locked on his, she slowly lowered herself onto his erection, taking him inside her inch by excruciating inch. She was sure that making love, no matter how often or how many times they had done it before, had never given her this soul-deep sensation of completeness.

"You're so *tight*," he said, his hands splayed across her hips, looking as though he was barely hanging on.

She rose up until only the head was inside her, then sank back down. Ash groaned as her body clenched down around him. He reached up and hooked his hands around her neck, pulling her down for a kiss. It was deep and reckless and more than a little wild. And in one smooth motion, he rolled her over so that she was the one on her back, looking up at him. And he was wearing a cocky grin.

She opened her mouth to protest the sudden change of dynamics, but at the same time he rocked into her, swift and deep—*oh, so deep*—and the sound that emerged was a throaty moan.

He pulled back again then rocked forward. Once, twice. Slooowly. Watching her face. This was just like the shower video, only better because she was actually feeling it. And it was everything she expected and more.

Faster, she wanted to say. *Harder.* But the words were getting lost somewhere between her brain and her lips. She felt paralyzed, poised on a precipice, and as he moved inside her, each thrust pushed her a little closer to the edge. Ash must have been able to tell that she was close. He picked up speed.

Her body began to tremble, then quake, then the pleasure took hold almost violently. It felt as though her body was turning in on itself. Toes curling, fingers clenching. She was still in its grip when Ash groaned and shuddered.

She was just starting to come around, to come back to herself, when he dropped his head on her shoulder. He was breathing hard, and she was having a tough time catching her breath, too.

Ash kissed her one last time then rolled over onto the mattress, drawing her against his side.

"Don't take this the wrong way," he said. "But that was without question the quietest sex we have ever had."

She knew from the videos that she had the tendency to be...*vocal,* during sex, but she just assumed she was saucing it up for the camera. She didn't realize she *always* acted that way. "I can try to be louder next time."

"Oh, no," he said quickly. "Quiet is good. I've stopped getting those I-know-what-*you*-did-last-night looks in the elevator."

She rose up on her elbow to look at him. "You're not serious," she said, but she could see by his expression that he was. Her cheeks flushed just thinking about it. He once said that she had voyeuristic tendencies, but come on. "I still have a hard time believing some of the things I did. And you know, I just assumed that when I got my memories back, I would go back to being the person I was before. But the truth is, I don't think I want to. I think I like myself better the way I am now."

"You know, I think I do, too."

She hoped he really meant that. That he wasn't secretly disappointed. "You don't miss the makeup and the perfect hair and the clingy clothes?"

"To be honest, I hadn't given it much thought. The clothes you wear look fine to me, and your hair is cute this way." He reached up and tucked a strand behind her ear. "As for the makeup, I never thought you needed it anyway."

"I think I was insecure as a child."

His brow furrowed. "You remember?"

"Not exactly. It's hard to explain. It's just a feeling I have. I look at the way I was and it's just so not me, so not who I am now. It makes me feel as though I was playing a role. Trying to be something that I wasn't. Which means I couldn't have liked myself very much, could I?"

"I guess not."

"Would it be okay with you if I bought some new clothes? Those lace push-up bras are like medieval torture devices. I'd honestly rather have smaller-looking boobs than suffer another day in one of those things."

He grinned. "You can buy whatever you need."

"I'll probably need you to take me, though. Since I'm not thrilled with the idea of taking the bus. In fact, I may never get on one again. You could just drop me off, and I could call when I'm finished."

"How would you feel about driving yourself?"

She thought about that and realized there was really no reason why she couldn't drive herself. She was off the pain meds and she wasn't getting dizzy any longer. "I guess I could. As long as you don't mind loaning me your car."

He got this adorable, mischievous grin. "I was going to wait until Monday when it got here to tell you."

"When what got here?"

"I wanted it to be a surprise, but I suppose I could tell you now."

"Tell me what?"

He jumped up, looking a bit like an excited little boy, and reached for his pants on the floor. He pulled his cell phone from the pocket, then flopped down on his stomach beside her. He tapped at the touch screen, but when she sat up and tried to see over his shoulder what he was doing, he rolled onto his back. "Just hold on."

He had such a sweet, goofy grin on his face, she was

dying to see what he was up to. When he finally handed her the phone there was photo of a car on the screen. A luxury mini-SUV in a rich shade of blue. "I thought your car was new," she said.

"It is."

"So why buy another one?"

He laughed. "For you. That's your car. Well, not that exact one, but one just like it."

"You bought me a car?"

"You need one, right?"

"Oh, my God." She threw her arms around his neck and hugged him. "Thank you!"

He laughed and hugged her back. "It's not that big of a deal."

"Maybe not to you, but it is to me."

"If you scroll left you can see what it looks at from other angles."

She sat back against the pillows, scrolling through the other shots he'd taken.

"It's so cute! I love it."

"It also has an excellent safety record. And I got the extended option package. It has everything."

She scrolled to the next page, but it wasn't of the car. It took her a second to figure out exactly what it was she was seeing, and when she did, her head began to spin.

One second Mel was all smiles, then her face went slack and all the color leeched from her skin. She lifted a hand to her mouth, as if she might be sick.

He sat up. "Mel, what's wrong?"

She shook her head and said, "I should be dead."

He looked down at his phone and realized she was no longer looking at her new car. She was looking at the photos he'd taken at the impound lot in Texas, of what was left of her old car. He had completely forgotten they were there.

"Crap!" He snatched the phone away, but it was obviously too late. He should have erased the damned things, or at least transferred them to his work computer. "I didn't mean for you to see those. I'm sorry."

She looked up at him, eyes as wide as saucers. "How did I survive that?"

"You were really lucky."

"Everyone kept saying that. But they always say that when someone has an accident and doesn't die. Right?"

He shrugged. "I guess sometimes they really mean it."

"Was it just the one picture, or are there more?"

"Half a dozen maybe. I'll erase them."

She held out her hand. "I want to see."

"Mel—"

"Ash, I *need* to see them."

"It'll just upset you."

"It will upset me more if I don't. *Please.*"

He reluctantly handed it back to her, and watched as she scrolled through the photos. When she got to the last one she scrolled back the other way. She did that a few times, then she closed her eyes tight, as though she was trying to block the image from her mind.

Letting her look had been a bad idea. He should have told her no and erased them. "Mel, why don't you give me—"

"I rolled," she said, eyes still closed.

"That's right. Into a ditch. Then you hit a tree. The doctor told you that, remember?"

Her brow wrinkled in concentration. "The interior was black, the instrument panel had red. Red lights. And the gearshift…" She reached out with her right hand, as if she was touching it. "It was red, too." She opened her eyes and looked up at him. "There was an air freshener hanging from the mirror. It smelled like coconuts."

There was no way she could have seen that kind of detail in the photo on his phone. She was remembering. "What else?"

"I remember rolling." She looked up at him. "I remember being scared, and hurting, and thinking I was going to die. It was...*awful*. But I do remember."

He wondered how long it would take before she remembered what else had happened, *why* she rolled into the ditch. Had she been conscious enough to know that she was miscarrying?

He put his hand on her shoulder. "It's over, and you're safe now."

She looked up at him. "There's something else."

He held his breath.

She stared at him for what felt like an eternity, then she shook her head. "I don't know. I know there's something there. Something I should know. It just won't come."

"It will," he assured her, hoping it never did, wishing she could just be content to let it stay buried.

Thirteen

Mel had a bad dream that night.

After a dinner of takeout Chinese that they both picked at, and a movie neither seemed to be paying much attention to, Ash walked Mel to bed.

He was going to tuck her in then go to his office and work for a while, but she took his hand and said, "Please stay." He couldn't tell her no. They undressed and climbed into bed together. He kissed her goodnight, intending it to be a quick brush of the lips, because he was sure that sex was the last thing on her mind. But her arms went around his neck and she pulled him to her, whispering, "Make love to me again."

He kept waiting for her demanding aggressive side to break through, but she seemed perfectly content lying there, kissing and touching, letting him take the lead. And he realized just how much he preferred this to the hot and heavy stuff.

Afterward she cuddled up against him, warm and soft and limp, and they fell asleep that way. It was a few hours later when she shot up in bed, breath coming in ragged bursts, eyes wild with fear.

He sat up beside her, touched her shoulder, and found that she was drenched in sweat. He felt the sheet and it was drenched, too. For a second he was afraid she'd developed a fever, but her skin was cool.

"I was rolling," she said, her voice rusty from sleep. "I was rolling and rolling and I couldn't stop."

"It was a dream. You're okay." He had no doubt this was a direct result of her seeing those photos and he blamed himself.

"It hurts," she said, cradling her head in her hands. "My head hurts."

He wasn't sure if it hurt now, or she was having a flashback to the accident. She seemed trapped somewhere between dream and sleep. "Do you want a pain pill?"

She shivered and wrapped her arms around herself. "I'm cold."

Well, lying between wet sheets wasn't going to warm her.

"Come on," he said, climbing out of bed and coaxing her to follow him.

"Where?" she asked in a sleepy voice, dutifully letting him lead her into the hall.

"My room. Where it's dry."

He got her tucked in, then laid there for a long time, listening to her slow even breaths, until he finally drifted off.

She apparently didn't remember the dream, or waking up, because she shook him awake the next morning and asked, "Ash, why are we in your bedroom?"

"You had a nightmare," he mumbled, too sleepy to even open his eyes.

"I did?"

"The sheets were sweaty so I moved us in here." He thought she may have said something else after that but he had already drifted back to sleep. When he woke again it was after eight, far later than he usually got up. Even on a Sunday. He would have to skip the gym and go straight to work.

He showered and dressed in slacks and a polo since it was Sunday and it was doubtful anyone else would be around the office, then went out to the kitchen. Mel was sitting on the couch wearing jeans and a T-shirt, her hair pulled back in a ponytail, knees pulled up with her feet propped on the cushion in front of her. If he didn't know better, he would say she wasn't a day over eighteen.

When she saw him she looked up and smiled. "Good morning."

He walked to the back of the couch and leaned over, intending to kiss her cheek, but she turned her head and caught his lips instead. They tasted like coffee, and a hint of something sweet—a pastry maybe—and she smelled like the soap they had used in the shower last night. He was damned tempted to lift her up off the couch, toss her over his shoulder and take her back to bed.

Maybe later.

When he broke the kiss she was still smiling up at him.

"Good morning," he said.

"There's coffee."

"How long have you been up?" he asked as he walked to the kitchen. She'd already set a cup out for him.

"Six-thirty." She followed him into the kitchen, taking

a seat on one of the bar stools at the island. "It was a little disorienting waking up in a bed I didn't fall asleep in."

"You still don't remember it?"

She shook her head. "I do remember something else though. The book I've been reading, I've read it before. I mean, I figured I had, since it was on the shelf. But I picked it up this morning after already reading almost half of it, and bam, suddenly I remember how it ended. So I went to the bookshelf and looked at a few others, and after I read the back blurb, and skimmed the first few pages, I remembered those, too."

This was bound to happen. He just hadn't expected it to be this soon. "Sounds like you've been busy."

"Yeah. I was sitting there reading those books, thinking how stupid it was that I could remember something so immaterial, and I couldn't even remember my own mother. Then it hit me. The picture."

"What picture?"

"The one of me and my mom, when I was thirteen."

He recalled seeing it in her room before, but not since they had been back. He didn't recall seeing it in her place in Texas either. "I remember you having one, but I don't know where it is."

"That's okay. I remembered. It just popped into my head. I knew it was in the front pouch of my suitcase. And it was."

Ash could swear his heart stopped, then picked up triple time. She remembered packing? "Your suitcase?"

"I figured I must have taken it with me on my trip."

"Right…you must have." Hadn't he checked her suitcases? So there would be nothing to jolt her memory? It was possible that he only patted the front pouches, assuming they were empty.

Oh, well, it was just a photo.

"I found something else, too," she said, and there was something about her expression, the way she was looking at him, that made his heart slither down to his stomach. She pulled a folded-up piece of paper from her back pocket and handed it to him.

He unfolded it and realized immediately what it was. A lease, for her rental in Abilene.

Oh, hell. He should have checked the damned outer pockets.

"I wasn't on a research trip, was I?"

He shook his head.

"I moved out, didn't I? I left you."

He nodded.

"I've been sitting here, trying to remember what happened, why I left, but it's just not there."

Which meant she didn't remember the affair, or the child. The limb-weakening relief made him feel like a total slime. But as long as she didn't remember, he could just pretend it never happened. Or who knew, maybe she did remember, and she was content to keep it her little secret. As long as they didn't acknowledge it, it didn't exist.

"You didn't leave a note," he said. "I just came home from work one day and you were gone. I guess you weren't happy."

She frowned. "I just took off and you didn't come after me?"

"Not at first," he admitted, because at this point lying to her would only make things worse. "I was too angry. And too proud, I guess. I convinced myself that after a week or two you would change your mind and come back. I thought you would be miserable without me. But you didn't come back, and I was the one who was miserable. So I hired the P.I."

"And you found out that I was in the hospital?"

He nodded. "I flew to Texas the next morning. I was going to talk you into coming back with me."

"But I had amnesia. So you told me I had been on a trip."

He nodded. "I was afraid that if I told you the truth, you wouldn't come home. I went to your rental and packed your things and had them shipped back here. And I…" Jeez, this was tough. They were supposed to be having this conversation when he was dumping her, and reveling in his triumph. He wasn't supposed to fall for her.

"You what?" she asked.

"I…" *Christ, just say it, Ash.* "I went through your computer. I erased a lot of stuff. Things I thought would jog your memory. E-mails, school stuff, music."

She nodded slowly, as though she was still processing it, trying to decide if she should be angry with him. "But you did it because you were afraid of losing me."

"Yes." More or less, anyway. Just not for the reason she thought. And if he was going to come this far, he might as well own up to all of it. "There's one more thing."

She took a deep breath, as if bracing herself. "Okay."

"It's standard procedure that hospitals will only give out medical information to next of kin. Parents, spouses… *fiancés*…"

It took a minute for her to figure it out, and he could tell the instant it clicked. He could see it in her eyes, in the slow shake of her head. "We're not engaged."

"It was the only way I could get any information. The only way the doctor would talk to me."

She had this look on her face, as if she might be sick. He imagined he was wearing a similar expression.

She slid her ring off and set it on the counter. At least she didn't throw it at him. "I guess you'll be wanting this back. Although, I don't imagine it's real."

"No, it's real. It's…" God, this was painful. "It's my ex-wife's."

She took a deep breath, holding in what had to be seething anger. He wished she would just haul off and slug him. They would both feel better. Not that he deserved any absolution of guilt.

"But you did it because you were afraid of losing me," she said, giving him an out.

"Absolutely." And despite feeling like the world's biggest ass, telling her the truth lifted an enormous weight off his shoulders. He felt as though he could take a full breath for the first time since the day he had walked into her hospital room.

"You can't even imagine how guilty I've felt," he told her.

"Is this why you've been avoiding me?"

Her words stunned him. "What do you mean?"

"All the late nights at work."

"I always work late. I always have."

"Do you always tell me you're at work when you really aren't?"

What was she talking about? "I've never done that. If I said I was at work, that's where I was."

"I called your office yesterday afternoon, to ask you about dinner, but you didn't answer. I left a message, too, but you never called back."

He could lie about it, say he was making copies or in a meeting or something, but the last thing he needed was one more thing to come back at him. "I was there. Brock and Flynn decided to throw an impromptu party. To celebrate our engagement."

Her eyes widened a little. "Well, that must have been awkward."

"You have no idea."

"I guess that's my fault, for spilling the beans."

"Mel, none of this is even close to your fault. I find the fact that you haven't thrown something at me a miracle."

"In a way, I feel like I should be thanking you."

"For what?"

"If you hadn't done this, I would never have known how happy I could be with you."

Not in a million years would he expect her to thank him for lying to her.

"But," she continued, and he felt himself cringe. When there was a but, it was never good. "If things stay the way they are, you're going to lose me again."

This was no empty threat. He could see that she was dead serious.

"What things?"

"You're always at work. You're gone before I get up and you come home after I'm asleep. That might be easier to stomach if you at least took the weekends off. I sort of feel like, what's the point of being together, if we're never together?"

The old Melody would have never complained about the dynamics of their relationship, or how many hours he worked. Even if it did bother her. And maybe that was part of the problem.

He couldn't deny that right before she left, he had been pulling away from her. He was almost always at work, either at Maddox, or in his home office. And it seemed that the further he retreated, the harder she tried to please him, until she was all but smothering him. Then, boom, she was gone.

Had it never occurred to him that he had all but driven her into another man's arms?

He knew that the sugar daddy/mistress arrangement wasn't an option any longer. She wanted the real thing.

She deserved it. But what did he want? Was he ready for that kind of commitment?

He thought about Melody and how she used to be, and how she was now. There was no longer a good Melody and an evil one. She was the entire package. She was perfect just the way she was, and he realized that if he ever were to settle down again, he could easily imagine himself with her. But relationships took compromise and sacrifice, and he was used to pretty much always getting his way, never having to work at it.

And honestly, he'd been bored out of his skull.

He wanted a woman who could think for herself, and be herself, even if that meant disappointing him sometimes, or disagreeing with him.

He wanted Melody.

"Mel, after everything I went through to get you back, do you honestly think I would just let you go again?"

Her bottom lip started to tremble and her eyes welled, though she was trying like hell to hold it back. But he didn't want her holding anything back.

He walked around the island to her but she was already up and meeting him halfway. She threw herself around him and he wrapped her up in his arms.

This was a good thing they had. A really good thing. And this time he was determined not to screw it up.

After seeing the pictures of her wrecked car, Melody's memories began to come back with increasing frequency. Random snippets here and there. Things like the red tennis shoes she had gotten on her birthday when she was five, and rides her mother let her take on the pony outside the grocery store.

She remembered her mother's unending parade of boyfriends and husbands. All of them mistreated her mother in some way or another, often physically. She didn't seem to know how to stand up for herself, when to say *enough*, yet when it came to protecting Mel, she was fierce. Mel remembered when one of them came after her. She couldn't have been more than ten or eleven. She remembered standing frozen in place, too frightened to even shield her face as he approached her with an open palm, arm in mid-swing. She closed her eyes, waiting for the impact, then she heard a thud and opened her eyes to find him kneeling on the floor, stunned and bleeding from his head, and her mother hovering over him with a baseball bat.

She hadn't been a great mother, but she had kept Mel safe.

Despite having finally learned that it was socially unacceptable, Mel had been so used to the idea of men hitting that when she'd started seeing Ash she'd always been on guard, waiting for the arm to swing. But after six months or so, when he hadn't so much as raised his voice to her, she'd realized that he would never hurt her. Not physically anyway.

When she admitted that to Ash, instead of being insulted, he looked profoundly sad. They lay in bed after making love and talked about it. About what her life had been like as a child, how most of her memories were shrouded in fear and insecurity. And as she opened up to him, Ash miraculously began to do the same.

She recalled enough to know that their relationship had never been about love, and that for those three years they had been little more than roommates. Roommates who had sex. She couldn't help but feel ashamed that she had compromised herself for so long, that she hadn't insisted on better. But they were in a real relationship now. They had a future. They talked and laughed and spent time together.

They saw movies and had picnics and took walks on the shore. They were a couple.

He didn't care that her hair was usually a mess and her clothes didn't cling. Or that she'd stopped going to the gym and lost all those pretty muscles and curves she'd worked so hard to maintain, and now was almost as scrawny as she'd been in high school. *Less is more,* he had said affectionately when she'd complained that she had no hips and her butt had disappeared. He didn't even miss the push-up bras, although he knew damn well if that had been a prerequisite to the relationship she probably would have walked.

He even forgave her for all the orgasms she had faked, during sex she didn't want but had anyway, because she was so afraid of disappointing him. And she was humbled to learn that there were many nights when he would have been happy to forgo the sex and watch a movie instead. He made her promise that she would never have sex if she didn't want to, and she swore to him that she would never fake an orgasm again. He promised that she would never need to, and in the weeks that passed, she didn't.

Despite all the talking they had done, there was still one thing that they hadn't discussed, something she had been afraid to bring up. Because as close as they had grown, there was still that little girl inside who was afraid to disappoint him. But she knew she had waited long enough, and one morning at breakfast, over eggs and toast, he gave her the perfect segue.

"Since your memory is almost completely back now, have you considered when you'll go back to school?" he asked.

She was suddenly so nervous that the juice she was drinking got caught in her throat. It was now or never.

"Not really," she said, then thought, *Come on, Mel, be*

brave. Just tell him the truth. "The thing is, I don't want to go back. I don't want to be a lawyer."

He shrugged and said, "Okay," then he took a drink of his juice and went back to eating.

She was so stunned her mouth actually fell open. All that worrying, all the agonizing she had done over this, and all he had to say was *okay?*

She set her fork down beside her plate. "Is that it?"

He looked up from the toast he was spreading jam on. "Is what it?"

"I say I don't want to be a lawyer and all you say is *okay?*"

He shrugged. "What do you want me to say?"

"After you spent all that money on law-school tuition, doesn't it upset you that I'm just going to throw my education away?"

"Not really. An education isn't worth much if you aren't happy in what you're doing."

If she had known he would be so understanding she would have told him the truth months and months ago. She thought of all the time she had wasted on a career path that had been going nowhere. If only she'd had the courage to open up to him.

"Do you have any idea what you might want to do?" he asked.

The million-dollar question.

"I think so."

When she didn't elaborate he said, "Would you like to tell me?"

She fidgeted with her toast, eyes on her plate. "I was thinking, maybe I can stay home for a while."

"That's fine. It isn't like you *need* to work."

"Maybe I could do something here, instead of an outside job."

"Like a home business?"

"Sort of." *Just say it, Mel. Spit it out.* "But one that involves things like midnight feedings and diaper changes."

He brow dipped low. He took a deep breath and exhaled slowly. "Mel, you know I can't—"

"I know. I do. But there's always artificial means. Or even adoption. And I don't mean right now. I would want us to be married first." He opened his mouth to say something but she held up a hand to stop him. "I know we haven't discussed anything definite, or made plans, and I'm not trying to rush things. I swear. I just wanted to sort of…put it out there, you know, to make sure we're on the same page."

"I didn't know you wanted kids."

"I didn't either. Not till recently. I always told myself I would never want to put a kid through what I went through. I guess I just assumed I would have a life like my mom's. It never occurred to me that I would ever meet someone like you."

A faint smile pulled at the corners of his mouth, but he hid it behind a serious look. "How many kids are we talking about?"

Her heart leaped up and lodged somewhere in her throat. At least he was willing to discuss it. "One or two. Or *maybe* three."

He raised a brow.

"Or just two."

After a pause he said, "And this is something you *really* want?"

She bit her lip and nodded. "I really do."

There was another long pause, and for a second she was afraid he would say no. Not just afraid. She was terrified.

Because this *could* be a deal breaker. She wanted a family. It was all she'd been able to think about lately.

"Well," he finally said. "I guess one of each would be okay."

By the time the last word left his mouth she was already around the table and in his lap with her arms around his neck. "Thank you!"

He laughed and hugged her. "But not until we're married, and you know I don't want to rush into anything."

"I know." They could hardly call three years rushing, but she knew Ash had trust issues. After his own cancer, then losing his mother to the disease, he'd had a hard time letting himself get close to people, then when he finally did, and married his wife, she had betrayed him in the worst way possible.

But Ash had to know by now that she would never do that to him. She loved him, and she knew that he loved her, even if he hadn't said the words yet.

It was a big step for him, but she knew if she was patient he would come around.

Fourteen

Ash sat at his desk at work, still smiling to himself about the irony of Mel's timing. Funny that she would pick today to finally broach the marriage and kids subject, when tonight he planned to take her out for a romantic dinner, followed by a stroll by the water, where, at sunset, he would drop down on one knee and ask her to marry him.

He hoped that if she had even the slightest suspicion of his intentions, he had dispelled that when he pretended not to be sure about wanting kids. Although admittedly, until recently anyway, he hadn't even considered it. He'd never planned to get tied down again, so it had just naturally never entered his mind. And his ex had never expressed a desire for children.

Now he knew, if they were his and Mel's, his life would never be complete without them. Natural or adopted.

He opened his top drawer, pulled out the ring box and flipped the top up. It wasn't as flashy as the ring he'd given his ex. The stone was smaller and the setting more traditional, but after Mel confessed how much she had disliked the ring for their fake engagement, he knew she would love this one. A sturdy ring, the jeweler had told him, one that would hold up through diaper changes and baby baths and dirty laundry. And with any luck that would be the scene at their condo for the next several years.

There was a knock on his office door. Ash closed the ring box and set it back in his drawer just as Gavin Spencer stuck his head in. "Am I bothering you?"

"Nothing that can't wait," Ash said, gesturing him in.

Gavin strode over and sank into the chair opposite Ash's desk. "It's getting really weird out there."

Ash didn't have to ask what he meant. The mood around the office had been tense for the past couple of weeks. He could only assume it was due in part to the security leaks. It wasn't openly discussed, but at this point everyone knew.

"That's why I stay in here," Ash said.

"You're lucky you can. You should try working with Logan Emerson."

"I did notice that he doesn't exactly seem to fit in."

"He kind of creeps me out," Gavin said. "It seems like every time I look up, he's watching me. Then I caught him in my office the other day. He said he was leaving me a memo."

"Did he?"

"Yeah. But I could swear the papers on my desk had been moved around. There's something not quite right with him. There are times when he doesn't even seem to know what the hell he's doing. Doesn't seem like a very smart hire to me. If it were my firm, you could bet I would do things differently."

But it wasn't. He knew Gavin dreamed of branching

out on his own, of being the boss, but talk like that could make some people nervous. Ash just hoped Gavin wouldn't undermine the integrity of Maddox and leak information to Golden Gate to suit his own interests.

Gavin's cell rang and when he looked at the display he shot up from his chair. "Damn, gotta take this. I've got a lead on a new client. I don't want to say too much, but it could be very lucrative."

"Well, good luck."

When Gavin was gone Ash looked at the clock. It seemed that time was crawling by today. It was still four hours until he picked up Mel for dinner. It was going to be tough sitting through the entire meal, knowing the ring was in his pocket. But he knew that the water was one of her favorite places, so that was where he wanted to do it. He'd timed it so that the sun would be setting and the view would be spectacular.

He'd planned it so precisely, there wasn't a single thing that could possibly go wrong.

Melody was running late.

She leaned close to the mirror and fixed the eyeliner smudge in the corner of her eye. Boy, she was out of practice.

Ash stuck his head in for tenth time in the past fifteen minutes. "Ready yet?"

"One more minute."

"That's what you said ten minutes ago. We're going to be late for our reservation."

"The restaurant isn't going anywhere. It won't kill us if we have to wait a little longer." It was their first real night out since the accident, and she wanted it to be special. She'd bought a new dress and even curled her hair and pinned it up.

"Mel?"

"Fine! Jeez." She swiped on some lipstick, dropped the tube in her purse and said, "Let's go."

He hustled her into the elevator, then into the car. Her new car sat beside his, and though she had been a little nervous at first being back in the driver's seat, now she loved it. She even made excuses to go out just so she could drive it.

Ash got in the driver's side, started the car and zipped through the garage to the entrance. He made a right out onto the street. Traffic was heavy, and Ash cursed when they had to stop at the red light.

"We're going to be late," he complained, watching for a break in the traffic so he could hang a right.

"What is it with you tonight?" she asked, pulling down the mirror on the visor to check her eyeliner one last time. "Are you going to turn into a pumpkin or something?"

He started to move forward just as she was flipping her visor up, and at the same time a guy on a bike shot off the curb and into the intersection.

"Ash!" she screamed, and he slammed on the brakes, barely missing the guy's back tire as he flew by in an attempt to beat the light.

"Idiot," Ash muttered, then he turned to look at her. "You okay?"

She couldn't answer. Her hands were trembling and braced on the dash, her breath coming in short, fast bursts. She suddenly felt as though her heart was going to explode from her chest it was hammering so hard.

"Mel? Talk to me," Ash said, sounding worried, but his voice was garbled, as if he was talking to her through water.

She tried, but she couldn't talk. Her lips felt numb and she wasn't getting enough air.

Out. She had to get out of the car.

The car behind them honked so Ash zipped around the corner.

He put his hand on her arm, keeping one eye on her and one on the road. "Mel, you're scaring me."

She couldn't breathe. She was trapped and she needed air.

She reached for the door handle and yanked, not even caring that they were still moving, but the door was locked.

Ash saw what she was doing and yanked her away from the door. "Jesus, Mel, what are you doing?"

"Out," she wheezed, still struggling to get a breath. "Get me out."

"Hold on," he said, gripping her arm, genuine fear in his voice. "Let me pull over."

He whipped down the alley behind their building then turned back into the parking garage. The second he came to a stop she clawed her door open and threw herself out, landing on her knees on the pavement. Her purse landed beside her and its contents spilled out, but she didn't care. She just needed air.

She heard Ash's door open and in an instant he was behind her. "Mel, what happened? Is it your head? Are you hurt?"

It was getting easier to breathe now, but that crushing panic, the instinct to run intensified as adrenaline raced through her bloodstream.

She closed her eyes, but instead of blackness she saw a rain-slicked windshield, she heard the steady thwap of the wipers. The weather was getting worse, she thought. Better get home. But then there was a bike. One second it wasn't there, then it was, as though it materialized from thin air. She saw a flash of long blond hair, a pink hoodie. She yanked the wheel, there was a loud thunk, then rolling—

"No!" Her eyes flew open. She was still in the parking garage, on the floor. But it happened. It was real. "I hit her. I hit the girl."

"Mel, you have to calm down," Ash said sternly, then she felt his arms around her, helping her up off the ground. Her knees were so weak, her legs so shaky she could hardly walk on her own.

"There was a bike," she told him. "And a girl. I hit her."

"Let's get you upstairs," he said, helping her to the elevator.

As the doors slid shut she closed her eyes and was suddenly overwhelmed by the sensation that she was rolling. Rolling and rolling, violent thrashing, pain everywhere, then wham. A sharp jolt and a pain in her head. Then, nothing. No movement. No sound.

Can't move.

Trapped.

"Mel."

Her eyes flew open.

"We're here."

Disoriented, she gazed around and realized she was back in the elevator, on their floor and he was nudging her forward. Not in the car. Not trapped.

He helped her inside and sat her down on the couch. He poured her a drink and pressed it into her hands. "Drink this. It'll help you calm down."

She lifted it to her lips and forced herself to take a swallow, nearly gagging as it burned a trail of fire down her throat. But she was feeling better now. Not so panicked. Not so afraid. The fuzziness was gone.

He started to move away and she gripped the sleeve of his jacket. "Don't go!"

"I'm just going to get the first-aid kit from the guest bathroom. We need to clean up your knees."

She looked down and saw that her knees were raw and oozing blood, and the sight of it made her feel dizzy and sick to her stomach.

She lay back and let her head fall against the cushion. She remembered now, as clear as if it had happened this morning. She was in the car, knowing she had to get help. She had to help the girl. But when she tried to move her arms something was pinning her. She was trapped. She tried to see what it was, thinking she could pry it loose, but the second she moved her head, pain seized with a vicelike grip, so intense that bile rose up to choke her. She moaned and closed her eyes against the pain.

She tried to think, tried to concentrate on staying conscious. Then she felt it, low in her belly. A sharp pain. Then cramping. She remembered thinking, *No, not there. Not the baby.*

The baby.

Oh, God. She had been pregnant. She was going to have Ash's baby.

The final piece of the puzzle slid into place. That was why she left Ash. That was why she ran to Texas. She was pregnant with Ash's baby, a baby she knew he would never want.

The relief of finally having the answers, finally seeing the whole picture, paled in comparison to the ache in her heart.

They could have been a family. She and Ash and the baby. They could have been happy. But how could she have known?

Ash reappeared and knelt down in front of her. He'd

taken off his suit jacket and rolled his sleeves to his elbows. "This is probably going to sting," he warned her, then he used a cool, damp washcloth to wipe away the blood. She sucked in a surprised breath as she registered the raw sting of pain.

"Sorry," he said. "This probably won't feel much better, but we don't want it getting infected. God only knows what's on the floor down there."

He wet a second cloth with hydrogen peroxide, and she braced herself against the pain as he dabbed it on her knees. It went white and bubbly on contact.

If she had known it could be like this, that they could be so happy, she wouldn't have left. She would have told him about the baby.

Now it was too late.

Ash smoothed a jumbo-size bandage across each knee. "All done."

"Is she dead?" Mel asked him, as he busied himself with repacking the first-aid kit. The fact that he wouldn't look at her probably wasn't a good sign. "Please tell me."

He sighed deeply and looked up at her. "It wasn't your fault."

So that was a yes. She pretty much knew already. And her fault or not, she had killed someone's baby. Someone's child. And she hadn't even had a chance to apologize. To say she was sorry. "Why didn't someone tell me?"

"The doctor thought it would be too traumatic."

She laughed wryly. "And finding out this way has just been a barrel of laughs."

He rose to his feet, the kit and soiled rags in hand. "He did what he thought was best."

It hit her suddenly that the doctor must have told him about the baby, too. He thought Ash was her fiancé. What reason would he have to hide it?

All this time Ash knew and he had never said a word. It was one thing to lie about engagements, and hide personal information, but this was their *child*.

"Is that why you didn't say anything about the baby, either?"

Ash closed his eyes and shook his head. "Don't do this. Just let it go."

"Let it go? I lost a baby."

He looked at her, his eyes pleading. "Everything has been so good, please don't ruin it."

"Ruin it?"

"Can't we just do what we've been doing and pretend it never happened?"

Her mouth fell open. "How can you even say something like that? I lost a child—"

"That wasn't mine!" he shouted, slamming the first-aid kit down so hard on the coffee table that she heard the glass crack. She was so stunned by the unprecedented outburst that it took a second for his words to sink in.

"Ash, who told you it wasn't yours? Of course it was yours."

He leveled his eyes on her, and if she didn't know better, she would think he was going to hit her. But when he spoke his voice was eerily calm. "You and I both know that's impossible. I'm sterile."

She could hardly believe what he was suggesting. "You think I had an *affair*."

"I had unprotected sex with you for three years, and with my wife for seven years, and no one got pregnant before now, so yeah, I think it's pretty damn likely that you had an affair."

He couldn't honestly believe she would do that. "Ash, since that night at the party, when we met, there has been *no one* but you."

"The party? I seriously doubt that."

He might as well have just called her a whore.

"If it *was* mine," he said, "why did you run off?"

"Because you had made it pretty clear that you had no desire to have a family, and you sure as hell didn't seem to want me. I figured it would be best for everyone if I just left. Frankly, I'm surprised you even noticed I was gone."

His eyes cut sharply her way.

Why was he being so stubborn? He *knew* her. He knew she would never hurt him. "Ash, I'm telling you the *truth*."

"And I'm just supposed to trust you? Just take your word for it when I know it's impossible?"

"Yes. You should. Because you know I wouldn't lie to you."

"I don't believe you," he said, and it felt as though a chunk of her heart broke away.

"Why did you even bring me back here? If you thought I cheated on you, if you hated me that much, why not just leave me in the hospital? Were you plotting revenge or something?"

His jaw clenched and he looked away.

She was just being surly, but she'd hit the nail right on the head. "Oh, my God." She rose from the couch. "You *were,* weren't you? You wanted to get back at me."

He turned to her, eyes black with anger. "After all I did for you, you betrayed me. I've taken care of you for three years, and you repay me by screwing around. You're damn right I wanted revenge." He shook his head in disgust. "You want to know the really pathetic thing? I forgave you. I thought you had changed. I was going to ask you to marry me tonight, for real this time. But here you are, *still* lying to me. Why won't you just admit what you did? Own up to it."

Own up to something she didn't do?

The really sad thing was that she suspected, somewhere deep down, he believed her. He knew she was telling the truth. He just didn't want to hear it. When the chips were down, and things got a little tough, it was easier to push her away than take a chance.

"Is this the way it is with you?" she asked. "You find something really good, but when you get too close, you throw it away? Is that what you did to your wife? Did you ignore her for so long that you drove her away?"

He didn't respond, but she could see that she'd hit a nerve.

"I love you, Ash. I wanted to spend the rest of my life with you, but I just can't fight for you anymore."

"No one asked you to."

And that pretty much said it all. "Give me an hour to pack my things. And I would appreciate if I could use the car for a couple of weeks, until I can find another one."

"Keep it," he said.

Like a parting gift? she wondered. Or the booby prize.

She rose from the couch and walked to her room to pack, her legs still wobbly from the adrenaline rush, her knees sore.

But they didn't even come close to the pain in her heart.

Ash sat at a booth in the Rosa Lounge, sipping his scotch, trying to convince himself that he wasn't miserable, wasn't a complete idiot, and not doing a very good job of it.

Mel had been gone three days and he could barely stand

it. And now that he finally realized what an idiot he'd been, he wasn't sure how to fix it.

He knew he had to be pretty desperate at this point to arrange this meeting, but there were some things that Mel had said that really stuck in his craw, and he had to know, once and for all, if she was right.

He checked his watch again and looked over at the door just in time to see her come in. Her hair was shorter than before, but otherwise she didn't look all that different. She scanned the room and he rose from his seat, waving her over. When she saw him, she smiled, which was a good sign. When he'd called her and asked to meet she'd sounded a little wary.

As she walked to the booth he saw that she still looked really good, and, wow, really pregnant.

"Linda," he said as she approached. "Good to see you."

"Hello, Ash." His ex-wife leaned in and air kissed his cheek. "You look great."

"You, too," he said. "Please sit down."

He waited until she slid into the opposite side of the booth, then he sat, too.

The waitress appeared to take her drink order, and when she was gone Ash gestured to Linda's swollen middle. "You're pregnant. I had no idea."

She placed a hand on her stomach and smiled. "Six weeks to go."

"Congratulations. You're still with…" He struggled to conjure up a name.

"Craig," she supplied for him. "We just celebrated our second wedding anniversary last month."

"That's great. You look very happy."

"I am," she said with a smile. "Everything is going great. I don't know if you remember, but Craig owned a gym in our old neighborhood. I talked him into expanding and we just opened our fourteenth fitness center."

"I'm glad to hear it."

"How about you? What have you been up to?"

"I'm still at Maddox."

She waited, as if she expected more, and when there wasn't she asked, "Anyone…*special* in your life?"

"For a while," he said, wanting to add, *until I royally screwed up.* "It's complicated."

She waited for him to elaborate. And though he hadn't planned to, the words just kind of came out.

"We just split up," he heard himself tell her. "A few days ago, in fact."

"I'm going to go out on a limb and assume that you asking to meet me is directly related somehow."

His ex was no dummy.

"I need to ask you something," he told her, rubbing his hands together, wondering if maybe this wasn't such a good idea. "And it's probably going to sound…well, a little weird after all this time."

"Okay." She folded her hands in front of her and leaned forward slightly, giving him her undivided attention.

"I need to know why you did it. Why you cheated on me."

He thought she might be offended or defensive, but she looked more surprised than upset. "Wow, okay. I didn't see that one coming."

"I'm not trying to play the blame game, I swear. I just really need to know."

"You're sure you want to do this?"

No, but he'd come this far and there was no going back now. "I'm sure. I need to know."

"Let's face it, Ash, by the time you caught me with Craig, our marriage had been over for a long time. It was only a matter of time before I left. You just didn't want to see it, didn't want to take responsibility. You wanted to make me out to be the monster."

"I guess I still believed we were happy."

"Happy? We were nonexistent. You were never around, and even when you were you were a ghost. You just didn't want to see it."

She was right. They had drifted apart. He didn't want to see it. Didn't want to take the blame.

"I know it was wrong to cheat on you, and I'll always be truly sorry for that. I didn't want to hurt you, but I was so lonely, Ash. The truth is, when you caught us, and you were so angry, I was stunned. I honestly didn't think you cared anymore. I felt as though I could have packed my bags and left, and you wouldn't have noticed until you ran out of clean underwear."

All of this was beginning to sound eerily familiar.

"So I drove you to it?"

"Please don't think that I'm placing all the blame on you. I could have tried harder, too. I could have insisted you take more time for me. I just assumed we were in a phase, that we had drifted, and eventually we would meet back up somewhere in the middle again. I guess by the time it got really bad, it didn't seem worth saving. I just didn't love you anymore."

"Wow," he said. Drive the knife in deeper.

"Ash, come on, you can't honestly say you didn't feel the same way."

She was right. His pride had taken a much bigger hit than his heart.

"Is that what you wanted to know?" she asked.

He smiled. "Yeah. I appreciate your honesty."

She cringed suddenly and pushed down on the top of

her belly. "Little bugger is up under my ribs again. I think he's going to be a soccer player."

"He?"

"Yeah. We still haven't settled on a name. I'm partial to Thomas, and Craig likes Jack."

"I always thought you didn't want kids."

"It's not so much that I didn't want them, but it never seemed like the right time. And it was a touchy subject for you, since you thought you couldn't."

"*Thought* I couldn't?"

She frowned, as though she realized she'd said something she shouldn't have.

"Linda?"

She looked down at her hands. "I probably should have told you before."

Why did Ash get the feeling he wasn't going to like this? "Told me what?"

"It was in college. We had been together maybe six months. I found out I was pregnant. And before you ask, yes, it was yours."

"But I can't—"

"Believe me, you can. And you did. But we were both going for degrees, and we hadn't even started talking about marriage at that point. Not to mention that we had student loans up the yin yang. I knew it was *really* lousy timing. So I did what I believed was the best thing for both of us and had an abortion."

Ash's head was spinning so violently he nearly fell out of the booth. "But all those years we didn't use protection?"

"*You* didn't, but I did. I had an IUD. So there wouldn't be any more accidents."

He could hardly believe he was hearing this. "Why didn't you tell me?"

"I thought I was protecting you. Believe me when I say I felt guilty enough for the both of us. And even if I had wanted to keep the baby, I knew you wouldn't. I didn't want to burden you with that."

That seemed to be a common theme when it came to him and women.

So Mel had been telling him the truth. She had been through hell and lived to talk about it, she had lost a baby, *his* baby, and he had more or less accused her of being a tramp.

He could have been a father. And he would have, if he hadn't been so selfish and blind. Not to mention *stupid*.

He closed his eyes and shook his head. "I am such an idiot."

"Why do I get the feeling you're not talking about us any longer?"

He looked over at her. "Do you think some people are destined to keep repeating their mistakes?"

"Some people maybe. If they don't learn from them."

"And if they learn too late?"

She reached across the table and laid her hand over his, and just like that, all the unresolved conflict, all the bitterness he'd shouldered for the past three years seemed to vanish. "Do you love her?" she asked.

"Probably too much for my own good."

"Does she love you?"

"She did three days ago."

She grinned and gave his hand a squeeze. "So what the heck are you doing still sitting here with me?"

Damn, the woman was good at disappearing. He had no clue where she was staying and she refused to answer her phone. But this time Ash didn't wait nearly as long to call the P.I. and ask him to find her again. But when Ash gave him the make and year of her car, the P.I. asked, "Does the car have GPS?"

"Yeah, it does."

"Then you don't really need me. You can track her every move on any computer. Or even your phone if it has Internet. I can help you set it up."

"That would be great," Ash told him. It was about time something went right. And thank God this time she hadn't gone very far. Within hours he was pulling into the lot of a grocery store a few miles away from the condo.

The idea of a confrontation inside the store seemed like a bad idea, so he parked, got out of his car and made himself comfortable on her hood. There was no way she would be leaving without at least talking to him.

She came out of the store maybe ten minutes later and his heart lifted at the sight of her, then it lodged in his throat when he thought of all the explaining he had to do. And the confessing.

She had one bag in her arms and she was rooting around in her purse for something, so she didn't see him right away.

She looked adorable with her hair up in a ponytail, wearing jeans, tennis shoes and a pullover sweatshirt. He was finding it hard to imagine what he considered so appealing in the way she looked before the accident. This just seemed to be a better fit.

She was almost to the car when she finally looked up and noticed him there. Her steps slowed and her eyes narrowed. He could see that she was wondering how he'd found her, especially when she had been dodging his calls.

"GPS," he said. "I tracked you on my phone."

"You realize that stalking is a criminal offense in California?"

"I don't think it can be considered stalking when I technically own the car."

She tossed the keys at him so forcefully that if he hadn't caught them he might have lost an eye. "Take it," she said and walked past him in the direction of the street.

He jumped down off the hood to follow her. "Come on, Mel. I just want to talk to you."

"But I don't want to listen. I'm still too mad at you."

Mad was good as far as he was concerned. Since he deserved it. She could get over being mad at him a lot easier than, say, hating his guts. Not that he didn't deserve that, too.

She was walking so fast he had to jog to catch up to her. "I've been an ass."

She snorted. "You say that like it's something I don't already know."

"But do you know how sorry I am?"

"I'm sure you are."

"It's not that I didn't believe you about the baby. I just didn't want it to be true."

She stopped so abruptly he nearly tripped over his own feet. "Are you actually saying that you didn't want it to be yours?"

"No! Of course not."

"You really are an ass," she said, and turned to leave, but he grabbed her arm.

"Would you please listen for a minute? I could live with the idea that you'd had an affair, that you had made a mistake, especially when I was the one who drove you away in the first place. But knowing that the baby was mine, and I was responsible…" Emotion welled up in his throat and he had to pause to get a hold of himself. "If I had treated you right, showed you that I loved you, you never would have felt like you had to run away. All the terrible things you went through never would have happened. Everything, all of it, is *my* fault."

She was quiet for what seemed like a very long time, and he watched her intently, in case she decided to throw something else at him. God only knew what she had in the bag.

"It's no one's," she finally said. "We both acted stupid."

"Maybe, but I think I was way more stupid than you. And I am so sorry, Mel. I know it's a lot to ask, but do you think you could find it in your heart to give me one more chance? I swear I'll get it right this time." He took her free hand, relieved that she didn't pull away. "You know that I love you, right?"

She nodded.

"And you love me, too?"

She sighed deeply. "Of course I do."

"And you're going to give me another chance?"

She rolled her eyes. "Like I have a choice. I get the distinct feeling that you'll just keep stalking me until I say yes."

He grinned, thinking that she was probably right. "In that case, you could hug me now."

She cracked a smile and walked into his arms, and he wrapped them around her. Even with the grocery bag crushed between them, it was darned near perfect. *She* was perfect.

"You know, deep down I didn't really think it was over," she said. "I figured you would come around. And of course I would be forced to take you back. *Again.*"

"But only after I groveled for a while?"

She grinned. "Of course."

He leaned down to kiss her, when a box sitting at the

very top of the grocery bag caught his eye. There's no way that was what he thought it was....

He pulled it out and read the label, then looked down at Mel. "A *pregnancy* test? What is this for?"

She was grinning up at him. "What do you think?"

He shook his head in amazement. *"Again?"*

"I don't know for sure yet. I'm only four or five days late. But my breasts are so tender I can barely touch them and that was a dead giveaway last time."

"I don't get it. I'm *supposed* to be sterile from the radiation."

"You might want to get that checked, because for a guy who is supposed to be sterile, you seem to have no problem knocking me up."

He laughed. "This is nuts. You realize that even if there are a few guys left in there, the odds of us going three years unprotected, then you getting pregnant not once but *twice,* is astronomical."

She shrugged. "I guess that just means it was meant to be. Our own little miracle."

He took the bag from her and set it on the ground so he could hug her properly. He didn't even care that people were driving by looking at them as if they were nuts.

As far as he was concerned, the real miracle was that he had let her go twice, and here she was back in his arms. And she could be damned sure he would never let her go again.

* * * * *

Don't miss the next KINGS OF THE BOARDROOM,
BACHELOR'S BOUGHT BRIDE
by Jennifer Lewis,
available March 2011
from Desire™.

2 FREE BOOKS
AND A SURPRISE GIFT

We would like to take this opportunity to thank you for reading this Mills & Boon® book by offering you the chance to take TWO more specially selected books from the Desire™ 2-in-1 series absolutely FREE! We're also making this offer to introduce you to the benefits of the Mills & Boon® Book Club™—

- **FREE home delivery**
- **FREE gifts and competitions**
- **FREE monthly Newsletter**
- **Exclusive Mills & Boon Book Club offers**
- **Books available before they're in the shops**

Accepting these FREE books and gift places you under no obligation to buy, you may cancel at any time, even after receiving your free books. Simply complete your details below and return the entire page to the address below. You don't even need a stamp!

YES Please send me 2 free Desire stories in a 2-in-1 volume and a surprise gift. I understand that unless you hear from me, I will receive 2 superb new 2-in-1 books every month for just £5.30 each, postage and packing free. I am under no obligation to purchase any books and may cancel my subscription at any time. The free books and gift will be mine to keep in any case.

Ms/Mrs/Miss/Mr _____ Initials _____

Surname _____

Address _____

_____ Postcode _____

E-mail_____

Send this whole page to: Mills & Boon Book Club, Free Book Offer, FREEPOST NAT 10298, Richmond, TW9 1BR